D0061465

Geraldine O'Neill was born in Lanarkshire, Scotland and has lived in County Offaly in Ireland since 1991. She is married to Michael Brosnahan, and has two adult children. She has published twelve previous novels.

Also by Geraldine O'Neill

Tara Flynn
Cara Gayle
Tara's Fortune
The Grace Girls
The Flowers of Ballygrace
Tara's Destiny
Leaving Clare
Sarah Love
Summer's End
Music from Home
A Letter from America
The House on Silver Street

Music Across the Mersey

GERALDINE O'NEILL

ORION

First published in Great Britain in 2017 by Orion Books,
This paperback edition published in 2018 by Orion Books,
an imprint of The Orion Publishing Group Ltd
Carmelite House, 50 Victoria Embankment,
London EC4Y 0DZ

An Hachette UK company

1 3 5 7 9 10 8 6 4 2

Copyright © Geraldine O'Neill 2017

A CIP catalogue record for this book is
available from the British Library.

ISBN 978 1 4091 6669 6

Typeset at The Spartan Press Ltd,
Lymington, Hants

Printed and bound by
CPI Group (UK) Ltd, Coydon, CR0 4YY

MIX
Paper from
responsible sources
FSC® C104740

www.orionbooks.co.uk

MUSIC ACROSS THE MERSEY

*Is dedicated to the memory of
the much-loved Merseyside Author and Historian,
Freddy O'Connor*

O love is the crooked thing,
There is nobody wise enough
To find out all that is in it,
For he would be thinking of love
Till the stars had run away
And the shadows eaten the moon.

W.B. YEATS

PART ONE

Chapter One

Dublin
March 1949

Ella Cassidy shifted the pot of boiling soup to a ring at the back of the cooker, then went out into the narrow hall, wiping her brow with the back of her hand. A thin, serious-faced girl of thirteen, blonde hair scraped back, apron tied around her waist, her demeanour was that of an older, careworn woman.

'Sean?' she called to her brother, a year older. He, and their younger brother and sister, were in the living room. 'Mind Larry and Hannah while I hang the washing out. Don't let them near the scullery.'

'They're grand,' he called back. 'They're drawing away on their books. Did Da say when he would be back?'

She leaned against the wall, suddenly weary. 'For the soup, around one. When I've hung the washing you'll need to take the ration book and go for a loaf.'

'Have you not made any soda bread?'

Ella felt her jaw clench. 'No,' she said. 'Mrs Collins said she'd have sliced bread in this morning and she would keep us a loaf.'

When did her brother think she had time to bake bread this morning? After making breakfast for everyone, she'd cleared up and then stripped the two younger children's beds and boiled water to soak and scrub the soiled sheets. Two-and-a-half-year-old Hannah was still in nappies, and, since their mother died two months ago – along with the baby she had just given birth to – four-year-old Larry had started wetting the bed again.

Apart from all that, she had the usual bucketful of nappies to wash. She did these every morning before school – on the days she was able to go to school. She missed more days than she attended as she had to stay at home with the younger children while her father went looking for work.

Ella went into the scullery, lifted the heavy wash basket up, then went out into the yard. She dropped the basket on the ground and looked up at the dismal grey sky. It would be another afternoon and evening of steaming, damp sheets and pyjamas drying around the fire, blocking out the comforting heat.

As she started to peg the washing out, she wondered what Nancy and Maeve were doing today. Her friends usually walked into the city centre on a Saturday for a look around the shops and, if they had money, had a cup of tea or hot chocolate some-where. If it was a fine day, they'd go to the zoo in Phoenix Park, as Maeve's uncle worked there and he could sneak them in free.

It was ages since she had done anything like that with her friends, not since the cold January day her beloved mother had died and Ella had taken over all the household duties. And she could not imagine a time when she would not be needed to do everything at home.

She began pegging the sheets on the lines, and was starting on the third when she heard boys' voices and laughter, and the sound of a ball being kicked against the fences at the front of the houses. She had almost finished when she heard Sean's voice outside, and irritation washed over her. He had gone outside and left the two little ones alone in the scullery!

How was it, she wondered, that he was older than her, and yet he had so little responsibility around the house? All he had to do was bring in turf or wood and set the fire in the small living room, and clean the grates and empty the ashes outside.

Well, Ella thought, as soon as she got inside she would run

him out to the shops for the bread and he could take the younger ones with him to give her ten minutes' peace.

Her thoughts turned to her father and she looked at her wrist to check the time on her mother's gold watch. Wherever he was, he should be home any time now. She started to peg the last few things on the line, then she heard Larry and Hannah laughing and giggling in the scullery. They were probably messing around, chasing each other – exactly what she had tried to avoid.

'I could kill our Sean!' she muttered to herself.

Ella had just turned back towards the house when she heard a piercing scream. Her heart stopped. It was Hannah! Then Larry was shouting and screaming too. Dropping the tea towel she was holding, she ran to the house.

She came to a halt at the scullery door. Hannah was lying on the floor, surrounded by a steaming puddle of scalding soup. Some of it had splashed onto the bare skin above her socks and on her knees and thighs. The boiling liquid had also seeped through the right sleeve of her cardigan on to her arm and shoulder. Her eyes stared up at Ella, her face chalk white, and her mouth open in silent shock.

Larry was standing up on a chair he had pulled over to the cooker. His thin body was shaking as he looked at Ella and pointed to the half-empty soup pot. 'It was an accident!' he sobbed. 'Honest – it was an accident! Hannah was hungry and wanted the soup and she tried to pull the pot down. I couldn't stop her...'

Ella rushed forward and swept Larry down off the chair. 'Run outside and get our Sean – then run and get Mrs Murphy!' No point in sending him to look for their father because he could be in any of the pubs within a two-mile walk.

As Larry tore out of the scullery, she looked down at her sister. A wave of panic engulfed her. She took a deep breath to steady herself. 'You'll be fine, my darling!' she said, trying to sound soothing and calm. 'We'll get you all washed and cleaned up and you'll be grand. You'll be as good as new.' How badly

5

burned she actually was, Ella had no idea, but she knew it was not good.

Hannah lifted her fair head and tried to sit up, but she fell back to the floor immediately and her eyelids fluttered and closed as she went into a dead faint.

Ella bent closer to try to move her sister, but then she noticed the raw, red skin on her legs was starting to break out in blisters. A sickening surge of fear rushed over her and she heard herself repeat in an hysterical, sing-song voice, 'You'll be grand, Hannah! You'll be grand.' *Holy Mother of God,* she prayed. *Please, please make her all right.*

She quickly moved over to the sink to grab the torn – but clean – towel she kept for drying her hands as she worked. She threw it into the stone sink and turned on the cold tap. When it was wet, she wrung the worst of the water out and rushed back to kneel beside her sister.

She went to put the cloth on Hannah's legs and then halted, her hands mid-air. Would the towel help, or would it make the burned skin worse? Panic rose inside her. *I don't know what to do!* she thought. *I don't know what to do!*

Hot tears trickled down her face. *Please Mammy,* she said in a silent prayer. *Please help me to do the right thing...* A heavy weight descended on her chest and she found it difficult to breathe. Just as she was gasping for air, the front door banged open and Sean came thudding towards them.

He paused, panting, his gaze moving from Hannah to Ella. 'Is she all right?' When he got no answer, he stumbled forward, dropping to his knees beside them.

Ella managed to find her voice. 'No, she's not all right... I *told* you not to leave them alone.'

'They were sitting drawing. I only went to answer the door...' As he looked up at her with wide eyes, Ella felt the greatest urge to slap his stupid, stupid face, but she knew that she had to keep calm for Hannah's sake.

'What are we going to do? There's no sign of Daddy...'

'We'll have to get her to the hospital—'

Before she had time to say any more, she heard a tap on the front door, then the sound of Mrs Murphy's comforting voice.

'Come in!' Ella called to their stout, elderly neighbour, almost weak with relief. 'Something terrible has happened to our Hannah and Daddy's not home yet! You'll have to help us.'

Rose Murphy appeared at the scullery door and her eyes widened in shock. 'Jesus, Mary and Joseph . . .' Her voice trailed off into a whisper.

Then, all the years of experience with her own brood took over and she stepped into the middle of the small scullery to galvanise the family into action. Within minutes Sean had been dispatched to the nearest shop to use the phone to dial the operator and tell her it was an emergency and that they needed an ambulance straight away.

She told Ella to get a clean towel and damp it with water, and then she sent the silent, terror-struck Larry upstairs to get a blanket to put over the shivering Hannah. 'We'll try to clean her up a bit, but we'll have to be careful not to put anything near the blistered skin,' she told Ella in a low voice. 'And where did you say your father was?'

Ella swallowed hard. 'I'm not sure . . .' she whispered. Her gaze shifted towards the door. 'I think he was going to see somebody about a job. He said he would be back around one, so he should be home soon.'

Mrs Murphy nodded but said nothing. She guessed that the last thing Johnny Cassidy was doing on a Saturday afternoon was seeing about a job. She liked a lot of things about Johnny. He had been blessed with one of the handsomest faces she had ever seen on a man. All women noticed him, even she, at the age of sixty-eight, who had long given up any thoughts about the opposite sex. He was blessed even further by a lack of vanity and always seemed surprised when anyone alluded to his looks. But an even better attribute, Rose thought, was his warm and kind nature. She knew that he loved his children and he had loved his wife – but all those fine points were overshadowed by his fondness for drink and the lack of stamina to stick at

7

any job. It was the quiet Mary who had been the worker, the backbone of the family who had held them all together.

Mrs Murphy looked down at poor Hannah who seemed to be coming out of her faint now, and was making low, moaning noises. God knows what injuries she had sustained.

A moment later Sean came bursting back into the house, breathless, and told them that the ambulance was on its way.

'Go outside and wait for your father,' Mrs Murphy told him. 'He'll be needed at the hospital.'

A long twenty minutes later the ambulance pulled up outside the house – and there was still no sign of Johnny Cassidy.

Chapter Two

Johnny Cassidy looked at the clock above the bar in the Brazen Head, then lifted his glass and drained it. He turned to the man beside him. 'I'd better be headin' off now, Andy.'

'You're not going already?' Andy Flynn looked taken aback. 'Sure, I've only just arrived.'

'Ah, the kids will be looking for me . . . you know what it's like.' The easy-going Johnny gave a knowing smile, which lit up his handsome face.

Andy gestured to the old lady behind the bar then pointed a gnarled finger at Johnny. 'Another pint for this man and a Jameson's for meself.'

Johnny waved his hand. 'I'm grand,' he said, buttoning up his coat. 'There's no need.'

'Indeed there is,' Andy said, standing up to find the coins in the pocket of his worn and stained trousers. 'It's the first time I've seen you since you buried your poor young wife. Buying you a drink is the least I can do.'

Johnny looked at the woman who was now pulling the pint of beer. He knew Andy didn't have money to be buying drinks, and he needed to get home to the kids.

Reading his thoughts, Andy tilted his head proudly. 'I won a few bob on a game of cards at the weekend. I've kept it quiet because you know how some people are when they think you have anything, but I was looking out for you ever since to have a drink with you.'

Johnny looked at him. 'That's decent of you now,' he said.

'But you might need it for yourself and the family. It doesn't go far when you have a houseful, especially with the rationing and everything.'

'Never mind that,' Andy said. He lowered his voice. 'There's a lad I know can get extra bits when you have the money, you know what I mean?'

Johnny nodded. Everyone knew about the black market.

'I won't refuse you then,' Johnny said. 'And I suppose another ten minutes either way won't matter.' Ella had asked him to come home around one; it was that time already and it would take him twenty minutes or more to walk from the Brazen Head to Islandbridge. He was aware of the trouble Ella would have gone to making the soup, because she knew how much he loved it. Her mother had made it most Saturdays, often with the extra vegetables they got from Mary's spinster cousin, Nora, who lived down in County Offaly.

A few weeks after Mary died, Ella got Mrs Murphy to come up to the house to check she had put all the right ingredients in the pot and was cooking it exactly the way that Mary would have done. It was a slow process, with the gas being rationed to only a couple of hours a day, but Ella had used every minute to get it boiling and leave it simmering away. Johnny had seen the pride in her eyes when the soup turned out right and she'd smiled properly for the first time since her mother had died when everyone told her how good it tasted. Since then, it had become a ritual on a Saturday for the five of them to sit around the table and have the soup with bread.

As he thought about it, Johnny felt bad about being late, but wouldn't it be the height of ignorance to refuse a drink from poor oul' Andy when he had a few extra pounds? And when the cold, creamy pint of Guinness was put on the bar counter, Johnny held the glass up in a gesture of thanks and took a long, deep drink.

Within a few minutes he could feel the alcohol in the fresh glass adding to the three other pints he had already drunk, and he was grateful, for it helped numb the raw wound of Mary's loss.

'Well,' Andy sighed, putting his glass back down on the bar counter. 'Any luck with work?'

Johnny shook his head. 'No, but I'm hoping for a few days down at the docks next week. And I've been asked to play at a dance in the Gresham next weekend, but I'm still thinking about it. It's hard to leave the children at home on their own. They're still young, and it's early days yet...'

'I'd go mad if I didn't get a few pints and a game of cards now and then,' Andy stated. 'Sure, hasn't life been miserable enough recently, with the war and the Emergency and everything?'

Although Ireland was a neutral country and so not directly involved in the war, rationing had been introduced, since many goods had to be imported. Bread was rationed, as was tea, butter, sugar, and everyday items such as soap, toothpaste and shoe polish, but many Irish people, including the Cassidy family, found tea the hardest to go without.

'It has indeed,' Johnny said.

There was a small silence now as they both thought of Mary, which had had a bigger effect on the Cassidys than any of the bombs the Germans had dropped early in the war.

Music was Johnny's other true love and the one thing he knew in his heart he was good at. His main instrument was the fiddle. His uncle Arthur had given him the beautiful instrument when his own hands were too bad with arthritis to play himself. After Johnny had mastered the fiddle, a friend gave him lessons on the banjo, and then he picked up an old mandolin in a second-hand music shop. Playing the string instruments came naturally to him, and he also had a more than passable voice. He loved the comradery of the other band members and the atmosphere in the smoke-filled dance halls and weddings that he played at.

Mary had been very proud of his musical skills; from the first day they had met, in a dance hall in Dublin, she had encouraged him to make a go of it and hopefully turn it into a full-time job. But Johnny didn't just have a fondness for music – he also had a fondness for all the socialising that went with it. And, by the end of the night, the thing he was most fond of was the drink.

Mary had known this flaw when she married him, but since Johnny Cassidy was the only man she wanted, she accepted it as part and parcel of him, and drinking didn't bring out any dark traits in him like it did with other men. If anything, it made him even mellower – and just a little stupid.

Andy clapped a hand on his shoulder. 'You should get out at the weekend and play a few oul' tunes to cheer yourself up. You'll surely have a kindly neighbour or someone close to keep an eye on the childer? And the few bob you get for playing will help out.'

Johnny nodded thoughtfully. It was hard to know what to do for the best. He worried about leaving the kids at night, especially while it was still dark in the evenings. Going out for a few drinks on a Saturday afternoon and a Sunday was a different matter. Sean and Ella were well able to look after the younger ones. Mary had shown Ella how to do basic cooking and sewing, and she was doing a great job of managing the household tasks on her own. He felt bad she was missing a lot of school, but the head nun in the girls' school was fairly understanding. And if Ella got stuck with anything in the house, there was always their neighbour, Mrs Murphy, who lived a few houses along, that they could call on for help or advice. Maybe, Johnny suddenly thought, he could ask her to keep an eye on them next Saturday night.

He finished his drink as quickly as he decently could, and made his way out onto the Quays.

The extra pint made all the difference, he thought, as he walked home. It brightened up a long, miserable Saturday, and made it easier to meet people face on.

Since Mary had gone, he had found the constant stream of people who wanted to offer their sympathies overwhelming. Women were the worst – often they started crying as they commiserated about his poor wife dying in childbirth, and then they would cry all the more thinking of the four motherless children left at home.

One who had taken Mary's death particularly badly was her cousin, Nora Lamb from Tullamore. An odd woman, who must be around forty, Nora had visited them up in Dublin every few weeks. It filled her lonely weekends as her parents and her beloved Uncle Bernard were all dead, and she lived on her own. Nora would arrive on the train around ten o'clock, bringing with her a bag filled with chops, or a piece of bacon, and potatoes and whatever other vegetables were seasonal. After a cup of tea, the two women would go into the little scullery and start cooking the meat, and then they would sit at the table chatting as they peeled the vegetables and put them on to boil. After dinner, Johnny would mind the children while Mary and Nora went for a walk in the Phoenix Park. Afterwards, Nora would treat them to a cup of coffee and a scone in one of the local tearooms. Later in the evening, Johnny would walk her down to the station, as she always went for the last train home.

Nora had come up to Dublin to see them a few times since Mary's death, but he knew that the visits would eventually dwindle away as she had only really come to see Mary. She wasn't a natural with children, although, in fairness, she was good in her own way. She often brought them second-hand books, or jigsaw puzzles and board games. They seemed happy enough to play the games, but they often got into trouble with their mother for skitting and laughing at their aunt after she left. Nora, Johnny noticed, found it hard to hide her old-fashioned view that 'children should be seen and not heard'.

Given that she was a straight-laced sort of woman, Johnny was always surprised at how relaxed and easy she was on their walk back to the station. She could chat well about things that men were interested in, like the farm she had inherited and rented out, or Manchester United, an English football team that she knew Johnny supported. In the beginning he had dreaded walking alone with her, but as time went on he had almost begun to enjoy the walk and the chat.

When the tragic loss hit them, there were a few local women who had offered to help the family out. Dazed with shock and grief, Johnny had welcomed their help. There were two women in particular who had made their presence felt. Cathy, a cheery barmaid he knew from the Barley Mow, and Bridget, a quiet, but kindly widow woman from Kilmainham that he and Mary used to go to the Catholic Mothers' meetings with. The women came down to the house most days and brought bowls of stew and anything they could get their hands on, like tea or sugar, to eke out the Cassidys' rations.

But within weeks of Mary's death, Johnny noticed that the initial sadness in their eyes had changed into a different kind of look.

Mrs Murphy confirmed his thoughts. 'Mark my words,' she warned, 'while they are useful enough, that pair are only biding their time until a decent interval has passed to take poor Mary's place.'

Johnny's heart had tilted at the thought. How could he even think of replacing Mary? He had no interest in any woman. Then Sean and Ella started to complain that Cathy and Bridget were around too often, were trying to take over the house and tell them what to do. Johnny saw the opportunity to use that to his advantage.

'I'm sorry now,' he told each of them, 'but the older kids are finding the house too busy, and want things back the way they were. Just our own little family.' He had brushed away any protests, saying, 'Of course they're grateful for all the help you've given, but I have to respect their wishes. It's going to take a while for us all to adjust, because Mary was an absolute saint.'

Bridget had gone off quietly, but Cathy had persisted. 'If you need anything at all, I'll be there any time you want.' Then she had looked Johnny straight in the eye, and added, 'Day or night.'

Johnny vowed to himself that he would be more careful, but he soon discovered that things were not so easy without the outside help. Initially, Ella had taken all the responsibility of doing the washing and cleaning, but as the weeks went on,

Johnny could see it was not easy work for a young girl, and the freezing wintry weather had not helped. At times he tried to give her a hand himself, but what did he know about putting clothes through a wringer and soaking nappies in bleach and the like?

The only solution was for him to get a decent job that paid enough to get a woman in to help, but jobs were as scarce as hen's teeth, and a decent, permanent job was even scarcer. Just months before Mary died he had been let go by Guinness's for bad timekeeping and missed days. He had been working with them for two years, and most men would have killed for a full-time job with the brewery, as it meant security for life along with other perks like a free drop of porter every day. But Johnny Cassidy was not most men.

Responsibility and thinking further than the next day had never sat easy with him. In most of his jobs, his mind was only half on work, while the other half was on the job he would have preferred – making music.

After he'd been let go, they had just about made ends meet with Mary's cleaning job and Johnny picking up a few pounds at the weekends from playing in the band. Mercifully, they had no rent to pay like many others in Dublin; they owned the terraced house outright, bought with the money Mary had inherited from her parents. But then the insurance money paid out on Mary's death hadn't amounted to much, once the funeral costs had been paid, and the rest of her savings were coming to an end.

As Johnny walked past Guinness's brewery now, he turned his head away from it to look out across the Liffey. He hated the reminder of the better life his family should have had – if he had been a better worker and husband.

As the terraced houses they lived in came into view, Johnny was surprised to see a black Ford car sitting outside. Somebody was getting a visit from a well-off relative or a boss, he thought, as none of the residents could afford a car themselves. It was somebody important enough who could get petrol to run a car, because there were few cars on the road these days with fuel still being rationed.

Someday, when the Emergency was over, if he could get a regular place with one of the top-class bands, he would save up and buy a car himself. He felt a sudden stabbing in his heart as he remembered the nights he had sat with Mary, telling her all his dreams about cars and other things. Nights when the house was quiet and the children asleep in bed. Nights when he explained why he found it hard to stick at ordinary day jobs when his mind was full of music. Mary was the only person in the world who seemed to understand him, and who did her best to encourage him. She had known him in a way that no other person ever had.

Even if his dream of owning a car came true now, it would not be the same. Mary would never sit in the car beside him. He would never see his wife again, never see her lovely face or hear her voice again. He was on his own. It was just him and the children from now on.

Chapter Three

Johnny quickened his step, thinking of Ella and the soup. He was almost half an hour later than he had said.

As he got near the house, the door of the car opened and Father Brosnan, the young curate from their church, stepped out. He was a nice young fella, Johnny thought. A decent, down-to-earth man, with no airs and graces – unlike the parish priest, Father Quirke. He had been very kind to the Cassidys since Mary had died, and had often dropped down to the house to see how they were getting on. On each occasion he had brought something – bread, cheese, tea, and a few slices of leftover cake. He had winked at the older children and said that it wasn't to be mentioned outside the house – and especially to Father Quirke. There was no fear of Sean or Ella mentioning anything to Father Quirke: they, and their friends, were all terrified of him.

Something about Father Brosnan's serious demeanour told Johnny that the priest was waiting to speak to him.

Thank God it's not Father Quirke, he thought to himself, *he could catch the smell of the beer at twenty paces.* The last time he had seen Johnny drunk at a neighbour's wedding, he had come around the following day and given him a sermon on wasting money. The young curate, Johnny guessed, would pass no remarks whether he smelled it or not. He knew life for the poor was hard enough without him adding to their misery.

'Hello, Father,' Johnny said, going forward with his hand outstretched. 'Are you coming into the house?'

'No, no,' Father Brosnan said. He wasn't his usual cheery self. 'I've actually been waiting on you.'

'Is there something wrong?'

'I'm afraid there is...' The priest sucked his breath in. 'We have to go down to the hospital straight away. Young Hannah has had an accident. She's been badly scalded.' He looked at Johnny. 'Hot soup, I believe.'

'Mother of God!' Johnny said. 'Is she all right? Did you see her?'

'No, Mr Cassidy. I got a phone call,' the priest went on, 'from one of the nurses at the hospital to ask me to bring you up to the hospital. I've been here for a quarter of an hour, so we'd best move quickly. We're only allowed to use the car in an emergency, but I thought this qualified as one.'

Johnny felt a wave of guilt wash over him, then tears rushed into his eyes. 'Ah, Jesus... the poor little cratur.'

I should have been home, he thought, *I should have been home and it wouldn't have happened.* Then he thought about Ella and how she would be feeling.

Father Brosnan put his hand on his shoulder and guided him towards the passenger side of the car. 'I think we'd better make a move now,' he said gently. 'They will be waiting for us at the hospital.'

Johnny got into the front seat of the car, and the two men drove out towards Kilmainham. They sat in silence until Father Brosnan reached into the glove compartment and brought out a packet of mints and handed them to Johnny. 'Have a few of these, for when you are talking to the doctors.'

When they came towards the entrance to St James's Hospital, Sean was there, waiting for them. He was stretched high on his toes, waving his hands about frantically, as though fearful they would not see him.

Johnny threw the car door open even before it came to a standstill, and then almost fell out as it came to a halt. 'How is she?' he called.

Sean ran to meet him. 'We don't know anything yet,' he said

breathlessly. 'The doctors and nurses have taken her away. They said she needed to go into special care.'

'They'll have to let me see her,' Johnny said, fear making him unusually assertive. 'I'm her father and will be down as her next of kin.' Saying the words *next of kin* filled him with dread as it rekindled memories of Mary.

Father Brosnan appeared behind them. 'I'll go in with you, Mr Cassidy,' he said. 'They might let us in when we're together.' He did not specifically say they would get preferential treatment because he was a priest, but they both knew that's what he meant.

Sean guided them down through the busy hospital corridors to the waiting room.

It was another hour before anyone was allowed in to see Hannah, by which time she was fast asleep having been sedated to allow the doctors to do their immediate work on her.

'I must warn you,' the Scottish doctor told them outside the room, 'she is a very sick wee girl. We took her down to theatre to clean her up a bit and see the extent of the burns.' He shook his head.

'Is she going to be all right?' Johnny asked, his voice barely a whisper.

'She has a long road to go.' The doctor walked towards the room where Hannah was and pushed open the door. He then looked back and gestured towards them. Johnny followed behind, and when the doctor went to stand by the small, iron-framed bed, he did the same.

Then he looked down at the sleeping form of his little daughter and his heart froze.

Chapter Four

Father Brosnan's car pulled up outside the terrace house and Johnny, Sean, Ella and little Larry all climbed out. Although Ella was weary and anxious about Hannah, it crossed her mind how unfair it was that the only times their family had a ride in a car was for a sad occasion. The last time had been at their mother's funeral...

Johnny lifted Larry out and told Sean to take him into the house.

'Don't go into the scullery, yet,' Ella said. 'I need to clean up the mess. Just get Larry washed and into his pyjamas and I'll mix up milk and a rusk for him.'

Then, Ella stood close behind her father, waiting to thank the curate. He often came into school and was always very kind to her and the other pupils. Unlike Father Quirke, who favoured those families who owned shops or pubs, Father Brosnan made no difference between the families. It did not matter to him whether the children were dressed in the best from Clerys or in hand-me-downs, or whether they only rented their houses instead of owning them.

Johnny, fully sober now, leaned back into the car. 'Will you come in for a cup of tea or milk or whatever we have, Father?'

'Ah no, thank you,' Father Brosnan said. He pushed the sleeve of his soutane to check his watch. 'Best to get back to the Parochial House and see if there are any other calls to attend to.'

When her father moved away from the car door, Ella took up his position. 'Thank you, Father,' she said solemnly. 'It was good of you to come up to the hospital, and then to come back again to bring us all home. And thanks again for the money you gave Sean to buy us the tea and chips in the café.'

'You're very welcome,' he told her, impressed with her manners given the situation. 'You were all a long time waiting there this afternoon, and needed something to keep you going.' As Father Brosnan looked at the thin-faced young girl, he could see tiredness and anxiety stamped on her face. If something wasn't done soon, if Johnny didn't shape up and sort things, Ella Cassidy's childhood would be at an end. She would end up taking on all the responsibility of the Cassidy family, and it would be the ruination of her.

When they got into the house, Ella and her father went straight into the scullery where they silently surveyed the scene of the accident. She turned then to look at her father, who was leaning against the door jamb. She could see he was trying hard to blink back tears, looked the same helpless way as he had done at her mother's funeral. She did not know what to do to make things better.

'I'll clean this place up,' she eventually said. She went to the sink and turned on the tap while Johnny stood in the doorway.

A knock came on the front door and Johnny went out to answer it. Mrs Murphy came back into the scullery with him, holding a circle of soda bread she had baked and wrapped in a clean tea towel, and a bottle of milk.

'The door was locked,' she said, 'or I would have let meself in and had it all cleaned up for you.' She held the bread and the milk out to Ella. 'I thought you might be needing this, since you've been out most of the day.' She paused, then she looked from Johnny to Ella. 'How is she, the poor little cratur?'

Johnny swallowed hard, his face was pale and drained. 'We'll just have to wait and see. Please God she'll be OK. Maybe a few weeks in hospital will help to heal the worst of it.'

'We just have to pray to God and his blessed mother,' Mrs Murphy said, making the sign of the cross over her aproned chest. She gestured to Johnny. 'You go on inside and see to the fire and I'll help Ella here.'

Later that evening, when Mrs Murphy had gone home and the house was clean and tidy again, Sean was sent out to buy them all fish and chips and a bottle of red lemonade. This had become a weekly treat since Mary had died, while there was still a bit of insurance money left. Tonight there was no sign of enjoyment from anyone as they all ate in silence around the coal fire, the washing left outside in the yard. Johnny sat in an old tapestry-covered armchair, Ella in a low nursing chair that her mother had used, and the boys on the wooden-framed settee. The fire was unusually bright as Sean had come home with a bag of coal the other night, which had been given by a friend's parents, but the comforting heat and the filling food was not bringing much cheer.

At half past eight, Ella took Larry up to bed. When she came back downstairs, she began to gather up the newspaper wrappings from the chippers.

'Sit down for a minute,' her father said. 'I want to ask you and Sean something.' There was silence for a few seconds then he said, 'I want to know what happened with Hannah when there was the two of you in the house, supposed to be looking after her. Why wasn't there someone there to watch her when you knew there was a pot of boiling soup?' He looked over at Ella.

Ella swallowed hard and looked over at Sean. He was looking down at the floor. 'It was just the way it happened,' she said. 'I was hanging the washing on the line...' She halted, waiting for her brother to step in, but he didn't.

'Surely,' Johnny said, 'you didn't leave them running around the scullery with boiling soup?'

There was a silence.

'Ahhh, Ella,' her father said, shaking his head. 'I thought you knew better than that.'

Tears flooded Ella's eyes.

'There's no good in crying about it now,' Johnny said. 'It's too late for that.'

There was a sudden sound upstairs and Johnny got to his feet. 'I think that's Larry moving about,' he sighed. 'I'll go up and settle him again.'

As he walked towards the door all three could hear Larry screaming, 'Mammy! Mammy! I want Mammy!'

Johnny went out into the small hallway, closing the door behind him and Ella looked over at her brother. A feeling of anger and injustice came over her.

She went over to the sofa and jabbed him hard on the arm. 'Why haven't you opened your mouth? Why haven't you told Daddy where you were when it happened?'

Sean shrugged her away. 'Get off me!' he said.

'I won't get off you!' She jabbed him again. 'And I'm not taking the blame for what happened to Hannah. You better own up when Daddy comes back down the stairs or I'm going to tell him myself.'

Sean grabbed her by the wrist. 'Don't say anything!' he hissed. 'I'm in enough trouble already! I don't need my father on my back over this as well.'

Ella pulled her arm away. 'What do you mean, you're in trouble? Who are you in trouble with? What have you done now?'

'It's none of your business. Feck off and leave me alone!'

The door suddenly opened and Johnny came in. He looked from one to the other. 'What's going on now?' he asked, his voice weary.

'Nothing,' Sean said. Then he took a deep breath. 'What happened with Hannah. It wasn't all Ella's fault.'

Ella stared at him in surprise.

Sean looked at his father. 'Like I told you earlier, I went to answer the door and – and I told them to stay quiet with their colouring books. I never heard them going out to the scullery. They must have gone as quick—'

Ella turned to him. 'You were meant to be looking after them. You knew I was hanging out the washing.'

'It wasn't my fault, I never asked the lads to call to the door for me. I thought it was Daddy or one of the neighbours.'

'You shouldn't have left them!' Ella repeated, her voice had a hysterical note in it now. 'Hannah is only a baby yet.'

Johnny threw his hands up in the air. 'Enough, for God's sake! Enough of the arguing. We're going to have Larry crying again and up all night. Haven't we had enough trouble in the house today without you pair fighting now?'

Sean moved to his feet now to face his father. 'None of this is fair,' he said. 'We're too young to be taking on the responsibility for Hannah and Larry.' He gestured towards Ella. 'And she's nearly killing herself trying to do everything. You need to do something – get somebody to help us.'

Johnny looked from Sean to Ella and bit his lip. 'Mrs Murphy is helping us—'

'She's too old,' Sean said. 'And it isn't fair to expect her. She's only a neighbour.'

Johnny threw his hands in the air. 'What do you want me to do?' His voice was anxious and guilt-ridden. 'We haven't the money to pay a woman to come in. It just isn't there.' He took a deep breath. 'I've been asked to play at a dance on Saturday night and that would bring in a few bob, but after what's happened to Hannah I don't want to be out of the house at night.'

There was a silence, and Ella could tell that her father was seeking permission from her or Sean to play at the dance: for him to be out the whole evening and then come home in the early hours of the morning, drunk, as he had often done when their mother was alive. But that had been different: they were in bed and whatever happened, day or night, they knew Mammy was there and everything would be all right. And even though their father might have a sore head or upset stomach the next day, he would have brought some money home and it would help towards food and fuel.

'I suppose it's too soon for me to be out at night,' Johnny said. 'I'm sure they will find somebody else for the dance...'

As Ella turned towards her father now, she saw the lost and helpless look on his face and her heart went out to him. Once again she felt the pain of his inadequacies and knew that he could not help the way he was, that there was something missing in him; she wasn't sure what it was, but it was something she knew was in most hard-working men and fathers, something that made them stronger and more dependable. Since she was a young girl, she had been aware of this and felt the same protective way towards him as her mother had.

Sean sat up straight, a dark frown on his face. 'Why don't you just forget about playing music, and find yourself a decent day job like other fathers do? And then you'll have the money to pay somebody.'

Sean had never dared to speak like that before.

Johnny took a step back, as if he had just received a blow. 'Am I not trying?' he said, his voice uncertain. 'I've to see a man down at the docks on Monday morning.'

'Monday morning,' Sean repeated in a mocking tone, shaking his head. 'That's what you always say. I just hope something turns up because we're going to need more turf or coal and – and ...' His voice thickened and he began to stammer. 'And we can't depend on other people to bring us things and do things for us.' Sean's eyes suddenly filled up and he pointed his finger at his father. 'You should have been here this afternoon and all of this wouldn't have happened. You're the daddy; *you're* the one that's supposed to fix all this for us!'

Ella whirled round at him. 'Don't you dare talk to Daddy like that! You would never have talked like that when Mammy was here.'

'That'll do now!' Johnny said, looking from one to the other. 'We're all tired now, and we just need a bit of peace and quiet. It might be the best thing if we all go to bed. We have to be up in the morning to see how poor little Hannah is.'

Ella watched Sean through lowered eyelids. There was more wrong with him than the argument tonight, she thought. Then she remembered what he had said earlier about being in trouble, and she felt her heart sink. *What kind of trouble is he in?* She asked herself. *What has he done?*

Chapter Five

It was Monday morning when Ella discovered what her brother had done. Ten o'clock. Well past the time when she and Sean should have gone to school.

She was busy in the kitchen when the knock came on the front door.

'I'll get it,' Johnny said, coming down the stairs. 'It might be Father Brosnan he said he would look in on us sometime today.'

Ella turned back towards the kitchen, taking off the apron she was wearing so she looked decent for the priest. Her father opened the door and she heard the voices. Her heart almost stopped when she realised that one of the visitors was Mr Rafferty, the headmaster from the boys' school. *Oh, no*, she thought. He had been out at the house a few weeks after their mother had died, saying that he knew things were difficult, but the law was the law, and both Sean and Ella should be back in school after a reasonable length of time. Now it seemed that time was up.

Hopefully her father would be able to explain about Hannah's accident and the headmaster would understand. Mr Rafferty was strict and took no nonsense in school, but Ella knew that he was fair. But then she head another man's voice. Someone she didn't know. She moved further down the hallway so she could stand behind the scullery door and hear what was going on but not be seen.

'Come in out of the rain, Mr Rafferty,' her father said, holding the door wide.

Ella listened as the men were guided into the front room.

'This is Garda Hennessey,' Mr Rafferty said. 'He called into the school this morning looking for Sean, and I had to tell him that he was missing school once again.'

Ella's hand flew to her mouth. They must really be in trouble if the Guards were calling into the school for them.

'I'm sorry Sean and Ella didn't make it this morning,' Johnny said, 'but there is a good reason. We had an awful accident yesterday, and the little one – Hannah – got badly scalded. She's in St James's Hospital, and we all need to go down there today.'

'I already know about it,' Mr Rafferty said, 'and I'm very sorry to hear what happened. We were told by some of the other children.'

The other man said something that Ella could not hear, then Mr Rafferty said, 'Is Sean here? It's actually him we've come about.'

'He is,' Johnny said. 'He's upstairs dressing the little fellow. Is it just about his school attendance, or is there something else wrong?'

The Guard spoke now. 'There is, I'm sorry to say, because I can see you have enough on your plate without me bringing more trouble to your door. It might be best if we have the young lad here to explain himself.'

'I'll go and get him now,' her father said, and Ella knew by the tone of his voice that he was anxious. She heard him go upstairs and then the murmur of his and Sean's voices, then a few minutes later both of them came downstairs.

'Now, Sean,' Mr Rafferty said, 'I believe you know Garda Hennessey?'

There was a silence.

'Ah, he does of course,' the Guard said. 'And there's no point in us wasting time here. I'll get straight to the point. Sean was caught breaking and entering a premises in Chapelizod on Friday evening just gone. A Guard was phoned to come out to

27

the place, and this fella here was brought to the station with two other lads.'

'Is this true?' Johnny asked.

Ella thought she might be sick.

Garda Hennessey answered for the dumbstruck Sean. 'Oh, indeed it is,' he said. 'I was on duty when we got the phone call from the coal merchants to say he had locked them into his yard. Him and two of his cronies. Seemingly, they had found their way in there several times recently, but this time the owner was ready for them. Once he knew they were in the yard, he crept around the back and locked the doors on them. There's no denying it, they were caught red-handed filling sacks with the man's coal.'

Ella's hand flew to her mouth. *That* was where the coal for the nice warm fires had come from – not from some friend's father.

Her father found his voice again, albeit an uncertain one. 'I don't know what to say, Mr Rafferty. We're a decent family. Nothing like this has ever happened before—'

'I beg to differ,' the Guard said. 'He's been at this caper a few times recently.'

'I meant nothing like this happened before his mother died. I'm not making excuses for him, what he's done is wrong, but it's been a tough old time since Mary died. It's been hard for us all.'

There was a silence.

'It's only a matter of weeks,' Mr Rafferty said. 'And I can vouch for the fact that they have always been a decent family. The parish priest and the curate will too.'

'I'm an understanding man,' Garda Hennessey said, 'but I still have to write a report up. I've been out to the other two lads' houses to give them a warning, and it wouldn't be fair on them to let him off too easily. He has to know he can't get away with this sort of carry-on. God knows where it could lead to.'

'There won't be any more trouble,' her father said. 'I can guarantee it.'

'I'd rather hear that statement from Sean himself – he's too quiet for my liking. Maybe he thinks he can get away with this sort of nonsense?'

'Sean!' Ella was surprised at the tone of her father's voice. 'Did you hear all that the Guard and Mr Rafferty have said? Nodding your head like a dummy is no good – you need to speak up for yourself. This is serious trouble you're in.'

Ella remembered the way Sean had spoken to her father on Saturday night. Surely he wasn't so stupid as to behave the same way now to the Guard and Mr Rafferty?

She began to say a silent *Hail Mary* but had only got through a few lines when an unexpected sound halted her: it was the sound of her brother sobbing. Sean didn't cry often. Even when their mother died, he hadn't cried until the day of the funeral. At the time she had thought it was as if he had pulled some sort of shell around him that kept him separate from all that was going on around him. Now the crying slowed down, followed by the sound of him blowing his nose.

Then, she heard his voice – hoarse and sort of strangled. 'I am sorry . . .' he said, 'but my father's not working and we're running out of money. We needed coal, and it was the only way I knew how to help.'

'For God's sake, Sean!' Johnny said. 'We weren't that desperate you had to steal.'

'It wasn't a man's house, it was only a business,' Sean snapped back. 'They have loads of coal there, we thought they wouldn't miss a few bags.'

'Stealing is stealing,' the Guard said. 'And breaking into private premises is a serious crime. Make no mistake about it. And if we were to send a report to the courts, they wouldn't be taking it too lightly. You could be looking at a stretch down in Daingean Reformatory. There are boys in there who have done a lot less. Are you getting the picture here, Sean?'

Ella closed her eyes. The thought of her brother being locked up in a place for bad boys brought a pain to her chest. And all for the sake of a few bags of coal.

'Are you listening, Sean?' Mr Rafferty said. 'Do you hear what the Guard is saying? Can you tell him that you're sorry and promise him you won't ever get involved in anything like this ever again?'

'He won't,' Johnny said, his voice unusually firm now. 'I can guarantee it.'

'I'm sorry,' Sean said. 'Don't make me go to the Reformatory – I didn't think it was so serious.'

'That's a bit more like it,' the Guard said. He paused, then, 'So we'll leave it at that, now, and I'll see what I can do. I can't make any promises, but I'll have a word with the sergeant and hopefully we can let it go.'

Ella heard Sean start to cry again and her heart went out to him. Before she could stop herself she moved quickly along the hallway and into the living room. She pushed her way past Mr Rafferty and the Guard until she was beside Sean and encircled him with her arms. 'You're OK,' she said in a soothing voice. 'You're OK, Sean. Nothing like this will happen again and everything will be fine.' In spite of everything – the terrible accident he had caused by leaving Hannah, and now the trouble he had brought to the door, she felt heart sorry for him.

The Guard and Mr Rafferty went towards the hallway, Johnny following behind. 'I'm afraid we'll have to notify the authorities about the little girl's accident,' the Guard said, 'and we'll have to mention what's happened here with Sean. Both the school and the law have a duty to inform them.'

Johnny's face was suddenly ashen. 'Surely you don't need to bring the authorities in?'

'Couldn't you get some help in the house?' Mr Rafferty said in a low voice. 'A relative or even a family friend?'

'It's not easy bringing another woman into the house... it's upsetting...'

'It will be more upsetting if the Health Board become

30

involved. You must surely have a niece or a cousin or someone who would help you out?'

Johnny gave a great sigh. 'I'll do my best to find somebody.'

'Do,' Mr Rafferty, said, putting an understanding hand on his shoulder. 'It would solve all your problems.'

Chapter Six

After he had closed the door on Mr Rafferty and the Guard, Johnny stood for a few moments in the hallway and then he squared his shoulders and came back into the front room. Ella and Sean were sitting side by side on the sofa with downcast eyes.

'OK,' he said, coming over to stand in front of the fire, 'what's done is done. There is no point in us going over everything again. We all know we need to make changes around here, and I'm going to make a start straight away.' He looked at the clock. 'I'm going down to the docks to see about work. After that, I'm going to find a phone box in one of the pubs and make a few phone calls over to England.'

Ella looked at him. 'Why are you phoning England?'

'To your uncles, to see if any of the girls can come over to give us a hand for a while. I'll be back in time for us to go to the afternoon visiting in the hospital. Hopefully, we'll see a good improvement in Hannah today.'

The job on the docks did not materialise, and the foreman asked him to come back the following day. With a heavy heart he walked all the way to the Barley Mow and used the payphone to ring the White Horse in Bootle to leave a message for his two brothers. He hated using the phone as he always felt self-conscious on it, but when he explained the situation to the friendly barmaid in the White Horse, she offered to go around to his brothers' houses that evening and let them know.

'It's not far from here,' she told him, 'and I know Charlie's wife well as I often meet her at Mass on a Sunday.'

Johnny felt himself relax a little. 'That's very good of you,' he said. 'Tell them if they can come to the bar later on tonight, I'll ring around half eight.'

In the afternoon the family all walked to St James's Hospital. It was a wasted journey because they were told they could not see Hannah for the next few days. With heavy hearts and hardly a word spoken between them, they all trudged back home.

Ella put the pan on and used up the last of Mrs Murphy's soda bread by frying it, and they all had it with a rasher of bacon. Afterwards, Sean wrapped Larry up in a woollen hat and scarf and took him out to the park to play football.

'Make sure and behave yourself when you're out,' Johnny said in a low voice. 'Straight there and back, no messing around in the streets.'

Ella shut herself in the scullery, and then kept herself busy with the pile of washing which had built up. When she had hung it out, she set the iron up and pressed shirts for her father and Sean.

Johnny sat in the armchair by the fire, nursing his thoughts about his sick daughter and trying to work out a way to keep the family together.

Later that night he walked back to the Barley Mow and, after having a pint of Guinness to bolster him up, he called Charlie and Joe. Charlie, his eldest brother, was waiting by the phone at the other end. Johnny quickly explained about Hannah and how the authorities were planning a visit. 'I'm afraid they'll say the accident was because there's no woman in the house. They might take the kids off me.'

'That's very bad,' Charlie said. 'Very bad indeed.'

'I was hoping that one of your girls might come over, or if not, maybe one of Joe's.'

'I'm sorry, Johnny,' Charlie said in a low voice, 'but we're in a bad way here ourselves. Even now, we're all still struggling with the mess from the bombings and the rationing. We were hoping everything would be fine once the war was over, but it's taking longer than we imagined and Patricia can't leave her job in the hospital. Since the men came back from the war, all the women are fighting to keep their jobs even in the hospitals.'

'What about Delia?'

'To tell you the honest truth, she's met a Yank. A big farmer from somewhere called Montana. As soon as all the paperwork is sorted, she's planning to get married and then head straight out to America. I can tell you now, she's broken her mother's heart, but she's hell-bent on going. And poor Annie has never got over losing Patrick in the war. She never will. Annie will never be the same again, her nerves are at her.'

Johnny realised that, because of the tragedy in his own life in the last few months, he had hardly registered the fact that other people were dealing with their own difficulties. He felt bad that Charlie had to remind him that they had lost their only son a few years ago. Johnny felt that he maybe hadn't been as sympathetic with his brother and his wife as he should have. Having endured the pain of losing Mary and the baby, he could now sympathise in a way he had never been able to before.

Johnny closed his eyes for a few moments. 'What about Bridie?' he asked. He was clutching at straws asking about Charlie's youngest daughter. She would not have been his first choice, as she was a giddy sort.

'Ah, she won't leave Liverpool,' Charlie said. 'The time we brought her over to Dublin, she couldn't wait to get back home.'

Johnny felt his heart sink. 'How are Joe's two daughters fixed?' Joe, a postman, was the middle brother and he had three sons and two daughters. Johnny's elderly father also lived with them.

'Well, I had a chat with him earlier,' Charlie said, 'and it's the same story. Catherine is in a factory and Lily is working in one of the big hotels and is getting married next year. They're all busy now and getting on with their own lives.' He paused. 'I know it must be hard for you with poor Mary gone, but in many ways, Johnny, you're better off in Dublin. Some of the families near us who had their houses bombed out are still sleeping on floors and in places that the charities are providing. Some of the places you wouldn't put a dog into. There are broken buildings all over the place.' He paused. 'And there were so many people killed in the bombings here – a lad I worked with lost three sons in the war. It's not been an easy time for any of us...'

They spoke for a few more minutes and then Johnny put the phone back in its cradle. He came back into the bar to drink another pint to help him gather his thoughts.

His last hope was Nora Lamb. And she was literally the last hope in every way. Not one of the family would have chosen her. Johnny knew that Mary had welcomed the solitary Nora as an act of charity – and the woman had no natural maternal instincts.

But he had to face the fact that no one else was available. It was Nora Lamb or the orphanage.

Chapter Seven

The following afternoon Johnny shaved, dressed in a white shirt and his good navy overcoat and hat, and got the twenty-past four train down to Tullamore. It was cold and windy with the odd spit of rain, so he walked briskly from the station to Nora's townhouse. It didn't cross his mind that she might be out. From her chats with Mary, he knew that, outside of work, her only regular outings were to the church and the shops.

The rain grew heavier and he was glad when he reached the house and saw the light within. He paused for a few moments to catch his breath, and then he lifted the brass knocker and gave it two firm taps.

He heard footsteps coming down the hallway, and he moved back a few steps.

Nora's eyes widened with shock, then her brow furrowed. 'Johnny,' she said, 'is there something wrong?'

He took his hat off and stood holding it. 'We've had a bit of trouble at home and I'm in need of your help.'

Nora stared at him, and then she suddenly realised she was keeping him on the doorstep. She quickly moved to step back and open the door wide. 'Come in, come in,' she said. 'I'm down in the kitchen. The kettle is boiled, so I'll make us some tea and you can tell me what it's all about.'

Johnny followed her down the dimly lit hallway with its mosaic-patterned tiled floor, remembering Mary remarking how gloomy and depressing the house was. He passed the tidy wooden coat stand, which had hooks holding Nora's hats and scarves, a drawer under the mirror for her keys, and a place at the bottom for her umbrellas. The saying, 'A place for everything and everything in its place' Johnny thought, was written for her. As they went along, he glanced at the dark green and maroon faded wallpaper, which was broken up with pictures of Our Lady, The Pope, and St Francis of Assisi surrounded by animals, and a variety of framed photographs of cheerless, deceased relatives. Nothing must have changed in the house, he guessed, since Nora's parents were first married.

'Oh Mother of God! The poor little thing,' she said when Johnny told her about Hannah and the accident, looking distressed. 'Will the burns heal all right? She won't be scarred or anything?'

'We don't know yet,' he told her. 'We have to wait and see how much the treatment helps.'

Nora asked him a few more questions about what the hospital were doing and then Johnny told her what Mr Rafferty had said about the authorities coming to see them.

'It's bad news, all right,' Nora said. 'No doubt about it.' She shook her head. 'It can't be easy managing those four children on your own.' She gave a sigh. 'And I'm sorry that I don't live nearer to help you out.'

She poured the tea into a mug for Johnny and a china cup and saucer for herself.

He looked at her, then gathering every ounce of determination he had, he laid his cards on the table.

'I wonder if you could get some time off work to come up to the house for a few weeks to help us out? I wouldn't ask, but we're in a desperate situation and I don't want to bring strangers in. The children are used to seeing you regularly.'

Nora's face was a picture. '*Me*?' she said in an incredulous, breathless voice. 'You want *me* to come up to Dublin and look after the children for you? You're not serious, are you? Even if I could get the time off work,' Nora said, 'I have no experience with children – I wouldn't know what to do. I'm too used to living on my own, have my own ways. They would probably be better off in an orphanage than being looked after by me.'

Tears gathered behind Johnny's eyes and slowly started to trickle down his face. He moved his mug out of reach and stared at it for a few moments until his sight was too blurred to see it. Then, silently, he folded his arms on the table and laid his head on them.

'Johnny?' Nora asked. 'Are you all right?'

He took a few deep breaths, trying to still himself, then his shoulders started to heave followed by dry, racking sobs.

Chapter Eight

Tullamore,
Co Offaly

Nora Lamb looked around her living room, checking that everything was in its place. Her parents' walnut clock was sitting straight in the middle of the black iron mantelpiece, as were the two brass candlesticks on either side. She had given the mantelpiece a last polish early this morning, although God knows the dust that would be on it when she came back. Her gaze moved downwards to the cold, empty grate that she waged war on daily. The sandy-coloured dust from the turf fires drove her mad. An ordinary duster did no good: it had to be a damp cloth first and then the polish afterwards.

She walked back into the hallway and down to the kitchen, checking once again that the back door was locked and the latches tight on the windows. The air was filled with the comforting odour of bleach and carbolic soap. She came back along the hallway and paused at the coat stand to check in the mirror that her tan hat was straight, the gold and red feather at just the right angle, and that the fur collar on her camel coat was sitting properly.

She looked at her face now. It was the best she could do with a touch of powder, a touch of rouge and a touch of pink lipstick. She had no illusions about her looks. She had never been a beauty, and at forty-two she was unlikely to become one now. Her thin nose was pinched-looking and inclined to redness, and

39

her blue eyes too faded. But she kept reasonably up to date with her clothes – she did not want to be thought of as old-fashioned by the other women at work. Bad enough she was referred to as a spinster. She had her mid-length auburn hair washed and set every Saturday morning so it was nice for Mass on Sunday, and she manicured her nails regularly.

She went upstairs once again, glancing around her bedroom to make sure it was still perfect, then went along to what had been her parents' room. It was exactly the way it had been since her mother died fifteen years ago, two years after her father.

She paused in the doorway to look over at the sepia wedding photograph. 'Wish me luck,' she whispered to the serious-looking young man and woman in the frame. 'And keep me safe up in Dublin.'

Her mother had always said the same sort of things to a picture of the Sacred Heart which was in the living room on the wall opposite the fire, and when she dipped her fingers into the Holy Water font at the front door. Nora had never got the same solace from religion as her mother. She observed her religious duties, went to Mass every Sunday and Confessions regularly, and all the other extras like October Devotions. But for all that, she preferred to talk to the photo of her parents, who still seemed much more real to her than God had ever been.

Her mother and father had wanted her to meet a nice, kindly man who would have married her and looked after her. Her mother, while she was in good health, had done her best to introduce her to anyone she thought might be suitable. But God, it seemed, had never had any plans for her in that direction. No matter how many candles she lit and prayers she said, asking for him to intervene, nothing ever materialised. All these years later, he still seemed happy enough to leave her rattling around in her lonely house on her own.

She heard the noise of the postbox now, and she moved quickly back down the stairs. There was a blue envelope on the mat which she picked up, immediately recognising the hand-writing and the stamp. It was from her cousin Imelda, who lived over in London. She put it into her crocodile-skin handbag to read on the train. Then, as she heard the walnut clock strike half past eleven, she decided that she would have to go now to be in plenty of time for the twelve o'clock train up to Dublin.

Nora's heart started to flutter. This trip to Dublin was the biggest thing she had done in years. She had, of course, had days up in Dublin visiting the Cassidys or for shopping or going to a show, but she had never left her house overnight for a long time.

She opened the front door and then lifted her grey and blue suitcase out onto the footpath outside, and then she locked the door. It was a strange feeling leaving the house and not being sure when she would be back.

She set off along the street. She had barely got into the rhythm of walking with the suitcase when she heard a voice saying, 'Off on yer holidays, Miss Lamb?'

It was Tony Healy, one of the porters from the hospital. Nora thought of him as a bit of a smart-aleck who liked the sound of his own voice.

'No,' she said, her brow deepening, 'I'm certainly not off on a holiday. I actually have a serious family illness in Dublin and I'm going up there to help out.'

'Oh, begod,' he said, clearly flummoxed by her news. 'I'm sorry to hear that. I didn't know you had relatives in Dublin.'

Nora was rewarded by his obvious embarrassment. 'Well, there's a lot people don't know about me.' She started to move forward again. 'I have to hurry for the train. There's a badly burned child in hospital that needs my care and attention. I know people are always complaining about the hospital authorities, but they have been very understanding. They told me not to worry about having the time off.'

'Sure, you're not one to swing the lead at work,' he said.

'I've not had a sick day off in ten years.' Nora's voice was proud. She guessed he was the type to take a day off when it suited him.

'When do you think you will be back?'

Nora stepped out to cross the road. 'That's something I just

cannot answer,' she said. 'It's in the hands of the man above.'
She smiled to herself as she walked smartly along towards the
station. That would give him something to talk about back at
the hospital, she thought. It would give them all a surprise to
know that she had a life outside of work after all. A life they
knew nothing about.

The train was on time for once, and Nora was grateful for it,
as the threatened rain had now started. She walked along the
corridor, dragging the case looking into each of the carriages
to find an empty one. She paused outside one which had just
one passenger – an old man who was reading his newspaper, a
well-dressed professional type who was unlikely to trouble her
with constant conversation. When she opened the door, the man
looked up and they gave each other a cursory greeting and then
he went back to his *Irish Independent*.

After a few moments, she reached to the seat beside her for
her handbag and she took out a book. It was one she had carefully covered with brown paper, as a student might do to protect
their textbooks. In Nora's case, she had covered it shortly after
she bought it, so as not to court any controversy. It was a copy
of *Gone with the Wind*. She had bought it in a second-hand
bookshop in Manchester when she was over a few years ago
for a funeral. She had read in the *Irish Independent* or some
other paper that the film had been censored, but she wasn't
sure whether the book was banned in Ireland or not. She had
no way of finding out without drawing attention to the fact she
had it in her possession, and she certainly did not want to take
a chance with breaking the law. She thought there was nothing
wrong with the book at all. She had read it several times and
loved it, and every so often she picked it up and read it from
start to finish again.

The train rattled on its journey. While she was not looking
forward to what lay ahead for her in the Cassidy household,
perhaps a break away from Tullamore and the people she
worked with would not be such a bad thing. It might actually
make them appreciate all the work she did. The typing, the

42

filing, writing up indecipherable doctors' reports, answering the telephone systems, posting reports back to patients' general practitioners.

But work had helped fill in all the empty hours she had had since her mother died. She had a few routines. Going to Mass before work and the walk there and back filled a small amount of time. Shopping filled another couple of hours, and was only necessary a few times in the week. Work had been her saviour. It got her out of the house and gave her a routine for five days of the week. But she could not say she actually enjoyed her work. At forty-two years of age, she worked roughly the same amount of hours in the week – and counted the minutes down in most of the hours until she was finished. And who really appreciated all the work she did? Who really appreciated *her*?

Recently, she had begun to see things she did as being more and more pointless, as though she herself was of no consequence. The ruminating had begun around the time Mary Cassidy died. She had never imagined that someone as lively and cheery as Mary could be there one minute and gone the next. Along with a tiny baby that had hardly had the time on earth to draw breath. It was hard to think of those tragedies, and it made her wonder if there was a God who could allow such a thing to happen.

While she and Mary had lived very different lives, they had got on well. And although Mary was seven years younger, they understood each other, Nora growing up as an only child, while Mary only had one brother who was much older than her, and who had emigrated to America when he was eighteen. They knew each other's family history and could talk about people, long dead, who no one else knew.

Nora felt a little guilty that she hadn't gone up to Dublin more often over the last years. In truth, the children had taken a lot of the pleasure out of the visits. They were too noisy and too lively for her and it was hard to have any kind of decent conversation with Mary with them around in the small house.

She had felt more comfortable as Sean and Ella had grown

up a bit and become more independent and sensible. They had quietened down enough to concentrate on books and puzzles, which Nora liked, and she began to enjoy talking to them about school work. Then Mary had become pregnant again and had two younger children within a few years, and Nora's visits had dwindled due to the racket they made.

And now Nora herself was going to step into the breach, into totally unknown territory. The Saturday afternoons she'd spent with the Cassidys were only a small window into the life that Mary and her family had led. And Nora knew that it was a carefully orchestrated window, designed to show them at their best. Johnny, when available, and the two elder children had been commandeered to help with the little ones during her visits to allow the women their long stroll around Phoenix Park. She guessed life, in the rest of the week, was far more chaotic and noisy than it was for her few hours' visit.

The Cassidy house was basic, but, to her credit, in spite of looking after four children and keeping a part-time job going, Mary had kept it spotlessly clean, and managed to have washing out every day – apart from a Sunday, of course. Nora knew she would now have to take over all those household chores, and, while she was used to running her own house, it would be much harder with five other people, especially with the mess that children made. She would miss the little comforts she had at home, but, in the short term, she would easily survive without them. And she could also bring back some of the smaller items on her visits back home, because she would insist that she had Saturday or Sunday to herself. She deserved one quiet day to look forward to.

As the green fields gave way to a more industrial-looking landscape as it neared the city, she realised that, strangely, she was looking forward to a new daily routine, and she liked the idea that nobody in Dublin knew her. Instead of wearing the invisible label of 'spinster', she could just be an ordinary woman. She could go about her business without fear of bumping into people like Tony Healy every five minutes, who thought they

44

knew every little detail of her life. She could walk about as a complete stranger who did not have to pass the time of day with anyone if she didn't feel like it. She did not have to explain herself to anyone or care what they thought about her.

In Dublin, Nora suddenly realised, she could be anyone she wanted.

Chapter Nine

At Kingsbridge Station, Nora walked along the platform, struggling slightly with the heavy case.

She wondered if a taxi might be in order, although it seemed an awful waste of money to her. Besides, she preferred to walk as it kept her figure trim and allowed her to wear the tight belts her women's magazines advised would draw attention to her slender waist.

As the crowd thinned, she saw a smartly dressed figure coming towards her with an outstretched arm.

'Hello, Nora, I thought I would come and meet you. I thought you might need a hand.'

She was taken aback to see Johnny Cassidy. He had never met her from the train before. He had only ever walked her back in the dark, winter evenings. She felt at a slight disadvantage, as she had not yet thought of what she might say to him when they first met. She was not good at off-the-cuff chat, and it was something she would have rehearsed on her slow walk to Islandbridge.

Johnny's arm reached out for the case. 'Oh, that's very good of you,' she said, feeling a little wave of relief at not having to carry it further.

His brows shot up as he took it from her. 'That's a fair weight.' He smiled at her. 'Did you bring half of Tullamore with you?'

Nora, not given to jokes, felt self-conscious. 'I put a bag with some fresh vegetables in it.'

'Ah, you're very good, as if it's not enough for you to come up here to help us out at such short notice.' He put the case back down on the platform. 'I can't tell you how much...' He paused, shaking his head. His eyes filled up and he took a deep breath to steady himself. '...how much I appreciate it. How much the whole family appreciate you coming to give us a hand.'

Nora could see his distress, but was at a loss as to what to answer. She could not say, 'It's no trouble,' or 'I'm delighted to be able to help you out'. Neither of which were true, and it would be almost reckless of her to give the impression that it was of no consequence. She gave a little nod. 'We'll see how it works out,' she said. 'We'll all put our best foot forward.'

'We will indeed,' Johnny said. He picked the case up again and they started to walk out into the main part of the station. 'And it's good news all round today. I was down at the hospital this morning and they told me that Hannah is coming on well. Please God, we could have her back home in a few weeks' time.'

'Oh, that's good news indeed,' Nora said. 'That will be all the prayers that people have been saying for her.'

'No doubt about it,' Johnny said. 'I've never been in the church so much in my life. Have you met our curate, Father Brosnan? He's the loveliest young fellow you could meet. He's been calling down at the house regularly since – since Mary died, and he's been visiting Hannah in hospital every other day.

'And we've done our best to get the house organised for you. We've moved the rooms around so the two lads are in with me, the girls will be in together when Hannah gets home, and you have a room and a bed for yourself. Is that all right?'

Nora tried not to show her relief. The thought of sharing a room – or even worse, a bed – had been one of her biggest dreads. 'That's very kind of you. I hope it's not put you all to a lot of trouble?'

'Not at all,' he said. 'You have a wardrobe there as well, and Sean and I lifted Mary's nice walnut dressing table in.' He paused. 'She would have wanted you to have it.'

As they walked out through the station, Johnny turned to her again. 'Are you OK to walk back to Islandbridge?'

'Of course,' she said. 'Don't I always?'

'I was just thinking of the handbag you are carrying, it looks a fair weight.'

'You have the case,' she said, 'and that is much heavier. I'm grand with the bag, it's the one I use every day for work—' She suddenly halted, realising she might be boring him with such small details of her life.

This was something she was very self-conscious about as she had overheard two of the younger, skittish staff laughing about a lovely carol concert she had been to the previous Christmas. The following day she had told them about it in some detail during their tea break. Afterwards, Nora had gone off to get a new box of carbon paper. She was returning to the office when she had heard her name mentioned. She had taken a few steps backwards and then frozen, the box of carbon clutched to her chest.

'Oh God!' one of the girls had said, 'Is that all poor oul' Nora has to look forward to over Christmas? I think I'd shoot myself!'

'Well, we are talking about *Miss Lamb*,' the other had laughed. 'I doubt if there will be many fellas looking to catch her under the mistletoe or trying to jingle her bells.'

They had then dissolved into giggles.

Determinedly, she pushed the cruel memory out of her mind.

'If you're sure the bag is not too heavy, that's fine then,' Johnny said, smiling at her.

The concern in his voice and his kindness suddenly lifted Nora's heart. It was nice to have someone to care how she felt about anything. But then, Johnny had always been a kind person. In that way, Mary had been very lucky. In other ways, she had been foolish putting up with his faults. And this was the very reason that Nora was up in Dublin, because Johnny had never been dependable in work. And because he didn't have a regular job, he couldn't afford to pay anyone. And so, he had come looking for help from her.

Nora was under no illusions.

Chapter Ten

Ella Cassidy stopped brushing her long, damp hair to study herself in the wardrobe mirror. She looked clean and tidy, which was the most important thing. Sean and Larry were sitting by the fire in the front room, washed and wearing their best clothes too. They had to make a good impression on Auntie Nora today. Good enough to make her leave everything she had down in the country, and move up full-time to Dublin to take the place of their mother. So far, her mother's cousin had only agreed to come for a month or so and Ella knew this could be their last chance to live as a family together, their last chance of staying out of the orphanage.

She closed her eyes, her heart suddenly racing, frightened at what the future might hold for the family, frightened at the thought of being separated from her father, from Sean and Larry and Hannah. There were times when Sean drove her mad, but next to her father, he was still the closest person to her in the world.

The day after her father had gone down to Nora in Tullamore, the authorities – a woman and an older man – had visited the house. They had spoken to Johnny and then brought Sean and Ella in and explained everything to them as well. They had to have a woman in charge of the house who would look after the younger two, and they both had to go back to school on a regular basis. A record would be kept of their attendance and their progress carefully monitored. If things did not work out, then they would all be taken into the custody of the Health Board.

Ella turned her mother's silver-plated hairbrush between her hands. She knew that however hard life was going to be with Nora Lamb, they had to make it work. She checked the time now on her mother's little gold watch.

She would go downstairs now and make sure that Sean had minded the fire, then she would put the kettle back on. She would double check that everything was clean and tidy. She would remind Sean once again to be cheery and polite, and help keep Larry entertained. She would impress upon him that they would have to do everything and anything to make sure that their Auntie Nora – for that was what they called their mother's cousin – would stay. A few minutes later, Ella knew he had got the message, because the minute he heard the gate creaking, Sean shot to get the door.

After her father had lifted the case and bag upstairs and Nora had taken her hat and coat off and hung them on the coat stand, Ella went to the scullery and made a pot of tea and brought it to the living room with mugs and Nora's special china cup and saucer. She set them down on the table.

'We have some scones that Mrs Murphy baked,' Ella said. 'A nephew brought her some flour and raisins.'

'I'll help you lift the other things through,' Sean said, getting up from the table.

'I can manage,' Ella said, but he followed her back to the scullery. 'Why didn't you stay and chat to Auntie Nora?' she whispered.

He shrugged. 'I never know what to say to her...'

'For God's sake, surely you could think of something for a few minutes?' Ella rolled her eyes. 'Well, you better start thinking, because she's going to be around all the time now.' She handed him a small china milk jug which had shamrocks on it and an equally small matching sugar bowl that her mother had always used for Nora. 'Take them in,' she said. 'It's the last of the sugar, so don't take any more than half a spoonful.'

When Ella went in with the scones, her father had put the radio on and a Glenn Miller song, 'In the Mood' was playing which made the living room seem unusually cheerful. After everyone else had taken a scone, Ella cut one in half and buttered it for Larry, then she lifted him up to sit on her knee.

'He's a very good boy,' Nora said. 'He's been sitting here quietly since I came in. Haven't you?'

Johnny ruffled his small son's hair. 'He's missing his little sister, aren't you, Larry? Will we go down to the hospital later to see Hannah?'

Larry looked at his father solemnly and nodded.

Nora shook her head and said quietly to Johnny, 'It must be very hard for him ... all the changes, and now me arriving.'

'He'll be grand,' Johnny said, taking a bite of his scone.

Ella lowered her gaze to the floor. It was hard for Larry. It was hard for them all.

There was a small silence, then Nora suddenly said, 'Oh, I do love Glenn Miller.' She swayed a little in her chair to the melody. 'His music is just lovely.'

'He was the one that went down in a plane, wasn't he?' Sean said.

'Yes,' she said, 'very tragic ...'

There was another silence. Ella threw a withering glance over at Sean for dampening down the atmosphere. He looked back at her with big eyes, having no idea why she was annoyed.

After they finished, as Ella started to clear up the plates, Nora said, 'I just want to get some things out of my case. I brought some meat and vegetables for the dinner tonight.' She paused, thinking it might look as though she were trying to take over already. 'Unless you had something else already planned?'

Ella felt her heart lift. It wasn't just that she hated asking her father for money, it was because, for the first time in ages, someone else was now involved in planning the meals. 'That would be lovely,' she said.

'Johnny,' Nora said, 'Would it be OK if I came to the hospital this evening? I don't want to push in ...'

'No problem at all,' he told her. 'She's allowed more visitors now she's been moved to the children's ward, and it would give her a chance to get used to you, for when she comes out.'

'That's what I thought. And I wonder, Sean,' she said, turning towards him, 'if you would be good enough to show me which room I'm in?'

Sean immediately moved to his feet. 'Of course I will.'

She followed him upstairs.

'This is it,' Sean said, stopping at the first room. He opened the door wide to show a bright room with freshly painted white walls, and a single wrought-iron bed. It was made nice with a cream crocheted cover. 'The bed was mine, but Da got a brand-new mattress and the sheets and things for you from Paddy Bracken.'

'Paddy Bracken?' Nora repeated.

'He has a second-hand shop down in Kilmainham.'

Nora's hand fluttered to her throat. She had dreaded the thought of using a mattress used by the children, but the thought of a second-hand one from strangers was even worse.

Sean read her face and rushed to reassure her. 'The mattress and sheets were brand new,' he said, 'and still in the wrapping. Paddy told Da that they were bought for a sick woman that lived in one of the big posh houses out in Ballsbridge, but she never came out of hospital again. Her family all have plenty, so they didn't want any of the stuff.'

Nora wondered about the cost of it all, and hoped Johnny had not over-stretched himself. 'Well, it looks lovely, I must say.' She went over to the corner of the room where Johnny had laid her case. 'Would you be a good boy and lift that up onto the bed?' When Sean did so, she unlocked it, and then took out the bag with the meat and vegetables and gave them to him.

'I won't unpack now,' she said. 'We have to get the dinner on so it's ready before we go to see Hannah.' *How busy things suddenly seem,* she thought, *and still the hospital visit to come.* 'You take that bag downstairs now, Sean, if you please.'

As his footsteps sounded down the stairs, Nora halted to look around the room. The single pine wardrobe, albeit scuffed and scratched, was clean and looked as though it would be adequate to hold all her things. It looked slightly at odds with Mary's shining walnut dressing table with the lovely triple mirrors, but it was more than she had imagined.

A little glow spread through her now. How thoughtful it was of Johnny to organise all this for her. She knew he did not have much, and what he had done was above and beyond what she had expected. She hoped he hadn't done it thinking that all the work would make her feel guilty and stay longer than she had planned, but then she dismissed it. He was just being nice, and she would make sure that she showed her appreciation.

She went back to look in her case again for the other things she had brought for the family. A short time later she came back downstairs carrying four books and a square, handmade, polished wooden box. She placed them on the table in the living room where Larry and Johnny were still sitting.

'Thank you, Johnny, for all the work you did getting the room ready for me. I can see you've even given it a fresh coat of paint.'

'It was the least I could do. Is it all right? Have you everything you need?'

'Absolutely,' she said.

'If you want to put a few pictures up or anything to make it more like what you're used to...?'

There was a silence.

'We'll see,' she said. 'I have all those things at home, really, and there's no point in taking them off the walls to bring back here, and then have to take them back home again later.'

'Whatever you want,' Johnny said. 'The room is yours to do whatever you want with it.'

She lifted one of the larger books, an Enid Blyton fairy-tale picture book and placed it in front of Larry. 'This is for you,' she told him. 'And we will all help to read it to you. I have another one here for Hannah.'

Larry looked at the book and then back up at her. 'Thanks,' he said, in a quiet voice.

Nora stepped out into the hallway. 'Sean and Ella,' she called out to them. 'If you have a minute, I have some small things here for you.'

'Ah, sure, there was no need,' Johnny said, gesturing with his hands. 'You're doing enough for us, you shouldn't have...'

She put her finger to her lips. When they came into the living room, she handed them a book each, saying, 'The lady in the shop told me that they are popular with boys and girls your age.' Ella's book was an American novel called *A Tree Grows in Brooklyn*, and Sean's was one of the 'Biggles' series. 'I thought, if you liked them, we might go down to the nearest library and borrow similar ones. The evenings are getting brighter and it will give us all somewhere to go and something to do. I spent a lot of time in Tullamore Library.'

Larry shifted his hand from his book to tentatively touch the top of the wooden box. 'What's in it?'

She smiled at him. 'Shall we open it and see?'

Everyone, including Johnny, crowded round as she slid the cover back to reveal a set of chess figures. Some of the pieces were in a light wood and some had been painted black, and they had all been varnished. 'They were my Uncle Bernard's,' she said. 'And he carved them all by hand, so they are very special.'

'We do woodwork in school,' Sean said. 'Could I hold one?'

'Of course you can,' Nora said, feeling a little warm glow in her chest again. She knew that he was going to be the hardest nut to crack in the house, and guessed the chess set could go either way.

Sean lifted a king from the box and then held it up to examine it closely. 'It's lovely,' he said. 'Look at the marks where he has carved it.'

Johnny lifted a piece now. 'It's a beautiful little set,' he said. 'You can see all the detail in it.'

'I don't suppose it's as perfect as a bought one, at least that's what Uncle Bernard said, but it's more special to me than any one that could be bought in a shop.'

54

'Do you know how to play?' Johnny asked. 'It's a game I never learned.'

'I do,' she said. 'He taught me and we used to play it on a Sunday afternoon after dinner. The games often went on until evening time.' She smiled and gave a little shake of her head. 'Oh, he was a great man. I miss him as much as I miss my parents.'

There was a silence then Ella said, 'I have the cooker on for the meat...'

'Ah, the meat, we'd better get a move on with it.' She gestured towards the chess set. 'We'll put this away now. When we have time later, we can look at it and I'll explain the rules.'

The next few hours passed as she and Ella sorted the bacon and vegetables and set the table in the living room. They then went out to get the washing from the line and bring it into the scullery and hang it over the clothes horse to finish drying. When that was done Nora went back up to her room and took two packets of tea from her case and a packet of digestive biscuits. Then she brought them down and made another pot of tea, using hot water they'd filled a flask with earlier – the gas was only on for a number of hours each day – and gave everyone a biscuit. She could see by the children's reaction that it was a great treat for them having tea twice in the afternoon.

The bacon bubbled away in the pan under the anxious eye of Ella, who could now see opportunities for accidents at every turn. Sean sat at the table reading the fairy-tale book with Larry, while their father dozed by the fire, so Nora went upstairs to sort out the things from her case.

She closed the room door behind her, suddenly glad for a few silent moments on her own. She sat on the edge of the bed to think over the happenings of the day so far. She wasn't sure what she had expected, but she knew that what had happened during the last few hours was not the way the Cassidys lived every day. She had seen it at work, with new members of staff, bright and falsely friendly to start until they knew what they were dealing with. After that, the incomers either fitted in with stronger personalities or they were left on the fringes of everything. She was one of the people on the fringe, on the edge of the conversations. She was older and too different in her ways to be included. There was always a stiffer, more formal atmosphere in the office when she was in their midst, as though they were waiting for her to go so they could relax.

There were only one or two people at work she had felt comfortable with. A nice man who had worked in the mortuary and a single lady called Veronica Fisher, who did the wages in the main office. Veronica had unfortunately moved to Dublin to be closer to her family and elderly parents, and Nora missed their little chats. It made her feel even more of an outsider, not having someone she felt she could relax with.

Nora got to her feet now to stand by the window. She hoped that would not happen with the family, that she would feel like an outsider again. She did not think Johnny would allow it – *could* not afford to allow it. She shrugged. In this instance, she held all the cards. She had her nice home and a life of sorts – a familiar routine at least – back in Tullamore. They had a lot more to lose than she did.

As she stared out into the backyard of the house and the yards of the houses at either side, she suddenly caught her negative, self-protective thoughts and began to chide herself for thinking of the poor, motherless Cassidys this way. They were only children, after all. Even the elder ones. She would do her best by them, Johnny included. She would do her best in memory of Mary. She would not give up easily.

Chapter Eleven

Ella looked around the table at the empty plates. 'It's twenty-five to six! We're not going to have time to do the dishes before we go to the hospital.'

'They'll wait,' Johnny said. 'The dishes will still be here when we come back.'

Nora looked at him and then bit her lip. 'I suppose they will...'

'It's a walk of around twenty minutes,' Johnny explained. 'So if we get ready to go now we should be grand. We don't need to be there dead on six. There are people coming and going in the hospital all the time.'

Ella could tell that her aunt was not comfortable leaving things untidy or rushing or being late. She moved to her feet. 'Come on, Larry,' she said, lifting him from his chair, 'we'll get you out to the toilet and then we'll wash your hands and face before we go to the hospital.'

'Can I bring my book to show Hannah?'

'If Auntie Nora says it's all right.'

'Yes, Larry,' Nora said, sounding pleased, 'you can bring your book and the one for Hannah.'

One after the other, each went quickly to the outhouse, then it was a rush to wash hands and faces at the scullery sink and put on outdoor clothing.

It was dry but cold, with a biting wind. Sean and Ella walked quickly ahead with Larry, Johnny and Nora coming behind at a more dignified pace. Every so often, the two elder children slowed down to take Larry by the hands and swing him up in the air.

'They seem in good spirits,' Nora commented, 'given all that has happened.'

'Ah, well, it's been a good day for them,' Johnny said. 'The best one in a good while.'

Nora felt that same warm glow inside her once more, and as they walked along, she thought how nice it was to have company to walk out with in the bracing air. She hadn't been part of a family like this since she was a child herself. Every so often she gave a sideways glance at Johnny, smart in his heavy coat with a woollen scarf tucked in at the neck, and wondered if people might mistake them for a couple. Probably not, she decided. Apart from the fact she was seven years older than him, she knew her more formal clothing and demeanour would make the age gap seem even greater.

Ella and Sean had slowed down a little now.

'We're going to have to go back to school on Monday or we'll be in trouble,' Ella stated. 'Daddy said as soon as we got somebody in to help, we'd be back full-time. I'm not looking forward to it – we've missed so much and we'll be really behind all the rest.'

'At least you're clever,' Sean said. 'You'll easily catch up. I haven't a hope, especially with the sums. I can't wait until I'm old enough to leave in the summer. It's feckin' stupid, they should just let me go now. What good is it doing me? Most of the other lads have left already and nobody is saying a word about it. It's only because the authorities and the Guards got involved. They are watching us now.'

Ella didn't correct him over his bad language, as she could tell he was in one of his touchy moods. 'I could help you with sums,' she offered. 'Or go and ask Mr Rafferty? I think he would be happy to help.'

'You can forget that.' Sean looked at her as though she were mad. 'Do you want the lads to think I'm some kind of eedjit licking up to the teachers?'

'OK,' Ella said, her eyes flashing in annoyance. 'I was only trying to help...'

He narrowed his eyes. 'Who asked you to stick your nose in? Don't forget who's the eldest here.' He jabbed his thumb at his chest.

Ella looked at him. He had always had an awkward side to him, but since their mother had died he always seemed that way.

When they came to the hospital entrance they waited to let their father and aunt catch up with them, Ella chatting away to Larry, ignoring Sean, glad when the adults joined them.

As they walked down the corridor, Nora asked what the visiting arrangements were, and how many could go in to see Hannah at a time.

'It depends on the sister who is on,' Johnny said. 'Some are stricter than others. I'll go in first and check, and then we'll know.'

Johnny went on ahead to see how the land lay, then a few minutes later he came back out, smiling and beckoning them. 'It's the nice younger one,' he said, 'Sister Gollogly.'

'Oh, that's an unusual name,' Nora commented.

'I think she said she was from Armagh,' Ella said. 'She's been very kind to Hannah.'

As they walked into the ward, Ella said, 'Hannah is in the first bed on the right. They keep her near the nurse's room so they can hear her if she needs anything.'

Nora felt a little pang of anxiety. She was not really used to children, and sick children she had no experience of at all.

The little girl was lying down flat on the bed, with just a slim pillow below her head. She had a light cover which came up to her chest, one heavily bandaged arm flat on top.

'And how's the little fairy today?' Johnny asked.

Hannah turned to look at them, and then a bright smile appeared on her face. 'Daddy!' she said. As she moved to sit up, a look of pain crossed the child's face. She moaned and lay back down again, crying.

Johnny moved to the top of the bed and put a soothing hand

on her head. 'You're OK, darlin',' he said. 'You just turned too quickly. Stay nice and quiet and you'll be grand.'

Ella went to the other side of the bed, murmuring more consolations. After a few minutes, when Hannah had calmed down, Johnny moved away to let Sean and Larry come to say hello to their little sister. Hannah was quiet to begin with, but then perked up a bit, and brightened further when Larry lifted his book to show her. Sean opened it for him and held it while the two younger ones looked at the pictures, with Larry pointing out the different characters and animals in the story.

Nora, unsure what to do, stood at the end of the bed holding on to her gloves and handbag and the fairy-tale book she had brought.

'Did the nice nurses put the cream on your arms and legs?' Ella asked.

'Yes,' she said, 'and they gave me some jelly.'

'Well,' Johnny said, 'aren't you the lucky girl? None of the rest of us have had jelly for a long time.'

Johnny turned to look at Nora, winking, and said in a low voice, 'She's in better fettle now, I'd say she'd be delighted if you give her the book you brought for her.'

She slid in by the bed to sit on the chair, then she turned to look at Hannah. 'Aren't you the brave little girl? And do you remember me? I'm your Aunt Nora from Tullamore...'

There was a silence as Hannah stared straight at her, as though trying to work out who she was. Nora watched now as the little girl's bottom lip began to tremble. Quickly, she lifted the fairy-tale book. 'Look what Aunt Nora brought for you? It's a lovely book all about the fairies. Would you like me to show you the pictures?' She forced herself to smile as brightly as she could, trying to win the child around.

Hannah's face crumpled. 'Don't like you!'

'Now, now,' Nora said, her smile fixed firmly. 'We know you don't mean that.' She opened the book and held it out. 'Can you see the lovely little fairies in the book? They live in that big magic tree.'

'Don't like you!' Hannah repeated. She started waving her good arm in the air as though pushing Nora away.

'Oh, dear!' Nora looked anxiously at the others, terrified the child would hurt herself. 'I don't want to upset her. It might be best if I left her now.'

Johnny moved towards the bed. 'No, she'll have to get used to you. Be a good girl now, Hannah,' he said in a gentle but firm tone. 'Be nice to your Aunt Nora.'

Nora stood up now, taking the chance to swap places. 'I hope you feel better soon, Hannah, and I'll keep this nice book safe for you at home.' Then, making one last attempt to win the child over, she leaned over the bed holding the book out to her. 'All the little fairies will be waiting for you in the enchanted wood—'

Then, before she could say any more, Hannah shouted, 'Don't like it!' and her good arm came flailing up and knocked the book flying.

Johnny moved quickly but the book moved quicker still. It descended with a hard thud on Hannah's nose and then bounced on her bandaged legs. Blood immediately began to trickle from her nose, down her face and onto the white bedclothes and the bandages on her arm. There was a shocked silence which lasted only moments before it was shattered by Hannah's piercing screams.

'Mother of Jesus!' Johnny gasped, grabbing the book and throwing it on the chair behind him. 'What have we done to her?'

Nora could hardly find the words. 'I'm sorry, it was an accident – you could all see that!' *What have I done?* she thought. *I was trying to do right and I've ruined everything.*

People in the ward were turning to look to see what was happening as Hannah continued to scream and sob at the top of her voice.

Johnny bent over his daughter, dabbing at her nose with a clean hanky. 'C'mon now, Hannah, you're OK, my little darlin'! It was only an oul' book that tipped you on the nose. Sure, haven't you had a nose bleed before? You'll be grand…'

Then, Larry suddenly ran around the bed to Ella and clung onto her leg for dear life, howling too.

Quick footsteps sounded and Sister Gollogly appeared at the end of the bed, her face aghast when she saw the blood. 'Good Lord, what on earth has happened here?'

Johnny took over the situation. 'She had a little accident with the book, Sister. She let it fall and it caught her square on the nose.'

Nora swallowed on the lump that had appeared in her throat and she closed her eyes. He had taken the blame from her – had understood it was a pure accident – and she felt almost weak with relief.

He put his hand on Hannah's head, her loud crying now dying down to a whimper. 'The bleeding has stopped already, hasn't it darlin'?' He moved to let the nurse past him. 'She'll be grand again soon, won't she? It's nothing too serious.'

Sister Gollogly stood for a few seconds, assessing the situation, then she looked back at Johnny. 'I think it would be best if you *all* left for the time being and let me sort her out.'

'Of course,' Nora said, putting her hand on Sean's shoulder, as though to guide him out but within a second of her touching him, he had moved out of her reach.

They all went out of the ward, under the watchful eye of the other visitors and into the long, cold corridor.

'I'm so sorry . . .' Nora said, once again.

Johnny held his hands up. 'It was an accident. You weren't to know what she was going to do. Hannah didn't know what she was doing. She's all mixed up . . . she's still only a babby in many ways.'

Nora nodded. 'Of course she is, poor little thing. And being away from home and everything . . .' But still, after the good day they had all had at the house, Hannah had put a fear in her now. What if the child really didn't like her? What if she didn't take to her at all? And if she didn't, what would happen then? She took a low, shuddering breath and told herself to calm down. She would cross that bridge if and when she came to it.

Sean suddenly drew his leg back and kicked the tiled wall. 'That nurse made things worse, showing us up like that in front of all those other visitors!'

Johnny's eyebrows shot up. 'That'll do you now!' he warned.

Sean moved down the corridor and then kicked the wall again. 'Throwing us out as though we were a load of tinkers!'

'Sean!' his father hissed. 'I've told you. That's enough. Behave yourself.'

Sean, eyes blazing, had his shoulders squared now and was shaking his head. 'I'm not going back in. They'll all be gawking at us and waiting to see if something else happens. I'm going down to Billy's house and I'll see you all later.'

'You'll go nowhere,' Johnny said. 'You'll stay here with the rest of us.'

Sean turned, and before his father could move forward to catch him, he tore off down the corridor.

Chapter Twelve

Ella woke in the early hours of the morning, the bedroom illuminated by a full moon. She lay still, the events of the previous night flooding back. What an awful ending to what had been such a positive day. Thankfully, when they all got back home, Sean had been back at the house waiting for them. Sitting in front of the fire, trying to look as though nothing had happened. Her father had taken him upstairs and given him a good talking to, and then he had come back downstairs and given a low, mumbled apology which a white-faced Nora had immediately accepted.

Ella turned her head into the pillow, trying to block the memories out. Then she lifted her arm to see the time on her watch. She gave a sigh – it was only half past three. She got up and stood for a while at the window, staring up at the night sky.

Her thoughts, as always, went to her mother. She clasped her hands together on the windowsill, closed her eyes, and said a silent prayer. She knew there was no point in praying for her mother's loss to become just a bad dream that they would all wake up from. She had prayed that for weeks after she died, and knew that that miracle was not going to happen. Her mother was in Heaven, along with their baby brother gone from them forever.

Instead, she prayed to Mary Cassidy to sort things out in the household she had left so abruptly. To let some good things happen to them instead of the never-ending problems that threatened to consume them. She prayed that Hannah would recover quickly and come home the sweet-natured little thing she had been when their mother was alive. She prayed that Sean would see sense and knuckle down and not cause any more problems than he already had. Ella then asked her mother to find her father a good job – a job that he would stick at, a job that would take away the worry of finding money for food and coal.

Her final prayer was to help her find something *really* likeable about her Aunt Nora, because so far she could find nothing in common with her. So far, she felt that when she was doing things like peeling vegetables with her and chatting to her, that she was only pretending to be relaxed with her...

Johnny was up early as usual on Sunday morning. He stole downstairs quietly to sort the fire and have the place warm for everyone coming down for Mass. He sighed as he did so, for there was only enough coal left for a couple of days and then he would have to draw a few more shillings out of the Post Office to buy more.

Sean had given them a small reprieve with the bags of stolen coal, but that carry-on was finished now and there would be no more.

Another week or two would see the account completely cleaned out. And then, he wondered, with a sinking heart, what would happen? He had to find money from somewhere to keep things going. And while it was unspoken, he knew that Nora was aware that things were tight, but he would be ashamed of his life if he had to admit to her he couldn't provide the very basics for his family. That would be the worst thing he could think of happening, as it might make her turn tail and catch the next train back to Tullamore.

The alternative scenario – equally humiliating – would be Nora Lamb offering to loan him money. He knew she was a woman of independent means and money would never be a problem to her, but she was already doing him a massive favour by coming up to help him in the house – to then ask her to pay for doing so would be beyond any reasonable thinking. There were no two ways about it: he would have to find work this coming week. How and where he did not know, but there was no other way out of it.

He got the fire going and went back into the scullery to wash his hands. He would have loved a cup of tea, but it was prohibited on Sunday mornings with fasting before communion, and anyway, the days of having a cup when you liked were long gone with the Emergency. There would be none until they come home from Mass when they all had their breakfast together. At least they had some rashers and eggs, which was more than many a family in Dublin. He gave a sigh and lifted a mug down from the dresser, filled it with cold water and drank it down in one go.

He took his good coat and hat from the back of the door and then lifted the ration book for the shop. He stepped outside into the cold dry air and headed out for a brisk walk to Kilmainham to buy the Sunday paper and get fresh milk and bread, if the shop had anything in stock.

Nora had listened as Johnny went downstairs. She lay on, giving him time to do all the little necessary tasks to get the house ready for the family coming down. She knew how important it was for people to have time and space for themselves, to let the mind settle without constant noise and talk.

Her mother had been an anxious sort of woman who talked continuously, who gave a running commentary on almost everything that she did from getting up in the morning until she went to bed at night.

Nora had seen how her father needed to escape in the evenings out into the garden or, in the colder months, to the solace of his shed hidden away at the bottom amongst the trees. Several times a week he also went to one of the local bars in town to have a few quiet bottles of beer. He went just after the pub doors opened, when there was little chance of running into other people. Other men left their homes later in the evening, to enjoy the company and the chat, and to play cards or dominoes. Thomas Lamb left his home to find peace.

Her Uncle Bernard – her mother's brother – had been a different sort of man. An old-fashioned bachelor, he liked the banter in the pub in the evening, and enjoyed the chat with the other farmers. But he was happy to spend most of the day entirely on his own on the farm. She herself needed that peace when she left the office – but an hour or two of solitariness a day would have been more than enough for her. That was the irony of it all. She had been left with the opposite problem – too much time on her hands.

But here she was now, in a house with more people than she had ever lived with before – and in the midst of it all, she would have to find time and space for herself. Thankfully, Johnny had organised it so she had the privacy of her own room, a sanctuary where she could escape to with her own thoughts. But it was a luxury he no longer had; now he was sharing his own room with Sean and Larry. Giving him a bit of time in the morning was the least she could do.

After a while Nora got up and, under the cover of her long winceyette nightdress and dressing gown, had her usual morning wash. She had dipped her flannel into the freezing water in the enamel bowl, shivering as she did so. It felt so much colder here in Dublin than it did in her house back in Tullamore. There was no electric fire to plug in while she got dressed and no hot water unless it was boiled in a kettle or pan.

She had taken off her dressing gown and then wiggled her arms out of the sleeves of her nightdress, and had managed to put her white cotton brassiere on underneath it without exposing her skin to the cold. She then sat in the chair to pull on a pair of soft cotton knickers which had tiny rosebuds on them, and then she fastened her white suspender belt and pulled on her 'Tempting Tan' stockings.

Giving a little shiver, she had put on the rest of her clothes, finishing with her green tweed skirt and fine-knit grey lambswool jumper, under the scalloped collar of which she put a double row of pearls. She slipped her stockinged feet into her black, fur-lined leather ankle boots with their tiny pearl buttons on the sides.

Warmed up a bit, she had taken her toilet bag and went to sit at Mary's dressing-table and then started to brush her shoulder-length auburn hair before organising it into a tidy bun.

Satisfied, she had reached for her compact and powdered her face, adding a touch of Vaseline on her eyelashes and a quick coat of *Pink Chiffon* lipstick – all little tips she had learned from the younger girls in the office in Tullamore. It was as little she could do to improve herself – but as much as she could get away with for Mass on a Sunday. She sat back and viewed herself.

As always, she felt a sense of disappointment.

With a little shake of her head she moved towards the wardrobe to get her suit jacket. Just then she heard the front door close behind Johnny. Surprised, she tiptoed out into the small corridor and crept downstairs, fearful of waking any of the children.

She went into the living room and over to the window to peer from behind the curtain, watching Johnny as he went off down the road. Had Johnny decided to go to an early Mass? If so, she was disappointed, for he had given the impression that they would all go to ten o'clock Mass. Surely he wouldn't leave her to go on her own with the children? The thought made her heart drop. She suddenly thought it would be a good idea to visit the outhouse while the others were not around.

When she came back, she decided she might as well set the table in the living room so that everything was ready when they came back to sit down to breakfast.

At home, if she woke early, she got up and went to eight o'clock Mass. Got it over and done with. Maybe when she got used to things here, she would be able to do the same thing, instead of waiting for everyone else for the later one. She went towards the window, wondering whether she should call the children or leave them until their father came back. Just as she glanced out, she caught sight of Johnny walking towards the house, the Sunday newspaper tucked under one arm, a brown bag in his other hand. Her heart lifted; he had only gone to the shop.

Then, in the few moments before he saw her, Nora noticed the slump of his shoulders and the sad, strained look on his face. He had a look about him that she realised was that of defeat.

'Another early bird,' he said in a low voice, as he came in. 'Anyone else stirring yet?'

Nora shook her head. 'Only me,' she said, smiling back.

He put the brown paper bag down on the dresser and lifted out a small bundle wrapped in greaseproof paper. 'Believe it or not, I managed to get half a dozen sausages,' he said. 'Mr Kirwin had them put by for a woman on Friday, and she never turned up. He said if they're not used today they'll go off.' He shrugged. 'And he wouldn't take any money for them. I tried, but what could I do?'

'That was very good of him,' Nora said. 'We could cook these sausages today and use them for a dinner tomorrow. If I did them with some onions and gravy,' Nora continued, 'it would go well with the potatoes. What do you think?'

'Sounds great,' Johnny said, relieved he didn't have to think about these things. 'There's some toilet paper there as well, and a packet of porridge. Sean and Ella can have it before going out to school.'

'Good, good,' Nora said. She could see a list of tasks forming in her mind now. Things to be cooked, things to be washed up afterwards, things to be done at certain times. Things that would keep her busy and give a framework to her day.

Johnny took his coat off and hung it over one of the chairs. 'I'd give my right arm now for a cup of tea.'

'I'm the very same,' she said. 'It's the one thing I miss on a Sunday morning.'

A noise sounded upstairs – Larry, laughing.

Johnny raised his eyebrows. 'That's the peace disturbed then,' he said, grinning at her.

Chapter Thirteen

They walked towards the church gate, Larry between Ella and Aunt Nora, each holding one of his hands, Johnny and Sean walking ahead. As usual, everyone wore their best Sunday clothes, which would be taken off immediately they got home and hung up until next week. Nora was wearing a grey velvet hat decorated with a black flower on the side, which matched her grey mohair coat.

As they walked along, Ella noticed that her father seemed to have lost weight and that Sean's head was almost past their father's shoulders now.

She also observed that Sean's trousers were suddenly high up on his ankles which meant he was growing again. His school trousers were probably the same, and she would have to get him to try them on today in case they needed letting down too – he would be feeling edgy and self-conscious enough going back to school, without another smart classmate or even a teacher passing a funny remark about his trousers. Her mother had been forever altering things for them as they grew taller and broader. It was one of her evening chores to sit in front of the fire, carefully unpicking stitches on seams to widen them or darning holes in socks and in the knees of the boys' trousers. Ella had often sat on the arm of the chair, watching as her mother worked away with the needle and thread.

She glanced now at her Aunt Nora, wondering whether she was any good at sewing or knitting. Then she heard her name being called. She swung around and saw Nancy McNamee and Maeve Kelly walking quickly towards her.

Ella looked at her Aunt Nora. 'It's my friends ... I just want a quick word with them.'

Nora gestured towards Johnny and Sean who had now turned in to the church gate. 'Go on,' she said, 'but be quick and catch up on us so we all get a seat together.'

'We haven't seen you for ages,' Nancy said as they came up.

'Well, I've had to help out at home.'

'Your hair looks lovely – it's much longer than when I last saw you,' Nancy commented, smiling warmly at her, 'and that coat really suits you.'

'Thanks,' Ella said. She noticed Maeve watching her closely. As usual, while Nancy gave all the compliments, Maeve said nothing. It was a wonder she hadn't said, 'Isn't that the coat you got for your mother's funeral?'

But then, new clothes weren't such a novelty to Maeve. Her father had a good office job on the railways, and she was the youngest in the family so everyone spoiled her. She had three older sisters who were working and they often bought her new clothes and passed down nice things to her.

Maeve looked at her now, as though she had been giving it great thought and said, 'That coat is very nice on you,'

Ella smiled at her and said thanks, immediately feeling guilty.

'Is that your aunt?' Maeve asked, pointing at Nora. 'The one that's come to mind you all?'

Ella felt her face flush. Maeve could be too nosey at times. 'Yes,' she said, 'it's our Aunt Nora.'

'She's a bit older than your mother, isn't she? And quite posh-looking. Is she a teacher or something?' Maeve asked, obviously intrigued.

Ella wasn't sure how she felt about Maeve's description of her aunt, but she supposed that her looking 'posh' was better than looking common. 'She's a secretary in a hospital,' she said. She had a feeling Maeve would be rushing home to tell her mother after Mass, as Mrs Kelly was every bit as nosey. She turned to

Nancy. 'I was going to call up to you this afternoon, just to find out what I've missed at school.'

'We haven't done anything you can't catch up on,' Nancy said. Then, she frowned. 'Well, maybe fractions, and some of the problems aren't easy.' She laughed. 'Well, for me anyway. If you come up around two o'clock that would be fine.'

'How is your granda?' Maeve asked Nancy.

Nancy's face fell. 'Ah, he's all right, but the doctor told him he can't lift anything heavy and he's to take it easy.' She looked at Ella. 'He had a bit of a bad turn last week. It's his heart, the doctors said.'

'Oh, I'm sorry to hear that,' Ella said. 'I like your granda, he's always great craic when we go over to their house.'

'We better get a move on,' Maeve said. 'Everybody else has gone in and the priest will be out on the altar. Remember, he was giving out the other week about people coming in late and he pointed down the back of the church to the ones that were standing. My mother will go mad if she hears I went in late.'

Ella thought that her father and Aunt Nora wouldn't be too pleased either. She hoped she could find where they were sitting in the church so she could join them.

As they walked up the steps to the church, Nancy caught Ella's arm. 'Do you remember me talking about my cousin, Danny? The one that's over in Liverpool?'

'I do,' she said. 'Isn't he about Sean's age?'

'A bit older; he's fifteen and finished school now.'

'What about him?'

'He came over yesterday to live with my granny and grandad and give them a hand around the house.'

'Didn't his mother get married again after his father got killed in the war?' Maeve said. 'And wasn't there talk about Danny not liking his new stepfather? I think your granny mentioned it to my mother.'

Nancy took a deep breath as they went in the door of the church. Maeve drove her mad at times, listening to the older

72

women talking and remembering everything they said. She leaned over to Ella and whispered, 'I'll tell you about it when you come down later.'

'Grand,' Ella said, as they went in. 'You two get seats for yourselves – I'll have to find my father and the others.' She went over to the holy water font, dipped her fingers, then blessed herself and went to the back of the church where she stood on her tiptoes for a few moments, trying to see where the rest of her family were. She spotted her Aunt Nora's hat in the third row from the back. There was one space left at the end of the wooden bench beside her. She genuflected and then slipped in beside her aunt.

She went straight to kneeling and started on a silent prayer to her mother to look after them all, especially Hannah. Then, just as she went to sit up on the bench, everyone else moved to their feet – the priest had stepped up to the altar. She turned sideways to look along the bench and Nora caught her eye and winked, whispering, 'Well done, you made it.'

When they got back to the house after Mass, Nora made a weak pot of tea and gave a cup to everyone to warm them up. Afterwards, she and Ella got started cooking and they all sat down to eggs and rashers and fried bread.

Johnny used the last piece of his bread to wipe the yolk from his plate then looked over at the clock on the mantelpiece. 'Visiting is at three this afternoon,' he told Nora.

She checked her knife and fork were uniformly in the middle of her plate, moved her chair back, and stood up. 'I think it might be best if you all went without me today,' she said, smiling. 'Poor Hannah was a little overwhelmed yesterday, so I'm happy to stay and have the dinner ready for you all coming back.'

'Is it OK,' Ella said, 'if I go down to Nancy's for an hour?' The words felt strange to her own ears; it seemed such a long time since she had asked that question.

73

'It's fine by me,' Johnny said, then he looked at Nora. 'Is there anything here that you need her for?'

'No, it's a Sunday, so we wouldn't be doing anything major around the house anyway.' She smiled at Ella. 'I think it would be nice for you to go and see your friend.'

Chapter Fourteen

When Nancy brought her into the house, Ella was taken aback to see the kitchen was almost full with people, all busy eating. She felt embarrassed to have called at the wrong time.

'You're grand, don't worry about it,' Nancy told her. 'I've finished eating anyway. They're neighbours, all here because my Uncle Charlie arrived up from Galway on the train.' She suddenly stopped. 'Are you hungry? Will I see if there's anything left?'

'No, thanks,' Ella said, 'I've just eaten before we came out.' She didn't mention it to her friend, but she also had an unusual, cramping feeling low down in her stomach which kept coming and going.

Nancy wanted her to come into the kitchen to say hello to everyone, but Ella shook her head. She suddenly felt awkward at the thought of going into a room full of strangers, especially Nancy's cousin. She wouldn't know what to say to an older boy. 'Maybe it would be better if I come back later...'

'Not at all, I'd already told Mammy you were coming about schoolwork, so she got Daddy to put a fire on up in the bedroom for us. We can go up now if you like.'

They had just started on the stairs when the knocker on the front door sounded. 'That'll be my cousin, Danny,' Nancy said, turning back. 'He went back over to the house to get Grandad's walking stick.'

As she opened the door, Ella quickly went up a few stairs so he wouldn't see her, then she heard Nancy say, 'Oh, Danny, this is my friend, Ella.'

Ella had no option but to turn back.

'Hi, Ella,' he said, in his strong Liverpool accent.

As she looked down the staircase, first at Nancy and then at her taller, dark-haired cousin, she suddenly felt more self-conscious than she had ever felt, and her face start to burn. 'H-hello,' she said, and could hear her voice had a strange crackling sound to it.

'I was just thinking that it would be nice if Danny got to know some lads,' Nancy said, smiling at one and then the other. 'I could bring him down to see your Sean and his friends. Maybe he could have a game of football or hurling with them sometime.'

'I'm not too sure about that,' he said, smiling, 'I'm not the world's best football player. Now, if it's swimming or tennis or even chess – that would be a different matter.'

As his deep brown eyes fixed on hers, something seemed to shift inside Ella. He had lovely hair, smooth and dark, almost black, and his brown eyes looked like velvet. Danny Byrne was the best-looking boy she had ever seen. The thought took her by surprise as she had never noticed boys in that way before. They all seemed like variations on her brother, Sean, and therefore held not the slightest interest for her.

But Danny was nothing like Sean or his friends. He was a different kind of boy. Even his clothes were different, she thought. There was something about them that made you look twice. He had on a grey shirt buttoned up to the neck with a sleeveless Fair Isle over it, knitted in grey, maroon and navy. She instinctively knew he was what the older girls described as a 'snappy dresser'.

She had heard some of the other girls she knew talking about boys being handsome, and one or two of the older ones – the more developed ones – talked about fancying them and even kissing them. But all of that had escaped Ella. She just didn't understand that sort of talk. Kissing boys was the last thing she'd wanted to do, and now, in the space of a few minutes, she realised she felt quite differently about it all.

'Well, I'm not sure if any of the lads have ever played tennis,' Nancy said, 'but I know they won't be swimming in the river until the weather is a bit warmer.' She gave a little laugh. 'And I definitely can't imagine Sean or any of the lads he mixes with playing chess.'

'You'll hardly believe it,' Ella said, her voice more normal sounding now, 'but we have a new chess set back at the house. My Aunt Nora says she's going to teach me and Sean how to play it.'

'Your Aunt Nora?' Nancy repeated. 'The one we saw at Mass this morning with the fancy hat?'

'Yes,' Ella said, 'the one that Maeve said looked very posh.' She found herself smiling. 'It was as if she couldn't believe we're related to someone like that.'

Danny's hand came up to his mouth and she could tell by his eyes that he was trying not to laugh.

'She said her uncle showed her how to play chess when she was a young girl and she loves playing.'

Danny clapped his hands and rubbed them together. 'Brilliant!' he said, 'That means when you and your brother learn, I'll have two people to play with.'

Slow footsteps sounded along the hallway now. 'Is that you back, Danny?' It was his grandmother.

'Yeah,' he said, walking down to meet her, 'and I've got me Grandad's walking stick.'

'I'll be hitting him over the head with the bloody thing, if he doesn't stop forgetting it. He's been told to take it easy, and the first time he comes out he leaves the stick behind.' She gave a wheezy laugh.

Mrs Byrne turned to look at her granddaughter and then at Ella. 'Ah, this is your friend from school. Ella Cassidy, isn't it?'

'Yes,' Ella said, nodding her head and smiling.

'How are you all doing, pet?'

Ella felt a little knot in her stomach. 'We're doing OK,' she said.

'Their aunt has come up from Tullamore to give a hand,' Nancy said.

'Ah, well, that will make all the difference,' Nancy's granny said. 'You need a good woman about the house.'

'We're just going up to the bedroom to do some schoolwork,' Nancy said, 'so I'll see you later, Granny.'

'OK, chicken,' she said, 'and nice to see you, Ella.'

They had only gone a few steps up when Ella heard the old lady say to Danny, 'That was a terrible tragedy what happened to that family. Did you hear about it?'

Ella could tell Danny was trying to quieten his grandmother down, so she wouldn't hear, but it was too late.

When they reached the steps at the top, Nancy turned to her. 'I'm sorry about my granny,' she said. 'But she's deaf and she talks really loudly, not realising everyone can hear her a mile off.'

'It's OK,' Ella said. 'I know she didn't mean any harm by it.'

They walked along the hall then Nancy said, 'Oh, I've just remembered, my schoolbag is behind the couch downstairs. I won't be a minute.' She disappeared down the stairs.

Ella didn't think she should go into her friend's bedroom on her own, so she went to stand at the bannister, then she heard Nancy's granny saying. 'Isn't Ella Cassidy growing up into a fine-looking girl?'

'Oh, she is,' Nancy said. 'She's the best-looking girl in the class, but she's not a bit vain about it. She's a lovely girl.'

Ella caught her breath at the compliments. She had never thought that people saw her in that way. She wondered if Danny Byrne was hearing them say such nice things about her.

'I'm glad to hear they have a woman helping them now,' Nancy's granny continued in a loud voice, 'because the father, God help him, isn't up to much. Johnny Cassidy is good-looking, to be sure, and a great fiddle player – but he's not what you would call a provider.'

Ella froze on the spot.

Mrs Byrne went on, 'Well, it's to be hoped that Ella takes after her lovely mother – a hard-working, decent woman. Because she'll get nowhere if she turns out like the father. It's a pity, you couldn't meet a nicer lad – but he's useless. All he wants to do is play music and drink beer.'

Ella's throat grew tight.

Then, to her embarrassment, she head Nancy saying in a loud whisper, 'Granny, will you keep your voice down! Ella is just upstairs.'

'Ah, get away with you,' the elderly woman said, in what she obviously thought was a lower tone. 'She'd have to have good ears to hear me from there. Anyway, I'm only speaking the truth. Sure, the poor girl must know what he's like. Everybody does.'

Ella felt hot tears rushing into her eyes. Who was *everybody*? She now wondered if Nancy's parents felt the same about her father as her granny did. Did Maeve Kelly's family think that too, or the people in the shops – or even Mrs Murphy? And what about Aunt Nora?

She suddenly got the strange nagging feeling low down in her stomach again, and then a small wave of pain took her breath away. Gradually, it started to ease off, but it left her feeling washed out. She wished she was back at home where she could just go and lie down on her bed, fall fast asleep and forget everything.

She closed her eyes as she heard Nancy's granny saying something else now, and she just could not bear to listen. She also didn't want her friend knowing that she had heard all those humiliating things her granny had said about her father. And that Danny Byrne – the first boy she had ever taken a notion for – had heard it too. She went quietly towards Nancy's bedroom and went inside and closed the door behind her.

Chapter Fifteen

On Monday morning Nora got up at seven o'clock and crept downstairs in her dressing gown and slippers, carrying the large jug. She boiled the kettle and then filled the jug to make her morning wash back up in her room more comfortable. Little things like that, she was sure, would make her situation with a colder house and outside toilet a little easier to live with.

Last night she had soaked enough porridge oats for everyone in a large pot, and now she left it simmering on the cooker while she then went upstairs and had her wash, then dressed in a plain, navy skirt with a wine, turtle-neck sweater and a pair of low-heeled navy shoes – all sensible for working around the house. Out of habit, she put on a single row of pearls and small matching earrings, and then she dabbed some powder on the shiny parts of her face and added a touch of lipstick.

When she came back down, Johnny was up and had the fire sorted, and then one by one the others began to appear. Neither Sean nor Ella, she noticed, was particularly talkative. Ella, she thought looked unusually pale, and didn't seem herself. Nora knew Sean was worried about going back to school, but she couldn't make out what could be wrong with Ella. When she thought about it, she had been quiet when they came back from the hospital the previous evening.

After dinner, as Nora cleaned up, Ella had ironed her clothes for school the next day and then had quietly asked Sean to bring his clothes down so she could press them. Ella had taken his school trousers and measured them against his Sunday ones, then she had gone to find her mother's tidy sewing-box as both pairs needed letting down.

When Nora put the dishes away she came to sit at the butcher's block beside Ella. 'I could do one of those trousers for you,' she said. Then, when Ella looked up, she noticed the pale face and the weariness in her eyes. 'Are you OK?' Nora said. 'You're awful quiet. You're not feeling sick or anything?'

Ella shook her head. 'I'm grand,' she said, 'I'm just a bit tired.'

Nora picked up the trousers and examined the hem. 'Are you worried about going back to school tomorrow?'

'Not really,' Ella said. 'I like school.' What she didn't say was that she was worrying about meeting Nancy after what her granny had said. When Nancy had come upstairs she had talked normally, as though old Mrs Byrne had never said anything. Ella didn't mention it either, and after an hour or so, Ella said she had to go or she would be late for visiting Hannah.

She looked at her Aunt Nora, through lowered eyelids. How could she tell her what Nancy's granny had said about her father? She was used to having a good job, and a nice big house, and money for anything she needed. She even had a farm, although she didn't have much to do with it. It was a miracle, really, that her mother's spinster cousin had ever agreed to come up to Dublin to help them out. And so far, Ella thought, things were going OK with her in the house, and she and their father seemed to be getting on well enough. If she heard what people thought of her father, Aunt Nora would probably start worrying and looking at him in a different light altogether, and cause an awkward atmosphere in the house.

After they had finished letting down the trousers, Nora said to Ella. 'You go off to bed now, and I'll press Sean's clothes. I have some shirts and bits and pieces of mine and Larry's so it will only take five minutes to do those.'

'Thanks,' Ella said. Her voice was so quiet, it was almost a sigh.

'You'll feel much better in the morning,' Nora had said, reaching over to pat her on the shoulder. Whatever was wrong with the girl, she thought, a day in school with her friends would probably cure it.

When Johnny left the house with Sean and Ella just before nine o'clock, Nora felt a sense of relief. That left her and Larry on their own, which suited her just fine, as she was anxious to get into a proper routine. She cleared up the breakfast things and then she got on with washing and ironing. She also thought it would be easier for her to get to know Larry better when they were on their own, as she felt stiff and self-conscious trying to talk to him when the family were around.

At the moment, he was happy in the living room with his colouring books and a jigsaw that Ella had brought back from her friend's yesterday. Nora went into the living room to check on Larry and wash down the table there and the window sills and doors. It was an easy house to keep clean because there were really only the basic, functional items in it. She wondered if it had ever occurred to Mary that she was going without things. Nora supposed the reason was having all those children, and that it would be more trouble than it was worth trying to keep little ornaments or precious books out of their way.

Later, as she started filling the sink with kettles of boiling water to wash the clothes, she wondered how things were back in the office in Tullamore. She presumed this Monday's routine was the same as every other one, and was surprised that she preferred to be here in Dublin doing washing, rather than her usual filing.

She brought Larry with her when she was hanging out the washing and then took him over to the corner of the yard where there was a thick growth of ivy climbing on the wall. She put a finger to her lips to warn him to keep quiet, and then she parted the leaves to point up to a nest that was hidden in a small cavity in the wall. 'We can't touch it,' she whispered, 'because the mammy bird is still building the nest and she might not come back to lay her eggs if she sees us near it.'

He nodded in understanding and copied her, touching his lips as she had done, then she let the leaves fall back and they both tiptoed across the small yard back into the scullery. The delight on his face gave Nora a warm, gratified feeling which stayed with her as she stood ironing shirts and sheets.

Johnny came back around eleven o'clock with news. 'I have four days' work down at the docks,' he said. 'I start in the morning.'

'That's great news,' she told him. 'Every little helps, and it's not the best time for anyone to find work in this country.'

Both of them knew that it was not a job she would have thought worthy of him, but beggars could not be choosers.

'How are you getting on here?' he asked. 'You have the place lovely and clean.'

'I'm doing whatever I see needs doing,' she told him. 'Just trying to keep things ticking over.'

'The hospital visiting is at two this afternoon. Do you want to come down with me and Larry? Hannah was in much better form yesterday, and I'd say she would be happier to see you.'

'I think it would make more sense if I go tomorrow,' she told him, 'when you are at work and Sean and Ella are at school. I'll walk down with Larry then and see her.' She gave a weak smile. 'I have a little bar of chocolate upstairs. I'll bring it in with me, and it might win her over.'

'Oh, you have the right idea,' Johnny laughed. 'I'd say you'll have no trouble at all when you produce the chocolate.'

When Larry went upstairs to have a nap around twelve o'clock, Nora made a cup of tea and an omelette with fried onions for her and Johnny. 'It's hard to know what to make at this time of the day,' she said, as they sat at the table in the living room, 'when we have so little choice with the rationing, but at least we can have eggs. I wonder will we ever get back to the days when we can have a cup of tea whenever we like?'

'Mary loved her cup of tea,' Johnny said, a far-off look in his eyes. 'She had terrible bad headaches when it was first rationed.' He smiled. 'She said she used to dream about drinking cups of tea, and in the end, we were laughing about it.'

'I remember her saying that,' Nora said, nodding her head.

'I heard a good few of them saying it at work, too, and I heard others saying the headaches were even worse when the cigarettes were rationed. I was always glad I never smoked.'

'I'm the very same,' Johnny said. 'The cigarettes never interested me. Although I have to confess I love a few pints – when we have the money to spare.' He paused, thinking. 'I've got the chance of earning a few shillings playing in the band at a dance on Friday and at a wedding on Saturday. I was wondering... would you be OK here on your own if I was to go?'

'Of course,' Nora said. 'It's work, isn't it?' While she didn't think playing music was the most regular of occupations, it would bring some much-needed money into the house. Along with four days' work down at the docks, it would make a big difference. The turf and coal had dwindled away to almost nothing.

Johnny nodded, hardly able to believe that she had agreed so quickly. 'Oh, it is,' he said, 'I get reasonably paid for it – more than a full day's work anywhere else – and if there is any food left over, the staff often give us a bit to bring home.'

'All the better,' Nora said. 'I'll be grand here with the children. I'm planning to go into town to get wool and a knitting pattern this week so I might take Larry with me tomorrow morning if the weather is decent – it will do the two of us good to get a good long walk along the Quays. I thought I might encourage Ella to do some knitting as well. It helps to pass the long evenings.'

'That's a great idea,' Johnny said. 'Let's hope that they tell us that Hannah is getting out of hospital soon, and that will be good news all round.'

The door went and Johnny came back into the living room, Rose Murphy following behind, carrying a parcel wrapped in newspaper. 'You've met Nora before, haven't you, Mrs Murphy?'

Rose's face tightened and she gave a little sigh. 'We met at the funeral, although there were so many people there we never got a chance to say more than a few words.' She smiled at Nora, then noticed her earrings and pearls. Where on earth did the woman think she was going, all dressed up like that, she wondered.

Nora viewed the older woman – heavy, with greying hair and a crossover pinny. She stood up and stretched her hand out, and Mrs Murphy shook it.

'Yes, it's nice to meet you again.' She remembered Mrs Murphy as a slightly gruff, old-fashioned sort of person, and was surprised that a young woman like Mary would want to be so friendly with her. In truth, she felt the neighbour was not quite in the same class as their own family.

Mrs Murphy looked at Johnny. 'Our Jack dropped me in three rabbits and I thought you could make use of a couple of them here.'

'That's very good of you, Rose,' he said. 'I'm sure we will.'

She turned to Nora. 'Do you think you would be able to make rabbit stew?'

Something about the way Mrs Murphy looked at her – as if she thought she was perhaps not used to doing anything domestic – got her back up. 'Oh, I'm sure I would,' Nora said. She was not going to admit to the fact she had never cooked one before. She thanked her and then, as she took the parcel from her, she felt the sides of it damp. When she looked down, she saw that the newspaper was all bloodstained, and she did her best not to shudder. 'We often had rabbit at home when I was growing up. Not in recent years, but my Uncle Bernard, God rest him, used to set snares for them on the farm.'

'Well, our Jack knows a lad who works out near the airport,' Mrs Murphy said, 'and, seemingly, the fields around are full of rabbits.'

'Imagine that,' Nora said. 'I wouldn't have thought that you would find rabbits in a city.'

'That's what makes Dublin unique,' Johnny said. 'It's a city surrounded by fields. We're not far from the sea or the heart of the country.'

The two women stared at him for a few moments, and

then Mrs Murphy said, 'You're a mine of information, Johnny Cassidy, that's for sure.'

He started to laugh. 'I don't know about that, but sure we can always make it up.'

She laughed along with him, and then she asked, 'Did Sean and Ella get off to school?'

'They did, thank God. I hope they've settled back in OK.'

'It's ridiculous – they should have let Sean off,' Mrs Murphy said. 'He's too old to be there when he has no interest in it. The master was hard on him, making him go back there for the sake of a few months.'

Nora was taken aback. The last thing she needed was Sean in the house all day. 'I'm not so sure it's a bad thing,' she said. 'I don't think education is ever wasted and it will get him back in a routine.'

Mrs Murphy folded her arms over her heavy chest. 'Indeed,' she said.

'Yes,' Nora said, feeling the blood from the rabbits seeping through the paper and onto her hands. Nora could see Mrs Murphy felt as though she had been put in her place and felt awkward about it. She didn't want to get on the wrong side of any neighbours, especially one who seemed to have been very good to the family. She looked down at the rabbit parcel and saw the blood trickling down through her fingers. 'Excuse me,' she said, 'I'd better get this into the scullery and into a dish.' She smiled warmly at Mrs Murphy. 'It was very good of you to bring the rabbits; they will be well appreciated.'

Mrs Murphy tilted her chin. 'You're welcome,' she said, turning towards the door.

As Johnny got up to see Rose Murphy out, Nora went quickly into the scullery and dropped the parcel in the sink, desperate to get the rabbits out of the wet newspaper and under the tap. She looked at her hands, covered in black newsprint and blood, and tutted to herself at the mess. Then she started to peel the paper back off the rabbits – and let out a scream.

Johnny came rushing into the scullery. 'What's happened?'

'It's the rabbits,' she said, a look of squeamishness on her face. 'They haven't been skinned – they still have their heads and all their fur on!'

'But that's the way we always get them,' he said, trying not to smile.

'I can't touch them,' she said, shuddering now. 'I can't even look at them.'

'Ah, sure, the poor little devils can't do you any harm,' he said, laughing now. 'And don't worry, I'll skin them for you.'

Nora turned her head away. 'Can you just lift them out of the sink, please? I need to wash my hands.'

'One minute,' he said, moving towards the hallway. 'I'll get a clean newspaper to wrap them in so the blood doesn't go on anything.'

The mention of the blood brought another little shudder. She turned sideways so she didn't have to look at them.

Johnny came back in with the newspaper then lifted the two rabbits out of the sink by the ears. He looked at Nora, and when he caught her eye, he jangled them in her direction as though they were doing a little dance.

She screamed again and ran out into the hallway.

Johnny put the rabbits down on the newspaper and covered them up, then bent double laughing. 'They're covered!' he called. 'It's safe to come back in.'

Nora stood with her back against the wall for a few moments to still her pounding heart then she gathered herself together and went to hover by the scullery door.

Johnny was standing with his hands on his hips, laughing. 'C'mon you're safe,' he said, beckoning to her. 'The little bunny rabbits are all covered up.'

'I really need to wash my hands,' she told him. 'And don't you dare come near me with those damned things again. It's not in the least bit funny.' Her eyes widened. 'If you do, I'll – I'll walk out that door and I won't come back.'

Johnny suddenly went silent and his face fell. What on earth had he done? He had obviously misjudged the situation really badly carrying on like that. 'Oh, God, Nora,' he said, 'I was only codding you – I didn't mean any harm at all. I was only teasing you. Having a bit of a laugh . . .'

He hadn't thought it through in any way, just let his instincts take over, having a bit of a laugh as he would with Mary and the kids or even Rose Murphy. He thought most women would scream and then laugh, as they would with a harmless little mouse running around.

He had not for a minute bargained on Nora's extreme re-action – and the consequences of it. While she wouldn't have been his first choice helping out – or even his third or fourth choice – in the short time she had been in the house with them, things had improved. Life felt safer now without the fear of the school or Guards breathing down his neck.

Nora went towards the sink, her gaze fixed firmly away from the rabbits, and turned on the tap.

Imagine if she went now, Johnny thought, and her having happily agreed to be at home at the weekend to let him go into town and play with the band. What kind of eedjit was he to have ruined all that? He cleared his throat. 'I'm sorry for acting the maggot, Nora. I didn't think you would be so frightened. You have every right to be angry with me.'

Her eyes narrowed in thought for a few seconds, and then she held her hands under the tap long enough to just wet them. As Johnny stood watching her, all anxious that he had upset her, she suddenly whirled around and placed one hand on each side of Johnny's face, leaving black and red fingerprints on both sides. Then she stepped back to observe the streaks of black newsprint mixed with blood.

'Now, Mr Cassidy!' she said, raising her eyebrows and laugh-ing, 'if we're going to start teasing, two can play at that game.' She indicated to the mirror over at the side of the window. 'Take a look at your lovely face.'

Johnny held his hands aloft and blinked his eyes several times. 'I don't believe it,' he exclaimed. 'You're a devil, so you are! All these years knowing you and I never guessed you had a bad bit in you.'

As she watched him checking his reflection, Nora felt more bubbles of laughter coming up into her throat. Then, as he turned towards her grinning, tears of mirth filled her eyes and she heard herself giggling in a way she had not done for years. It was so long ago since she had laughed that hard that she could not remember it. It could be as far back as when she was a young girl in boarding school, and it was certainly before she had started work in the hospital.

'I didn't think when I caught you with the rabbits,' Johnny said, 'because Mary and I used to have a bit of carry-on like that every now and then. I got a real fright when you turned on me and said you were leaving.'

Nora wiped the tears with the back of her hand and then turned back to the sink. 'I've decided to give you a reprieve,' she said, 'but you'll know not to do it again.' She rinsed her hands under the cold water and then she lifted the bar of washing soap and rubbed it over both palms and let the water run over them until they were clean.

'I will,' he said, 'I certainly will. I've learned my lesson all right.'

She lifted the towel and dried her hands. 'I think we've both learned a lesson,' she said. 'A bit of a laugh does you the power of good.'

And when Johnny went off to the hospital with Larry in the afternoon, Nora sat down in the living room and stared out of the window. This was the third day she had been in the house and each day had been totally different. The office already seemed like a different world. And she was beginning to feel like a different person.

Chapter Sixteen

Sean and Ella arrived back from school before Johnny got home from the hospital. Nora thought that Ella looked slightly brighter, but Sean looked almost like a different boy.

'How did you get on?' she asked, expecting little in the way of a reply.

'Grand,' he said. 'One of the teachers is going to teach me to play the piano. Our headmaster, Mr Rafferty, organised it. This music teacher, Mrs Keating, is coming in every Monday. Since I don't have to go to Irish, they've said she'll give me exercises to do on the piano in the hall. And she says she'll check on Mondays how I'm getting on, and if I'm doing OK she'll give me harder exercises.'

'And why don't you have to do Irish?' Nora asked.

Sean looked down at the floor. 'Well, I missed too much being off, and I'm too far behind to pick it up now. I'm no good at it anyway,' he shrugged. 'Mr Rafferty said I've got a good ear for music and singing, and that learning the piano would be better for me. He says I can go into the hall to practice any time I'm not in class, and that I can do it during the dinner break, or even stay after school.'

Nora thought Mr Rafferty seemed a sensible man, keeping idle hands busy. 'And are you interested in music?'

'Oh, I am. I can play the fiddle a bit, Daddy showed me, and the tin whistle, and I like singing too.'

Ella came to stand at the scullery door. Nora could see the girl looked pale again. 'And how did you get on at school?'

'Fine,' Ella said. 'I managed the arithmetic and everything all right. I've got homework to do tonight, reading and questions for English.'

'Well, that all sounds good,' Nora said. 'And Sean was telling me all about him learning the piano.'

Ella felt her stomach tighten at the mention of it. She was embarrassed that a special case was being made out of Sean, and she knew it was because Mr Rafferty was trying to keep him in school and out of trouble. When the girls' school was out in the yard at break, they could see over the fence to the music room in the boys' school and they saw him through the window, practising on the piano.

'Isn't that your Sean?' one of the girls asked. 'What is he doing?'

Ella had shrugged and said she didn't know, but Maeve had made a great laugh of it, saying, 'Would you look at him, sitting there at the piano? He must think he's Frank Sinatra or Bing Crosby.'

Ella was grateful when Nancy stuck up for him. 'I don't know about his piano playing, but Sean can sing, Maeve, I've heard him. He's brilliant.'

Maeve had turned to Ella. 'Your father plays the fiddle in a band, doesn't he? I saw him at my cousin's wedding. Maybe Sean will form a band with your father.' She started to giggle. 'You could join them too. Can you imagine? The Cassidy Trio.'

'Very funny,' Ella had said, trying to look as though it hadn't bothered her, but it had.

She looked at her aunt now and decided to ignore the mention of Sean and the piano. 'Do you need any help?' she asked.

'I think we're fine,' Nora said. 'We have a rabbit stew for dinner with potatoes and carrots. It's been on a few hours and it should be ready for around five o'clock. Are you hungry?'

When there was no reply, she turned to look and saw Ella, her eyes closed, sliding to the floor.

'Jesus!' Nora said, rushing over to her and she and Sean helped Ella sit up.

'If you hold her,' Nora said, 'I'll get her a drink of water.'

As she came back from the sink, Ella was trying to move, slightly disorientated, and her skirt rose up to her knees. Nora went to kneel beside her to pull it down and protect her modesty, and saw the small stain on the girl's white knickers.

I should have guessed, she thought. *I should have asked her about her periods.*

They got her into the living room and onto the couch, and Nora rubbed her hand, asking a very concerned Sean if he would take Larry into the scullery and blow bubbles with him.

'You know what's wrong with you, don't you?' Nora said. 'What's been upsetting you for the last few days – making you feel a bit off colour.'

Ella stared at her aunt, her eyes dazed. 'How did you know about what Nancy's granny said about Daddy?'

'Nancy's granny?' Nora was totally confused now. 'Did she say something nasty about your father?'

Ella bent her head and started to cry. 'She was talking about him not having a proper job and—' She suddenly halted, as though just realising what she was saying.

'Don't pay any attention to people like that,' Nora said. 'They need to take care of their own business and stop minding other folk's. It's not an easy time for anyone, finding work with the Emergency.'

Ella slowly nodded. She suddenly felt reassured now with the way her aunt had reacted, and the fact she had stood up for her father. But even so, she didn't want to discuss it any more, because just thinking about it made her feel upset. 'I don't feel well. I've a headache and a stomach ache.'

'You don't need to worry, what you're feeling is all normal. That's what I was trying to tell you.'

Ella looked up at her. 'What?'

'Your monthly period.' Nora spoke in a low voice. 'Have you had one before?'

Ella shook her head. 'Is that what it is?'

'Yes. When you fainted I noticed you had a little patch of blood on your knickers...'

Ella's face flushed and she drew her legs up under her, embarrassed.

'Nobody else saw you,' Nora said reassuringly, 'Sean wasn't there at the time. Do you know about girls having their periods?'

She nodded. 'Mammy told me that I would have it some time, and some of the girls in school have them. I don't know what to do. Will it make me sick every month?' She started to cry again. 'I wish my mammy was here now.'

'She's up in heaven now,' Nora whispered, 'and she's looking down on you, watching and helping you with everything. Every time you think of her, just remember that, and you will feel she's with you all.' Nora put her arms around the girl now. 'I've been praying to her to guide me in doing things the way she would have done, so I know we're going to manage everything just grand.' She rocked Ella gently from side to side. 'You don't need to worry about anything. And next month you'll be prepared. I have some sanitary towels up in my case, and I can buy you some more at the chemist's tomorrow.' She patted Ella, then moved back. 'Now, I'm going to go upstairs and get those towels for you, and a small sanitary belt to hold them on. I left some clean underwear on your bed earlier, so I'll get you a pair of knickers, and you can go out to the outhouse and sort yourself out.'

'Thanks,' Ella said in a muffled voice.

Nora went out to the hallway and then she stopped and went to the stand where she had hung her handbag. She opened it and came out with a packet of Beechams Powders, which she kept in case of an unexpected headache or if she felt off-colour when it was that time of the month herself. She went into the scullery and got half a cup of milk and then came back in to Ella and instructed her how to take it.

Ella was in bed when Johnny arrived back from the hospital with Larry. He said that the visit had gone well and that he saw an improvement in Hannah. Nora took a deep breath and explained as delicately as she could why Ella was lying down. He had looked concerned, but not as embarrassed as she had imagined, and, when she thought about it, she realised that after helping produce four children – five counting the baby that was lost along with Mary – he probably knew more about the workings of the female body than she did herself.

Upstairs, Ella eased herself up in bed and sat with the bedclothes tucked around her, her long blonde hair loose over her shoulders. In the two hours she had slept, everything seemed to have magically improved. Her head and stomach were no longer sore, and although she felt a bit embarrassed for fainting and then crying over what Mrs Byrne had said, she felt reassured after the chat with Aunt Nora.

She heard a tap on the door and then her father's voice saying, 'Can I come in?'

'Yes,' she called, pulling the covers up to her chin.

'How are you doing?' he said, coming in to sit on the side of the bed. 'Your Aunt Nora told me you weren't too well.'

'I'm all right now – I think the sleep and the Beechams Powders helped me.'

'That's good,' he said, patting her leg. 'If you need any women's things or anything like that, just ask Nora.' He smiled. 'Are you coming downstairs for something to eat? Nora has kept something hot for you. The gas will go off soon, so if you're not up to coming down, we can bring it up to you.'

'I'll come down.' Then, as her father went to turn back to the door, she said. 'How did you get on with the job you went to see about this morning?'

'Grand,' he said, nodding. 'I start in the morning.' Then he shrugged. 'It's only for the week, but sure, something will turn up for next week.' Then he gave her a big smile and a reassuring wink. 'I have two nights – Friday and Saturday – playing in the band and that will help. And your Aunt Nora will be here to make sure you're all well looked after.'

Ella tried to smile back, but her face just didn't seem to do it naturally. Her father had turned towards the door and didn't see.

She lay back down and closed her eyes. She could hear him going down the stairs singing 'Swinging on a Star'. She hadn't heard him singing like that for ages, not since their mother died.

He must be feeling a little bit happier again, she thought, and she knew it was because he was looking forward to going out with the band at the weekend. And she knew he would come home having drunk too much after it. It was all the things that Nancy's granny had said about him.

But Aunt Nora was not easy-going like her mother and she was not used to having a man who came in talking nonsense about all the tunes they had played and all the people who came up to congratulate the band or to ask them to play special requests. What if Aunt Nora told him she was going back to Tullamore? What would happen to them all then?

Ella turned around and buried her face in the pillow.

Chapter Seventeen

On Tuesday afternoon, Nora washed and dressed Larry into his Sunday clothes, and then changed from her house clothes into her tweed suit, a blouse and pearls. As they walked along towards the hospital, she felt the sun warm and thought it a hopeful sign that spring was on the way.

She and Larry had begun to settle into a routine. It had surprised her to discover that he was a serious and sensitive little boy, and she felt a bit guilty thinking that she had never taken the time to get to know him or Hannah at all. She supposed it was no wonder that the sick little girl had been awkward with her, this aunt who was almost a stranger. When she had visited the house, her main aim had been to spend time with Mary without the children getting in the way.

There were only a few books and toys in the house suitable for a boy of Larry's age – a few miniature cars, a teddy bear, a kaleidoscope, and some building bricks and it crossed her mind that the Cassidy children had a lot less toys and books than she had had growing up, less than their mother's family too. And it wasn't just because of rationing, it was down to Johnny not having a steady job to afford the things a growing family needed. Mary had kept them spotlessly clean and reasonably well dressed, but no family should have to worry about having turf or coal in during the winter as the Cassidys obviously were.

As they walked along the road up through Kilmainham, Nora pointed out the numbers on the doors of the houses and the colours of any that were painted, and got Larry to repeat them back to her. They passed a newsagent's shop that had comics and a few children's bits and pieces in it, so she bought Hannah a cardboard dressing-doll set. It was flimsy and light and unlikely to cause any damage if it were dropped, unlike the hardback fairy-tale book that still filled her with guilt. She bought Larry a small bottle of bubbles, which she thought was safe enough and might help to entertain his little sister.

She was anxious about seeing Hannah again, and had decided that if she was as fractious as she had been on the last visit, she would leave as quickly as possible. They were walking towards the main entrance of the hospital when Nora felt a hand on her shoulder.

'Nora Lamb? It *is* you, isn't it?'

Nora turned to find herself looking at Veronica Fisher, one of the few women she had got on with in the hospital in Tullamore. 'Veronica!' she exclaimed. 'I don't believe it – I was just thinking about you recently and wondering if I would ever see you again.'

'Well, here I am, as large as life, and twice as bad,' Veronica said, laughing.

'You're looking very well,' Nora said. 'You've hardly changed since I last saw you.' She still had the same short and curvy figure, dressed in a black coat and hat, with a bright blue scarf and a pair of stylish navy shoes. She always wore high heels, Nora remembered; being small, she must have thought they gave her a bit of a lift.

'It must be a good five years since I last saw you,' Veronica said. 'I often wondered how you were getting on.' She looked down at Larry. 'And who is this fine little fellow along with you?'

Nora moved closer and quickly whispered the situation to her.

'Ah, that's very sad,' Veronica whispered back, nodding in Larry's direction. 'Always worse when there's children involved.' She gave a little sigh. 'Well, I was in a similar position as you know – I came back to Dublin to help look after my parents who were both in their eighties.'

'And how are they?' Nora enquired.

Veronica's face fell. 'They both passed away two years ago – within months of each other.'

'Oh, I'm sorry to hear that,' Nora said. 'And you didn't move back to Tullamore?'

'No,' Veronica said. 'I've got used to being out in my parents' house in Ballsbridge, and I have a brother, Dominic, out in Donnybrook, so it suits me fine. There's a lot more going on up here than there is in Tullamore, and it's easy enough to get in on the bus here to work.'

'Oh, you're back working again?'

'Yes,' Veronica told her. 'I was lucky enough to get in the main office here. I'm in personnel now, so you get to meet all kinds of people.'

'Well, I'm glad it all worked out for you,' Nora said, very impressed. 'They've held my job open for me in Tullamore, but I've no idea when I will get back.'

'The change will do you no harm. Whereabouts are you?'

'Islandbridge, opposite the Phoenix Park.'

Veronica nodded. 'Very central for you for getting into Grafton Street and O'Connell Street.' They chatted for a few more minutes, Veronica asking after anyone she remembered from the hospital and Nora bringing her up to date with news. Then Veronica looked at her watch. 'I'd better get back to the office – I was just out at the post office with a few letters. We must meet up for a cup of tea when you have some time to yourself – or maybe we could meet some evening for the pictures?'

'Oh, that would be lovely,' Nora said. 'Maybe if we have the cup of tea first we can plan the cinema for another night?' She thought for a few moments. 'How would Saturday afternoon suit? We could meet in Bewley's – I love their coffee.'

'That would be grand.' Veronica told her. 'Two o'clock?'

As they parted, Nora was glowing from having met her old friend, and the fact she had something lovely to look forward to for the weekend. She couldn't remember the last time she had a social outing with a friend.

They went into the ward now, Nora holding Larry's hand

tightly, and turned towards the area where Hannah's bed was. Sister Gollogly was with her again today and had her sitting up in the bed.

Nora hesitated, wondering if the nurse would refer to her previous visit. 'Oh, have we come at a bad time?' she said, taking a step back. 'Do you want us to come back later?'

'Not at all. You've come at just the right time,' the nurse said. 'We've just put cream on Hannah's arm and legs and nice fresh bandages. She's been a very good girl, haven't you, Hannah? And she hasn't cried once today.' She smiled at Nora. 'She's in better form today than she was at the weekend. I think the worst of it is beginning to heal up now.'

Nora felt a wave of relief. 'Oh, that is good news.'

As the nurse moved out to let her in to the chair at the side of the bed, Nora kept a grip on Larry, afraid he would launch himself at his sister.

Larry held his little bottle up so Hannah could see it. 'Bubbles!' he said, looking back at Nora and smiling. 'Auntie bought me bubbles!'

A warmth spread through Nora now. At least she had one on her side so far.

'Me! Me!' Hannah said, smiling and holding her good arm out.

Nora relaxed a little. Hannah might be all right today. 'Oh, I have something nice for you too,' she said. 'Some nice little dollies.'

For the next hour she sat with both children, showing them how to blow bubbles without dripping the soapy liquid everywhere. Then she very carefully pressed out the cardboard boy and girl and their clothes as they both watched her with great rapture.

When the visiting bell sounded, she reached for her bag, grateful to have got through the afternoon without trouble. Then, just as she was saying goodbye to Hannah, the ward sister came over to the bed again. 'I've just had a meeting with Hannah's doctor and he said he's pleased with her progress. You can tell her father that Hannah might be ready to go home in the next couple of weeks, when the last of the blisters have dried out. We can send a nurse to the house to change her dressings.'

Nora tried not to look taken aback. Although she was relieved the poor child was well enough to come home, she had not expected it so quickly. She was just getting into a nice little routine with Larry and the others, and she was afraid that having a younger, more unpredictable child, was not going to be easy. But home with the rest of her family was where Hannah should be and Nora would somehow manage 'Well,' she said, smiling now. 'That is good news.'

Johnny arrived home from work around six o'clock. He was tired from all the heavy lifting, but there was a light in his eyes, knowing he was bringing in some well-needed money.

When the dinner was over, Nora went into the scullery with some of the dishes while Ella gathered up the rest and any cutlery that was left.

Johnny caught Ella's hand and squeezed it. 'How are you today?'

A slight flush of embarrassment came on her face. 'Grand,' she said, moving her hand away to pick up a knife.

'Did your Aunt Nora tell you that the visit with Hannah went well today? The nurses said she might be out in the next week or two.'

'That will be great,' Ella said, smiling at the thought.

'Seemingly, a nurse will come in and sort her bandages for a few weeks and after that, she should be ... well, almost as good as new.'

There was a small silence now, as both knew that Hannah would never be the way she was before the accident. The doctors had already explained to Johnny that she would be left with scars on her arm and legs, which would fade in time, but would never wholly disappear.

'Hopefully, things will improve all round now.'

Chapter Eighteen

On Thursday, as Ella was walking out of school with Nancy and Maeve, they were all laughing at a story Maeve had just told them about one of her older sisters going on a blind date with a lad she had met through the Penfriend's column in the *Ireland's Own*. She had always been a great storyteller, and when she was in one of her good moods she was very funny and entertaining, and it always reminded Ella why they were friends.

'The lad was from out Kildare way,' Maeve said, 'and my mother said he probably had a big farm there and plenty of money, so Anna better get herself all dolled up.'

'Had she seen a photo of him?' Nancy wanted to know.

Maeve shook her head and started to laugh. Then she held her hand up. 'Let me tell it in the right order or I'll forget.' She giggled then went on, 'So there was Anna, going through all her clothes and then Maggie and Bridget's, and saying she had to find something really special.'

'So what did she wear?' Ella asked, intrigued.

'Well,' Maeve said, 'she eventually got a green satin dress that Bridget had worn as a bridesmaid a few years ago, so she spent hours taking it in and adding flowers and beads at the neck and all that kind of thing.' Maeve bit her lip. 'Then she went to the hairdresser's to get her hair done all fancy, and then she spent more hours painting her nails and putting on make-up. Everybody waved her off to get the bus into town to meet the rich Kildare farmer under the clock at Clerys in O'Connell Street.'

She suddenly stopped and put her hand over her face, laughing hysterically.

'What happened?' Nancy urged.

Ella started to laugh too. 'Did the heel break off her shoe or something?'

'He wasn't a rich farmer at all!' Maeve finally gasped out. 'He was an old fella with long, straggly hair and he turned up wearing a pair of wellington boots covered in cow shite!'

As the three girls neared the gate, hanging onto each other, laughing helplessly, they suddenly became aware of a boy standing watching them. When Ella realised who it was, her heart began to race and she could feel herself blushing. She slowed her walking down so she was hiding behind the other two, afraid he would see her red face.

Nancy took a deep breath to still her giggling. 'What are you doing here?' she asked.

Her cousin Danny lifted an amused eyebrow. 'That must have been some great joke,' he said, 'I was just watching you all roaring with the laughter.'

'Were you waiting on me?' Nancy asked.

'Sort of,' he said. 'I wanted to catch your friend here and ask about organising a game of chess with her brother.'

'Sean Cassidy?' Maeve's tone was incredulous. She turned to Ella. 'Is your Sean playing *chess* now? I thought it was the piano he had taken up.'

Ella felt her cheeks burning and tried to think of something smart to say in return, but nothing came to mind. 'He's only learning chess,' she said, lamely.

'Well,' Danny said, smiling, 'if he can play the piano, I'm sure he'll manage chess.'

Maeve looked him up and down. 'And are you some kind of an expert at chess?' Her tone was mocking and slightly flirtatious.

'Nah,' he said, as if he hadn't noticed Maeve's manner, 'I'm not an expert at anything, but I like it, and it's something to pass the evenings.' Danny looked at Ella. 'Is your brother coming out of school now?'

'Yes,' she said, 'he usually walks home around the same time as me.'

'OK,' he said, 'I'll walk over to the boys' school with you.'

Danny nodded his head in Nancy and Maeve's direction. 'See you later, girls.' He started walking ahead and Ella had to move quickly to catch up with him.

'It's a nice day and I was bored in the house,' he said, 'and I just thought I'd take a walk down to see if we could arrange this chess thing.'

She was thinking all sorts of things, but she needed to clear this subject up before an embarrassing situation arose. 'Sean's not really got the hang of chess yet, so you might be disappointed,' she told him. 'You actually sound like you know what you're doing, and we're only learning the names of the pieces and where you can move them.'

'That's how everybody learns at first.' He shrugged and smiled at her. 'I'm not that bothered about how good you or your brother are. To be honest, it's really just an excuse to get out of the house and I thought you and me got on fine, so I thought I might get on with your brother too.'

She didn't know what he would make of Sean, because they were two very different types of lad. 'Sometimes me and Sean don't get on,' she told him. 'Sometimes we could nearly kill each other.'

He started to laugh. 'That's brothers and sisters for you,' he said. 'I think they're all like that, arguing and everything, especially when they're around the same age. Mine are only little, so it's easier to be nice to them.'

'I'm the same with Larry and Hannah,' she said. 'Larry's four and Hannah's nearly three.'

'Nancy told me about your little sister,' he said. 'Is she getting better now?'

Ella nodded. 'Yes, she's a lot better, but she needs to stay in hospital for a bit longer.'

He was silent for a few moments, and then he said. 'She told me about your mother as well – I'm sorry.'

His words suddenly hit her as though she had just received a blow in the stomach. It was always the same, when she suddenly was reminded about what had happened, especially if she was in any way relaxed or on the verge of feeling something akin to happiness.

Then, as though he could sense her reaction, he quickly said. 'I know what it feels like because I lost my father during the war. We were waiting on him to come home for Christmas – I was only seven at the time – and then we got a telegram to say he was missing in action. It wasn't a very good Christmas, because my mother wasn't interested in anything else but going to church with my granny from Liverpool, and praying all the time that he would be found. There was no Christmas tree and no presents because she said it was all stupid if my father wasn't home. Granny brought us up to her house for the day, and she had some presents wrapped for me and pretended that Father Christmas had got mixed up and left them there by mistake. Then, a few weeks later, army officers came out to the house to say he had been found. He'd been killed in the trenches.'

It was all so sad, Ella didn't know what to say now, so she just repeated what he had said to her. 'I'm really sorry ... It must have been hard being just the two of you, because it's been really hard even with five of us. I think we all kind of tiptoe around it.'

Danny nodded. 'In a way, I understand how my mother was, she was in shock and it was terrible for her. She didn't really talk to *me* about it, but she was always talking about it to other people when I was there. I think she thought I didn't understand a lot of it, but I did.'

They walked on in silence towards the entrance to the boys' school, and it occurred to her that she had never spoken much about her mother to anyone until yesterday when she talked to Aunt Nora after she fainted. And now, she was talking about it to a stranger. It just seemed so big and overwhelming for her to talk to her father or Sean about it – like a monster lurking in the shadows – that it was easier to pretend it wasn't there at all.

As she looked back at him, their eyes locked and Ella felt

her face really flush now and she had the same fluttery feeling in her stomach. He was lovely, she thought; his face, his gorgeous brown eyes, and his lovely, cheery Liverpool accent. And although something made her think that he liked her, she couldn't be sure. She was about a year and a half younger than him, and maybe he thought that was far too young to be a proper girlfriend. Up until she met Danny Byrne, she would have thought the same herself. But now things seemed very different. *She* seemed very different. As her eyes moved down towards his mouth, she suddenly wondered what it would be like if he kissed her. Her face flushed even redder and she had to turn away from him now so he wouldn't guess what she was thinking.

The boys were all trailing out of the gates now from the various classes – some in groups, some alone, different heights, different ages. Eventually, all the boys had gone and they were still waiting.

'Do you think he's gone home already?' Danny asked.

Ella shrugged. 'I don't know, he might be in that music room again.' She looked at him. 'I don't want to meet the headmaster or any of the teachers, they don't really like girls coming over to the boys' school.' She especially didn't want to bump into Mr Rafferty, as he might say something about his visit out to the house. 'They'll just start asking us questions and wanting to know who you are, and what you're doing in the school.'

He started to laugh. 'I'll just tell them you're my girlfriend.'

She looked at him in shock. 'What?'

'I'm only taking the mickey,' he said, hitting his elbow against hers.

Half of her was thrilled he had said such a thing, but the other, more careful side of her, knew that he might be teasing.

'If you did say something stupid like that, you'll get both of us in trouble.' Her voice was serious now. 'You're not in England now, you know.'

'I was only kidding,' he said, 'and for your information, Miss Bossyboots, I'd be in trouble for saying it in Liverpool as well.

Teachers are strict there too, you know. We had a headmaster who would cane you as quick as look at you.'

'Well, why did you say it?' she asked.

He looked at her with narrowed eyes. 'Well, maybe I was thinking that when you're a bit older, I would like to have a girlfriend like you. I liked you the minute I saw you. I think you're nice-looking and you're a nice girl. Is there anything wrong in saying that?'

Ella looked back at him and she could tell by the way he was looking at her, that he was serious. 'No,' she said her heart suddenly beating quickly, 'there's not.'

'Well, that's OK, then.'

'Daddy would probably go mad if he saw me going around with boys,' she said.

'I know, but you won't be going around with anyone. I could see you at the house if I was playing chess with your brother or your auntie,' he said, 'couldn't I? There's nowt wrong with that, is there?'

Ella didn't know what to say to him. It all felt a bit confusing. Then she suddenly felt uncomfortable, and it made her remember her period and the sanitary towel she was wearing. She had already changed two in the school toilet today, but she had heard of girls getting their clothes stained with blood. 'I need to go home,' she said, starting to walk away. 'I think our Sean must have left earlier.'

'Will you tell him about the chess?' he said. 'And maybe I'll see you again soon.'

'I'll tell him,' she said, and then she rushed off leaving him staring after her.

Sean arrived home almost an hour after Ella.

'Where were you?' she asked him accusingly. 'I was waiting outside the school for you, but there wasn't a sign of you.'

'I was in with Mr Rafferty and Mrs Keating, the music teacher. They wanted to talk to me about something.'

'What?' she asked, still annoyed.

Just then Nora called out from the scullery. 'I got a tin of cocoa today and I'm making Larry a cup. Would you both like some now, or do you want to wait until bedtime?'

'Now!' they both said together, and walked down into the scullery.

Nora put the milk on top of the cooker to boil, and then poured another drop of the milk into a jug and started mixing the cocoa powder into it to make a paste.

'I've got a bit of a job,' Sean said. 'Mrs Keating came into the school to see me and ask if I could go out to her house in Inchicore to help with the garden. Her husband has something wrong with his back and he's been told he's not allowed to do any bending or lifting. She said she'll give me five shillings a week, plus a free piano lesson any time I'm out there after school, and any Saturday morning. I've to go out there tomorrow, straight from school.'

'Well, that's very good news,' Nora said. 'She must have taken a shine to you. You're obviously behaving well for her.' She went to the dresser now and took four mugs off the hooks.

Sean shrugged, embarrassed. 'She keeps saying I'm the best piano student she's ever had. Mr Rafferty said the very same thing when he heard me. I don't know what to make of it. I can't tell if I'm good or not, but I really like playing the piano.'

As soon as the milk started to show signs of boiling, Nora whipped the pan off the heat and poured it into the mugs. 'The sugar is finished,' she told them before they complained, 'but it's nice enough without it. We'll go in and drink it at the table in the living room. Larry is in there playing with a packet of cards.' She looked from one to the other, smiling. 'We've an hour before your father comes in from work, so I could teach you both a bit more about the chess if you like.'

Ella had to stop herself from saying it was a great idea, thinking that it might look a bit too obvious, but as soon as they sat down, Sean turned to her. 'What were you looking for me for anyway?'

Ella took a deep breath, not sure how her news would be

received by her brother or aunt. 'It wasn't me that was looking for you, it was Nancy's cousin. He was telling Nancy that he wished he had another boy to play chess with.'

'Chess?' Nora said, all interested.

Ella shrugged, trying to effect disinterest. 'Yes,' she said. 'I was telling Nancy about you teaching us how to play, and she must have told him.' She made a little face which she hoped would look as though she thought it a ridiculous idea.

'If he can play chess, he must be a decent sort of a lad. It takes concentration and self-discipline. I wouldn't mind a game with him myself.'

Ella took a drink of her cocoa as though the conversation was of no interest to her.

'What's the boy's name?' Nora asked.

'Danny,' Ella said, feeling a little thrill run through her at the sound of his name. 'Danny Byrne.'

'Well, why don't you ask Danny to call down to the house on Sunday after dinner?' Nora suggested. 'It might be a good idea if he and I were to play a very basic game, while you and Sean watch, so you get the hang of it.'

Ella took another drink. She wasn't at all sure about playing chess, but if it was the only way she could get to see Danny Byrne, then it was worth the effort. 'OK,' she said, 'I'll mention it to Nancy at school tomorrow.'

Chapter Nineteen

On Friday night, after Sean and Ella went to bed, Nora settled down in front of the fire with the radio on low and her copy of *Gone with the Wind*. She had poured herself a cup of tea from the thermos flask, and felt tired but contented. She thought that her first week had gone well and that things had moved a long way since her arrival. Johnny had worked all week and had come home on Friday night with a big barrow load of turf, which he had got from someone he knew.

When she went around the back of the house to open the gate for him, he told her, 'I've bought three barrow loads. I'll empty this one and then go back for the other two.' Sean went along with him, and on the final run back with the turf, he had carried another bag of it on his back. The sight of it, plus the money Johnny had brought from his four days' work had cheered Nora up immensely. He had placed the small envelope with the few pounds down on the butcher's block in the scullery, just as he used to do with his wife.

'That will buy whatever you can get for the house with the ration book,' he said, 'and hopefully it will give enough to keep us all going for the week.'

'That's grand,' she told him. 'And if you can manage here, I thought I might go down to Tullamore on Sunday and pick up some more rashers and eggs and I might even get a boiling fowl.'

'You're very good,' he told her, 'and it's all appreciated. Everything you do is appreciated.'

'That's all right. I came up to Dublin to help, and that's what

I'm trying to do.' She paused. 'We've no meat this evening with it being Friday, so I thought I would fry up some potatoes with an egg and onion? Will the children eat that, do you think?'

And Johnny, in higher spirits with his week's work finished and two nights' playing music ahead of him, was in the mood for celebrating. 'I thought we might send out Sean and Ella for some fish and chips.'

'Won't that be expensive? We could maybe put the money to greater use.'

'Ah, the children all love that, and sure, I'll make the money up with working over the weekend.'

Nora had been about to ask, what about the following week? And all the weeks to come? But, she did not want to spoil his treat. If it happened more regularly she might have to say something, but she would treat this as a special occasion. And the thought of fish and chips did appeal to her.

By seven o'clock they were all sitting listening to a children's radio programme, having eaten well and drunk a glass of milk each with the fish and chips. Johnny looked at the clock and then he gave a stretch. 'Right,' he said, 'if anyone needs to use the outhouse, go now, because the scullery will be out of bounds for the next half an hour.' He clapped his hands together and smiled. 'The pots and kettle of water should all be boiling now, and I'm going to go and have a nice soak in the bath.'

'I've left the white shirt you asked me to iron in your wardrobe,' Nora told him, 'and I gave your good suit a light press.'

Nora had not imagined herself doing things like this for a man when she agreed to come and help. She had imagined Johnny and the older two doing for themselves, but she had soon realised that being part of a family meant doing what was needed if it helped everyone else. Johnny was going out again tonight to work and bring in more money, after a day's hard physical labour and she knew he needed to look spick and span when he was playing in a band.

*

She had been sitting reading for around half an hour when she heard Larry crying and then footsteps upstairs, so she went quickly upstairs in case he needed to use the chamber pot. When she tapped on the door, she found that Sean was already dealing with him.

'It's OK,' he told her, adjusting the half-asleep child's pyjamas. 'He woke and needed to use the pot. I'll bring it down to the outhouse and empty it.'

'No,' she said, 'I'll do it. You go back to sleep.'

'Thanks, Aunt Nora,' he said quietly. 'You're very good looking after us.'

'That's all right,' she said. 'That's what I'm trying to do.'

A short while later she returned the pot upstairs and peeped in Ella's room.

'It's OK, I'm awake,' Ella said. 'I woke when I heard Larry crying.'

Nora went into the room and pulled the door over after her. 'Sean sorted him out and he's grand now, and his bed is still dry.' She paused. 'How are you? Has your period got any lighter?'

'Yes, it's a lot easier now.' She paused. 'It's not as bad as I thought it would be. After the first day everything got better.'

'That's the way it is for most women,' Nora told her. 'I still have mine, regular as clockwork, every month.'

Ella looked surprised. 'When does it finish?'

Nora sat down on the end of the bed. 'It varies from woman to woman, but usually late-forties to fifties.'

'Does it stop when women are too old to have babies?'

'Yes,' Nora said. She could not remember ever having had a conversation like this before, but she realised that it was something she should address with the young girl. She was sure it was what Mary would have done. 'And you do know that when you start your period, it means that your body is getting ready so that when you are old enough, you can have a baby.'

Ella sat up now, leaning against the wooden headboard. 'I heard something like that, but I wasn't sure if it was true.' She stopped and then she whispered, 'I don't know if I'll ever want a baby. I'd be afraid, after what happened to Mammy.'

Nora felt a little stab in her chest. 'Try not to think like that,' she said, in a soothing tone. 'Your mother had four healthy children and what happened was very sad and very unfortunate...' She paused, trying to get the right words. 'And very rare.' She put her hand on top of the blanket where Ella's feet were. 'From what I know of your lovely mother, she would not want it to have a bad effect on you. She would want you to live your life the way that's natural for you. To make your own plans and have your own family.'

There was a silence then Ella said. 'Do you mind me...' She hesitated. 'Do you mind me asking you a personal question?'

Nora felt herself tense up. She had no idea what she was going to have to answer – or, indeed, if she had any answers. 'What do you want to know?'

'I just wondered why you never got married. Did you not want to have a family – or do you prefer to be on your own?'

Nora pursed her lips together, then let out a long, low sigh. 'Oh, that's a hard question, Ella – and a very grown-up one.' She looked over to the window, where a sliver of moonlight came through the curtains.

Ella suddenly became fearful of the silence. 'I'm really sorry, Aunt Nora,' she said. She could just make out her aunt's profile, and something about the set of her jaw and the way she was just staring at the window worried her. 'I shouldn't have asked you something like that. I never thought... it was too forward of me.'

Nora shook her head. 'No, no, it was a natural enough question to ask.' Her finger came up to press on her lips, then she suddenly smiled and nodded her head. 'The answer is, I never planned *not* to get married. I never planned *not* to have children. It's just the way my life turned out.' She thought again. 'There was a time when I thought I might get married...'

'What happened?'

'I was only young, really, sixteen or so.'

Ella was glad the room was dark so the surprised look on her face was not seen. She could not in a million years imagine her aunt being that age. 'And where did you meet him?'

'He was from Wicklow, but he had had relatives down in Tullamore, and he helped out on the farm one summer. He was a student, up in Dublin, studying to be a vet.'

'What did he look like? What was his name?'

'His name was James Meehan. He was taller than me, thin with reddish hair. He was a shy kind of a boy.' She paused. 'He wasn't everyone's idea of handsome, but he had a nice smile and he was a very decent sort. I remember him being particularly gentle with the animals; I thought he would make a very good vet.'

Ella suddenly thought. 'And was he older than you?'

'Oh, yes,' Nora said, nodding her head. 'He was nineteen.' She shrugged. 'And that was the problem. When my mother and father found out about it, they weren't happy at all. They thought he was too old for me, and said that he would go back to Dublin and forget all about me.' She looked towards the window. 'We had a lovely summer; I used to go down to the farmhouse and cook the dinner, and then I used to bring tea out to the fields for them.' She gave a little far off smile. 'And we both went with Uncle Bernard to the fair days in town.'

Ella was riveted to the story now. 'So, what happened afterwards?'

'Well,' she said, 'when he went back to university in Dublin, he wrote to me for a while. In fact, he wrote to me right up until he left university.'

'Did your parents mind you writing to him?'

'At first,' she said. 'Even though I let them read them and they could see it was all innocent, I discovered my mother had burned a few of the letters, and I was very upset. By this time, I was working in a solicitor's office in town, and plenty of girls had boyfriends and were going to dances and that kind of thing, but my mother didn't like me going anywhere. We had some big rows, and I got my Uncle Bernard to talk to them. He said James was a decent, well-educated lad and they would be hard-pushed to find a better match. He came down to see me at Christmas, and they allowed me to go to the pictures with him. And then I was planning to meet him one Saturday up in Dublin, but the day before I got very ill.'

'What was wrong?'

'They said it was glandular fever,' Nora said, 'but it was more than that, because I was sick with it for over two years. I lost my job – naturally they couldn't keep it open for that long. I lost a lot of weight, had no strength, and I was sleeping all the time. I didn't even have the strength to write to him.' She shook her head. 'Oh, my poor mother was worried out of her mind. She contacted James's relatives and asked him to come down to see me. She thought it would liven me up a bit. I think she would have done anything to see me looking back to my old self, but when he came to see me, I was so sick, he didn't know what to say.'

'Did you see him again when you got better?' Ella asked.

Nora shook her head. 'No,' she sighed. 'He wrote for a while, but something happened at university and he left and went to England. I never heard from him after that.'

'Did he ask you to get engaged?'

'Not in so many words,' Nora said. 'But I think he might have if I had seen more of him.' She shrugged. 'Things just didn't work out...'

'And did you never meet anyone else?'

'No,' she said. 'After that, I never really met anyone else. My mother and father weren't very well, and then I helped to look after my Uncle Bernard too. I was lucky that I got the job in the hospital office when I recovered. But I still wasn't really well when I went back to work, so I didn't get out much to meet anyone else.' She stood up now. 'But, I often thought of James and wondered what would have happened if we had lived nearer each other, or if I had been older when we met and could have made my own decisions.' She patted Ella's arm. 'Life doesn't always turn out the way we expect it,' she said. 'Or the way we want it to. But you already know that, Ella.'

Ella felt sorry for her now. It sounded as though her Aunt Nora had led a very lonely life. She lay down in the bed. 'Goodnight, Aunt Nora.'

'Goodnight to you, Ella,' she whispered as she closed the door.

Chapter Twenty

Nora was dozing by the dying fire, her flask empty and her book lying on the small table beside her, when she heard the front door opening. She moved quickly to reorganise her skirt and twinset.

Johnny came into the living room carrying his fiddle case in one hand and a brown paper bag in the other. 'You're still up?' he said, smiling at her. His blue eyes were sparkling from the glasses of beer he had drunk and playing the music he loved.

'I was just going to go to bed, and I must have dropped off for a few minutes.'

He put the bag down on the table. 'I'm glad you didn't. I've got a pile of fancy sandwiches and sausage rolls that they gave me and the other lads at the end of the night. And,' He went into the bag and came out with an almost full bottle of white wine, 'they gave me this as well. Nobody else wanted it, and I suddenly thought you might have it. What do you think? Have you ever drunk wine before?'

Nora nodded. 'Yes, I had some at a wedding and another time at a funeral in Manchester.'

'I've never tried it, but I'm game to have a go,' he said. 'I think we have some brandy glasses somebody gave us one time. We've only used them a couple of times.'

'You don't mean us to drink it now, do you?'

Johnny smiled and shrugged. 'The waiter told me that, once it's open, you have to drink it or it will taste like vinegar.'

Nora looked at the clock. 'But it's nearly twelve o'clock...'

'Sure, it's Saturday tomorrow,' he reminded her. 'There's no big rush on anything.'

She thought for a moment. She had never been in this kind of situation before, and her instincts were to react the sensible way her mother would have done. But, after the conversation with Ella tonight – after the reminder of how her mother had made so many decisions for her – she decided to make up her own mind. 'Go on,' she said. 'What harm can a glass do? I've heard wine can be medicinal for you.'

'We'll have a few sandwiches as well,' he said.

Nora looked in the bag at the slightly squashed sandwiches, which were cut into dainty quarters. 'They must have got white flour from somewhere,' she said. 'There are always people who know where to get things.'

'Money talks,' Johnny said. 'It always has. I'll get those glasses now and a couple of small plates.'

He came back a few moments later and he poured them both a glass of the wine, and then he opened the bag out properly, so they could see what was in the sandwiches. 'There's enough for us to have a few and we can keep the rest for the children in the morning.'

Johnny held his glass out to Nora and gave her a warm smile. 'Sláinte!'

Nora held her glass out to his and repeated the Irish toast. They both took a mouthful of the wine.

Johnny pulled a face, held the glass out as though examining it, and then took another, bigger mouthful. 'Ah,' he said, 'it kind of grows on you.'

Nora had forgotten how sour wine tasted and wondered if she had actually tried more than a sip on the occasions she had had it before. She took another little drink, and agreed with Johnny that it wasn't as bad as the first. As a younger woman, she would never have forced herself to eat or drink anything she didn't like, but since the Emergency had been in operation, sometimes there simply was not that choice.

Johnny went over to the radio and fiddled about for a few

moments until he found a station that was playing some sort of American jazz music. He turned it down low so it gave a nice background sound but would not waken the children. As he came back to his chair, he did a little dance shuffle – just a few steps – and he and Nora started to laugh.

'The music earlier must have gone to your head,' she said, taking another mouthful of the wine.

'Begod, I think you could be right!' It was the sort of non-sense he and Mary used to get up to after his nights out. She listened as he told her stories of the people who had been at the dance, as he recounted the banter amongst the band members and anything of note about the fancy hotel or dance hall he had been playing in. Apart from singing, Johnny also loved dancing, and on a few occasions he had come back and shown her a few of the new dance moves he had seen on the floor, then he had got Mary up and they had waltzed and laughed their way around the small living room floor.

It brought a pain to his chest to think of her now and those nights together that they would never have again. And earlier, as he had played his violin and laughed along with the other lads, at the back of his mind he felt guilty for enjoying the night out, knowing he would not be coming home to her. But, he did not know what else to do. He sorely missed his easy-natured wife more than he could ever have imagined, but he had to live for the children, and there was no point in living half a life.

He could only carry on and make the best of things. The night out at the dance had brought that back to him with a force. Seeing all the well-dressed people, laughing and generally enjoying themselves, made him think of how frighteningly fleeting life could be.

Mary was not a selfish woman, and she would not have wanted him to pine away at home when he could be out earning money doing the one thing he loved – making music. It wasn't as if he was interested in any of the women who came up to chat to the band at the break and give him special dance requests for the band to play. There had been only one love in his life and she was gone. And if he were to meet someone else, it would be a long way off in the future. He was not looking for anyone to fill his wife's shoes. His family, and finding enough work to keep them in a half-decent situation until they were grown up, was all he was interested in. His nights out at the weekend, having a few bottles of beer, and being able to play music, was the only thing he asked for himself.

Nora took a bite of a chicken sandwich and thought how lovely it was, and then had another sip of wine, which now tasted quite pleasant. By the time she had eaten a second sandwich, Johnny had refilled both their glasses.

'Tell me more about the dance,' Nora said, sitting back comfortably in her chair.

Johnny beamed back at her. He had not imagined that she would accept the drop of wine so favourably, and then sit back so relaxed, enjoying the bit of music on the radio. As he had walked back along the shadows of the quays, humming to himself, he had envisaged her having gone to bed early to read from her well-worn, leather-backed prayer book.

Even just a week ago, Nora Lamb would not have been the company he would have chosen to spend the remnants of a good evening with, not in a million years. It was strange, Johnny thought, how things could suddenly change. This plain, old-fashioned cousin of his wife was the perfect company for him at this particular point in his life. She had been here all night looking after his children while he was out, and she expected nothing in return apart from enough money to put food on the table and keep the house warm. If his boat ever came in – if he ever made it big in the music world – she would be on the top of his list of people he would treat.

He looked over at her now, quietly singing along with Billie Holliday's 'These Foolish Things'. He smiled to himself. Poor Nora, he thought, had probably never done a foolish thing in her life. If she had, she had kept it very quiet because she didn't smoke and rarely drank, and Mary reckoned she hadn't had a boyfriend since she was a young girl.

He thought she looked more relaxed tonight and, in a strange kind of way, younger than he had ever seen her before. She had always seemed so uptight and correct, her life so perfectly ordered. Old before her time.

Johnny wondered now if being with the children was maybe as good a thing for her as it was for them. It had given her a change of scenery being up in Dublin, and a change of routine, and, he then remembered, she was meeting up with an old friend in Bewley's tomorrow which was something he had never heard of her doing before.

He lifted the bottle of wine up to the light and saw there was only enough to give them another couple of mouthfuls each. He held it out to Nora and she smilingly lifted her glass up to let him pour.

'The wine was actually lovely,' she said, a slight slur in her voice. 'I hope they give you more to bring home another night.'

'I hope so too.' He drained the end of the bottle into his own glass and gave a little sigh before swallowing it all down.

Johnny wished they had given him another couple of bottles of wine; he wished he could have stayed out later and found one of the bars along the quays or in Kilmainham that had a 'lock-in'. Bars that would allow him to drink as much beer as he could afford to buy, or consume enough to take him into some sort of oblivion that would help him to forget all that had happened to him in the last three months. That would help him forget all the responsibility he now carried on his shoulders.

Chapter Twenty-One

As the sun came up, Nora, lying in bed with her hands folded behind her head, felt a wave of anticipation and excitement about the day ahead, something she had not expected to feel at this stage in her life. Even a week ago she would not have believed she would have been full of such optimism.

She had a social engagement with a friend. A *proper* friend. Veronica Fisher actually liked her. She did not just tolerate her as the other staff in the hospital had.

When they had worked in Tullamore – both in different offices – they never had the occasion to mix with each other socially. Their relationship had been limited to quick chats when Nora had a reason to go over to the main office, but they were of a similar age, both unmarried and older than most of the other female staff they worked with; they both dressed in smart, good quality clothes, although Veronica was fond of brooches and colourful jewellery, while Nora veered more towards the sober side, lifting her work outfits only with pearls or a jet necklace of her mother's.

They did not have the same subjects to chat about as the younger ones, because of their different fashion taste, and neither of them had dances to discuss or nights at the pictures with boyfriends. At least, Nora presumed that Veronica did not have that side to her life, because she'd never spoken about it. If she ever had a boyfriend, she'd kept it private. It was more dignified, Nora thought, for older women to keep any late romances discreet, and she knew that was the sort of person that Veronica was.

But Nora's optimism about the day ahead was not solely linked to meeting up with her friend. When she had gone to bed in the early hours of the morning, she had felt slightly giddy with the effects of the wine she had drunk and the enjoyment of the music they had listened to on the radio. Jazz was something she had never really understood before, and the unexpected pleasure she had felt from actually listening to the words, as Johnny had encouraged her to, and concentrating on the tempo and different instruments, had been a revelation. She had no idea that he was so passionate about it, and somehow, over the sandwiches and the wine, it had transferred in a small way to her.

As they sat, the wine relaxing her, Nora had asked him about his personal favourites.

'I love all sorts of music – classical, jazz, traditional Irish music, big band, and all the up-and-coming singers like Frank Sinatra and Perry Como. Just listening to them takes me into a whole different world.'

'I can tell,' she said. 'Your whole face lights up when you're listening, and you can't help yourself singing or humming along with almost everything that comes on the radio.'

'Oh, you have a feel for it yourself,' Johnny had said, winking at her. 'I heard you singing along to the Billie Holiday song and last week you were enjoying the Glenn Miller radio programme too.'

'You're right,' she said. 'I suppose, in my own way, I do enjoy music – I just never thought about it much before.'

Nora had asked him how he had learned to play the violin, and Johnny told her how his family had all loved singing and how he had various relatives who played instruments of every type. 'My brothers over in Liverpool tell me my father can still knock out an old tune on the mouth organ and tin whistle. Hopefully, when things settle down, I might get across to see them all again.'

She, in turn, told him how her mother loved listening to the radio, and that she herself felt it gave a life to an otherwise empty house. Then, impulsively and aided by the wine, she confided a regret she had rarely shared. 'I would have loved to have had a dog, a small one for company in the evenings. Just a little thing to nurse on my knee.' The tone of her voice spoke of her deep disappointment. 'But I thought that it was unfair to leave the poor thing alone when I was out at work all day.'

The jazz programme finished and a new radio programme started with general music, and when 'I'm Looking Over A Four-Leaf Clover' came on, both their faces lit up.

'Oh, I love this one,' Nora said, smiling and nodding, all sad thoughts of the dog she never had banished.

Johnny clicked his fingers together. 'Art Mooney and His Orchestra! He also had that hit last year, "Baby Face".' He curled his lip up at one side in parody of the American singer and sang a few bars of the popular song.

Nora clapped her hands and laughed. 'Oh, lovely!'

They sat listening and chatting for another half an hour until Nora realised with a shock that it was half past one in the morning. 'I must go,' she said, suddenly flustered. 'I have so much to do in the morning before catching the bus into Grafton Street to meet Veronica.'

'Ella will give you a hand,' Johnny said. 'Don't be worrying about things here, we'll all be grand.'

She turned to look at him now. 'Thanks,' she said, 'and thanks for—' And halted, realising she had been about to thank him for his company and for listening to the radio with her. For talking and being nice to her – all the things that no one else had taken the time to do with her in years. But she realised that would sound as though she were a pathetic sort of person who was not used to doing the simple, ordinary things in life. Instead she said, 'Thanks for the sandwiches and the wine. It was a nice little treat.'

After she got into bed, she lay there humming the songs, and wondered if her elevated mood was a result of the wine. While she was sure it had something to do with it, it came to her that the main reason was sitting talking with Johnny.

The night had given her a glimmer of hope that, while they were living in the shadow of such an awful, unexpected tragedy, nice things could happen unexpectedly too.

The morning went even quicker than Nora had expected and she felt she was running to catch up with herself. Johnny went to the shop for the paper and came back with a bag of brown flour, milk, and their tea and sugar rations. Nora mixed a loaf of soda bread and, while it was in the oven, got on with the washing. By the time Sean and Larry and Ella came downstairs, the bread was ready and Ella supervised a pan of boiled eggs while Nora hung the washing out to dry.

Later, all her tasks finished, she washed and changed into her blue suit with the tie-belt jacket and kick-pleated skirt. And, as she did up the buttons on her mauve silk blouse, she decided she was going to ask Veronica Fisher for advice today. Advice on her hair and make-up. Veronica always looked nice, and seeing her earlier in the week had made Nora think that maybe she needed to make more of an effort herself. She knew she wasn't any kind of beauty, but lots of women her age still met men.

Last night, talking to Ella about James Meehan, had got her thinking about meeting a nice man. And it was strange that later she would spend so much time chatting with Johnny. Of course he was a few years younger than her and they were different in many ways, but nevertheless, they had conversed very well. She felt she had passed herself off well, been able to chat and even let her hair down a bit having the few glasses of wine. Being in Dublin, in a place where no one knew her, might just open up new opportunities to meet men that had previously been closed to her. She wasn't foolish. She knew she was plain, and wasn't in her youthful bloom any more, but she wasn't an old woman either.

She wasn't sure where she might meet a suitable man, but she had a much better chance in Dublin than she did in a small country town. And there was no harm in looking her best, just in case. Who knows, she thought, maybe Veronica might be keen on going to a dance some night, or maybe the theatre. Nora wasn't sure if there were many social events going on in Dublin with the Emergency still on, but she would soon find out.

Chapter Twenty-Two

Nora enjoyed the walk up from O'Connell Street to Grafton Street. The day was bright and sunny and gave the impression that summer was just around the corner, but she had put her warm raincoat on over her suit anyway. Better to be safe than sorry. March was one of those months where it could be sunshine one day and snow the next.

She arrived at Bewley's early, and while she was waiting for her friend at the small table in the corner, she discreetly glanced around at the other tables. There were few men, mainly young students from the university and colleges, and groups or pairs of women. There was one man around her age she noticed, who was sitting at a table drinking coffee and reading the *Irish Independent*. There was a striped scarf on the empty chair beside him, which made her think he might be an academic or a professor from the university. She cast glances his way as he finished his coffee and then reached into his pocket for a pipe. Smoking wasn't something she cared for, but she was sure that in time she could get used to sharing a house with someone who did.

Veronica arrived dead on time and after a look at the menu they decided on coffee and a cream cake each.

'It's a treat,' Veronica said, when the waitress arrived with their order. 'I just love a nice bit of cake.' She gave a little laugh. 'It's the one good thing about the rationing; at least it's helped to keep me a bit trimmer than I was before. Not having sugar and as much fatty stuff definitely helps the waistline.' She put her finger in the waistband of her skirt. 'I'm sure I was over almost a stone and a half heavier when I was in Tullamore.'

'Well, you always dressed very well,' Nora told her, taking a sip of her coffee. 'And I never noticed you ever being particularly heavy.' In truth, Nora was being kind because back then she had always noticed that Veronica had a blocky sort of shape. She seemed more in proportion now.

'I've a sweet tooth, that's my problem,' Veronica laughed. She studied Nora for a few moments. 'You never changed a bit. You've always had a lovely slim figure and nice legs. And you don't look any older.'

Nora felt herself flushing at the unexpected compliment. 'Well, that's very nice of you to say so...' She put her cup down in her saucer. 'Actually, talking about looks, I was going to ask your advice on buying some make-up today. Maybe a new shade of lipstick and some mascara? I've never worn it and I thought that while I was here in Dublin I might go mad and try a few new things.'

'We'll have a look in one of the chemist shops when we're finished here,' Veronica said. 'I could do with some new perfume myself.' She suddenly paused. 'I've just remembered, I brought you a nice recipe for a sponge.' She went into her handbag and came out with a slip of paper with the hospital heading on it. 'It has carrot in it, so you don't need to use as much flour. I thought it would be useful as you have so many to feed in the house.'

Nora thanked her, delighted that Veronica had been thinking of her during the week. Copying out a recipe was only a small thing, but it was the thought that counted. The thought of a friend.

'Tell me,' Veronica said. 'How is the little girl? Hannah, isn't it?'

Nora nodded. 'We think she is getting out at the end of next week. Her legs and arms are healing up nicely, although they will be scarred. Thankfully, she is too young to know any better about it at this stage.'

Out of the corner of her eye, she saw the man over at the

table fold his newspaper then stand up and lift his scarf, and wrap it around his neck. He gave a glance around him as though checking to see if he knew anyone, then his eyes moved over to where the two women were sitting. His gaze did not linger on them. A few seconds later he moved smartly towards the door.

'I was wondering,' Nora said, turning back to Veronica, 'if there are any suitable dance halls for women of our age?'

'Dance halls?' Veronica repeated, most surprised.

Nora smiled at her. 'I've just taken a notion I would like to go to a dance. Have you any interest?'

Veronica looked flustered, then she smiled. 'You've caught me there, Nora. I wasn't going to say anything just yet, but to be honest, I'm busy at the weekends. You see, I've met a man. We've been going out for the last year or more at the weekend.' She made a little, embarrassed face. 'We meet up for walks on a Sunday after Mass, go for a cup of tea, dancing, the occasional meal,' she shrugged, 'that sort of thing.'

'And, do you mind me asking, where did you meet him?' Nora found herself suddenly intrigued.

'At the hospital,' she said. 'He's a supervisor in the maintenance department. We got to know each other when he was sorting new shelves in the office. His name is Frank – Frank Morrison.'

'Well, that's lovely news,' Nora said, genuinely delighted for her. 'Good for you! And has he never been married?'

Veronica shrugged. 'No,' she said, 'but he told me he was going out with a girl for a long time.' She lowered her voice. 'Nearly ten years.'

'And were they engaged?'

'No, seemingly they were saving up for a house. Frank wanted to buy it outright, no mortgages or loans. She had a good job in one of the banks, but of course if they had got married quicker, she would have lost her job. They only had another year or two to go, and between them they had enough money to buy a nice-sized house. Then she turned up one night and told him it was all off.'

'And what was the reason for that?' Nora asked.

Veronica shrugged. 'The usual, she had done the dirty on him with one of the fellows that worked beside her in the bank. A younger chap.'

'It seems like Frank got a narrow escape. She sounds a right flighty piece.'

'You've hit the nail on the head – and that wasn't the worst of it,' Veronica whispered. 'It turned out she was already expecting a baby to the other fellow, and they were married within a month of her telling Frank.'

Nora's hand came up to cover her mouth. 'That's unbelievable,' she said. 'All those years stringing Frank along while he's working and saving hard, and then she ups and marries someone else, just like that.' She clicked her fingers together.

'Well,' Veronica said, 'it's her loss and my gain.' She smiled at Nora now. 'You don't mind me not going out with you to the dance?'

'Not at all,' Nora said. 'How could you? It wouldn't be right going to a dance like a single woman, when you're courting.'

'It's no problem us going to the pictures next Saturday afternoon, or even during the week, because I only see him on a Wednesday night. He's very sensible about money and he's still saving to buy a house.' She leaned in closer to Nora. 'But of course, if things were to get really serious with us...'

'You mean engaged?'

Veronica nodded. 'Well, of course I already have a house. Just like yourself, I'm in a secure position. I don't really want to hang around for too long, especially if it's not going in the right direction. When you get to a certain age... you understand, what I mean, Nora. You're in the same boat. We don't have that many years left if we are thinking of having children. If Frank isn't going to make a move soon, then I might have to reconsider things.'

Nora swallowed hard. She had given up any thought of having children a long time ago, and her recent thoughts had been more to do with someone to spend the long, lonely evenings with, someone to chat to, to sit and eat with. She knew, of course, that the physical side might be still a factor, but she hadn't given it any great thought. Finding a suitable man was the first step.

As the two women were saying their goodbyes on Grafton Street, a thought came into Nora's mind.

'Do you ever get to hear of jobs going in the hospital?' she asked.

'For you?'

'No, for men. My cousin's husband needs a decent, secure job that is near enough to home.'

Veronica looked thoughtful. 'I know one of the women who deals with vacancies – Peggy Carr – I'll have a word with her if you like. Although I can't promise anything.'

'I understand,' Nora said, 'and I'd never have asked about anything like this before, but he's finding it hard getting full-time work.'

'What sort of work do you think would suit him?'

'Oh, anything at all,' Nora said. 'He's a very adaptable man, cheery and willing to put his hand to anything.'

Nora got off the bus and walked back towards the house. Her day out had been one of the best she had had in years. She had enjoyed the great chat with Veronica and she was also pleased with her cosmetic purchases. She thought she might use some of the Pan Stick foundation for going to Mass in the morning. The girl in the chemist had put a touch on Nora's reddish cheeks and nose and when she looked in the mirror, she immediately liked the way it evened out the tone of her skin and made it softer and younger looking, but also looked as though she had nothing on her skin at all. Veronica had then suggested she have the girl show her how to put mascara on, and again, when she saw the difference it made, she wondered why she had not had the confidence to try it out before.

She shied away from buying eye shadow. 'No, Veronica,' she'd said, shaking her head, 'It's just that bit too much for me. To be honest, I would feel like a clown going out with a colour on my eyelids.'

She did allow herself to be talked into a slightly bolder colour of lipstick, though.

'As long as it's not too obvious,' Nora said. 'I'll be afraid to wear anything bright.'

The girl found the exact shade – Dusty Rose – which satisfied both Nora and the other two. Her cheeks burned as Veronica complimented her and said that the make-up took years off her.

'We deserve to treat ourselves now and again,' Veronica told her. 'Haven't you worked hard all these years, and you're now working even harder looking after a big family? It's a credit to you.'

As she walked towards the row of terraced houses, one of the doors opened and Mrs Murphy came out. Nora slowed to a halt, her good mood making her sociable. 'Lovely day, Mrs Murphy, isn't it?'

'It is, thank God,' she said. 'Any news about Hannah?'

'We're expecting her home later this week or the week after.'

'That's good news,' she said. 'The poor little cratur, having that happen to her.' She paused. 'You seem to have things ship-shape in there. I see Sean and Ella going off to school in the mornings and they seem happy enough.'

'Sean's learning to play the piano. I think it's to keep him out of harm's way as he's so behind with lessons, but he's delighted, and it's keeping him occupied.'

'Well, there's bound to be music in his blood,' Rose said. 'He didn't lick it from the stones, and as you say, it'll keep him out of trouble.' She paused. 'I'm glad I caught you, because someone called to the house yesterday afternoon, but there was no one in.'

'I was at the hospital with Larry. Do you know who it was?'

Rose nodded her head. 'Do you remember the pair that were helping out at the house after the funeral? The two women?'

Nora's brow furrowed. 'I can't say I do, there were so many people there.'

'Well, if looked to me as if they had their eye on himself.' She nodded her head in the direction of Johnny Cassidy's house.

Nora's eyes widened. 'So quickly after poor Mary? I don't believe it!'

'Especially that one from the Barley Mow. She brought bottles of beer down here, and after she did a bit of ironing, she was sitting in with Johnny in the evenings. It was obvious what was on her mind – I could see it as plain as day with me own eyes – but he was in such a daze, it didn't occur to him. The other one, from the Catholic Mothers Association, wasn't as brazen, but still, you could tell she was trying to make the place her own.'

'And was it one of the women who came to the house yesterday?'

'The one from the church. She brought a present for Hannah and I thought I would wait until I saw you and give it you.' She stepped back into the hallway, to a half-moon table, and lifted a small parcel wrapped in paper decorated with pictures of teddy bears. She handed it to Nora. 'She said she saw you at Mass with Johnny and the children last week, and she was asking to know who you were. You might think Dublin is a big place compared to Tullamore,' Mrs Murphy said, 'but churches are the same everywhere. It would surprise you what some people notice when they should be saying their prayers.'

'Do you mind me asking what you told her?'

Rose folded her arms high up on her bosom. 'I said it wasn't my place to go talking about other people. I just said that Johnny had made arrangements now, and had a very decent, respectable woman living in the house who was taking care of everyone.' She gave a little laugh. 'Oh, she was desperate to know who you were, but I wouldn't please the likes of her to go explaining anything. I'm not saying that Johnny has to make a saint of himself forever, and I know he's the sort that women would go mad for, with his looks and the music and everything. But there has to be a decent length of time, doesn't there? It looks very bad when you see anybody that's been widowed out and about with someone else within months. It shows no respect at all.'

Nora made a tutting sound in agreement.

'Bringing you here was the best day's work Johnny Cassidy ever did.' Rose shook her head. 'Between you and me, men are weak. On his own, and after a while, he would get lonesome. It would only take a night when he had a few too many drinks for one of them to take advantage of him.' She held her hand up. 'The next thing is there would be another little Cassidy on the way, and before he knew it, the bans would be up in the church. Believe me, I've seen it happen time and time again. Women are the devils when they get a notion for a man.'

Nora digested the words, weighing them up carefully. 'Well, let's hope nothing like that happens,' she said in a fearful voice, 'because it would be nothing short of a disgrace to poor Mary's memory.' She looked down at the parcel now, wondering what was in it. It felt soft, like a little dress or maybe pyjamas. No doubt something to curry favour with little Hannah, which would in turn win favour from her grateful father. The thought of these women who were now biding their time to warm Johnny's bed filled her with alarm, women who were scrutinising her as she walked up the aisle to receive Holy Communion. She gave a little cough and looked up at the sky. 'It's getting overcast now. I'd better get back home and see to the supper.'

'How did you get on with the rabbits?'

She had to stop herself from laughing when she remembered the carry-on she and Johnny had over them. 'Grand,' she said, 'it was very good of you.'

'If I get any more I'll drop them down.'

Nora gave her a grateful smile, but as she walked away, she wondered if Mrs Murphy knew what her reaction to the bloody animals had been, and was having a little joke at her expense.

Chapter Twenty-Three

Around eleven o'clock that night, Nora was sitting sewing quietly when Johnny arrived in from the wedding, drenched through.

'It's a shocking night,' he said, shaking the drops of rain from his coat. 'I just missed a bus, so I started walking and then the sky opened.'

Nora looked over to the window. 'I didn't even notice,' she said. 'I was busy here altering this skirt for Ella. I hope it's not as bad in the morning or I'll have to forget going down to Tullamore.' The thought of walking from the station down to the house was not appealing.

Johnny glanced at the skirt in her lap, then a shadow crossed his face. 'Is it one of Mary's?'

'Yes,' Nora said. 'Ella was upstairs earlier going through the wardrobe and she found this and asked me if I could take it up for her.' She realised he was still staring at the skirt, a glazed look in his eyes, and then it dawned on her. 'I never thought to ask you if it was all right... Ella asked me if I could sort it for Mass in the morning. Maybe you don't want her things touched yet?'

'It's all right,' he said. 'It's better Ella has it if she needs it.' As he turned to go back out to the hall, he almost lost his balance and had to catch his hand on the door handle to steady himself. He straightened up and then went out to the hall to hang up his coat. Then he came back to hover at the door. Nora thought he seemed a very different man from the night before.

The skirt had obviously upset him and she wondered what she could say to make things seem more normal. 'I kept some tea in the flask for you,' she said, then, attempting to lighten things further, she added, 'I wasn't sure if there would be wine left over from the wedding.'

He gestured towards the hallway as though she had not spoken. 'I'm just going to the outhouse.'

As she watched him turn awkwardly again, Nora caught her breath as she realised he was drunk. Before, she would have had no great sympathy for an intoxicated man, but there was something about his face tonight that reminded her of her Uncle Bernard when he had to shoot an old sheepdog he was very fond of. Later that night Bernard had come back early from the pub and staggered into their house, tears streaming down his face. Her mother had had to make him strong tea and when she wasn't looking, her father had slipped a miniature bottle of brandy into it. She was around fourteen years old, and for the first time ever, she had seen a naked vulnerability about her uncle and had felt a wave of compassion for him. It was so strong, she had wanted to go over to him and put her arms around him to comfort him. But they were not that kind of family. She now felt the same compassion for Johnny, but there was still that sense of helplessness that there was nothing she could do.

A while later, the rain battering on her bedroom window and the sound of the wind howling made Nora's mind up about not going to Tullamore. Perhaps, she thought, she could go one day during the week with Larry. It would mean missing a visit to Hannah, but if Johnny had not found work, he would be going anyway. Ella had also reminded her that the young lad who played chess was coming round, and it might be best if she was there.

Soon, she fell into a deep sleep. When she woke, her heart was pounding, and the words *two years* echoed in her head. Disorientated, she was unable to tell if something had actually really happened, or whether she'd had a strange dream. She lay for a while longer, her heart beginning to slow down. Her face felt hot, her neck and chest, under her arms – and also, she realised with a pang of alarm, between her legs. She also had a throbbing feeling in the pit of her stomach which she had not had since James Meehan – and recognised it as physical desire. All the feelings that she knew were unholy and wrong for a single woman to have.

She looked towards the bedroom door. It was tightly closed. She listened to see if there was any noise, any footsteps along the hallway. All was silent.

Overwhelmed, she turned and buried her face in the pillow. Had it been real? Had Johnny Cassidy come into her room? She could picture him now, sat on the side of the bed, stroking her face and telling her how grateful he was for all she had done for the family and for him personally. He said he was lucky that such a clever, independent woman would give up her time for them. All things he had said in as many words before, apart from the fact that this time he had also said he found her a very attractive woman, the sort of woman he would at some time in the future like to marry.

'Marry!' she had said in shock.

It was all so vivid. Was it possible it could be real?

'I know I'm a few years younger,' she could remember him saying, 'but what does that matter? We get on so well together, we have the same outlook in life. Look at the bit of craic we had the other night, and we make a great team with the children. They are the important things in life, aren't they?

'I like the way you are fit for me,' he said, 'and don't just agree with everything, the way some women would do it just to please or *plámás* you.'

'But Johnny,' she had told him, 'I'm not that kind of woman. I have never thought of you like that. I'm not like the women who have been chasing you since poor Mary was buried.'

'That's why I have no interest in them,' Johnny had said. 'Those type of women are not like you or my Mary. You two stand head and shoulders above all others. I know Mary would prefer I was with you than anyone else.'

Nora could remember lowering her head at the mention of her dear cousin's name. 'It still feels like a betrayal – and even if I was to consider it,' she whispered, 'it's far too soon.'

'You're right. It is too soon,' he said, 'and I am not thinking of replacing Mary. I'm not suggesting that we do anything wrong or disrespectful to her memory.'

'What are you suggesting then?' Nora had asked.

'I just wanted to state my case before another lad gets in before me. Sure, a fine woman like you – a classy woman of independent means – would have her choice in Dublin.'

'Now, Johnny,' she had said, waving his flattery away with her hand.

'I'm suggesting we have a private arrangement that only you and me know about. I'm suggesting that we put Mary's memory first and foremost, but that we know, after two years, we can then do the right thing for the family, the right thing for our own happiness.' He had taken her hands in his. 'Promise me – two years.'

She had turned towards him and, as he moved closer, she had gently put her hands on either side of his handsome face. 'Two years,' she heard herself whisper back.

And then, as his lips barely fluttered against hers, she felt a thrill run through her, and the words *two years* echoed again and again.

Now she lay under the covers, going over the scenario; looking for proof that what seemed so vivid was indeed a reality, any sign that might indicate Johnny Cassidy had actually been in her room. Gradually, a coldness descended on her as she realised it was all a trick of her mind, she had had some kind of strange, erotic dream, a dream which had deceived and deluded her in the worst possible way. The feeling of shame and embarrassment she felt now at even thinking it could have been real was overwhelming. So overwhelming she would have preferred to awaken from a terrifying nightmare.

Chapter Twenty-Four

Johnny was up later than usual, and he raked the fire and carried the ashes outside, dreading Nora coming downstairs. He had a vague memory of being quiet and withdrawn when he came home from the wedding last night. She had been good enough to save him some tea, and had possibly waited up for him, but she had gone off to bed very quickly after he arrived home and he guessed it was because she felt uncomfortable with him having had a few drinks.

Ella came downstairs wearing her mother's warm dressing gown, checking for hot water to fill her jug for washing. Seeing the dressing gown jogged his memory and he remembered his rather melancholy reaction to Nora altering one of Mary's skirts for Ella.

He shook his head. He couldn't remember whether Nora had cast the skirt aside or whether she had finished altering it. There was no sign of it downstairs, so he would have to wait until she was down to get ready for Mass.

As Ella was passing her aunt's room with the steaming jug, she heard a movement and paused to tap on the door. 'It's me,' she called. 'I just wondered if you did the skirt?'

The door opened and her aunt, also in her dressing gown, held the skirt out. 'I hope it's OK,' she said. 'I decided to just use tacking stitches at the sides in case it's not right.'

Ella held it out. 'It looks perfect to me, Aunt Nora,' she said, smiling. 'Thanks.'

Nora noticed the jug. 'Could I have a drop of that water,

please, Ella? It would save me going downstairs.' It would also save her meeting Johnny while the memory of the dream was still so clear.

Ella handed it to her. 'Pour it into your bowl and I'll go down and fill it again. There was still a good bit in the kettle.'

'That's kind of you, I won't be a minute.' She came back with the empty jug. 'Is your father downstairs yet?'

'Yes,' Ella said. 'I think he's going to the paper shop soon.'

By the time Nora was washed and dressed, and had taken her time carefully applying her Pan Stick and a bare touch of mascara, she felt braver than before. She could not put off going downstairs any longer, and when Johnny arrived back home, Nora already had Larry washed and dressed and sitting in the scullery with a piece of toast and some milk.

Johnny put a pint of milk and the newspaper on the table, and then he looked over at Nora. 'Not the best of mornings,' he said, 'but the rain is not as heavy as last night.'

She caught his wariness and glanced out of the window. She guessed he felt bad about his manner from the night before. A flush came over her as she thought of the dream again; thank God he knew nothing about it. She cleared her throat. 'I suppose we have to be thankful for small mercies.'

Ella came rushing downstairs when she heard her father. 'What do you think of the skirt?' she said, standing at the doorway. She turned around so they could get a better look.

'It's lovely,' Johnny said. 'Well wear it.' He paused. 'If you want to have a look in the wardrobe and see if there's anything else, you might as well. I'm sure your mother would be delighted to see you putting them to good use.'

Nora felt a little mollified by this, but on the way to church she deliberately walked ahead with Ella and Larry and left Sean behind with his father. She knelt and stood and prayed aloud when everyone else did the same, but her mind was oblivious to the actual ritual of the Mass. In her head she said her own private prayers, asking forgiveness for whatever weakness and silliness had brought about the visions of the night before, and imploring that she never had to suffer such delusions again.

As they were coming out, Nora stopped on the steps to sort her umbrella. Sheltering under the arch of the church door, she noticed a woman coming over to talk to Johnny. She was a small, tidy woman with short dark hair, wearing a brown suit with fur at the collar and cuffs, carrying a crocodile handbag. Nora could tell that Johnny was trying to get away. Then the woman turned around so she could get a better look at her. So, Nora thought, was this one of the women who thought she could fill dear Mary's shoes? Filled with curiosity and an unusual sense of confidence, Nora found herself stepping over to join them.

'Nora!' Johnny said, sweeping an arm around her to bring her into the small circle. 'I was just telling Bridget here what a great help you have been to us. Only a week in the house and she has us all knocked into shape.'

The woman observed Nora for a few moments then she held her hand out. 'It's great news that Johnny has some help around the house. And he was telling me that you are related?'

'Yes,' Nora said, shaking her hand. 'I'm a cousin of Mary's from Tullamore.' She looked over at Ella and the younger ones then she turned to Johnny. 'Would you check that Larry is OK? I thought he looked a bit fretful.'

'I'll go and get him now. He'll be fed up at this stage and looking to go home.'

As he went off, Nora turned back. 'Of course, Johnny and I are not blood relations, but we get on just grand. We always did.' She gave a little smile. 'And how did you come to know the family?'

Bridget flushed. 'Oh, I know them going to Mass, and Mary and I were in the Catholic Mothers Association.'

'Ah, yes.' Nora gave a smile. 'You must be the lady Mrs Murphy told me about. She said how helpful you and some of the other women were to the family after the funeral.' She touched the woman's hand. 'It was very good of you, and

Johnny and I appreciate it, but thankfully there's no need for help now. I was able to get leave of absence from my job to move in full-time.'

'I suppose a few months off is as much as they will allow?'

'I can take as long as I need.' Nora leaned towards her and said in a low voice, 'You see, the bosses are very understanding.' She shrugged. 'But even if things were to change, I'm lucky enough to be in the position where I could give up work if needed.' She shook her head. 'You needn't worry, I won't let Johnny and the children down. I'll be here as long as they need me.'

'Oh, well...' the woman said. 'That's a great help for them.'

'If you see that other lady who was very kind – the barmaid – you might let her know that we're just grand now and won't need any more help. She's a friend of yours, isn't she?'

'No,' the woman said. 'Sure, I only met her at the house.' Her eyes narrowed and she looked uncomfortable. 'She's not coming around now, is she?'

'No, no.' Nora lowered her voice. 'Between you and me, from what I heard, I think that one took a little notion for Johnny. Can you believe it? And poor Mary not cold in her grave.'

Bridget gave a little gasp. 'I'm not surprised; she was a brassy sort of a woman. Disgraceful to be playing up to a man so soon after his poor wife has just gone.' Bridget's face was solemn again. 'It's different after a decent interval.'

Nora saw Johnny coming back towards them with Larry and Sean.

'I should have thanked you for the present that you gave Mrs Murphy for Hannah, and I'll see she gets it when we're in visiting this afternoon. That was very kind of you.'

'That was a terrible accident. I must call in to see her when she gets home.'

Nora raised her eyebrows and smiled. 'Don't put yourself to any trouble, Bridget,' she said. 'As soon as she's well enough, we'll bring her to Mass. Lovely to meet you,' Nora said as she turned to leave. 'And no doubt I'll see you again.'

As they walked out of the church gates, Johnny said, 'You look as though you had a great chat to Bridget. She's a nice enough woman, isn't she?'

'She is,' Nora agreed. 'And I thanked her for the little present she left for Hannah.' She paused. 'Have you any word about work this week?'

Johnny lifted his eyes to the grey sky. 'I'll be down at the docks in the morning and see if there's anything going.'

'You did well over the weekend with the music,' she told him, 'that was more than most men earn in a week.'

His face brightened. 'Playing in a band is good money. If I could be sure of getting the work every weekend, it would suit me down to the ground. It would give me more time at home and I would be able to give you more of a hand with the children.'

She could see that her words of encouragement had lifted him up, and she could also see his point about the money being very good. But she wasn't so sure about him being around the house all week. It couldn't be a good thing for a man, and especially for one who was fond of a drink, as it could lead to him spending more time in the bars. And that might just lead to him spending more time with the women who worked behind the bars.

Then, as they walked along with Larry between them, chatting away, she suddenly realised that she felt fine again with Johnny. The silly dream of the night before had faded away and so had any lingering awkwardness she felt about it. She supposed people had dreams like that all the time – the mind could be very strange – but who was going to go talking about anything so personal? And she certainly wasn't going to go confessing it to the priest. She wasn't to blame for a dream. It would be different if she had been like Bridget and that barmaid one, where she had actually had notions about Johnny Cassidy.

She cast a sidelong glance at him now and, as he turned and caught her eye he smiled at her. The way he had smiled at her in the dream last night. A heat came to her face and her heart started to beat quickly. She could not deny it: he was a handsome, attractive man. And although he and Mary had been as happy as a couple could be, it would only be a matter of time – hopefully a *decent* length of time – until he was snapped up by another woman. A heavy weight suddenly descended on Nora as she thought it through.

All the work she would have done with the children and the house would be forgotten. *She* would be forgotten. A new woman coming into the house would make sure of that. That's the way things were. The saying came into her mind – *A new broom sweeps clean.* Then she thought about the often forgotten ending – *but an old broom knows the corners.*

She already knew the corners of the Cassidy family. Of course it had been poor Mary she knew best, but in the short time she had been part of the family, she felt she was getting to know Johnny and the children just as well.

No doubt the barmaid would be a more forward, brassy type, who would use any trick in the book to ensnare Johnny. Nora imagined her as a cheap sort, her hair bleached so often that it would have the same texture as candyfloss, skirts tight around the backside and blouses straining at the chest. But some men were easily fooled by women like that, especially when drink was involved, and it would only take one night, when Johnny was in a vulnerable state, for someone like the barmaid to make her move. She caught her breath at the thought. Those poor children being brought up by someone like that! All the work that Mary had done completely discarded – all the decent Catholic values made a mockery of.

Within no time, Sean would be completely out of hand, probably drinking and getting into trouble with the Guards again. Poor, clever Ella wouldn't stand a chance. She would feel in the way, and let down by her father marrying a woman who was beneath their mother, and would probably grasp at the first young man who gave her a kind look to get away from home. It had happened to many a decent young girl. And what would happen to the two little ones? Nora could not bear to even think of that.

As they crossed over the road towards Islandbridge, a thought struck her. She wondered if maybe – given the respectful length of time – that she would be the right and proper person after all to take over where poor Mary tragically had left off. Maybe she shouldn't dismiss her dream, after all.

She wondered, now, if she herself could be that new broom.

Chapter Twenty-Five

The Sunday dinner plates had been washed and tidied away, and the kettle was boiling when a knock came on the front door. Ella, doing a jigsaw with Larry and Aunt Nora, felt her heart lurch. She forced herself to pick up a piece and then study the picture to see where it might fit in. Sean went to answer it and he came back into the living room with Danny Byrne, a brown paper bag in one hand and a book in the other, following behind.

'Ah,' Johnny said, from his place by the side of the fireplace, 'the Liverpool lad who is the chess champion.'

Danny grinned. 'I don't think the word "champion" was ever mentioned when we met after church this morning, but I give it me best shot.'

Ella felt a little thrill at the sound of his Liverpool accent, and lifted her head to look at him. He gave her a quick wink, unnoticeable to anyone else, and she looked away, her cheeks burning.

Johnny gestured towards Nora. 'This is Sean's Aunt Nora.'

'Nice to meet you,' Nora said, nodding at him; he must have met the others when she was talking to that Bridget. He looked a smart young fellow, she thought. You could tell by the bright, intelligent eyes.

'And nice to meet you too,' he replied. He held out the bag. 'Me granny gave me a cake to bring down. She said to tell you it has coffee in it, but it's not too strong.'

'Coffee?' Nora said, sounding impressed. She looked inside

the bag. 'I'd say that will be really lovely.' She stood up. 'You sit down here while I go and make the tea and we'll all have a slice of that to go with it.'

Danny turned to Sean and handed him a book titled *Chess Made Easy*. 'That's the library book I was telling you about. If you have a look at the beginning, it explains all the pieces and the moves and things.'

'Thanks,' Sean said. 'I'll have a look through it now.'

Nora looked at Danny. 'Do you go to the local library here?'

'Yes, I just joined the one in Inchicore last week.'

'I think it's the best thing you can do. I've been meaning to join myself, but I'm a member in the Tullamore library, and I'm not sure if you are allowed to borrow from two libraries at once.'

'I'm sure they will let somebody like you,' Danny said, 'I mean, it's not as if you're the sort that's going to do a runner on them with loads of books.'

Johnny started laughing. 'I'd say Nora is the last person to run away with anything.'

'I must go down to the library this week,' Nora said, smiling at Danny. 'As soon as we get a nice day, Larry and I will go.'

'The weather is to pick up this week. It's dried up in the last hour,' Danny said. He started to laugh. 'Me granny wanted me to bring her umbrella with me in case I got wet walking down here. Bad enough with the Scouse accent without anyone seeing me with a flowery brolly!'

Everyone laughed and Ella thought how, in only a few minutes, Danny Byrne had really brightened up their house.

Danny lifted the lid of the jigsaw box and studied the picture they were trying to make, then he looked down at the part they had completed so far. 'C'mon!' Danny said, 'or we'll never get this finished and get the chess started.'

They chatted and laughed as they put the pieces together, helping Larry to add the more obvious bits that he could do. Then later, as they were drinking the tea and eating the cake, Johnny sat beside Danny and asked him about Liverpool.

'And do you know Bootle well?' Johnny asked him. 'I have brothers and my father living there. He moved over to live with one of my brothers when my mother died.'

'I wouldn't know Bootle well at all,' Danny said, sounding apologetic. 'I've only been out there a few times, like.'

After the tea and cake, the finished puzzle was put away and then Nora had Sean, Ella and Danny all sitting around the table with the chess set in the middle. She and Danny played a simple game, explaining each move they made and why they did it. Any time they didn't understand anything, Danny showed them the diagrams in the book and quickly explained it.

Several games later, Danny looked at the clock. 'God, it's nearly nine,' he said, 'I'd better go home and walk the dog or me granny will be going mad.'

'How long are you staying in Dublin?' Johnny asked.

The boy shrugged. 'I'm not sure. I'm helping out with me grandparents just now, but when Grandad's a bit better, I'm going to start looking for a job.'

Sean looked over to him. 'You're lucky, I wish I could start work. I hate school.'

Johnny ignored him. 'So you're going to stay for a while, Danny?'

'Yeah, I'm in no rush to go back to Liverpool.'

Nora was curious. 'And have you family still there?'

'Me mam and me younger sisters. Me mam got married again a few years ago. Me dad was killed during the war.' He paused as though he was going to say something else, but then changed his mind. 'I like it over here, and Granny and Grandad need me to help with things.' He turned now and glanced around the room, taking everyone in. 'Thanks for the tea and the game of chess. I really enjoyed it.'

Nora could not but be impressed by both his manners and his quick brain, and she felt he was the sort of young fellow who would be a good influence on Sean. 'You can come down again to play at the weekend,' Nora said.

'That would be great,' Danny said. 'It can get a bit quiet, especially on a Sunday.'

'The evenings are getting longer,' Johnny said, 'so you can wander down any time.'

Nora smiled to herself. They were both singing from the same hymn sheet where Danny Byrne was concerned.

Chapter Twenty-Six

On Monday Nora set off for the hospital with Larry. Johnny had gone out of the house at eight o'clock to see about some casual work in a furniture warehouse. Hannah was down at physiotherapy when they arrived, so Nora sat Larry down with a comic she had bought on the way.

After about ten minutes, the physiotherapist brought Hannah back to the ward and Nora was delighted when the child came walking straight over to her with a big smile on her face. She bent and kissed her.

'Did you bring me anything, Auntie Nora?' Hannah asked.

'Of course I did. I have a bag of nice sweets for you, and if you're very good you can have some.'

'Isn't she the lucky girl?' the physiotherapist said, smiling.

The young woman helped Hannah back into bed, and Nora watched closely. She observed how Hannah approached the bed backwards going up on her toes, and then how the physiotherapist gently put her hands on her waist and lifted her into a sitting position on the bed. Hannah then used her good arm to turn carefully.

'She's made great strides since last week,' the physiotherapist said. 'She's able to walk almost easily now and is doing everything we would hope for at this stage. If you call down to the ward office, they should be able to let you know about her being discharged.'

'Is it this week, do you think?' Nora asked.

'I'd say so, but nearer the end of the week. We'll be giving you the special creams and some exercises that she has to do every day.'

Nora nodded. A week ago she'd been daunted at the thought of having the responsibility, but she felt more confident now and was looking forward to having the whole family together again – a family she was now beginning to feel part of. Halfway through the visit, she was surprised to see Johnny coming into the ward. He explained that he had only been needed for a half day as some of the lorries had been held up at the docks in England.

He shrugged. 'I've to go down again in the morning and see if they have arrived yet.'

As he spoke, Nora caught a whiff of whiskey on his breath. 'What time did you say you finished?'

He lowered his head and lifted up Larry's comic. 'Around half twelve, I think it was.' He did not look in her direction. 'I met a lad when I was walking home, a fellow who hadn't seen me since Mary passed away. It's the custom to buy you a drink...'

Nora closed her eyes. She should have known there would be a reasonable explanation.

When visiting time was over and they walked down to the ward office, Nora went into her handbag and came out with two mints which she handed to Johnny. She then gave another to Larry and put one in her own mouth. Johnny gave an embarrassed smile and mumbled something in thanks.

A short while later they came out of the office. Johnny turned towards Nora and said in a low voice. 'Thanks be to God and His Blessed Mother, Thursday she will be out.'

'Thanks be to God indeed,' Nora repeated.

'I'm glad you were with me,' he said. 'I hadn't realised that the Guards had given them all the information about the accident. If you hadn't been there with me now, they might not have agreed to let her home.' Johnny stopped and took Nora's hand in his. 'I'll do everything in my power to make sure this works. We owe you so much.'

As her hand tightened around his, she felt a flame light within her and race right through her body. She lifted her eyes to meet his, and as she did so, she heard a voice close by calling her name. She turned her head and saw Veronica standing in the corridor, staring at them in shock.

'Nora...' she said, her voice faltering, 'I wasn't sure if it was you or not.'

'Johnny,' Nora said, moving her hand out of his. 'This is Veronica – the friend I was telling you about. The one I worked with in Tullamore.'

Johnny moved forward to shake Veronica's hand, while she was still staring at Nora, as though seeing her for the first time.

'Sorry,' she said, turning to him to shake his hand. 'I'm pleased to meet you, Johnny.' She shrugged and gave a little laugh. 'I suppose I'm still not used to bumping into Nora in Dublin yet. It's like seeing a different woman now.'

Nora smiled. 'I suppose we're all getting that bit older.'

'It's the other way around,' Veronica told her. 'It's younger you're getting. That mascara and lipstick are lovely on you.'

Nora flushed with the compliment, feeling slightly worried that the make-up was a little more obvious than she had intended.

'She does look very well,' Johnny agreed. 'It must be the Dublin air.' Larry tugged at his hand, and he bent down to see what was wrong. 'Oh,' he said, 'I think we need a little visit to the gents.' He turned to Nora. 'I'll meet you outside.'

'Well,' Veronica said as she watched the father and son going off hand in hand, 'I've seen him around the hospital lately, and I can't believe that's the man who's house you're living in.'

'Why?' Nora said.

'He's like a film star,' Veronica said.

'Ah, you're joking now,' Nora said. 'I know he's not bad-looking, but I wouldn't go that far.'

'I was going down to the canteen with some of the women from the office and they all commented on how good-looking he was.' She shook her head. 'You seem to be getting on very well with him...'

'Well, I've known Johnny for years, and I have got to know him much better in the last few weeks. I suppose it's only natural living in the same house.' Nora did not want to say anything that would give the wrong impression. 'I'm so busy with the children and running the house, I hardly have time to think about it.'

'He looks very fond of you, when I saw you walking together along the corridor ...'

Nora inclined her head now. 'We had just got good news that little Hannah is getting out of hospital on Thursday.'

'Oh, that's great news,' Veronica said. She suddenly looked at her watch and said, 'Sorry, Nora, I need to run. I'll see you at the pictures on Saturday afternoon.'

As she rushed off down the corridor, Nora realised that she hadn't asked her if she had had a chance to enquire about any job vacancies, then she thought that maybe it was just as well. It was still early days, and she didn't want to appear too pushy about it. She walked out towards the entrance now, all the things Veronica had said running through her mind.

Chapter Twenty-Seven

On Tuesday, after school, Ella was just about to cross the road when she saw Danny Byrne walking towards her with his grand-parents' dog – an uncertain breed of terrier. She felt her heart quicken, but took a deep breath so as to appear unaffected by his appearance.

'Hi Ella!' he said, raising his hand in greeting.

'Hi,' she said, suddenly tongue-tied as he came towards her. It felt funny, after sitting beside him at a table for hours the other evening, to now feel so shy and awkward again.

'I thought I might see you coming out of school. I'm out walking Prince for me granda, and I hoped I might walk a bit of the way back home with you.'

He obviously didn't feel in any way shy with her. 'How is your granda?' she asked, not able to think of anything else to say.

He shrugged. 'He's getting a bit better, but Granny keeps tell-ing him off for doing things he shouldn't be doing, so I try to keep out of it when she starts. The dog gives me a good excuse.'

Ella imagined that she would need lots of excuses to get out if she had a granny like his. They started to cross the road now, Prince straining at the lead. When they got to the other side Danny looked at her with a lopsided grin.

'Well,' he said, 'how do you think the chess went the other night?'

She nodded. 'It was good, it was something different – a bit of craic.'

'I bet Sean was glad when I left. He looked dead bored at times.'

'Sean gets bored with everything if it's not to do with sport – and now music since he's learning to play the piano.'

Danny shrugged. 'Everybody is different. Your auntie is a nice woman, isn't she?'

'Yes, she is,' Ella said. 'She can be a bit old-fashioned and strict at times, but I suppose it's because she's been used to living on her own for so long.'

'Nancy said she came to help your family after you lost your mother. That was good of her.'

Ella felt a little jolt at the unexpected mention of her mother. She bit her lip and nodded her head.

He touched her arm. 'I'm sorry. I should know better than to put me foot in it. I know what it's like, when you're suddenly reminded. I still feel like that when someone mentions me father unexpectedly. Nobody understands until it happens to them.'

A lump came into Ella's throat and for some reason she suddenly felt like crying. At home and with her friends, she somehow managed to hide her huge sorrow, but Danny Byrne understood and she didn't have to pretend. She swallowed hard. 'How long is it since it happened?'

'About eight years,' he said. 'I can still remember the day me mam got the telegram. She hardly had time to get used to it when our row of houses was hit with a bomb and we had to move out to me other gran's in Anfield.'

'That must have been terrible,' she said. 'It's really hard to imagine what it must have been like. There was some bombing in Dublin, but it wasn't near us.'

'I was only little, but even I could see that the war changed everything,' he said. 'It's like you had a life before the war and a different one after it. I was in Wales for a while when all the kids were evacuated, that was a big change.'

'What was it like?'

'I was just outside a seaside place called Rhyl, with a nice family, two elderly teachers, Mr and Mrs Hughes. Their family were all grown up and married, and they had a house with a spare room, down near the shore. They were very good to me, and I still keep in touch with them with the odd letter. I sent them a postcard the other day to let them know I had moved over to Dublin.'

'Do you think you'll ever see them again?'

'Yeah, when I'm working and I've enough money saved up, like.' They walked along in silence for a while and then he said. 'The biggest change for me – apart from me dad getting killed – was when me mam got married again.'

Ella looked at him and he caught her eye. 'Me and me step-dad, Eric, don't get on. In fact, I hate his guts. He treats me totally different to my two little sisters because they are his and I'm not. I think I remind him of me dad. They knew each other when they were growing up, from what I've heard when they're arguing. Me mam and Eric went out for a while and then she met my dad and broke it off with him. Every time they have a row Eric brings it up saying that she only took him as second-best. He goes on about it all the time, especially when he's drunk, and I can't stand it.' He looked at Ella now. 'The last time he was shouting at her I went in and told him to stop it, and we ended up in a fight. He was so horrible to Mam I felt like killing him. That's partly why I've come over here, to get away from everything.'

Something told Ella that even Nancy didn't know all these details, and hearing about Danny's family troubles made Ella feel better about overhearing his granny going on about her father. Danny had met him and got on great with him, so he obviously hadn't paid any heed to her.

A woman with a small poodle came towards them now, and Prince started growling and barking and Danny had to use both hands to pull him out onto the road and away from the other dog.

'He's a right little spitfire,' Ella said, when they got back onto the pavement.

'That's why my granny wants me to walk him, she's afraid that one of these days he'll pull Granda off his feet.'

When the terraced houses the Cassidys lived in came into view, Danny slowed down. 'I better head back,' he said, 'but I'll maybe come down tomorrow evening or Thursday for a game of chess.' He halted. 'If that's OK? If you don't mind me coming.'

She smiled at him. 'It's OK by me.'

He looked straight into her eyes now and she didn't look away, then they both started to laugh.

'See you then,' he said, pulling Prince around to head back in the opposite direction.

Ella walked towards the house, smiling all the way.

Chapter Twenty-Eight

The following day Nora and Larry walked down to the library. The librarian listened to what Nora told her about being up in Dublin for the foreseeable future and said it was fine to join the Inchicore branch there and then.

She was allowed three books, so she picked two romance books and a picture book for Larry since he was too young to join himself.

As she walked back to the house, she thought she would definitely go down to Tullamore this coming weekend. She would go on Saturday, she decided, when Hannah had settled in at home, and when Johnny and the children were all there to take care of her. She would go on the morning train to give her plenty of time. Apart from picking up her tea and sugar rations, she would get any meat and vegetables she could get from the local shops or Tim Dunne, the bachelor farmer she let the land to. She decided she would bring the case with her as she also wanted to bring back her own lace bedspread and pillowcases and other little things she missed.

Later, at the hospital, Hannah was bright and cheery and talking about coming home. With the nurse's help she slid out of bed and then Nora took her carefully by the hand, and the three of them took a little walk down to the playroom.

Nora was showing them how to look into a kaleidoscope when her friend Veronica gave a little tap on the door then opened it. 'Can I come in for a minute?'

'Of course you can,' Nora said, pleased to see her.

'I have some news for you,' she said. 'I was talking to Peggy Carr this morning, and she told me they have a theatre porter's job going. She's asked if Johnny could come in for an interview tomorrow morning at eleven o'clock. She spoke to the man in charge and she's put a good word in for him.'

Nora caught her breath. 'Oh, that's very good of her.'

'Peggy is a very decent sort.' Veronica nodded towards the children and said in a low voice, 'I've explained his sad circumstances and told them I can vouch for him, knowing you so well.'

'Oh, Veronica, you've no idea how grateful I am to you.'

'Well, we're not home and dry until he's had the interview tomorrow.' She took a sheet of paper out of her pocket. 'Peggy has given me a list of some of the questions he'll be asked, so he'll have time to prepare for it.' She handed it to Nora. 'There's a few notes after each question, to give him an idea of what they want to know. There's nothing really technical about the job or anything, it's really just about handling people and knowing the right thing to do in an emergency or who to call for.'

Nora bit her lip.

Veronica noticed the worried look on Nora's face. 'It's not the sort of thing Peggy or me would normally do, but plenty of others help their friends to get a foot in the door with jobs – and often they're not the sort that's needed at all. We have one porter who is the most miserable man God ever put breath into, and he's working there because his sister, who's a nurse, got him in. He's not a bit suited to the job.'

Nora nodded now. 'I'm very, very grateful.'

'Johnny seems a lovely, friendly man, and that's the sort you want working with people when they're nervous going down to theatre for an operation. There's no harm in helping him if he's the right person.'

'I'll give him the notes,' Nora said, smiling warmly at her friend, 'and thanks again.'

Veronica touched her on the shoulder. 'I hope it all works out – you deserve a bit of luck.'

Chapter Twenty-Nine

Johnny arrived back from the hospital the following morning, beaming from ear to ear. 'I got the job,' he said. 'I start next Monday morning, and it couldn't be handier with fixed day-shifts and only a ten-minute walk down the road.'

Nora closed her eyes and joined her hands together as though in prayer. 'Thanks be to God,' she said, turning away so he wouldn't see the tears in her eyes.

This, she thought, was as decent a job as he would ever get.

She also noticed Ella's similar reaction when she came in from school and heard the news. Sean just nodded his head as though his mind was elsewhere, which it often was. But the look of relief was plain on Ella's face.

The second piece of good news came when Johnny and Nora went to the hospital to bring Hannah home. She was to travel alone with Nora in the ambulance, but when Johnny told the ambulance man he was starting work at the hospital, he told him and Larry to hop in and they could all get a lift back to the house.

Nora had managed to save enough flour to make the cake recipe that Veronica had given her, and she decorated it with icing sugar and buttercream and a small packet of coloured sweets to celebrate Hannah's arrival back home. She'd put it in a cupboard to bring out as a surprise for the little girl after they had all eaten their dinner.

Just around six o'clock, Danny Byrne turned up at the door, so Nora sent him and Ella along to Mrs Murphy's to invite her up for a cup of tea and a bit of the cake. She thought it was a good thing to keep the neighbour on side. Though Rose was a bit too rough and outspoken for Nora's liking, she had, in all fairness, been very good to the family.

'Begod, this is getting more like a party,' Johnny said, clapping his hands together, when Rose arrived ten minutes later, armed with a large bag of sweets for the children and a bottle of sherry for the adults.

'Don't ask where I got them,' she said, touching the side of her nose.

Johnny's eyes twinkled as he took the gifts from her. 'You've no need to worry, Rose, I have no intentions of asking.'

The evening took on a really celebratory feel as Johnny filled three tumblers halfway up with the sherry. The cake was cut into the right number of slices for everyone, and the sweets were shared out equally amongst the children. Ella went upstairs and got colouring books and crayons for Larry and Hannah and she and Sean and Danny sat at the table beside them and helped them colour the pages.

Johnny fiddled around until he found a station on the radio with lively music, and then he and Nora and Rose Murphy sat sipping on the sherry and chatting. Nora asked Rose about where she grew up and tried not to show her surprise when she learned that the neighbour had an uncle who was a priest in England and an aunt who had been a nun in a convent in Galway.

'My mother's side were of better stock than my father's side,' Rose explained, as though reading Nora's mind, 'although my father's side were warmer-hearted and good and decent people. The Flannerys were all very religious, but they were cold fish. It's all very well going to church and everything, but at the end of the day, it's how you treat other people, friends and neighbours, that count.' She smiled brightly at Johnny and then Nora. 'Wouldn't you say so?'

'Indeed I would,' Johnny laughed and held up his glass, 'especially when they come bringing sherry.'

Rose held up her glass now and then Nora leaned forward and they all touched glasses.

'To Hannah's continued good health,' Nora said.

Then, Johnny, his face serious now, said in a low voice, 'And to absent friends who will always be missed...'

As she swallowed down a mouthful of the sweet alcohol, Nora felt a stab of guilt at the reminder of poor Mary. It felt sharper as it came in the midst of her enjoying Hannah's small homecoming celebration. But wouldn't it be a desperate situation for the children if they all sat in misery and sadness? Surely Mary would not have wanted that?

The days were flying by so fast, and so many things happening, that she often didn't have time to think of her cousin for hours. But, when she did, she always thought of her with the greatest sadness. And no matter how busy life became – how big the gaps became – she always would.

Chapter Thirty

The good news of the previous days was dampened down on Friday when Sean appeared home from school with blood all down his shirt. Johnny got it out of him that he had been in a fight with some lads who had left school the previous summer, lads who had nothing better to do but hang around the streets, who had been goading him into a fight for days, taunting and mocking him for playing the piano and being the 'teacher's pet'.

'I'm not going back,' he told Johnny. 'I've had enough.'

'You have to. You only have to stick it out until the summer.'

'I don't care,' Sean said. 'I hate going there. I hate the lessons and the teachers. I hate everything. I'm too old for it.'

Johnny was still wondering what to do with him when Mr Rafferty and Mrs Keating appeared at the house an hour later and asked to speak to him in private.

Mr Rafferty started off by reiterating the story Sean had told, and Johnny was taken by surprise at the headmaster's response.

'He wasn't to blame,' Mr Rafferty said. 'Those boys have been coming into the yard after school and banging on the windows and taunting poor Sean. To be honest with you, I'm surprised he didn't snap before now. Many a lesser boy would have done.'

'It's an awful pity,' the piano teacher said, 'because he's the most gifted music student I've come across – given the length of time he's been learning. I have taught hundreds of pupils and not one could touch him.' She shrugged. 'But he's refusing to play the school piano again. He can't take the comments and the ridicule from the ignoramuses that are only jealous of him.'

Johnny looked from one to the other. 'What's to be done about him? He still has another two or three months until school finishes for the summer.'

'I think we might have an answer to it,' the headmaster said. 'We called in to see Father Brosnan before coming down here and we all had a serious discussion about Sean. He's done what we asked, he came back to school as willingly as he could, even though we all know he's not cut out for formal education.'

'I won't argue with that,' Johnny said. 'You can't knock learning into him if he isn't interested.'

'Well, he's not going to learn much more in the next few months, and there's no point in putting him through any more misery,' Mrs Keating said.

'Exactly,' Mr Rafferty agreed. He held his hands out, palms up. 'The upshot of it is that we feel he should leave school now.'

Johnny's eyebrows shot up. 'What about the Guards? The one that came down here with you before was adamant he should be back at school.'

Mr Rafferty jutted his chin out. 'He was only following me and the priest, trying to frighten Sean after the trouble with the coal yard. Sean is of an age where he can leave school now, especially if he is found some sort of work.'

'And where is he going to find that?' Johnny said. 'Who's going to give Sean a job?'

'My brother, Martin,' Mrs Keating said, smiling at him. 'He has a music shop down off Henry Street. He sells all kinds of instruments and books and sheet music and that sort of thing. He also has an instrument repair service.'

A smile broke out on Johnny's face. 'Sure, I know the very shop. They did a nice job repairing my fiddle last year.'

'Well, I am sure that Martin could do with a fit young lad to help him around the shop and to collect and deliver instruments to people from the big houses. He would be delighted to have somebody like Sean, who has a real interest in music himself.'

'Do you think so?' Johnny said. It was like him landing the porter's job in the hospital – it all seemed too good to be true.

After the run of bad luck and tragedies the family had endured recently, it was hard to believe that good things might happen to them.

'Yes,' she said, 'I'm sure Martin will take him on. The only thing is, I don't think the pay will amount to much – a few shillings a week is about as much as he can expect.'

'Anything will do,' Johnny said. 'As long as it's something that keeps Sean's interest and keeps him out of trouble. Sure, there are plenty of young fellas who have to learn trades and get paid nothing for it.'

'Well, there's more to it than just the job. As you know, I've been teaching Sean the piano for the last few weeks and he's coming on in strides, and I've also got him singing scales. He has a very fine voice with a good vocal range. I think, with the right training, he has the making of a good career playing and singing.'

Johnny was shaking his head in disbelief. The only trait that he saw in his son at the moment was awkwardness. The thought that he had a real talent for music was a revelation to him.

'If Sean continues to help me out with the garden and any household chores, I will be happy to give him the piano lessons and the voice training free. It's the only way to make a professional living out of it. He will stand out from the rest of the performers if he has the proper training, especially if he can sing and accompany himself on the piano.'

Visions of Sean on the stage in a bow tie and suit now came into Johnny's head. Visions of the sort of career Johnny would have loved for himself.

'The other thing is that Sean could practice on the pianos in the shop when it's quiet. Martin is a good pianist himself and will keep him right.'

'It's very good of you.' Then Johnny's eyes narrowed in thought. 'But I don't really understand why you and Mr Rafferty here would do all this for him.'

'I wouldn't like to see his unique talent wasted,' she said, 'but it's also because Mr Rafferty told me how the family had been through a difficult time recently, and I couldn't get it out of my mind. Something told me that it was the right thing to do.'

This was the answer to all his prayers. Somewhere up in Heaven, Johnny now firmly believed, Mary had managed to work this all out for the family. She had sent Nora to them, and now she was sorting out work for him and Sean.

'Well, I'm grateful to you both for helping us all out. I don't mind admitting that things have not been easy recently.'

'I was telling Mrs Keating that you're a talented musician yourself,' Mr Rafferty said. 'I've heard you at several weddings and at a dinner dance in the Gresham. You can fairly knock out a tune with the fiddle.'

'That's very kind of you,' Johnny said, feeling a glow of pride at receiving a compliment from someone like the headmaster of the school. 'Of course, I never had any real professional training myself, but I grew up in a family that loves music – aunties and uncles and all that – and we all learned from each other.'

'Well, that's good training in its own way,' the music teacher said. She stood up. 'I'll see Martin this evening, and I'll let you know when Sean can start in the shop.' She held her hand out.

'That would be grand,' Johnny said, shaking her hand and seeing them out to the door. As he closed it behind them he heaved a big sigh of relief.

Was it possible that things were going to settle down for the Cassidy family?

Chapter Thirty-One

When she saw the red sky on Friday night, Nora told Johnny she was going down to Tullamore in the morning. 'Hannah seems to be settling well back at home, and we managed putting the cream on her arms and legs. It's just a case of everyone keeping an eye on her.'

'Off you go,' Johnny said, 'we'll manage here fine for the day. Are you sure it's no trouble coming back on the five o'clock train? I wouldn't like to rush your first visit home.'

'That train suits me grand,' Nora said. 'I'll get everything done I need to in that time.' He had told her about another night's work he had got playing in the band, and she knew he needed her in the house, especially now that Hannah was back home.

'I can always depend on you,' he said, giving a little grateful sigh.

On her way to the station, carrying her empty case to refill with any items she thought would be useful, Nora bought herself the latest copy of *Woman's Life* to read on the train. It was very quiet, so she had a carriage to herself and she enjoyed the peace as she sat looking out of the window or reading through her magazine. She looked at the fashion page, which gave ideas on how to update clothes already in your wardrobe by adding little bows here or a bit of braiding there. This was nothing new, she thought, it was more or less what all the women she knew had been doing for years. She put the magazine down on her lap and stared out of the window, wondering when rationing would end and clothes be in full supply again.

She flicked through the magazine, halting at the make-up page, looking at all the suggestions they made for a woman to look more glamorous and sophisticated, then she turned the pages until she came to a knitting pattern for a slim-fitted jumper with pockets, which she felt would suit Ella. Nora was sure there was a hardly worn, pale blue cardigan at home that her mother had knitted in the same fine, four-ply wool. If she could find it, she would bring it back to Dublin and they could spend an evening carefully ripping out the cardigan, then press the strands of wool and wind it up into balls again before knitting it into the new style. Ella would be delighted with the idea, and it would give them something to do together. The idea brought a smile to Nora's face. She went back to reading her magazine, studying recipes, looking at smiling babies and older children in mothercraft pages, and ideas for making the home a nicer place to live. She noted that most of the ideas were aimed at the families with plenty of money, and smiled ruefully when she read the article on exercise to maintain a slim, healthy figure.

'Rationing and running after a family will soon knock off any extra fat,' she said in a loud whisper to the empty carriage.

She then moved onto the page where women Nora perceived to be silly wrote in for advice on their problems. If the problems were real of course, she thought, and not made up by some cynical man sitting at a desk in the magazine office, laughing his head off at the readers.

According to the young women in the office in Tullamore, this was the most popular page in the magazine. She scanned over the problems about a gambling husband, ungrateful children, and a spiteful mother-in-law, sighing. She had read variations on these problems dozens of times in various magazines. Her gaze moved to a problem posed by an unmarried woman in her late thirties, asking for advice on how to attract a man. The usual suggestions were given, such as keeping your hair in a youthful style, wearing make-up that was discreet but perfectly applied, and always acting in a ladylike manner. Being over-friendly or familiar with strange men was not encouraged as it was likely to attract the wrong types. A line at the end of the paragraph suddenly caught her attention. *Man is by nature a discoverer. It is not beauty which holds his interest, but rather mystery and charm...*

Nora mulled it over in her mind. It was the most encouraging thing she had read in a long time. She had always presumed that when it came to men, beauty would win over anything else. How, she wondered, could she cultivate mystery and charm? Charm was easier as it was simply being nice and pleasant to people. She had always been taught that being polite was very important, but she supposed she could make a point of being consciously pleasanter than usual. Being mysterious was something she had no experience of at all. In fact, she did not know any woman who would qualify as being mysterious. The only time she came across women who were any way mysterious was in films like *Casablanca* or *Rebecca*. Under what circumstances would an ordinary Irish woman become mysterious? As she looked out of the window at a field of sheep, she thought becoming mysterious would not be easy.

As she went inside, the house felt exactly the same as she left it, apart from a few envelopes which were on the floor in the hallway just behind the door. She put her case down and then closed the door behind her and picked up the mail. There was nothing of great interest apart from a letter from a cousin in Manchester.

She quickly went round, checking all the downstairs rooms. She lingered at the door of the bathroom, imagining what it would be like to have one in the house in Dublin. It was easily the convenience that she missed most. She had adapted well enough, because in her early years she had grown up using an outhouse. It was only when she was around eight or nine that her father had brought builders in to add a bathroom off the scullery.

Nora stared at it for a while, thinking, then she went upstairs to check the three bedrooms and was pleased to see that everything was fine.

Without having taken her coat off, she lifted her handbag and gloves, and went out of the house again.

A short while later she was leaning back having her hair washed in her hairdressers in High Street.

'I'm glad I could squeeze you in,' Ellen, her hairdresser said, wrapping a towel around her head. 'You were saying you would like your hair changed, have you anything in mind?'

'Not really,' Nora said, her voice uncertain, 'I thought maybe something a bit more up to date.'

Ellen frowned thoughtfully. 'I think we could go for a Lauren Bacall style. Slightly shorter at the front, a side parting, and done in waves. What do you think?'

Half an hour later Nora looked in the mirror and was amazed at the change. The loose waves softened her features and she liked the way it draped down one side.

'It really suits you,' Ellen told her. She narrowed her eyes. 'You look different, and it's not just your hair, although I think the style takes years off you.' She clicked her fingers. 'You're wearing make-up, aren't you?'

Nora flushed. 'Just a touch,' she said. 'I hope it's not too noticeable? A friend talked me into it.'

'Well, listen to your friend,' Ellen said, 'because you look the best I've ever seen. It's just the right amount without being obvious, and with your new hairstyle, you look really terrific. A different woman altogether.'

Nora smiled at her reflection. She did look better, she thought, although she wasn't deluding herself that she looked anything like a film star. She just wanted to look the best she could. And, if she was honest, she wanted to look better than Bridget or the barmaid – or any of the other women that might try to tempt Johnny Cassidy away, before a decent length of time had passed to let her show her own hand.

Two years would be a long time to wait before any link between them could be recognised in public, but in the meantime she would have the advantage of being with him every single day. And she would quietly work away at helping Johnny become the decent, hard-working sort of man that she knew he was capable of being.

Two years, Nora thought, would be worth the wait. It would see the biggest and best change in her life.

When she had cleaned up the scullery after their lunch of sausages and fried bread, Ella told her father she was going to take Hannah out in the pushchair. 'I might walk down to Nancy's for half an hour,' she said, 'or I might just go straight down to the Memorial Park and have a nice long walk around it.'

'That's a grand idea,' Johnny said. 'The nurses said to get her out in the fresh air.'

'What about Larry?' She didn't want to sound as if she didn't want to take him, but it was easier if she only had one child to keep amused.

'Me and Sean were talking about bringing him to the hurling match in the park down the road. We'll let him have a nap now and wake him up when we're getting ready.'

'My Aunt Nora said he's not taking a sleep every afternoon now.'

Johnny nodded. 'That's good. I think he needed the little naps when he wasn't sleeping as well at night after – well, after your mother went.' He gave a deep sigh, and then he shrugged.

Ella looked at him and her eyes suddenly filled up.

Johnny went over and put his arm around her. 'Are you doing OK?' he asked.

She rubbed her fist to her eyes and then nodded. She leaned in on his chest and he automatically wrapped his arms around her, as he had done since she was a little girl. They just stood there in silence for a few minutes and then Ella moved out of his embrace. Her heart was heavy, but there was no point in starting crying again, it just gave her a sore head and made everyone else upset too.

As she dressed Hannah for going outdoors, it struck her that the house was different without Aunt Nora around. Although her aunt was a quiet woman, she was a definite presence and was now a real part of their family.

Ella knew things would never be the way it was when their beloved mother was alive, but they were a lot better than they were a few weeks back, and most of it was down to Aunt Nora. If she hadn't come they could all be in an orphanage, and her father could be drinking himself into an early grave. Instead, her father was starting a regular, good job at the hospital. It was a job that Ella could feel proud of when she was talking to people like Nancy's granny, and it would keep him too busy to be wandering into pubs in the middle of the day. Almost as good was the fact that Sean was getting away from school and starting work down at the music shop. She had prayed to her mother to help find a solution to these things and now believed that her mother had sent Aunt Nora to sort everything out.

And as she walked along the road to the Memorial Park, where she had a loose arrangement made to meet up with Danny, she thought how funny it was that even playing chess with her aunt had given her a perfect excuse to see him on a regular basis. She turned in the gate now and could see him coming towards her with the dog on the lead. He was smiling and waving, and just seeing him made her heart soar. Danny Byrne was like a ray of sunshine on the darkest day.

It wasn't just that he was good-looking and funny, he was clever and sensitive too. She could talk to him in a way she had never talked with anyone else.

She knew of course that they were too young – *she* was too young – to be a proper girlfriend and boyfriend. But in two years things would be different. She would be heading up to sixteen, working and earning her own money. Sixteen was a respectable age for girls to be going out to dances and to the pictures with boys. In the meantime she was lucky that she could see him almost every day.

Two years, Ella thought, wasn't that long to wait.

PART TWO

Chapter Thirty-Two

December 1950

'Well,' Johnny asked, 'how do we look?'

Ella felt a surge of pride as she looked at her father and her brother. 'Like one of the bands you would see in the films.' They were both wearing new black suits, white shirts and bow ties, and shiny patent black shoes. They were almost identical apart from Sean wearing a spotted bow tie and his father plain black.

Nora's steps could be heard coming down the stairs then she came into the living room carrying her camera. 'I have to get a photo of you,' she said. 'We have to have something to remember Sean's first performance on a big stage.'

'Big *solo* performance,' Johnny said, clapping a hand on his son's shoulder. 'This time he's going to be singing and playing a good few numbers on his own. There's not many lads his age get to play in Wynn's Hotel at a dance during the Christmas week. They said the tickets were sold out early in the month, so it will be packed to the rafters.'

Ella watched Sean as he gave a nervous smile and dug his hands deep into his trouser pockets. She could tell he was anxious about going on stage – he always was. But he took his music so seriously that she knew he would have practised over and over again to make sure he had it all off perfectly.

He was hardly in the house at all these days; if he wasn't at the music shop he was at Mrs Keating's house. He was allowed to go there any time he needed to practise a new tune or have her listen while he tried out a new song. At home he was always upstairs in his room, learning the words of songs, and he had more or less taken over the radio in the living room, listening out for big hits in Ireland or Britain or America.

As she looked at him now, his fair hair dampened down, the front in a quiff like his idol Frank Sinatra, she could hardly believe how grown-up and handsome he was. All the girls said he was actually more handsome than Frank and any of the other film stars they all idolised, and Maeve had stopped all the jeering comments about him playing the piano. They all took him and his music seriously now, and any questions about him were asked with genuine interest. Since leaving school he was like a different person. He no longer hung about with the boys he had got into trouble with, and his easily inflamed bad temper seemed to have settled – although he still had his moments.

He and his father had found common ground with music and spent hours chatting about the latest popular tunes on the radio and in the dance halls. Spending so much time with Mrs Keating and her very clever, but slightly eccentric, brother had obviously had a good effect on him.

He poured all his pent-up energy into practising on the piano every spare minute in the shop or in the Keatings' house. He also had access to any sheet music he needed, and while the brother and sister tended to steer him in the classical music direction, Johnny kept him up to date with the more popular tunes.

Martin had a radiogram in the shop and he often played classical music as they worked, but since it was now the middle of December he had switched to Christmas carols. Sean had also advised him to play a record called *Christmas Songs by Sinatra*, as hearing it would encourage younger ones to buy a copy when they came into the shop. It also helped Sean learn all the lovely festive songs like 'Have Yourself A Merry Little Christmas' and 'Winter Wonderland' off by heart, as he heard them being played time and time again.

'Those suits and the bow ties are lovely on you,' Nora said. 'You're like something out of a magazine.' She lifted the camera now, and started fiddling around with the lens. It was the last birthday present she had got from her Uncle Bernard before he died, and she had hardly used it until becoming part of a family when she suddenly felt the urge to capture key moments like tonight.

Johnny laughed and touched his fingers down the lapel of the jacket. 'God bless the man down at the docks who found us the material, and God bless the tailor that ran the suit up in jig time.' He turned to Sean. 'And I've explained to this fellow that you're taken more seriously if you're turned out well. You never know, any night, if there could be a talent scout in the audience. Things are starting to get back to being more normal now and they say the Emergency could be over in the next few months.'

'They've been saying that for the last two years,' Ella said. 'God knows when it will eventually finish.'

Nora focussed the camera now. 'OK,' she said, taking a few steps backwards, 'we're all ready, so keep nice and still.' She took another shot just in case the first one was blurred.

When she had finished, Sean said, 'I wouldn't mind having a go at the camera.' He came over to stand close to her now. 'If you show me what button to press, I'll take one of you with my dad all dressed up now.'

Nora thought for a few moments. She was wearing a nice enough red twinset with her black jet beads and she had just had her hair set that morning. She had long since decided that going up and down to Tullamore to have it done had become too much trouble, especially since she had transferred all her ration books and post office accounts to Dublin.

As she smoothed down her black skirt, she reckoned she was as decent looking as she was likely to be, and it would be lovely to have a photo of her with Johnny in his suit and bow tie.

Sean took the camera and held it up to look through the lens. Nora showed him the various buttons to press and how to make the lens focus in closer or move further back.

'Practise it for a minute until I get my lipstick,' she told him.

Johnny looked at the clock on the mantelpiece. 'We'll have to get going soon to catch the bus.'

'Take a photo of your father and Ella while I'm gone,' Nora said, knowing it would give her a few more minutes.

She quickly ran upstairs, trying not to make any noise that would waken the two younger ones. They went to bed earlier and easier on the darker nights and they both slept soundly most nights. Although the scars on Hannah's arms and legs still looked bad, they had healed nicely over the twenty-one months and no longer hurt her, and Larry didn't wake as often crying for his mother. Nora thanked God for that, because it had made her heart sore listening to him, and she now felt that in a small way she had helped to heal the scars the serious little boy carried deep inside.

Nora tiptoed over to the dressing table where she had her make-up items neatly laid out. She lifted her eye-shadow box and then, with her little finger, applied it to her eyelid. She added a quick brush of mascara before putting on her deep red lipstick which she felt would show up better in the photograph.

She heard everyone laughing and chatting downstairs and knew she could linger a few extra moments to make sure she looked her absolute best beside Johnny. She went over to the wardrobe mirror and studied herself. She didn't look bad at all. Her new shorter hairstyle, she reckoned, was the best change she had ever made. She had seen the picture in one of her magazines and had taken it to the Kilmainham hairdresser who said it would suit her perfectly. It was similar to her Lauren Bacall style, but cut to just below her chin, and in the same soft waves. Even Mrs Murphy had said it gave her face a great lift.

When she came downstairs, Sean turned around and gave a loud wolf whistle. 'That red lipstick looks lovely on you.'

'Will you be quiet!' Nora said, but she was smiling and her face was flushed with delight at the compliment.

Johnny beckoned her over. 'Quick now, we need to get a move on.'

Nora moved into position beside him, both standing straight and staring into the camera.

'Get in a bit closer,' Sean told them, 'and give me a nice big smile.' He stepped back, and crouched down a little, as he thought a professional photographer might do.

Nora caught her breath as she felt Johnny's arm move around her waist and a spontaneous smile broke out on her usually serious face.

Sean clicked the camera. 'Great,' he said, moving a little closer, 'and one more to be sure I've got it right.'

'Come in for this one, Ella,' Nora beckoned, 'stand in at the other side of your father.'

Johnny's other arm went in around his daughter, and he pulled them both in closer to him.

Chapter Thirty-Three

It was almost twelve o'clock when Johnny and Sean came home that night. Ella and Nora were sitting by the fire, knitting and talking and listening to the radio, waiting on them. Ella was trying to finish a blue sweater which had a lace diamond pattern across the chest which Nora was helping her with. Christmas Day was over a week away, so she had time to finish it for wearing to Mass on the day.

The kettle had been boiled earlier and they had decided to take a chance on leaving the kettle on the glimmer light, to make a celebratory cup of tea when the musicians arrived home. Ella had also baked scones which they were waiting to have.

'Ah, he was the star of the show, no doubt about it,' Johnny said. 'And he has got the band another booking back there in the New Year. The manager said he could give us one of their big nights as long as we brought the young piano player too.'

Nora clasped her hands, delighted. 'They must have been very impressed with Sean.'

'They were, no doubts about it,' Johnny nodded, his eyes shining. 'And you should have seen the younger women hanging about the stage to chat to him during the break. They were asking for his autograph and everything – you would have thought he was Frank Sinatra himself.'

Sean laughed, an embarrassed look on his face. 'I have no interest in women at the minute; I have enough on my plate, I have no time for them at all.'

'That's what they all say,' his father said, 'until one catches your eye.'

Ella wondered how her father would feel if he knew that she had caught Danny Byrne's eye. Even though Danny was around Sean's age, she guessed that he would be happier not to know that for a while longer.

Danny had become almost part of the family. He called to the house regularly, and though they were rarely on their own as there was always someone in the house with them, in rare snatched moments he took the chance to hug or kiss her, although she made sure they sprang apart when they heard anyone about.

She helped her aunt bring in the tea and scones now, proud that Sean had done so well. Things had improved so much in all areas of their lives in the past year or so. Her father had settled well into the porter's job and had continued to play odd nights with the band, usually when he wasn't working at the hospital the next morning. On the few occasions he played before a work day, he always reassured Nora that he would only have a few pints during the night to quench his thirst, and come home straight afterwards. He had a few dances he was to play at over Christmas and New Year, and he said those particular nights would give the extra money needed to buy the children a few toys at Christmas, and any special food or clothes that might be needed.

Although he seemed to have improved, Ella still dreaded the nights her father went out. She could always tell the next morning, by the heavy look in his eyes and the redness of his face, when he had drunk too much. She also knew there were still odd nights when he had not come straight home after playing, but gone to one of his old haunts to extend his drinking hours. Her biggest worry was that he would start drinking heavily on the nights before work, and then not be fit to get up the next day. But that hadn't happened since he had started in the hospital, and tonight he and Sean had come straight home after the dance.

On the Saturday before Christmas Nora went into town to meet up with Veronica, who had suggested that, for a treat, they meet up in the fancy Shelbourne Hotel around two o'clock. She had decided to wear a plum-coloured suit she had got for a wedding some years ago, just before clothes coupons had come in, and she had rarely had the occasion to wear it since. It was a dressy suit, with a black velvet collar, and she liked the way the skirt flared out when she walked, making the most of her slim legs.

She had brought most of her things up to Dublin, and a good few of them were now hanging in the wardrobe in Ella's room, having been taken in to fit the girl. The suit however, when Nora tried it on, fitted perfectly, and she felt it looked even nicer on her now with her shorter hair and with the right sort of make-up.

It was a dull winter's afternoon with an icy breeze, so she needed to wrap up warmly for the twenty-minute walk from the bus stop to the hotel. Her heavy camel, swing-style coat was stylish enough for the smart hotel, and roomy enough to wear over the suit. She gave a nod and smile to the uniformed doorman, then, slightly intimidated by her plush surroundings, she walked along the thickly carpeted hallway towards the door of the hotel lounge. As she peered in, Nora was surprised to see Veronica sitting with a well-built, balding, smartly dressed man. She hesitated for a moment, wondering if this was Frank, the man that Veronica was seeing. Veronica saw her and waved her over. She walked to the table rather self-consciously, hoping the man wasn't going to stay, as she didn't want to play gooseberry to them.

'Nora,' Veronica said, standing up, 'this is my brother, Dominic. He was coming into town and I asked him if he would like to join us. I knew you wouldn't mind.'

Nora felt a little wave of relief. She smiled at her friend and then turned to look at the man, who was now standing up too, taken aback to notice that he had a red birthmark on his forehead and down the left side of his face. It was what she had heard people refer to as a 'port-wine stain'.

He held a big, square hand out to her, smiling, but she could sense a nervousness about him. She guessed he felt self-conscious about the mark on his face, and she wondered if he found it difficult every time he was introduced to someone new. She intuitively felt he was a kind man and wanted to put him at his ease. She took her glove off now to shake his hand, smiling warmly.

'I've heard a lot about you, Nora,' he said, 'and it's very nice to meet you at last.'

'It's nice to meet you, too,' she said, 'and lovely that you could join us.'

A waiter came to take Nora's coat from her, and Dominic moved to hold the chair out for her, then they all sat down.

Veronica smiled at her. 'I hope you don't mind me saying, Nora, but your suit is absolutely beautiful. And I love the shorter hairstyle on you too.' She looked Nora up and down, smiling in approval. 'You're looking very well.'

Dominic looked around for a few moments trying to catch the eye of a waiter, then he moved to his feet again, saying he would be back in a few minutes.

When he was out of earshot, Veronica moved to sit on the edge of her chair to be nearer Nora. 'I hope you didn't mind me bringing Dominic along? You see,' she gave a sigh, 'he's very shy. He always has been. I suppose you noticed the birthmark?'

'Well . . .'

Veronica made a little waving motion with her hand. 'It's the first thing most people notice, and I would have warned you if I'd known in advance that he was coming into town.'

'I wouldn't give it any more thought,' Nora said. 'He seems a very nice man, and that's what matters.'

The two women sat chatting about trivial matters like make-up and fashion and then they moved on to any news that either of them had. Nora talked about the children, and how clever she thought Larry was because he could already read quite well.

She then told her friend about how well Sean and his father had looked, all dressed up in their suits and bow ties.

'I actually took a few nice photos of them on the camera,' Nora said, 'and I'm going to put the film in today to have it developed.'

'Make sure and bring them with you when we meet up after Christmas, I'd love to see them.'

'I will, of course,' Nora promised, 'and you'll see how big Hannah and Larry have got since you last saw them.'

'You've grown very fond of them, haven't you?' Veronica said. 'I can tell by the look on your face when you're talking about them.'

Nora looked thoughtful. 'Yes, I am fond of them all. It wasn't easy in the beginning, but I can hardly imagine my life without them now.'

'Do you think you'll stay in Dublin? Or will you go back to Tullamore when Ella has done her school certificate and can look after the younger ones?'

Nora looked out towards the entrance of the hotel now. 'I honestly don't know, but I'm going to have to make some decisions in the New Year. I don't think they will hold my job much longer. It's been over a year now, so I think I'll have to resign at some point.'

'Have you talked to Johnny about it?'

'No, not recently. He knows they are keeping the job open, but we haven't talked about it really since I moved up.'

'But what if you give your job up and then Johnny goes and meets someone and decides to get married again? What would you do then?'

Nora caught her breath. Veronica had just touched on the rawest nerve. She had asked something that Nora could not bear to ask herself. 'Well,' she said, 'that would of course change everything.'

Then, before any more could be said, Dominic appeared at the table, with a waiter behind him carrying a tray with three schooners of sherry. 'It's Christmas,' he said, 'so I thought a little celebratory drink was in order.'

Nora looked up at him with forced gaiety. 'Oh, how lovely,' she said, grateful for his timely intervention. She turned to Veronica, still smiling, as though her mind was miles away from their earlier conversation, trying to ignore the anxious feelings that her friend had awakened. She put the crystal glass to her lips and swallowed deeply. As the golden liquid slid down her throat then began to warm in her chest, she felt it immediately comforting. She took another mouthful and when she put her glass back down on the table, noticed that she had drunk almost half of it already.

She glanced at the other two – still holding almost full glasses – and wondered if they had noticed how much she had drunk so very quickly. Veronica was busy remarking to Dominic about how busy the city was. Nora lifted her glass from the table and held it in her hand, thinking they were less likely to notice it than if it were on full display on the table.

By the time she had finished the last of her sherry, the earlier conversation about Nora's future had drifted to the back of her mind. Over sandwiches, mince pies and a large pot of tea, the women recounted stories of working together in Tullamore to fill Dominic in on how they came to know each other. Dominic was then urged by his sister to tell Nora about his garden landscape business.

'I don't do any of the actual gardening myself these days,' he explained, 'I have four or five men working for me who do that. But I do go out to the houses and talk to the owners and then I come home and draw up the plans. When the gardens are finished, the men go out to some of them every few weeks to keep them well-maintained.'

When Veronica went to speak to someone she recognised at another table, he told Nora about the big houses he had worked for around Dublin.

'And has it all stopped now with the Emergency being on?'

Dominic had raised his eyebrows. 'Not completely,' he told

her. 'It would surprise you, at times, to discover there is still money around for certain people. The laws that apply to us do not always apply to others.'

Nora had nodded her head. 'Well, as we know, there's always been one law for the rich and one law for the poor.'

'And then,' Dominic said, 'there are those of us that float around somewhere in the middle, trying to make the best of things.' He waved a hand around. 'There are plenty of poor souls who would never see the inside of a place like this, and it behoves the rest of us to appreciate our good fortune. We might be struggling with rationing and missing the way life used to be, but we are not in the dire position some families are.'

'Exactly,' Nora said, delighted to hear that he had a social conscience and did not shirk from expressing it.

They chatted on for a while about how Christmas gave a great lift to everything with the trees and the decorations, and how it helped people through the dark winter.

When the waiter came to clear the table of the tea things, Dominic asked him to bring three more sherries. 'Just to warm us up before facing out into the cold again. That breeze could cut you in two at times.'

'It could,' Nora agreed. 'It can be brutal coming over the bridge.' She was delighted that he had ordered another drink. She would never normally dream of drinking alcohol during the day, but it was Christmas, after all. When the waitress came back with the sherries, they toasted each other again, and then sat back in their chairs, chatting.

Dominic glanced around him, then he turned towards her, his face serious. 'I've enjoyed meeting you and talking to you, Nora.'

'Well, thank you,' she said, taking another warming mouthful of the sherry, 'and I can return the compliment. I've very much enjoyed talking to you.' Nora was surprised that she felt so comfortable with Dominic after such a short time. She held her glass up. 'And thank you again for the festive drink, very kind of you.'

'I wondered,' he said, 'if you were free some evening... some weekend... if you might like to go to the pictures or to a concert or something like that?'

Nora felt herself freeze. Had she somehow misled this poor man into thinking that she had some sort of interest in him? She took another little sip from her sherry to stall for time. She had only been polite to him, had chatted to him as she might have chatted to Veronica – aimless, easy chat. Had the sherry loosened her tongue so much that she had unwittingly given the impression that she had a romantic notion of him?

And then it dawned on her. Veronica had devised the whole thing. She had deliberately brought her brother along, thinking he might be a suitable match for her.

She looked at Dominic now and could see from the little tic which had just developed on his cheek that he could almost read her thoughts.

Nora took a deep breath, 'That is very kind of you, Dominic,' she started, desperately trying to find the right words – the kind words to let him down. 'But unfortunately, I don't get much time to myself...'

Then, out of the corner of her eye, she saw a figure to the side of her, and was relieved when Veronica slid back into her chair.

'Sorry about that,' Veronica said, smiling from one to the other. 'It was one of the doctors from the hospital. He was there with his wife and I couldn't get away from them.' She looked down at the sherry and then she turned to her brother. 'You're a devil,' she said, 'but I won't argue since it's Christmas.' She took a sip from the glass then she looked over at Nora. 'Is Johnny going to the Christmas party tonight?'

'Yes,' Nora said. 'He is.' He had told her about how all the porters were going for a few drinks with the staff from some of the other wards. She looked at Dominic now, anxious to check he was all right. She guessed he knew he had been rebuffed, but she wanted him to know that she liked him as a friend. 'Johnny is my cousin's widower whose house I live in out near the Phoenix Park. I help to look after the children.'

Dominic nodded his head. 'Veronica told me, and said how

good you were to come up to Dublin to help them all out.' He gave a sympathetic smile. 'Shocking a young family losing their mother like that.'

'They keep me very busy,' she told him, grateful that he was not holding the rejection against her. 'There are times I hardly have time to bless myself. I'm lucky to squeeze a few hours every so often to meet up for a cup of tea with your sister.'

'I heard some of the nurses talking about the party,' Veronica commented now. 'They're hoping to get Johnny to play a few tunes on the fiddle, and I think they've asked if his son will drop in and give them a few songs. Johnny has been telling them all about him at work.' She shook her head laughing. 'But in truth, I'd say there will be a few of them hoping to catch Johnny under the mistletoe. He's a big hit with all the women.'

Twenty minutes later Nora was walking back down a wintry Grafton Street, her heart still racing. She could hardly remember what they had talked about leading up to their goodbyes.

The main thing she could remember was the picture that Veronica had painted of the handsome, widowed Johnny at work, surrounded by all the young nurses. The young nurses who would have no thought to decency – no thought to waiting two years for him. As bad as that Bridget from the church and the brazen barmaid. They would be there tonight, waiting to get their chance with him under the guise of Christmas high spirits. The thought of it made her feel sick.

Had all the time she spent these past months – keeping a respectable distance between them in the house – been a total waste of time? Was some bold and brassy nurse going to step in now and take her place?

This time next year – over two years since Mary's passing – would she be preparing to go back to her own, lonely house in Tullamore? She would have lost her job by then and what would she have to go back for? She would also have lost the four children, who she now realised she had grown to love almost as her own.

The cold nipped at her ears and nose. She slipped her handbag higher up on her arm then moved her hands to pull her hat down tighter. She tried to walk as quickly as possible, sometimes walking in a zig-zag pattern to avoid bumping into people. And then she moved too far to one side and went over on her ankle. She caught her breath, knowing that her unsteady walk had not been helped by the sherry she had drunk too quickly. The pain only lasted a few moments, and then began to ebb away, so she knew that she was all right. Tears began to fill her eyes and she turned away, pretending she was looking in a shop window.

She took her hanky out and dabbed at her eyes, and then she took a few deep breaths to steady herself. She opened her eyes and found herself looking into a window filled with lovely ladies' silk nightdresses, satin pyjamas and dressing gowns. Silky, feminine items, nothing like the warm winceyette ones she wore under her heavy woollen dressing gown with the plaited cord belt. She stared at them for a moment, then wondered if she had her clothing coupons in her handbag. She remembered – she had put them safely in a zipped inside pocket.

She straightened herself up, held her head high and opened the shop door.

Chapter Thirty-Four

Ella came home just after half past ten from a Christmas concert in the church hall to find her aunt on her own in the living room. She was quietly sewing a skirt she had made for Hannah to wear on Christmas morning.

Nora smiled at her. 'Well, how did it go?'

'It was great,' Ella said. 'We really enjoyed it. There was a lot of singing and there were a few funny sketches, so it was a good laugh.'

'I'm glad you had a good night. Did Danny go with you after all?'

Ella moved her gaze to the skirt her aunt was sewing. 'Yes,' she said, 'he came with Nancy.' She halted, embarrassed at talking about him. 'Did Sean come back yet from Daddy's hospital do?'

'Yes, around ten o'clock. He said he only stayed long enough to play half a dozen songs, as the piano wasn't great – some of the keys didn't work and you know what he's like if things aren't perfect. He said the best bit was the sausage rolls and sandwiches. He's gone to bed as he said he was tired.'

Ella stood for a moment. 'I'm tired myself.' Then her eyes lit on the blue jumper she had been knitting. 'Oh, you finished the jumper for me!'

Nora had sewn up the seams and carefully pressed it, then left it folded on the back of one of the chairs.

Ella lifted it from the chair then held it up in the air, examining it. 'Oh, thanks, Aunt Nora, it looks really lovely. I can't wait to wear it to Mass on Christmas Day.'

'I put your hot water bottle in half an hour ago, so your bed will be nice and warm.'

Ella's face crumpled a little as though she might cry at the kindness, but she smiled instead. 'Thanks – and thanks again for doing my jumper. You're so good to us, and you hardly have any time for yourself.'

'Well, I had a nice afternoon in Dublin with my friend.' She paused and then she smiled. 'And I had a lovely hot bath when you were all out. I bought a bottle of bath oil today and I put some of that in the water.'

'I thought something smelled nice. Well, I'm glad you treated yourself.'

'You can have a drop of it when you have your next bath.'

Ella smiled as she went out, wondering if Danny would notice if she smelled all fancy with the bath oil.

Nora was waiting up when Johnny came home at one o'clock in the morning. He put his fiddle case down in the hallway and hung his coat up, then came in to join her. She had kept the living room fire on all night, so the room was lovely and warm, and she had changed into her nightclothes. She could tell immediately by his glazed eyes and slow movements that he had drunk a lot more than usual, and as he came to sit opposite her at the fire she could smell whiskey on him. On other occasions she might have been angry with him, but not tonight. It would be unreasonable to complain about a Christmas night out, and she was grateful that he had come home at all and not been lured away.

'Well,' she said, smiling warmly. 'Did you have a nice night?'

'It was grand,' he said. 'A good enough oul' night. A bit of singing and a few of them even had a bit of a dance.' He looked at Nora now and said, 'Sean came down and gave us a few tunes.' He said it in such a way it sounded as though she hadn't known anything about it, even though she had been there when

Johnny left and he was making Sean promise to come down to the pub.

'He belted out a few songs for them and they were all delighted.' There was a definite slur in his voice. 'The women were going mad for him. They all think he should be singing in London or New York, he's that good.'

'And were there many there?'

'Ah, around forty or fifty.'

Nora took a deep breath. 'Well, I'm glad you enjoyed the night.'

'Everyone here all right?' he asked. 'The young pair OK?'

'All grand.' She halted. 'When I was in Dublin today, my friend gave me a present, and I thought you might like to share it with me.' She stood up. 'It's in the scullery, I'll get it now.' As she went out into the hallway, she blessed herself for telling a lie. She had bought the bottle herself. The two drinks she had had in the Shelbourne had helped her relax through the awkward part of such an elegant afternoon, and she thought it might help her in a different way tonight.

Johnny looked at her with bleary eyes as she passed him by. A minute or so later she came back in carrying a bottle of sherry and two tumblers. His eyes widened when he saw the bottle. He straightened up in his chair and rubbed his hands together. 'Well, that was very good of your friend.' He looked up at her. 'Are you sure you don't mind opening it tonight?'

'Better we enjoy it when the children aren't around,' she said. 'Why don't you find a nice music station on the radio?' She opened the bottle and poured two good measures.

'Ah, sure what's the harm? And isn't it Christmas on Monday?'

It suddenly crossed Nora's mind that they should be fasting from midnight to go to communion in the morning, but since Johnny had said nothing about it, she decided she would ignore it too. She had spent her whole life living by the church's teaching and always doing the right and proper thing. Where had it got her? And what difference did an hour either way make? It was all nonsense. It was rules made up by priests who were only men, to suit themselves. To keep the common herd of the church congregation bowing and scraping to them. Would Jesus himself actually care if they had a glass or two of sherry? Nora thought not. The Bible was full of stories of people drinking wine and enjoying each other's company, and Jesus gently telling Martha off for putting work and duty before people. Jesus had no problem with people enjoying themselves.

And, as she and Johnny touched their glasses together, she thought of how Jesus really just wanted people to be kind and to comfort each other, as she and Johnny were now.

Half an hour later, Johnny went to the outhouse, and as he came back into the living room he staggered against the door jamb. The main light was off and there was only the glow from the fire illuminating the room. The Ink Spots had just come on the radio singing 'Whispering Grass'.

'Oh, I love this,' Nora said, getting to her feet, her glass still in her hand. 'It's so beautiful, it makes you want to dance.' She started to move slowly around the small room now, her eyes half closed, her free hand waving in the air in time to the music. As she moved, she pictured Johnny dancing with the nurses earlier that night. She took another long drink of the sherry to push the image from her mind.

She beckoned to Johnny now. 'Dance with me...' She went to put her glass down on the mantelpiece, and he came into the room, unsteady on his feet. The shadowy darkness, the warmth from the flickering flames, and the musky perfume that Nora had put on after her bath gave an unfamiliar ambience to the room. A welcoming ambience, not unlike the small function room in the bar from earlier in the night, with the dim lights and the low music.

The dancing there had started when Sean got up on the piano stool. By then, Johnny had had a few hours of beer and had moved on to drink whiskey. All the women had clapped and cheered as Sean sang the opening lines of 'Santa Claus is Coming to Town', and then reached for any available men to dance with, laughingly pulling and dragging them away from the bar and onto the floor. Several had headed in the handsome Johnny's direction. It was a Christmas party, after all, and these were the people he saw every day in work, so it would be seen as terrible bad manners not to. And so, he had danced with them.

Two women in particular, one a nurse, one a woman from the maintenance office, had made their attraction to him obvious. They had pressed tightly against him as they danced, and one had wound her arms around his neck. She was curvy and attractive and sweet-smelling – as Mary had been – and there was a point when drink and nature had almost taken over. Johnny found he had to make an effort not to pull her tighter to him or bend his head and kiss her. But respect for his departed wife – and the knowledge that Sean was just across the dance floor from him – had kept his responses well muted.

Nearly two years had passed since he'd held a woman in his arms like this; more in fact, for he had kept a caring and gentlemanly distance from Mary in the latter weeks of her pregnancy. And when she was taken from him without warning, intimacy had disappeared completely from his life and his only natural urge had been to survive and protect his family. Even when the barmaid from the Barley Mow had offered her comforts without any ties, he had found himself lacking in any desire. But the days since losing Mary had passed and life with his beloved Mary was beginning to feel like a dream which belonged to a different time, to a different world. And, now working full-time in the hospital, he was beginning to feel like a different Johnny Cassidy. And it was this different man, who, having drunk half a bottle of sherry, was now in a drunken stupor. So drunk, he was oblivious to the fact that the woman he was now dancing with was one of the plainest women he had ever come across – Nora Lamb.

The two large glasses of sherry had done its work on Nora too, both physically and mentally. Just as she had planned. All her thoughts from earlier in the day had come tumbling back, and she knew, without a doubt, that if she did not make herself available to Johnny Cassidy, another woman surely would.

As they moved in a shuffling fashion around the floor, out of time to a second Ink Spots' number – 'I Don't Want to Set the World on Fire' – she had to grip onto Johnny's shoulders to keep him upright. As she reached up to wrap her arms around his neck, her dressing gown fell open, revealing the dove-coloured satin nightdress decorated with delicate grey lace. It had thin straps, and was cut low in the neck then gathered in such a way underneath that it scooped her breasts and made them look surprisingly full. Nora moved out of his reach for a few seconds and shrugged the dressing gown off her shoulders, letting it fall to the floor.

She now felt the very same desire she had felt when she'd woken from the erotic dream all those long months ago, and this time it overtook any feelings of guilt. In the darkness of the room, her heart racing, she found her way back into Johnny's arms. As they shuffled around, his eyes closed now, she felt her body start to shake as his hands slid up and down the silky material on her back. Perspiration broke out on her face, between her breasts, under her arms, and the throbbing low down in her stomach intensified to such a pitch that her thighs were wet with wanting. When his hands moved to the front to fondle her breasts, she had to bite her lip to stop from moaning aloud.

At the back of her mind a little voice struggled to be heard, warning her that she was a woman in her forties who had never been with a man before; warning her that losing her virginity might hurt. How much, she had no idea. It was not a subject that she had ever discussed with anyone, and the scant knowledge of it that she had from library books or magazines gave her no real idea of what to expect. The little voice was warning her that it might hurt so badly that she would find herself calling out, and the children might hear them. But the blood pounding through her head now drowned out everything but the rush of desire she had successfully ignored for most of her adult life.

And without a care for any consequences, she reached for his hand and guided him over to the couch. As he flopped down on his back, Johnny's eyes fluttered open for a few seconds then closed again. Nora leaned over him, and her hands roamed over his shoulders and then his chest. At first there was no response, and for a few moments she thought he was asleep, but when she manoeuvred herself to lie on top of him everything suddenly changed.

His hands reached out for her and began to move down her arms, around her waist, and then run back and forth over her breasts. He did it almost in slow motion, but Nora felt every imprint his fingers made on her body, shuddering with pleasure at his touch. This was what she had dreamt about, read about. Nervously, she moved her mouth down on his and, as he kissed her back, she felt like the sensuous, passionate women she had read about, the sort of woman she felt she was destined to be.

At some point Johnny manoeuvred her around on the couch so she was now lying under him. His breathing was coming heavy now, and as his weight came down on top of her, she could feel the extent of his arousal as he pressed hard against her thighs. She felt a victorious wave wash over her as she felt the tangible evidence of his desire for her. The idea that such a handsome, younger man would find her so enticing gave her a thrill all of its own.

Johnny moved to slide his braces down and unfasten the buttons on his trousers and she lifted her hips and brought her slippery nightdress high up on her bare breasts. Then, as she felt his hot, hard, naked flesh on hers, she arched her body to let him move inside her.

At first she felt a sense of panic as he met with some resistance, and her natural urge was to pull away in case it hurt. But, determination to make sure everything was as it should be for him, made her move her hips to meet him. He thrust a few more times which made her feel sore and gave no pleasure at all, then something seemed to give and he slid inside her with ease.

And then, as a wonderful feeling she had never experienced started to spread through her, and was building up into some

had when Cathy from the Barley Mow had made a play for him. And that was where all the confusion lay. How – when he had resisted temptation so easily from other, more attractive women – had he come to be in the position he was in now?

He could have got away with it if he had been a less honest man. If he had played his cards differently. When he woke at five in the morning after that first time he could barely remember anything. The thumping headache from all the drink had been more dominating, and the details of their encounter were so sketchy that he had convinced himself it had all been a weird dream.

It was only when he moved to go to the outhouse, before going up to bed, that he noticed the blood on his shirt and trousers. Absolute terror had run through him as he realised it had all been real. He had not only had sex with Nora, but there was a possibility that he had done something even more awful to her. He had, in some way, hurt her. He'd closed his eyes, trying to make sense of it all. He knew he was not a man who would physically hurt a woman. He didn't have it in him.

And then it suddenly struck him. It was her first time with a man. She had been a virgin! Johnny had somehow managed to pull himself together to go up to bed, but he had lain awake, dreading what the following day would bring.

The morning routine passed the same as any Sunday. He and Nora greeted each other, though without making any eye contact, and they walked down to Mass and back with the children. They talked about general things, each carefully avoiding any discussion of the night before. When Ella asked how Sean had got on, playing at the hospital 'do', both he and Johnny gave their account of it, with Sean laughingly complaining about the old wreck of a piano that had half the keys missing.

As she served breakfast and then dinner later in the day, Nora chatted to him and looked him in the eye as she normally did, as though nothing untoward had happened. Gradually, as the day wore on, they got back into the same routine.

The only difference Johnny noticed, was that as she went

about her chores, Nora was quietly humming to herself, which he found disconcerting. It seemed she was happy, and he wasn't quite sure why. In one way, Johnny had felt a sense of relief that she wasn't blaming him for doing something terrible to her, but in another, he felt a sense of trepidation, as though something terrible might befall him.

He had made the decision that they would never get into that position again, that he would be careful, when drinking, to make sure he was sober enough to know exactly what he was doing. Christmas came and Nora was generous with gifts for the children. She also bought a few bottles of whiskey and sherry and when Mrs Murphy and Father Brosnan called, Johnny poured small measures and waved away any suggestion of a second drink.

Winter moved into spring and Nora took a trip down to Tullamore one Monday morning when Ella had just started the school Easter holidays, and was available to look after the younger ones. When she came back that evening, she told Johnny that she had officially handed in her notice at the hospital. 'They were good, keeping it open for me for two years,' she said. 'And to be honest, after being away for so long, I don't feel I really want to go back.'

Johnny felt a sense of foreboding. 'What about when Hannah starts school?' he said, 'won't you miss work then?'

'If I do, I might find a job in the hospital,' she said. Secretly, Nora hoped she would never have to work again when she and Johnny got married.

He had then broached the subject of money with her, checking that she would be OK in the future without her wages.

'I'm grand,' she said. 'The money I get from the farm keeps me going. And you know, things are ticking over well enough here with your own job and anything extra you bring in from playing at the weekend. Sean also helps out, now he's playing regularly at the weekend. It covers all the basics, so I'm not spending as much money living here. And while we're talking about such things, I wanted to make a suggestion about Ella...'

She had then gone on to say that she had been looking into the cost of Ella continuing at school for another year or two. The nuns in the girls' school had said she was too clever to leave school early, and that they recommended she go into 'Secondary Tops' which would give her a certificate that would help her to go into something such as nursing or even teaching. And while no one was suggesting that money was plentiful with a house to run with six people in it, if they budgeted carefully, and she put in a regular amount, they could afford the money necessary to keep her on.

Johnny had to agree with Nora that Mary had always hoped that the clever Ella would get the chance to do something more than the menial jobs she had done. He had also calculated that, by the time Ella was finished at school, the younger ones would be well settled in school themselves and Nora's help would no longer be needed. And so he had agreed, knowing that she would be a fixture in their lives for another few years. After that, he would waste no time in encouraging her to go back to her house in Tullamore. She deserved to live a nice, easy life after all the work she had done for the family.

The next physical collision happened that Easter Monday, when Johnny played at a dance in town with Sean. When the band was packing up, Sean had told him and the other men that he would no longer be playing with them. He had been offered a regular weekend booking playing the piano in one of the bigger hotels.

'I'll be playing more classical stuff,' he told them, 'while the guests are eating dinner in the evening. Mrs Keating said I need to broaden my repertoire if I want to get on in my career, rather than sticking to just playing in dance halls.'

Johnny had taken the news that Sean was striking out on his own badly. He had imagined that Sean's growing talent would lift the profile of the band and take them to a wider audience. His private dreams of playing in bigger and better places, and of he and Sean playing and singing together, maybe even recording records, were suddenly dashed.

He had gone to the bar that night and drunk several large whiskeys in a row to dull the disappointment. And he had then gone to a bar in Kilmainham that he knew did a lock-in, saying he needed to see a man about a booking the following week. He had tried to keep a smiling façade, and whether Sean had sensed his father's upset or not, his desertion of the band was not mentioned.

Johnny had met up with several people he knew, and with his night's payment burning a hole in his pocket, he bought rounds for them. He drank more large whiskeys and several beers, until he was seeing double and was told to go home by the bartender. Nora was waiting for him again – Sean had warned her that Johnny had been drinking heavily and had stopped off to have more – so she was waiting with the low music and the room lit only by the dying firelight, her confidence bolstered by another new nightdress – black satin this time – and the leftover Christmas sherry and whiskey. He was so far gone that he hardly needed any encouragement to have another glass, and as he sat on the couch, eyes closed again, she ran her trembling hands over him again and again, until nature did its work and he found his body responding.

When he awoke downstairs again, his clothes in disarray, he knew exactly what had happened. As before, the incident was never referred to between himself and her, but it left him feeling disgusted with his weakness and even more concerned about the situation than he had been the first time. A recurring image of the flimsy black nightdress had led him to do some investigations in Nora's room the following Saturday afternoon when she had gone to meet her friend and Sean was at work in the music shop and Ella had taken the younger ones out.

Johnny had never been further than the doorway since she moved in, and the room was very different from the way it had been when she moved in. She had brought cushions and curtains from Tullamore, and even carried a small fancy bedside table up. She had pictures on the wall and a French-style lamp with fringes so she could read in bed.

Then he went over to Mary's dressing table. He slid a drawer open which contained neatly folded silk scarves and some items of jewellery. But when he opened the second drawer, his heart sank. There was the black satin nightdress he remembered, and peeping from underneath, a delicate dove-coloured one. He pulled the drawer out further to reveal a peach-coloured bra with fancy matching silk knickers. Without touching a thing he shut the drawer quickly.

He came downstairs, mulling over his finds, and came to the conclusion that nothing that had happened had been accidental. Nora Lamb, it seemed, had orchestrated the encounters on both nights, and had been ready and waiting for him coming home. His weakness in it all, he concluded, was drink. He would have to be more abstemious, because if he didn't – God knows where it might lead.

This most recent encounter with Nora was the one which had driven him again to the confessional box. He had received a message from one of his brothers in Liverpool, via Father Brosnan, that his father had suffered a stroke and was in hospital, and they weren't sure which way things were going to go. Johnny had rung back the following day and was told that the old man seemed to be making a recovery, but had lost the power of his speech and the use of his left arm.

Guilt over not seeing his father for a few years – and the knowledge that when he did see him again there would be no chat and banter – sent him to seek comfort in whiskey again. This time he did not wait until night to drink; he went out on a Saturday afternoon and did not return until well after everyone except Nora was in bed. When he staggered in, he started a speech that he had rehearsed all night. A speech which he hoped would lead to him suggesting that Nora move back to Tullamore and he get in an elderly, paid housekeeper who would go home to her own place at the end of the day. He didn't know how he would find the money, but he would do it somehow – and he would certainly cut out the drink, which would save a few shillings.

He started off apologising to Nora for taking advantage of her when he had been previously drunk. How he knew what a despicable thing it had been and how sorry he was, and how he promised never to do such a thing again. And then he had shed genuine tears, saying how ashamed he was and how upset poor Mary would be to know of his disgraceful behaviour. Nora had sat there in her dressing gown, listening to every word, and then she had quietly told him that he had nothing to be sorry about. She said if it hadn't been her who had received his amorous overtures, it might be some woman who would use the situation to pressurise him into marriage far earlier than he was ready for.

She then disappeared into the scullery, coming back with a bottle of sherry with two glasses gone from it and whiskey for Johnny. And when she held it out, the enticing smell of the golden liquid made him weaken in seconds.

She then poured her third glass of sherry of the night, took a deep drink, and sat down beside him. She had leaned in closer to him and said, in a soothing voice, 'We both respect dear Mary's memory, and what has happened in this room will stay between the four walls. We're not harming anyone else.'

'But what about you?' Johnny had drunkenly asked. 'Surely you don't want to live in a house with a man who has done such a thing to you? A man who is still dedicated to the memory of his beloved wife? A man who might never be able to love someone else?' He had taken another gulp of whiskey. 'Wouldn't it be better if you got away and lived your own life, and maybe met a more deserving man?'

Nora had told him she would be there as long as the little children needed her, and pointed out that they would be upset if she was to suddenly disappear. It would seem to the poor little mites that they had lost two mothers in only a few years. And, she added, she would miss them as much as they missed her.

Johnny had looked lost then, hearing the truth in her words. He lifted his glass and drained it and silently allowed her to fill it again.

As he walked down Grafton Street now, he was emphatic that

this time had to be the last. And, he realised there was only one answer to the situation he was in – watching every mouthful he drank. He knew he only had himself to blame. He was the author of his own misfortune – and had allowed a dark web to be wound around him.

Chapter Thirty-Six

On her fifteenth birthday, Danny Byrne bought Ella a gold chain with a small heart-shaped locket. When she showed it to her father and Aunt Nora, she expected a shocked reaction, but they didn't look in the least bit surprised. All her efforts to treat him like only a friend when he came to the house, and try not to talk too much about him, had not fooled anyone.

Sean had laughed and jeered. 'As if we didn't notice that he had his eye on you, and all the times he's been coming, pretending he wanted to play chess.'

Ella had flared up at him. 'He wasn't pretending! Danny genuinely loves playing chess. He'd have to be some kind of eedjit to be coming up to the house and sitting with Aunt Nora and the rest of us for hours playing if he didn't like it.'

'Well,' Sean said, 'it was you that mentioned the word eedjit, not me.'

And when she then tentatively asked her father if it was OK to go to the pictures with him, he smiled, and said, 'I suppose you're old enough now, and he's a decent enough lad. Just make sure that you both behave.'

'Of course we will,' she said, a hurt tone in her voice. But he hardly seemed to notice. Her father, she thought, seemed changed these days. Older and quieter. He had stuck well at his job in the hospital and had curbed his heavy drinking habit. In many ways Ella was grateful for the changes and it was what she had prayed for. She didn't have to worry about him disappearing to the pub all day on a Saturday – he now spent more time with Larry, taking him to the park or to football or hurling matches. Sometimes they went into the city to the Natural History Museum because her younger brother was fascinated by the animals on display and wanted to know all the countries they came from. But there was a change in her father that worried her. He seemed quieter and low in spirit. He had also lost weight recently, which was unusual since there was more food available now that the rationing was officially over. Ella guessed not drinking might have made him lose a bit of weight, but other than that, she couldn't come up with any answers.

Her aunt had bought her a lovely handbag and some perfume for her birthday, and her father had given her money to buy a new pair of shoes that she had had her eye on in Clerys' window. Tall and slim now, her blonde hair almost down to her waist, Ella Cassidy drew admiring glances wherever she went. She laughed off any compliments, as the only boy she was interested in was Danny Byrne. She still had to catch her breath at times when she saw him.

Delighted that the announcement of their romance had met with no resistance, Danny started calling in most evenings after work, dressed in his smart coat and hat. A year before he had got one of his younger cousins to take over the household jobs for his grandparents, to let him get out and earn a proper living, and eventually, having walked the streets searching, was offered a three month's unpaid trial at a printing firm, to see if he was up to the job. Within weeks he proved he was, and almost a year later he was earning reasonable money, and enjoying the buzz of daily life in the city.

When Ella asked him if he ever thought of going back to Liverpool, he always shook his head. 'I miss me mother,' he said, 'and I will go back to see her and the younger kids when I've saved enough money, but I'll never go back to live there while she's married to that rat of a husband.'

It was almost two months later when Father Brosnan came down to the house on a Sunday evening to tell them that a call had come from Liverpool to say that Ella's grandfather had suffered another massive stroke and been given the Last Rites. Ella was sorry to see how upset her father was. After the priest left, he went up to his bedroom and closed the door. Aunt Nora had gone up with a glass of whiskey for him and knocked on the door, and Ella had been shocked when she heard her father's voice raised and saying, 'You can pour that down the sink. That's the last thing I need!'

She had never heard him speak so sharply to her Aunt Nora. That evening, he went back and forward to use the phone in the pub and he eventually arrived home with the news that his father had died.

Johnny went into work on Monday, and when he came home he announced that he and Sean were going to go over to Liverpool on the boat the following night. He told them he didn't know exactly when the funeral was as they took much longer in England, but he needed to be over there to support his brothers and for the Rosary in the house in the evenings.

'It's the least I can do,' he told Ella and Nora, 'because I never got to see him when he was sick. You'll all be grand here until we get back. I would say we won't be much more than a week – maybe ten days or so.'

Ella noticed her Aunt Nora looked shocked. 'But what about your job?'

'The hospital is fine about it and so is the fella in the music shop. Sean let the hotel he plays in know as well, so we're all covered.'

Ella had wondered if her grandad's death might make her father more morose, but from the minute he planned the trip over, he actually seemed happier. It was as if a weight had been lifted off him. He and Sean went out after work and bought black ties and white shirts to wear with their good black suits, and new black hats.

Unknown to Johnny, Ella had made up her mind that she wasn't going back to school after the summer holidays. Having seen Danny enjoying work in the city so much, she decided she wanted to do the same. She had never been that keen on being a nurse or a school teacher anyway. She wanted something more exciting. She confided in Nora on the Tuesday evening, and the older woman, disappointed, tried to talk her into staying on for another year, but Ella was adamant that she wanted to find a job in Dublin and earn her own money.

'You've been more than good to me,' Ella said, 'helping to pay for me to go to school and buying me clothes and books. It's about time I got out and started working. Maeve and Nancy left school last year and they're able to buy their own things now.'

Nora had made a decision too, after her last visit to Tullamore, and now told Ella she had business down in Tullamore on the Wednesday afternoon, and asked if she and the children would like to come down for a day out with her. Her business would only take half an hour or so, and they could wait for her in a nice tearoom.

Ella had already filled in some application forms for work, and was waiting to hear back. She had half planned to spend the Wednesday going around the shops, hotels and offices to see if they had any notices up about needing staff, but she felt that she had disappointed her enough by leaving school.

'That would be lovely, Aunt Nora,' Ella said, 'and Larry and Hannah will enjoy going down on the train.'

They first went to the house, and Nora did all her usual checks and found nothing untoward, and then they walked down High Street to the tearoom. Nora let them pick a cake each and a drink, and when they were settled she set off to the bank, where she had arranged to meet the man who she had rented her Uncle Bernard's farm out to.

She had just entered the bank and was looking around to see which desk to go to, when she felt a hand on her shoulder.

'Nora?'

She turned around to see a dark-haired woman a few years younger than herself, smiling at her. Nora recognised her but couldn't think of her name or where she was from.

'I thought it was you,' the young woman said, smiling warmly at her. 'You're looking really well, I hardly recognised you.' She could see Nora was trying to work out who she was. 'It's Kate, Kate Thompson. I work on the reception desk at the hospital.'

Nora's face suddenly brightened. 'Oh, Kate,' she said, 'My mind went a blank for a minute.' She laughed. 'Old age setting in! How are you?'

'Grand,' Kate said, rolling her eyes. 'I came running down here in my dinner break.' She stood back to look at Nora's floral-patterned, long-sleeved dress with its wide red belt and flared skirt. 'Your outfit is gorgeous,' she said. 'I've never seen you wearing anything like that before.' She looked her up and down appraisingly, noting the fashionable shoes and bag – and the make-up. 'But then, it's a good while since I've seen you. I heard you're not coming back, is it true?'

Nora nodded. 'I'm all settled up in Dublin now.'

'Well, you were very well thought of in the hospital. Always regarded as a great worker.'

This was news to Nora and it gave her a little lift to hear it. 'Well, I suppose I tried to do my best.'

'Haven't you the house up there, just off High Street?'

Nora glanced around her, checking that no one she knew was within earshot. 'Yes, I kept it just in case.' She felt her heart quicken now. 'But I doubt if I'll need it again – I've met a lovely man and he works in one of the bigger hospitals in Dublin...' She smiled almost coyly now, imagining the looks on the faces of the other women in the office when they heard the news. 'We're actually planning to get married in the next year or two. He's widowed this last few years, but still, we don't want to rush things too quickly out of respect to his late wife and family.'

'Well, isn't that the lovely news! The best of congratulations to you both. I'm absolutely delighted for you!' Kate tried not to show how shocked she was. Everyone regarded Nora Lamb as a confirmed spinster, and yet here she was, all dressed up to the nines in the latest fashion with her hair looking lovely, telling her that she was getting married.

A big, red-faced man came rushing towards them. 'I'm sorry

I'm late, Miss Lamb,' he said. 'I got caught with the vet who came out to see one of the cows.'

Nora turned towards him. 'We're in no rush, Tim,' she said reassuringly. 'If you don't mind checking at the desk who we have to see, I'll be with you in a minute.'

'I'll check right now,' he said, 'and I'll let you know.'

Nora turned back to the receptionist. 'It's the farmer I let the land to,' she said, in case Kate might think it was her intended husband. As if there was any comparison between Johnny Cassidy and poor Tim Dunne, who was the typical old-fashioned bachelor. She had to stop herself from smiling now. 'I hope you don't mind, but I have to go now. I have business to see to.'

Kate put her hand on Nora's arm. 'Well, I'm delighted to have seen you, and I must mention you to any of the girls I see from your old office, tell them how well you looked and how well you are doing. They will be delighted to hear.'

'Oh, do, please,' Nora said, feeling slightly light-headed now. They would all be surprised when they heard the news. If only they could see the young, handsome Johnny. Any one of the young women in the office would have been delighted to catch him themselves. And it was she, Nora Lamb, who now had one up on them all. 'It was so lovely to see you,' she told Kate, 'and do make sure to give them all my best.'

Chapter Thirty-Seven

When they arrived back in Dublin, there was an important-looking, long white envelope addressed to Ella. She held her breath as she opened it. 'I've got an interview in Clerys on Friday!'

'Clerys?' Nora repeated, impressed. 'Oh, that's great news altogether. That would be a lovely place to work.'

'That's what I thought myself,' she said, feeling all excited. 'I've to be there for eleven o'clock in the morning.'

'Is there any particular department you would like to work in?' Nora asked, as they walked through to the scullery to start the evening meal.

'I would be happy with anything at all. Just the thought of working in such a big, glamorous place would be brilliant.' She halted. 'What will I wear to the interview?' There was a note of panic in her voice. 'I haven't really got anything good enough.'

Nora held her hand up. 'Now don't start worrying. We'll go into town tomorrow and buy you something perfect to wear – in fact we'll go into Clerys itself. It will give you a chance to look around and see the lay of the land.'

'But we can't afford to buy clothes in Clerys – it's really expensive in there.'

'We can,' Nora said, tilting her head. 'I got a little windfall today, and it would be lovely to treat you to something nice.' She smiled.

Ella looked at her quizzically. 'Are you sure?'

Nora nodded. 'I'll go down to see Mrs Murphy later on, and

see if she wouldn't mind keeping an eye on Larry and Hannah while we're in town. We can bring her a little gift back to thank her.' She touched her hand to Ella's arm. 'I'm proud of you for getting an interview there, and I know your father will feel the same when he gets back. You've done very well.'

On Thursday night Ella had a bath and washed her hair, and was up early on Friday morning, her clothes all laid out on the chair in the corner of the room. It was a warm, sunny morning and her new cornflower-blue dress and jacket would be absolutely perfect. She couldn't believe how kind her Aunt Nora had been buying her a complete outfit. She had even bought her a full set of underwear, including two new brassieres – one plain, everyday one, and one which was decorated with lace.

As they had made their way through the store, Ella had thought she would love to work on almost every floor and in almost every department they came to. She felt so excited being in such a glamorous place that even if they asked her to work on the tobacconist counter – or the one in the food hall selling the strange-smelling German sausages – she would grab the opportunity with both hands.

As she walked into the store now for her interview, she thought again how grateful she was to her aunt for not only buying her the lovely, classy clothes, but for suggesting that they spend the afternoon wandering around the store, getting to know the departments and then having afternoon tea up in the gorgeous restaurant.

'It's just doing a little bit of homework about the place before you go in,' Nora had whispered to her as they stood at the perfume counter. 'And to let you get a feel for the place, so you won't be overawed tomorrow.'

Her aunt constantly surprised her with the things she said, and Ella realised that they had gained far more than they ever imagined when Nora had come to live with them. It wasn't just the day-to-day household duties that she had willingly set about, it was the care and attention she gave to all aspects of their lives, without interfering too much. Whenever problems arose, she always stepped back to let their father deal with them in his own way. And, she was not the old-fashioned, 'Holy Mary' sort that Sean, in particular, had worried about; in fact, she often made comments about things she thought were wrong about the church, and how priests were only human like the rest of us, and should not sit in judgement over anyone.

Ella was also grateful that her aunt had not interfered in her going out with Danny, and was actually encouraging him by inviting him to stay on in the evenings for supper, or telling them about a new film she'd heard was coming to the picture houses in Dublin. She was surprised when her aunt asked her if she knew how lucky she was, to have met someone who obviously thought so much about her. Nora also said that Danny was very intelligent but, more importantly, he was kind and considerate, traits not often found in young men. Neither she nor her aunt made any mention of the moody Sean, who was so wrapped up in his own musical world that he hardly had time to notice if anyone else needed help.

Once inside the ground floor of Clerys, Ella stopped one of the uniformed staff to check where she should go to ask for Miss McFarland, as her letter had instructed. As she followed the woman, she knew that if she hadn't been around the store yesterday, she would have been terrified.

Miss McFarland was younger than Ella had imagined, and very attractive, wearing an elegant black dress with several strands of pearls of varying lengths. Her long blonde hair – similar to her own, Ella noted – was pinned back in a neat, but stylish, chignon and she wore subtle make-up and lovely perfume. As she looked at her and listened carefully to everything she said, Ella made up her mind that, when she had money, she was going to dress like that.

After asking Ella lots of questions, Miss McFarland said, 'I don't know if you have any preferences about which department you would like to work in, but at the moment we have vacancies in haberdashery and ladies' handbags...' She stopped to consult her notes. 'And the gents' shoe department and on the perfume counter.' She then looked up at Ella. 'We also need staff in the restaurant.'

Ella stared at her for a few moments before she realised she was being offered a job and being asked where she would actually like to work. 'Oh,' she finally said, taking a deep breath, 'I would be happy to work anywhere.'

Miss McFarland's beautifully shaped eyebrows lifted in surprise. 'Well, in that case the restaurant need—'

Ella suddenly thought of the perfume department where she would have loved to work, but she knew little or nothing about the beautifully displayed bottles of exotic and expensive perfume. She imagined all the well-dressed, wealthy women she would have to serve and thought she might feel overawed by them. Then an image of the female staff in the restaurant, wearing white overalls and hairnets, flew into her mind. It was one of the places, she realised, she would not want to get stuck working in. Once in the catering line of work, she guessed, she might be there forever. She thought she would like somewhere in the main part of the store, where she would see people coming and going. Where she might see Nancy and Maeve and be able to have a few words with them. A lively, cheery sort of counter she would feel confident working on.

'The bag department,' Ella suddenly heard herself say. 'If it's still OK, I think I would really like it there.'

Miss McFarland looked at her and smiled. 'You can start on Monday. There will be a letter going out in the post to you today with all the details about your training period and your wages.' She pushed her chair back. 'I'll take you downstairs now and we'll sort out your uniform.'

Chapter Thirty-Eight

Johnny walked down Richmond Street, glancing at all the pubs and shops as he went along. His brothers always laughed about the local saying, 'In Liverpool there's a pub on every corner' – in this street, Johnny thought, there was one pub after another, never mind the corners.

Today, however, the bars weren't Johnny Cassidy's main interest. Today he was more interested in finding the place he and Sean had visited yesterday morning when they first arrived, the Strand Café. They had stayed out at his brother Charlie's house in Bootle last night, and when they left the house this morning, Sean had told his father, in no uncertain terms, that he would not be staying there again – funeral or no funeral.

'If I have to sleep in the feckin' road, I'm not sleeping in that kip again tonight,' he had said. 'I thought England was supposed to be miles ahead of us?'

'Don't be so ignorant,' Johnny had told him in a low voice. 'You know the people in Liverpool have just been to hell and back with the war. You can't expect their houses to be like mansions.'

'The state of that house has nothing to do with the war.' Sean pulled a face. 'You can tell it's never been kept clean. They're lucky to have a bathroom and toilet inside, and they don't even look after it. And the scullery! My stomach was turning, trying to eat the breakfast this morning sitting in there.'

'It's easy to complain, but the poor divils have still got rationing on over here,' Johnny told him, 'and the neighbours were good enough to give over some of their food for you and me this morning.'

'We didn't come with one arm as long as the other, did we? We brought over a big piece of bacon and chops and biscuits and chocolates,' Sean argued. 'And we'll be out buying drink, and whatever the shops will let us have, to take into the house for the wake.'

'You know what's wrong with you? You're spoiled, with your nice clean bed at home and your mother and then Nora running after you with ironed shirts and everything.'

'I could do with having my own room at this stage,' Sean said, 'I'm still sharing with you and Larry.'

Johnny let out a weary sigh. 'If you'd seen the way we grew up,' Johnny said now. 'I never had the luxury of my own bed. We had three in the one bed and at times my mother had to throw the old coats on top of us, but you would never have heard any of us complaining. You don't know you're born.'

'Ah, don't start with the oul' sob stories,' Sean said. 'I'm still not staying another night in Bootle.'

'Surely you can stick if for a few days?' Johnny said, his voice more beseeching now. 'Just until the funeral is over and we can catch the first boat back home.'

Sean had turned to look at him. 'I'm not complaining about Liverpool, it's the kip we're staying in that I'm complaining about. We need to find somewhere else to stay while we're here. It's not fair on them, for they haven't got the space for us and Auntie Annie can't look after her own family, never mind us. She seems overwhelmed with everything. Every time one of us speaks to her she looks as though she can't make out a word we say. Our Dublin accents can't be that bad she can't understand us.' He looked at his father. 'It's the truth, isn't it?'

'The poor woman hasn't been well since they lost Patrick in the war.'

'I know, and I feel sorry for her,' Sean said, 'but I think having us as well as a coffin in the house is too much for her. I want to go into a bed and breakfast. I know you said it's only throwing money away, but I'll pay for a room for the two of us somewhere in the city.'

'But the rest of the family are out in Bootle. We'll have to keep getting the bus in and out.'

Sean shrugged. 'I'd rather be where there are decent bars and places to go into. The ones out where the family live are dog-rough.'

Johnny had clenched his teeth together. He hadn't noticed before what a snob his son was turning into and wondered if Sean had maybe spent too much time with Mrs Keating and her brother. Although they were nice enough people in their own way, Sean was taking on their posh way of speaking and dressing, and talking like an expert about the food and wine he got in the fancy hotels he played in.

Another thing that was turning his head was the money he got from playing the piano in the various hotels and restaurants in the city, three or four nights a week now – and he was in such great demand that he could pick and choose whoever offered him the most money.

As they walked along in strained silence, Johnny wondered what his wife would have said if she could have given him advice. And then it came to him that she would say something like, *Didn't we always hope the children would do better than us? Didn't Sean work hard to pay for his own piano lessons this past year and bring home any money he had to help out at home? Didn't he help out paying for Ella to go to school, and buy clothes and toys for the younger ones. You can't expect him to mix in a totally different, wealthier world, and not take on some of the ways.*

Whether Mary had put the answer in his head or whether he came up with it himself, Johnny felt better, though the thought of going in amongst strangers didn't appeal to him. Then he remembered seeing a notice about accommodation when he was in the Strand Café. The thought cheered him up a bit, because the owners had been so welcoming any place they recommended had to be OK.

Sean said he wanted to have a walk around the city for an hour on his own to have a look at any music shops, and they arranged to meet later in the Queen's Head at the corner of Richmond Street.

By that time, Johnny hoped that Sean would be more relaxed and easier company.

He also hoped that his own patience would be completely returned.

Chapter Thirty-Nine

Sally Mather was behind the counter in the café, busy making a pot of coffee when the doorbell sounded. She turned around and then a smile broke out on her face. 'Nice to see you again – I didn't think we'd see you so soon.'

Johnny took his hat off. 'If I'm honest, neither did I.' He was pleased to see the cheery owner of the café was working again today. When he and Sean had arrived off the boat early yesterday morning, they were the first customers. The petite, dark-haired Sally and her son, David – who didn't look that much older than Sean – had come over to the table to chat to them. They'd guessed straight away that they had come off the boat.

'Well, find yourself a seat, love,' Sally said now, 'and one of us will be over to you in two ticks.'

Johnny looked around. There was a table in the corner, over by the window.

A few minutes later, Sally made her way over. 'Is everything going OK with the funeral arrangements?' she asked in a quiet tone. 'You were saying yesterday morning you didn't know when everything would happen.'

Johnny looked up at her. 'It looks like it's to be next Friday,' he said, 'but they should know for definite this afternoon.' He halted. 'Can I just ask you about the notice you have on the door about a bed and breakfast in Richmond Street? Where is it? I remembered seeing the notice yesterday, and I was looking as I was walking along this morning, but I didn't see anything.'

'Well, there's actually a few,' she told him. 'Some of the pubs have rooms above them.' She smiled. 'But the notice is about here. I have a few rooms upstairs and I've started letting them out.' She shrugged. 'It's a big enough house and now the kids are married, there's only me at this time of the year.'

She didn't look old enough to have kids who were married, he thought. 'And have you any vacancies at the moment? I'm looking for a room for me and Sean.'

She shook her head. 'Not tonight, but from tomorrow night I have a twin room free.' She suddenly stopped then she said, 'Hold on a minute and I'll just check with David.' She went back to the counter where her son was making up sandwiches. They spoke for a bit and then Sally came back. 'We've managed to juggle things around. David and his wife, Joanne, have a spare room that they sometimes let out, and the fella that was going into the twin room can stay at their house. He's stayed there before and they'll be glad of the extra money, and the lad can come and have his breakfast here, so it won't be any real bother.'

'Ah, no . . .' Johnny shook his head. 'Sure, that wouldn't be fair at all. I don't want to put anyone to any trouble.'

'But he's only staying for one night, while you and your son need the room for a few nights, don't you? And I have a nice big sitting room with a radiogram that the guests can use.'

As Johnny looked at her now, he was suddenly reminded of his wife, even though they were completely different looking. Sally was much smaller and had different-coloured hair. He couldn't put his finger on what it was, but whatever it was, it had given him a real start.

'Are you OK, luv?' she asked. 'I hope I wasn't pressurising you or anything. Maybe you would prefer to be in one of the pubs?' She pointed out into the street.

Under other circumstances Johnny might well have preferred to be in a room above a bar, but he knew the drink might prove too much of a temptation – and there would be enough over the days leading up to the funeral. His brothers were the same as himself, they all enjoyed a few drinks any time it was available.

'I think the room you have will suit us best,' he said, 'if you're sure we're not putting you out too much.'

'Not at all,' she said. 'I'll take your order now and then I'll let David know.'

Johnny lifted the menu. There was a good range on offer and cheaply priced, although he noted there were a lot of little stars beside some of the items. When he read down further, he realised the stars meant that certain things might not be available, and that margarine would often be served instead of butter. The thought of the oily, awful-tasting spread made Johnny's stomach heave a little. 'I've had breakfast not that long ago, so I might just have a scone and jam and a pot of tea if that's OK?'

'Of course it is, luv,' she said, smiling at him. 'You can have whatever you want, as long as it's not rationed.'

He smiled back at her. 'Between you and me, the tea we had out at my brother's was like dishwater.'

'Ah, you're spoiled with the strong tea in Ireland,' she told him. 'All the Irish folk that come in here tell us that. I'll see if I can squeeze a few more leaves into the pot.'

'That's good of you,' Johnny said. 'And if you don't mind, I'll just have the jam on its own – no margarine.' He suddenly felt he was acting like Sean now. 'I've never liked margarine – or butter – or anything like that.'

'Whatever you want, luv,' she said, smiling at him.

As she walked away, Johnny thought how long it seemed since he'd felt relaxed enough to even look at a woman in case she took him up the wrong way. After what had happened with Nora, he couldn't take the chance on leading someone else on. He had managed to make a mess of his whole life now, and he only had himself to blame. Just thinking about it brought a heavy feeling into his chest. He turned his gaze towards the window and the busy street.

As he sat drinking his tea, the café gradually filled up. When he had finished, he got up and made his way to the till.

'Me mam will be here in a minute,' David said, 'and she'll tell you the arrangements about the room.'

It suddenly dawned on him that he hadn't asked how much it would be. Then he shrugged to himself. Sean was insisting that he would pay, so why should he worry?

Sally came over to him. 'You can drop your bags off here any time,' she said. 'We're open until ten o'clock tonight.'

'That's a long day for you.'

'Oh, I'm not running this place on me own,' she explained. 'David and his wife, Joanne, and me daughter, Karen and her husband, Kevin all work here as well. The kids have been helping me since they were only nine or ten, just after the war started.'

Johnny quickly calculated that her son and daughter must be around twenty, so she could be forty, just a few years older than himself

When he left the café, Johnny went for a walk around the streets, shaking his head at the state of the lovely old buildings that had been badly damaged, some even brought to piles of rubble and stone. As his brother, Charlie had said, it would be years before the areas were cleared and rebuilt, but Liverpool, he firmly believed, would rise again as a beautiful city. Dublin had really got off lightly during the war. At the time everyone was in shock that places like the Phoenix Park could have been bombed by the Germans, and twenty-eight people killed in one incident. But, in comparison to the thousands that were killed in Liverpool and even more in London, it was actually very little. He looked at his watch now and decided he better get a move on or Sean would be complaining again. He turned around to see exactly where he was, and realised he had lost his bearings.

Johnny arrived in the Queen's Head in a bit of a sweat, and in an unusually foul mood. He had gone around in a circle several times, until he eventually decided to stop someone to ask if they could direct him back to Richmond Street. The man he asked was reasonably smart – the sort of man who you would expect to be civil and understanding of people in a strange city.

'What did you say?' the man had asked, with narrowed eyes.

'Sorry now, I was just asking if you could tell me the way to Richmond Street,' Johnny repeated, smiling at him.

'And do you live here?' the man asked. 'Do you live in Liverpool?'

Johnny shook his head. 'No,' he said, smiling amiably. 'I live in Dublin for my sins, although it has to be said it's not the worst place in the world.' He paused for a moment, then his face grew solemn. 'I'm actually over here for my father's funeral. He was living here for the last number of years, and my two brothers are over here as well. He died a few days ago, the Lord have mercy on his soul.' He made a small gesture of the sign of the cross.

The man looked at him and then said in a low, but clear voice. 'I never met one Irishman that I liked. They're all inbreeds and thieves and liars, to a man.' He halted, taking in Johnny's shocked face. 'And one less of them alive in Liverpool is good news as far as I'm concerned.' The man leaned in closer now. 'Now fuck off back to your stinking bog on the next boat and leave this country to the decent men it belongs to.'

Normally, Johnny would have been lost for words, but something in him reacted quicker than usual. 'Is that what you think? Well, I'll tell you something,' Johnny replied, 'we're from the land of saints and scholars, and I've never come across a man in Ireland who was as ignorant as you.' He straightened up and pushed his shoulders back. 'And after what our country has suffered at the hands of the likes of you, I'll still say to you, goodbye and good luck.' Johnny had then turned on his heel and walked off in the opposite direction.

Twenty minutes later he was standing at the bar in the Queen's Head, trying to calm down. The barman was a friendly young lad, but it had been hard for Johnny to break a smile to him as he ordered his drinks, far less get into casual banter. He had never come across anyone who had been less than friendly in the bars in Bootle, although he had heard from his brothers that abuse happened regularly on the building sites and if you wandered into the wrong pub. Whether it had been good luck or what, Johnny had never suffered such a thing himself, but he now knew what it felt like to have had his country and nationality attacked for absolutely no reason.

It had taken him two large glasses of whiskey in quick succession to still the racing of his heart. He had drunk the first one straight down at the bar, and then taken the second glass over to a table in the darkest corner, feeling that he wanted to hide away until he had gathered himself together again. He was thankful that the bar was almost empty. The insults that had been hurled at him kept whirling around in his head and he wondered now if that was the general opinion of Irish people in Liverpool. If it was, he wanted out of it. As soon as the funeral was over he wanted out.

He had eventually calmed himself down and had just been back to the bar and ordered a pint of ale when Sean came rushing in the door.

'I know I'm a bit late,' he said, clapping a hand on his father's shoulder, 'but I got caught up with some fellas.'

Johnny's heart jumped and he whirled around. 'What happened? What did they say to you?'

Sean stepped back, surprised. 'What are you talking about?' He looked at the empty whiskey glass in front of his father and rolled his eyes. 'Don't tell me you've been stuck in here drinking all the time I was away? I was just trying to tell you about the great chance I've just been given.'

Johnny took a deep breath. 'No, I was in that café from yesterday morning again, and I just got here a short while ago,' he said, 'Go on, I'm listening.'

Sean related how he had gone into a music shop and got chatting to a friendly fella, who told him all about the night life in the city. Sean had said he was interested in hearing any pianist or singers when he was over, to hear the sort of stuff they were playing, and the shop owner had shown him a board behind the counter which had notices about dances, concerts and also adverts for all sorts of musicians wanted, and others from artists looking for bookings.

He had then given Sean a card and said, 'This is a booking agent I know well, and he told me he is looking for singers who can do Frank Sinatra stuff.'

'When I left the shop I went into the first phone box I saw,' Sean said now, 'and I phoned the number and got straight through to him.'

'And what did he say?' Johnny asked.

Sean looked at his watch. 'He wants me to meet him in the Adelphi Hotel at three o'clock this afternoon.'

'The Adelphi? Begod, that's one of the fanciest hotels in Liverpool.'

Sean shrugged. 'I've played in the Shelbourne, haven't I? It can't be much posher than that.'

'That's true for you,' Johnny said.

The barman came with Johnny's ale and Sean ordered one as well.

'I might as well go and meet the booking agent,' Sean continued, 'because I'll get to know what sort of acts are doing well over here, and I might learn something that will help my own career and keep me ahead of the rest.'

'What's his name?'

'Ricky Hamilton. He sounded a nice enough fella on the phone. I think he's from London.'

'What if he offers you something? Would you think of moving over?'

Sean looked at his father as though he was mad. 'Not a chance. I'm getting on grand in Dublin, why would I move here? I just want to see the lay of the land.'

'How have you found the people so far?'

'Grand. All very friendly.'

Johnny thought back to the man who had been so aggressive towards him for being Irish. He was just going to tell Sean about it when the barman came over with Sean's drink and made a friendly remark about the weather, so Johnny thought he wouldn't bother mentioning it. Even thinking about it made him feel on edge, and there was no point in making Sean feel the same. It was best to keep things on as even a keel as possible.

'You'll be happy to know I've sorted us out with digs down here.'

'Where?'

Johnny could hear the suspicion in his voice. 'The café we were in yesterday morning. They have rooms above it.'

Sean thought for a few moments. 'That will be grand,' he said. 'It seemed decent enough and it's central for everything. I'm planning on spending more time down here in the city than back in Bootle anyway, so it's ideal for me.'

'Oh, well, that's all that matters, isn't it?' Johnny said, holding his hands up. 'As long as it suits you and your big music career, never mind about the reason that brought us here. We're only burying my poor oul' father in a few days' time.'

Sean looked at him. It wasn't often that his easy-going father reared up on him. 'I didn't mean it like that.'

'I never even got to see him before he died.' Johnny's voice was hoarse now. 'And I feel bad I didn't see him while he was still in the whole of his health, but with one thing and another I didn't have the money.' His eyes filled up. 'And then what happened to your poor mother and the little one she was carrying. It's not been the easiest few years.'

Sean felt a wave of sympathy. 'I didn't mean that the way it sounded,' he said, placing a hand on his father's shoulders. 'We'll be out at the house for the wake and the funeral and everything. We'll make sure we do all the right things.'

Johnny closed his eyes and nodded. 'None of the others have said anything, but I know they must be thinking bad of me for not being here.' He felt in his coat pocket for one of the hankies that Nora had carefully ironed and folded in neat squares for him. 'But with me starting at the hospital last year and trying to keep things going at the house . . .'

'I know it's not been easy on you,' Sean said, 'and I know there's times when I'm so busy I might forget, and I'm sorry if it came across the wrong way or anything.'

Johnny waved away his apologies, blew his nose, and then gave a watery smile. 'We're all doing our best,' he said. 'And the truth is, at times it's not good enough. But what can we do? Only keep trying.' He lifted his glass and took a big gulp out of it.

Sean did the same and they then sat back in silence for a few minutes, each with their own thoughts.

'It could all have been worse,' Sean suddenly said. 'Imagine what would have happened if my Aunt Nora hadn't come to look after us all when she did. Hasn't she been great?'

Johnny's stomach clenched.

'She would never take Mammy's place,' Sean went on, 'but she's looked after us as good as many other mothers. There's nothing she wouldn't do for us.' He looked up at his father's pale face. 'Isn't that right?'

'It is,' Johnny said. 'She's a great housekeeper, all right.'

'Ah, she dotes on Larry and Hannah,' Sean said, glad to get on to a safer, more positive subject now. 'You'd think they were her very own the way she goes on. She never missed a day or night putting the cream on Hannah after her accident, and she's brought Larry out of himself. We all know he's clever like Ella, but he's getting more confident in himself, he's a cheerier lad and everything.'

Johnny sat silent now, just nodding his head.

'Weren't we blessed that she came to live with us?' Sean said. 'Weren't we blessed?'

Chapter Forty

Mrs Murphy slowed down as she came up to the Cassidys' house. There was a builder's van outside and the front door was wide open. She wondered what could be happening, especially with Johnny away in England. He had called in before he left, but he hadn't said a word about any work that was needed doing in the house.

When Mary was alive, she would just have tapped on the open door and walked in to see what was going on, but it was different now. In fact, as she thought about it, she wouldn't have had to ask, because Mary would already have told her any news or anything different that was happening. Her cousin, Nora Lamb, on the other hand, would tell you nothing.

Rose didn't hold it against her. Nora meant no harm, and knew no other way of working. Mary Cassidy herself had told Rose what a private, closed person her cousin was, and said that even though they had known each other all their lives, that there were still a lot of things she didn't know about her cousin.

Rose had seen how hard the woman had worked, and how she had transformed from the uptight spinster aunt who hadn't a clue about children to the caring mother figure she had become to the family. And it hadn't escaped her notice either, the changes that had occurred with Johnny himself. He was up and out to work at the hospital every morning and was bringing home the money needed to run the household.

He had changed in other ways too. It was rare now that Mrs Murphy saw him drunk on a Saturday afternoon or Sunday – or hungover the following mornings – as he used to be. He was more likely to be out walking in the park with the two younger ones or walking them into the city centre to let Nora get on with the housework. In fact, when the weather was decent, Rose noticed that he was hardly ever in the house at all.

She heard voices now and footsteps coming to the front door, so she took a few steps backwards not to be meeting them head on.

'This afternoon is fine by me,' she heard Nora say. 'We want the outside work done as quickly as possible, and the plumber's shop will bring all the things I've bought as soon as you've got everything done.'

'I'll get back to the yard now,' the man said, 'and I'll have the lads out to ye with the bricks and the cement-mixer around twelve o'clock.'

As she turned to go back into the house, Nora saw Mrs Murphy. She paused, then folded her arms and said, 'Isn't it another lovely morning?'

'It is, thanks be to God. And how are they all?'

'Oh, grand,' Nora told her.

'Ella enjoy her first day in Clerys?'

'She said that she loved it.'

'Grand, grand, I'm sure she'll do well. Any news when Johnny will be back?'

Nora shook her head. 'I'm sure we'll hear soon.'

'I'm just walking down to the bakers; can I bring you anything back?'

'That's good of you, but I was there yesterday and I think we'll manage until tomorrow.'

There was a small silence, during which Rose thought she would be damned if she was going to ask about the builder's van. 'Ah well,' Rose said, hitching her shopping bag up on her arm, 'I'll be seeing you then.'

'We're having a bit of work done while Johnny is away,' Nora suddenly said.

'I saw the builders' van, right enough – the roof didn't fall in or anythin'?'

Nora gave a little smile. 'No, thank God. We're having a bathroom built off the scullery downstairs. They're starting this afternoon.'

Rose looked at her in amazement. 'A bathroom? Like the ones at the other end of the terrace?'

Nora nodded. 'Seeing theirs gave me the idea how it could be done, so I just went to the same builders and plumbers.' When the neighbours at the end had had theirs finished, they invited all the neighbours in to view the small square bathroom with the toilet, bath and sink. 'To be honest with you, it's the one thing I've struggled with, being used to my own bathroom down in Tullamore.'

Mrs Murphy nodded her head. 'Naturally,' she said, 'you would be bound to miss that if you were used to it. Well, for the likes of me, I couldn't afford it, and I suppose what you never had you never miss. Johnny never mentioned it, but he probably had enough on his mind.'

Nora's face suddenly became serious. 'He doesn't know,' she said. 'I was just thinking about mentioning it to him, when he got word about his father.'

'Well, it will be a lovely surprise for him. I can't imagine anyone not happy to have an inside closet, unless he's worried about the money. I know he has the good job now, of course, but he could be anxious committing himself to it.'

'Johnny doesn't have to worry about it,' Nora said. 'I'm paying for it. I decided to sell two fields.' She was talking quicker now, as though it was all very exciting. 'You know I have the farm down in Tullamore? Well, the farmer who rents it has been asking me for years to actually sell him a few fields next to his own, and I was just wondering how we could afford the bathroom, and then it suddenly hit me the other night in bed, that I could sell the fields and put the money to better use in the house here up in Dublin.'

'Begod, that's great news!' Mrs Murphy said. Imagine this

woman – only a cousin of Mary's, not even a sister – selling land and everything to help the Cassidys out. She'd never heard anything like it. 'I'll tell you something, you've been the making of that family. God was good the day he sent you up here to Dublin.'

A pink tinge came to Nora's cheeks. 'Do you think so? Do you really think I've made a difference?'

'Indeed I do,' Rose Murphy said. 'Those poor children were lost before you came, Ella was like a little skivvy and Sean was running wild. To see the difference now in a couple of years is unbelievable.' She leaned in closer. 'And it's not just the childer, the difference in Johnny Cassidy is obvious too.'

Nora's hand came up to her throat. 'In what way?'

'Between you and me, drink was getting to be a problem with him, even when Mary was alive.' She shook her head and made a little hissing sound. 'After Mary died I thought he would go to the dogs altogether, but the accident with little Hannah must have hit him badly, the fact that he wasn't here that day, that he was down drinking in the pub. That put a bit of a halt to his gallop, but I think it's the steady job in the hospital that has sorted him out, and again – that's all thanks to you.'

'Well, it's very good of you to say so. There are times when you're not sure if you're doing the right thing or not, especially when you were never blessed with children yourself.'

'You would never know it,' Rose said, 'you're a natural with them.' She paused. 'I can see you're busy so I'll let you go.'

'It was nice chatting,' Nora said. 'If I'd known I'd bump into you, I'd have had the kettle on. You must come in for a cup of tea another time.'

As she walked away, Mrs Murphy wondered about all the big plans and changes going on in the house just down the road from her, and her not knowing a single thing about it. Rose always thought she could read people well, but Nora Lamb had certainly taken her by surprise today, and it wasn't the first time. She had made change after change in the house, bringing fancy stuff back from Tullamore, buying good-quality, second-hand chairs and cupboards from Paddy Bracken for the scullery and bedrooms. And although Nora said they didn't cost much, Mrs Murphy wondered now if they were really as cheap as she had described. She knew that the spinster was fairly well off, but handing out all the money needed to add a bathroom onto the house was a whole different matter. It was an awful big investment for a house that wasn't her own, a house that she might only be living in for the next few years. It made Rose wonder what Nora's plans for the future were, when Johnny Cassidy eventually remarried. He had everything going, and now he had a steady job and knocked off the hard-drinking, there's few women who would refuse him.

Surely Nora wasn't planning on living with the family for ever? A new wife might have different plans. She thought of the old saying – a new broom sweeps clean.

And Nora was the old broom.

Chapter Forty-One

Ella stood back to check how the cream leather bag with the polished bamboo handle looked. She had put it in the middle of the display attached to railings at the back. She tilted her head left then right, checking that it was straight.

Miss Roarty, the head of the department narrowed her eyes. 'You have it more or less perfect, just check that it's secure.'

Ella went to check and was happy all was fine. She then took up her duster and went around the displays straightening things and then giving them a rub over. She had done that every single day since working in Clerys, and so far, had not found a speck of dust. There was the odd fingerprint on the patent leather bags, but nothing much else. She would have been surprised to have found anything dirty or dusty with the amount of staff that were squeezed into the section.

It crossed Ella's mind that there were more staff than needed on a lot of the counters, but she kept herself busy – or looking busy when there was nothing to do. She was out at the front of the counter, dusting the shelves there, when she heard her Aunt Nora's voice.

'Well,' her aunt said, 'so this is where you work.'

'It is,' Ella smiled at her aunt then glanced around to see if Mrs Roarty was there, and when she could see no sign of her she turned back to her aunt. 'We're not supposed to talk unless we're serving customers,' she said in a low voice, 'but if you move over to the side there, nobody will really notice.'

'The men finished the roof on the bathroom today,' Nora said, her eyes shining. 'They only have to put the bathroom suite in and link up the pipes, then tile the floor and it's all done. I left Hannah with Mrs Murphy so I could come in and buy some nice new towels and some mats for the bathroom.'

Ella flicked her duster over a shelf, 'I can't believe it,' she said. 'We've got our own brand new bathroom! Daddy is going to be over the moon when he gets back.'

Nora's brow furrowed. 'I just hope he doesn't mind I went ahead without telling him. I didn't mean to, I didn't expect them to do it all so quickly.'

'He's not going to mind, he'll love it the same as everyone else.' Ella paused to glance behind her again, and then she whispered, 'I've just seen Miss Roarty, our boss, at the other side of the counter, so I'd better look as if I'm busy.'

'You can serve me,' Nora whispered. 'I might even treat myself to a new bag.'

'Well, that's grand then,' Ella said, putting her duster behind the counter. She smiled and placed her hands flat on the glass counter. 'I can't get in trouble for chatting to a customer, because Miss Roarty is always saying we have to help and encourage them to buy a bag.' She waved her hand to the bags on display on a stand on the counter and then over to the ones at the other side. 'Have you seen anything that caught your eye? What colour and style were you thinking about?'

Nora pointed to a small navy bag with white piping which was standing on the counter. 'Could I have a look at that one, please?' She moved along the counter, checking the bags, then she indicated a plain navy clutch which was on a hook on the railings. 'And that one too.'

Ella lifted the first bag and gave it to her aunt to examine, then went to get the other one. As she was unhooking it, she saw two youngish women coming towards them.

'Nora Lamb!' one of them exclaimed. 'Fancy meeting you in here. How are you?'

Ella watched as her aunt turned around and saw the colour drain from her face.

The other woman said, 'We heard how you're all settled in Dublin now – and the good news about you getting married soon. Are you in looking for something for the wedding?'

Nora turned back to Ella. 'Thank you,' she said, without looking at her, 'I'll be back shortly . . .' Then she moved away from the counter, the two women following closely behind her.

Ella looked at her aunt open-mouthed. Who were the women, she wondered, and what on earth were they talking about? Aunt Nora obviously knew them, Ella thought, and she could not understand why she hadn't told them straight away that they had been misinformed. Why, instead, she wondered, had her aunt gone off with them?

A while later her aunt came back to the counter. 'I think it's best if I leave the bag until another time,' Nora said, checking her watch. 'It's more important that I get the things for the bathroom that we need, and then get back home to collect Hannah. I wouldn't like Mrs Murphy to think I was taking advantage of her.'

'Did you know those two ladies?' Ella asked. 'The ones you went off with earlier?'

'Yes . . . I used to work with them in Tullamore.' Nora threw her gaze to the ceiling and said, dismissively, 'They're a gabby, giddy pair. They've never changed a bit.'

'I thought they said something about you getting married?'

Nora's eyebrows raised. 'Me? I think you must have heard them wrong.'

There was a small silence, then Ella noticed Miss Roarty looking down at her. 'Don't forget I won't be home after work. I'm meeting Danny for something to eat and we're going straight out to the pictures.'

'It was strange that Aunt Nora said I'd heard it all wrong,' Ella told Danny later as they sat in a café in O'Connell Street eating fish and chips, 'but I'd swear I heard them talking about her getting married.'

Danny shrugged. 'Maybe somebody said it to the women for

a bit of a laugh, and she might have guessed that and been embarrassed. Women can be horrible to each other at times.'

'Do you think so? You don't think she's met someone and doesn't want to tell us?'

'What?' Danny shook his head. 'Not a chance. She's a lovely woman, a real lady, but – an' I don't want to be disrespectful – she's a bit past it, isn't she? I mean, if she was ever going to be married, it would have been a good many years ago. She's kind of missed the boat there, if you know what I mean. And when would she ever get the time to meet anybody? She's in the house every night.'

'What about during the day when Daddy and me and Sean are all at work and Larry's at school? She could take Hannah with her.'

'Nah,' Danny said, shaking his head. 'I just can't see it.'

When they left the café they walked up to a public phone box and rang the number of the Strand Café in Liverpool as Nora had asked Ella to find out what was going on with Johnny and Sean. The noise at the other end was loud, but eventually Ella understood from the man's voice that both her father and Sean were out in Bootle, and that, if she rang back around ten o'clock, there was a good chance she would catch them.

After they came out of the cinema later, they walked down O'Connell Street chatting about James Cagney's brilliant performance in *White Heat*. Then Danny said, 'I hope it didn't upset you, all the talk about mothers in the film.'

She looked at him.

'I think about my mother every single day,' she told him. 'And it's not just the film, there are reminders about mothers everywhere, every day, so you can't really ever get away from it.' She paused. 'You must think about your mother too.'

'I do,' he said, 'I miss her, and she's only a few hours away on the boat, but I can't get to see her because of her bastard of a husband.'

'Oh, Danny...' Ella squeezed his hand.

'I try not to think about it,' he said, 'and I am saving up to go over sometime.'

'I'll go with you,' she said. 'We could go next year. I could stay with one of my uncles, I'm sure.'

He stopped. 'Would you really come with me?'

'As long as my father lets me. He should be OK if I'm staying with relatives.'

'That would be the gear,' he said, drawing her into his arms. 'Absolutely the gear.'

Ella smiled and rolled her eyes. She always thought it was funny when he used the Liverpool saying.

Danny bent his head now and kissed her gently on the lips, then he pulled her tighter and his kisses were harder. When he moved away, he looked very serious. 'You know, Ella Cassidy, I don't know what I'd do without you. I love you with all my heart.'

'And I love you too,' she whispered. 'The very same.'

They walked down until they came to a phone box and went inside and tried the café number. This time a woman answered and after a few minutes Johnny came on the line. 'Sorry I missed you earlier, Ella, I was out at your Uncle Joe's house. How are things back at home? How are the little ones?'

'They're both grand,' Ella told him. 'But they keep asking for you and Sean. When are you coming home?'

'Well, the funeral is in the morning,' he said. 'And we'd planned on coming back the day after, but the only thing is that Sean has been asked to play next weekend in a big hotel here and the money is terrific. It's around three times what he gets in Dublin.'

'That sounds a lot,' she said. 'But what about his work here? And what about the hospital?' Ella suddenly felt concerned for her father's job. Sean would be fine, the man in the music shop was easy-going with him. Her father was in a different position, she couldn't bear the thought of him losing it after all the trouble he had had finding a decent one.

'They're OK,' he reassured her. 'We've phoned the hospital

and the music shop and they've said it will be OK. Sean phoned the hotel he was playing in and they're getting somebody to cover him.'

'I'll let my Aunt Nora know, then.'

'Is everything in the house OK?'

'It's grand,' Ella said. 'In fact, there's a surprise waiting on you.'

'What?' he asked. 'Is there anything wrong?'

Ella thought there was an edge to his voice, as though he was anxious. 'No, no, it's a good surprise.' She couldn't tell him about the bathroom as her aunt was determined that it should be a big surprise. And the way he sounded now, it didn't seem the right time to tell him about her new job. 'We're all fine,' she said, 'Aunt Nora's been great.'

There was a silence.

'Daddy?' Ella said. 'Are you still there?'

'I am,' he said, 'but this must be costing you a fortune, so I'll get off now. You can let everybody know we'll be home on the boat a week on Monday morning. It's not worth coming home, so me and Sean will go straight into work.'

The pips suddenly sounded on the phone, and they just had time to say goodbye then Ella placed the receiver back in the cradle.

Chapter Forty-Two

Sally was sitting on the sofa in the sitting room with a glass of Babycham on the coffee table in front of her, and beside it there was a glass of beer.

'Everything OK, luv?' she asked. 'I've poured you a drink.'

'Oh, thanks,' Johnny said, looking a bit distracted.

'Are they all OK at home?'

He nodded. 'Well, Ella said the little ones are asking for me, but everything is fine.'

'They sound well looked after with their aunt and big sister, I wouldn't worry.'

'Thanks,' he said, holding the glass up. 'It's great to have a quiet few minutes.'

Sally drew her legs up under her. 'I often feel like that,' she said. 'But it's nice having a bit of company at this time of night. I know I often have people staying, but most of them go to bed early, and if I'm working in the café at night I don't see them until the morning.' She smiled. 'But it's always nice to know there's someone else in the house apart from meself.'

'Do you mind me asking about your husband? You were saying that he's gone for a good bit of the year?'

Sally shrugged. 'He goes youth hostelling. He sets off around March and is gone until the weather starts to get very cold in October.'

Johnny looked at her in amazement. How could any man leave such a cheery, lovely woman? Lovely in every way, he thought. Lovely natured and lovely to look at. Tonight, he thought, with her tiny, petite, figure and her dark hair tied back in a ponytail, you could almost take her for a girl instead of a woman in her late thirties. But, in the short time he had known her, he had begun to think that she was one of the most capable women he had ever met.

'I hope you don't mind me saying, but when I heard you and your son talking about you living on your own, I thought you were either widowed or divorced.'

Sally sighed and took a drink from her Babycham. 'In a lot of ways, I might as well be.' She bit her lip. 'I hate talking bad about poor old Bill, because it's not his fault. He doesn't choose to be the way he is...' Her eyes filled with tears.

Johnny put his drink down on the table and instinctively moved over beside her and put his hand on her shoulder. 'You don't need to talk about it,' he said. 'I understand. I know how I felt after Mary died. There were days when I saw somebody we knew and I'd walk a mile around in a circle to avoid having to talk to them.'

She shook her head, smiled, and then wiped a stray tear away. 'Aw, look, it's just a bloody disaster and I'm just one of thousands of people in Liverpool affected by that bloody war. The poor old city took a right bashing – you'll have seen all the houses and buildings that came down – and God knows when it will all be sorted and back to normal. I don't think it ever will, it just goes on and on...'

They sat for a few moments in silence then Johnny said, 'We just have to keep hoping that one day we'll feel happy again, but it's not easy to believe it at times.'

'People understand when somebody dies,' Sally said, 'but it's a different situation altogether when you're left with a person who is nothing like the one you knew.' She looked at Johnny. 'Bill used to be an absolutely brilliant husband and father. He was clever and a great laugh, and when he went off to fight during the war, we were just grateful we weren't one of the families that got telegrams too saying "killed in action".

'I thought we were really, really lucky that he came home

looking the same as he went. But,' she gave a great sigh, 'looks can be deceiving. He didn't get a scratch on him, but what he saw and what he went through changed him forever.' She lifted her glass again. 'It was all the usual things you hear about war but you don't think too deeply about, until you know somebody that's been there and seen it first-hand, and they tell you all about it. Bill saw so many of his platoon blown to bits and the upshot of it all is that his nerves have totally gone. Most nights he can't sleep, and then he's always exhausted, in a kind of daze. It's not helped that his ears were badly affected by an explosion late on, and when he came home he had to get hearing aids.'

'Oh, God – and does that help him?' Johnny asked, thinking how awful that must be for a relatively young man.

'Most of the time it helps, but they can irritate him by making the wrong noises louder. He went back to work in the café a few weeks after he came home, but every noise startled him. The door banging, the coffee machine, the sound of lorries going past, loud music.' She shook her head. 'And everything annoyed him if things weren't exactly the way he wanted them, and if you asked him what was wrong, he didn't want to talk about it. It got really difficult with David and Karen. They didn't know what to say or do at home or in the café without him over-reacting. Eventually, after a big blow-up in the café about some noise that he couldn't handle, I dragged him to the doctors. They explained a lot of soldiers were the same coming home from the war, and that it might be best for him and the family if he gave up working for a bit and took some time to himself. I was surprised when he agreed, and he started reading more and then he started walking.'

'Well, that's got to be good for him,' Johnny said. 'After Mary died I started walking more myself. I didn't plan it, but if I went out to the shops I would go the long way round just to be out and looking at anything, except the empty space she had left in the house. At times I would be gone for hours, and if it hadn't been for the children, I don't think I would have come back.'

Johnny lifted his glass and took a drink. He wondered what

Sally would think if he told her that his walks invariably took him to the pub, and that's where he had been the day poor Hannah got scalded. And of course, that had all led to Nora Lamb coming to living in their house. 'At times,' he said, 'we men just aren't good at handling things.'

'Well, Bill's long walks grew into practically morning until night, and we never knew where he went. Then he started cycling, and he could go thirty and forty miles in a day, without any great reason for going to the place he had been to. He said he needed to tire himself out so he would get a decent sleep, because he kept waking with nightmares. And he preferred the quiet of the country and the fact there weren't bombed out houses to remind him of the war. He heard about youth hostels and started doing overnights, then long weekends away. After he did a week-long cycle trip around the Lake District, he began going off for weeks on end. He would work out the route he was taking, and which hostels he was staying in, and then get in touch with post offices and organise to pick up his pension at different places.'

'And does he keep in touch while he is away?'

'Oh yeah,' she said, 'he sends postcards from every place he is in to let us know he is all right. Every couple of weeks he phones as well, so we always have an idea where he is. A couple of years ago he did a tour lasting months; he took his bike on the train down to some place near Land's End and then stayed in hostels all the way up to John O'Groats.'

'That was some cycle,' Johnny said, not knowing whether he should be impressed or commiserate with Sally.

She gave a weak smile. 'His time away has got longer and longer,' she said.

'Did you argue about him going?'

'At first I used to get really upset, but if he was here for long there would be rows and big silences.' She shrugged. 'The kids would tiptoe around him, and after he went things would get back to normal and we were all more relaxed in the café and at home.' She finished the last of her Babycham. 'I don't think I've told all that to anybody in years… All our family and friends know what's happened, and they kind of understand it, but we don't really talk about it. Bill can't help the way he is, and we've just had to get on with things. David and Alice both got married young, both at eighteen.' She made a little face. 'I don't know why, we weren't exactly a good example to them. You've seen the two of them work in the café with their other halves.'

'Well, that seems to have worked out well,' Johnny said. 'They must all get on great together, and from what I've seen, David and Karen obviously think the world of you. It sounds as though you have it all well worked out. It's a good business, always busy every time I look in.'

'It was Bill's idea,' she said. 'We'd just bought it before the war broke out. We had this house first – it was Bill's mam's and she left it to him when she died. The café came up for sale and he was dead keen, so…' She put her empty glass on the table. 'I thought I'd just work in it for a few years, and that Bill would take on other staff. I never envisaged I would end up running the place.' She gave a long sigh. 'To be honest, it's not the dream I had when I was young. It's not how I imagined my life turning out.'

Johnny got to his feet now. 'Well, I can agree with every single word you've said there. The situation I'm in now is not what I imagined, not at all.'

For a moment he thought he might pour out the story about all the difficulties he had gone through in the last few years. That he might even confide in her about the situation he faced now. But no… He looked at her and smiled. 'Thanks for the drink, I'd better head off to bed now to make sure I'm out in Bootle early in the morning.'

'Are you very sad about it, your father's funeral?' Sally asked. 'I know, depending on their circumstances that to some people it can actually be a relief.'

'To tell you the truth, I don't know what I feel.' He ran a hand through his brown hair. 'Probably guilt more than anything. And regret. I wish I'd got over to see him before he died.'

He did not add that he already lived every day with guilt and regret. Sally Mather was a lovely woman, but she had enough problems without him telling her all about himself. And while her problems were ones she didn't deserve, Johnny knew he deserved absolutely everything that happened to him.

He walked over to the door and then he turned to look at her. 'I hope that at least some of your dreams come true. You deserve it.'

She looked at him now. 'That's very nice of you.'

'Well,' he said, 'I know what it's like to have dreams that are taken away from you...'

Their eyes met and Johnny knew, in that moment, that she liked him as more than just friends. He liked her too. But he reminded himself, Sally's husband might not be around, but she was still married to him. And then there was the problem at home with Nora. She would be there, waiting for him.

The thought sent a shiver through him.

He smiled then he put his hand on the door knob. 'I'll say goodnight to you now.'

Chapter Forty-Three

Sean looked at the music sheets and nodded his head. 'They all look grand,' he said. 'I've played a few of them before in the Shelbourne. If it's OK to come into the hotel to practice like you said, then I'm sure I'll be fine.'

'No problem,' Ricky Hamilton said. 'I've got it all sorted for you. The hotel is looking for a pianist cum vocalist on a regular basis, someone who can do all the new American stuff. They were really keen when I told them about you.' He tapped a finger on the song sheets. 'I thought we should mix up the different moods – a bit of Sinatra, Nat King Cole, and The Ink Spots – all that kind of romantic, but classy stuff that the women like to listen and dance to.'

'Have you told them I'm not available on a regular basis?' Sean said. 'I'm only here next weekend and I don't know when I'll be back.' He was suddenly feeling a bit out of his depth.

'It would be worth your while coming over at weekends,' Ricky told him. 'The money is better than anything in Dublin. You can even fly over and it will still be worth your while. They'll put you up in a nice room here in the Adelphi – it's top notch. And there are other upmarket hotels in Liverpool that will pay good money for a class act. All that voice training you've done makes you stand out from the usual acts.' He held his hand out and moved his fingers as though playing a piano. 'Just think about it, your music could be heard all across the Mersey. And you don't know who might hear you and offer you a contract.'

'You mean making records?' Sean imagined his records in the music shops in Dublin, a picture of him sitting at the piano on the record sleeve.

'You could be heading down to the Big Smoke with me,' Ricky elaborated. 'You know you're good enough, don't you?'

Sean gave an embarrassed smile and a shrug. This was all going a bit too fast for him. Liverpool was a big enough change, and from what he'd heard of London, it sounded a bit much for him. He had only been looking around to see what the music scene was like in the big English cities. He'd never imagined meeting a booking agent so quickly, and one that would have all these big ambitions for him.

'Look,' Ricky said, 'I know you're still young and coming over here from Ireland must be a bit overwhelming. But think of it this way: starting earlier means you'll have a longer career. If you want to move over here, I'll look after you. I'll make sure you're seen and heard in all the right spots. What do you say?'

Sean's eyes narrowed in thought. 'We'll see how it goes on Saturday,' he said once more.

He lifted his hat and coat. His father was probably in bed now back in Richmond Street, and would be wondering where he was. Tomorrow was the funeral out in Bootle, and he would have to meet up with all his uncles and cousins again, and say and do all the right things.

It was a miserable, wet morning as father and son got into the taxi outside the Strand Café. As they drove along through the grey city streets, Johnny rubbed a circle in the steamed-up window, to let them look out. As he stared at the big buildings and then at the docks, his thoughts shifted from Sally Mather to his father, then across the sea back home to the children.

'The Germans did their best to wipe poor old Liverpool out, didn't they?' Johnny commented as they passed more and more devastated buildings.

'I don't know how your brothers have stuck it out here with the state everything is in,' Sean said. 'You would have thought they would have wanted to get out of it and come back home to Ireland.'

'Sure, how could they?' Johnny said. 'Their wives are from Liverpool and all their families were born and have grown up here. And where do you think they would live if they came back to Ireland?'

'I heard some of them saying they only rent the houses, so they could move over and rent a house in Dublin.'

'You make it sound easy,' Johnny said, an edge to his voice. 'Where would they find work? You saw how hard I had it trying to find a full-time job. There's a lot of rebuilding going on here, so at least there will be work for some of them.'

'What are we doing after the funeral?' Sean asked, as they drove along Stanley Road towards the church in Bootle. He had been asked out to drink in some of the pubs in Bootle with his cousins, but had managed to avoid it because he felt it was not the sort of night out he was used to. Having spent time with his uncles and cousins, he realised he had nothing at all in common with them, and he knew that his father's barbed comments about him being more used to mixing with the hierarchy, the Keatings and their type, actually had a note of truth in it.

'We're going straight out to the cemetery after the funeral Mass,' Johnny said, 'then we're going to a pub beside it for soup and sandwiches. One of Jimmy's daughters organised it and we're all giving something towards the cost.'

'I'll give towards it too,' Sean said. 'What I get paid for playing in the Adelphi will more than cover the whole trip over and the stay in the bed and breakfast.'

'Well, that's something,' Johnny said.

'Weren't we lucky to stumble on that café with Sally and then get digs with her? She's a lovely woman, isn't she?'

'We were, and yes, she's very nice.' Johnny deliberately kept his comments brief as he did not want Sean to know that he had got to know Sally Mather better than he realised.

The taxi drew to a halt and they stepped out opposite the Catholic church where the funeral Mass was to be held. Sean paid the taxi and then they crossed the road and walked over into the church.

As Johnny knelt in the front pew of the church, his eyes closed, he went back in his mind to when his father was a younger man and their mother still fit and well – before the family took their own paths in life. While he was very sad now at this newest loss, he could take comfort from the fact that they had been a happy enough family, and, even after being widowed his father had lived a good and long life.

He watched as Joe went up to do a reading on the altar, followed by one of Charlie's daughters.

Johnny turned at one point to glance at Sean and noticed his eyes were filled with tears. He was surprised, thinking that the boy hadn't known his grandfather well enough to feel so upset. Then it dawned on him that Sean was probably thinking of his mother's funeral. A heavy weight came down on Johnny's chest as he thought back to that awful day, and he wondered if his own family would ever regain the happiness they once had when Mary was alive.

Chapter Forty-Four

Johnny thanked the uniformed man for holding the door open for him as he left the Adelphi. As he walked down the steps of the impressive building, his hand running along the polished brass railing, he felt a swell of pride when he thought of the reaction that his son had got that night. Frank Sinatra couldn't have gone down better he thought. And he couldn't believe how confident Sean was, knocking out all the songs on the piano without a wrong note, his voice was better than he had ever heard it.

Johnny had been in two minds about going when Sean asked him to come for at least part of the evening. He'd dreaded the thought of going on his own, but Ricky Hamilton had said he could join him, and he would keep a table at the side of the room where they would be near the piano. The Adelphi was too fancy for him – it was not the sort of place he had ever been socially. It was a very different situation when you were playing with a band, which gave you a right to be there. But for Sean's sake, he had to be there. The boy was only just seventeen, and although he was now as independent as he would ever be, Johnny knew the way the music business went, and although Sean was full of all the exciting possibilities that the booking agent had described, Johnny knew things often came to nothing.

It had crossed his mind to ask Sally to join him but he'd decided against it. He would be sitting drinking with her, and he would probably have to dance with her. He couldn't deny that the thought of holding the petite, attractive woman was a nice one, but he knew there was no point in getting any friendlier with her.

It was a dry evening so he had walked down through the streets, taking care not to look directly at anyone, remembering what had happened before when he had innocently engaged with a stranger.

He had mentioned the incident to Sally in one of their chats, and she had nodded and said, 'Yeah, there are some people who don't like the Irish or the Welsh, or even folk from Manchester. They just don't like anyone who's not from Liverpool. I think the war didn't help, the Irish not getting involved in the war.'

'It's understandable,' Johnny said, 'but there's a terrible history of the Irish being persecuted by the English. You must know all that with your granny coming from Galway.'

'I do,' Sally said, 'but me granny was always careful talking about anything like that.'

Ricky Hamilton was nicer than he imagined, and straight-talking. He had bought Johnny a whiskey which made him feel easier in his surroundings, although he was conscious that he couldn't get too relaxed and slide into a night of heavy drinking. He had to keep things on an even keel as he had somehow managed even on the day of his father's funeral.

His brother Joe had got totally scuttered, and so had a lot of the others, but that was only to be expected after burying their father or grandfather who had lived with them and they were going home to their own houses and beds. Johnny couldn't risk anything going wrong back at the bed and breakfast. Drink had become his enemy. It had betrayed him too many times and left him fearful. He had drunk all right, but he had drunk slowly and carefully.

Tonight it was important that he didn't put a foot wrong. He sat in the palatial ballroom, listening to Ricky Hamilton reiterating all the things that Sean had already said about how he could launch his career in Liverpool.

'I don't think he's ready to make such a big move yet,' Johnny said. 'He's still got a lot of ties in Dublin, and he's got his whole life ahead of him.'

'Hopefully he has,' Ricky agreed, 'but he won't have the unique value of being only seventeen or eighteen for too long. That's the thing that's getting them here: the crowds all love to see a new, up-and-coming act that they think will hit the big time. You must know that, being in the music business yourself?'

As Johnny listened to the music agent, he realised that his own ambition was more limited than Sean's. He loved playing – and he would still love to do it full-time – but he was happy in the familiar surroundings of the Dublin venues, playing the same tunes every week, drinking and chatting with the other lads in the band, picking up his few shillings at the end of the night. He was a fairly decent fiddle player – nothing more, nothing less.

And tonight had underlined what he already knew. His son was in a different league altogether. He looked Ricky in the eyes. 'Do you really think Sean could make it big?'

'With the right management – undoubtedly.' Ricky said. 'I cover a lot of acts, but if I find someone special, they will get all my attention to make sure they get every opportunity that's going. I think Sean could be up there with the best, making records and everything.'

Sean came to the table, anxious to hear what they thought of his performance.

'Excellent,' Ricky said, clapping him on the shoulder.

Johnny agreed and said he had never heard him sing better, and that he could now add the Adelphi to his list of big-name places he had played in.

Sean lifted his beer and took a good drink of it. 'I thought it went well,' he said, 'but it's good to hear it from somebody else.'

Johnny said he was leaving after the break and told Sean to be careful walking back to their bed and breakfast later.

'I'll be grand,' Sean said, rolling his eyes as though his father was showing him up.

Ricky had winked at Johnny and said, 'I'll arrange for a cab to drop him back.'

Johnny had walked back himself, glad to be out in the fresh air. He walked down Ranelagh Street then crossed over to Church Street. As he walked along, he went over the events of the past week in his mind, the wake out in Charlie's house, and then the funeral. He thought of all the people he had talked to – about how their lives had been so devastated by the war in so many different ways.

But the one thing that had struck him had been the way the people of Liverpool had picked themselves up and put their lives together again. People like his own family, and countless others like Sally Mather.

As he walked towards the Queen's Head, he thought about his father and the fact he wouldn't see him again, and then he thought about Mary. Then he went inside and ordered a double whiskey. And just as the barman lifted a glass, he changed his mind.

'Sorry now,' he said, 'forget the whiskey. I'll just have a pint.'

An hour later Johnny walked into the Strand Café, planning to sit down and have fish and chips and a cup of tea before going up to his digs. It was absolutely packed with the crowds of people that had just come out of the cinema. He stood for a few moments, trying to decide what to do.

David Mather was just coming back towards the kitchen having served a table, and came over. 'You're going to be a while here if you want a seat.' He thought for a minute. 'What are you having?'

'Fish and chips,' Johnny said. 'The plaice if you have it.'

'That's two shillings. If you pay me now and go on upstairs, I'll send, Cyril, the Saturday lad, up to you with it in ten minutes. And me mam's in, so she'll likely make you a cup of tea.'

As he went upstairs to the big living room, Sally came out from her bedroom.

'Ah, it's only you, Johnny,' she said, smiling at him. 'You're back fairly early.'

He explained about the fish and chips.

'I'll go and make the tea,' she said, and laughed. 'I'll butter a slice of bread and I'll steal a few of your chips to make a butty.'

A few minutes later a knock came down the hallway and as Johnny came out of his room, Sally was ahead of him. 'If it's the young lad,' he said, 'tell him to keep the tanner change.'

'He'll be delighted,' she said, 'it's usually threepence they give.' She came back with the steaming parcel wrapped in newspaper. 'You get started,' she told him, putting it down on his plate, 'and I'll bring the tea and bread and butter in now.'

When they were sitting down she said, 'Go on, tell me how it all went.'

'Ah, he was great,' Johnny said, 'no doubt about it. He never missed a note and the crowd loved him.'

'You must be very proud of him,' she said. 'If they're saying he's good enough to get a recording contract, it sounds like he could end up really famous.'

'The only thing is, he'd have to move over here, and I just feel he's too young. I know they're saying that could be a good thing, but Sean can be awkward and temperamental at times.'

'Well, kids can all be like that,' Sally said, 'I've gone through some rough patches with my two, and having to deal with Bill as well...' She smiled and raised her eyebrows. 'They do grow up eventually, and get past all the nonsense, and Sean seems a lovely lad to me, and you and him seem to get on well.'

'It's not just the music, Sean made a bit of a fool of himself in the pub after the funeral.'

'What did he do?'

'Well, he was feeling guilty about not spending more time with his uncles and cousins.' Johnny sucked his breath in through his teeth. 'So without saying a word to me, he went to the lad behind the bar and said he was buying everybody in the pub a drink.' He shook his head. 'It just wasn't the time or the place to go and do that sort of thing. Most of the men were twice his age and could hardly afford a drink for themselves, and the young lads were the same. None of them are in the sort of jobs that earns much, and they live hand to mouth.' Johnny held his hands up. 'I'm not making little of them – I've had plenty of times where I didn't know where the next penny was coming from. So, I knew what they were all thinking with Sean playing the big "I am".'

'What reaction did he get?'

'The one I was afraid of,' Johnny said. 'After they'd all drunk what he bought them, and a good few more, you could hear the comments being made in the background about how he'd spent little or no time out in Bootle with the family. And of course he'd told one or two about playing in the Adelphi and when that got around they were sniggering and calling him Frank Sinatra.'

'Oh, God,' Sally said. 'I can see what you're saying, but I think some of those lads sound like right scallies.'

'Sean was ready to turn on them – I told you he had a bit of a temper – and I had to get him out fast or we'd have had a fight on our hands.' Johnny let out a long, low sigh. 'That was all I needed at my father's funeral.'

'Did you have a row?'

Johnny rolled his eyes. 'There's no point. He just doesn't get it. He thought he was being nice and friendly to them, so I didn't make too much of it, because he had his big night ahead of him and all the practice it entailed, and I didn't want him raring up on me and getting all upset. No doubt I'd have been blamed if anything went wrong. I just want to keep the peace until we're home.'

'Are you looking forward to getting home?'

Johnny nodded, finishing off the last of his chips. 'I'm really looking forward to seeing the children. I've never been away from them for long before, and I suppose I worry about them.'

'You said it was an aunt looking after them?'

Johnny's throat tightened. 'Well, a cousin of my wife's they call aunt.'

'That's good of her. And does she help you out often?'

He suddenly felt he could not breathe properly. 'Nora lives in the house with us.' He spoke slowly and deliberately. 'She came after Mary died because we were told we had to have a woman in the house and she's been with us since.'

'That must have been a great help to the kids, and to you as well.'

Johnny closed his eyes for a few moments, then shook his head. 'If you don't mind, I don't really want to talk about it.'

There was a silence, then Sally said, 'Oh, God, I'm sorry, I didn't mean to upset you.' She leaned across the table and covered his hand with hers. 'Are you OK?'

He looked up at her now. She was a nice, sensible woman who had been through a tough time herself. Maybe she would understand and could help or advise him. Who else could he talk to about it? 'I've got landed in the most dreadful situation with Nora. She's been good with the children – God knows she has. Nobody could have been better. She's got to love them as if they were her own, and she's given up her job in the hospital where she lived. And there are times when she helped us out financially and everything.'

Sally nodded her head slowly, digesting all he was telling her. 'And is Nora around the same age as yourself?'

'She's a bit older,' Johnny said, 'maybe seven or eight years.'

'Has she ever been married?'

'No,' he said. 'Never. She owns a house and a farm in Tullamore – just over an hour on the train from Dublin. She used to go down there often at the beginning, but she only goes occasionally now or if she has business.'

A picture was beginning to form in Sally's head. 'Do you think,' she said in a low, sensitive tone, 'that she might have a notion for you?'

He closed his eyes for a few seconds and then nodded his head. 'That's what's worrying me.'

'And do you have a notion for her?'

'Not in a million years! She's a lovely woman, kind and help-ful, but she's the last woman I would think that way about.' He felt as bad as he could about himself now. If Sally knew what had happened between himself and Nora, she would think what a liar and awful hypocrite he was. She would feel he had used the poor woman. And yet, he felt he was honestly telling the truth because at no point had he had a notion for her.

'Well, there have been plenty of people who have ended up married because of circumstances like that.'

'I couldn't,' he said, giving a shudder. 'I just couldn't . . .'

At no point had he planned what had happened. But he knew, from the evidence of the bottles of sherry and whiskey, the flimsy nightwear, that Nora herself had carefully planned it. Drink, he knew, was the major player in what had facilitated it. Drink and the long months of celibacy. And while it was easy to point the finger at her, at the end of the drunken day he had given in to some dark corner in his nature. A dark corner he would never visit again, if he was to live and die the life of a priest.

'The longer she's there, the more settled she will feel,' Sally said, her face sympathetic.

'That's exactly what I'm worrying about.'

'What about your daughter, Ella? Wouldn't you think of her taking over for a few years, until the little girl's at school?'

Johnny hadn't considered it before, as he still thought of Ella as a child herself. But, she had grown up in a lot of ways, including the romance between herself and Danny Byrne. 'You might have hit on the right idea,' he said, smiling at her. 'It would let Nora go back to her own place, because it's what she's going to have to do sooner or later.'

'Let the poor woman down gently,' Sally said. 'Don't push her out too quick. It sounds like she's made the family her own and she's going to find it hard to go back to the life of an older, single woman.'

'I wouldn't do that,' he said. 'It wouldn't be fair. I feel guilty enough as it is. Not having talked about it we've led her to believe – *I've* led her to believe – that she was a part of the family for the long-term.

'You see, when she came to help, after Mary died, my only thought was keeping the family together. I couldn't see any further than the next day, the next week. I never thought it through – at the time I wasn't seeing things clearly. I never thought what it would mean down the road for us and for her. I was just getting by as best I could, then it dawned on me that she was all settled in Dublin and thinking...' He shook his head.

'I think you need to talk to her,' Sally advised. 'And you need to do it sooner rather than later for everyone's sake.'

There was a loud bang and they both looked towards the door, and then they could hear the sound of heavy feet coming up the stairs. Sally pushed her chair back and went towards the hall.

'Mam?' David's voice called. 'Are you there Mam? We've just had a phone call from the police!'

'I'm coming!' Sally rushed out to meet him.

Johnny suddenly felt alarmed. Was it Sean? He looked at the clock. Had something happened to him on his way back from the hotel? No, he reasoned, that agent had said he would get him a car home.

He heard Sally cry out and, with his heart thudding, he went out to see what was happening. David was standing with his arms around his mother. More footsteps and voices were coming up the stairs now.

'It's me dad,' David said, his eyes wide with shock. 'He's in a hospital somewhere in Scotland. He was found out near a youth hostel in Loch Lomond.'

Johnny looked from one to the other, not knowing what to say. 'How is he?' he finally ventured.

'He's dead,' Sally sobbed. 'He was lying out in a field for days, and they've only just found him.'

Chapter Forty-Five

As he and Sean walked from the bus stop towards Islandbridge, Johnny made a concerted effort to shift his thoughts away from the tragedy that Sally had suffered in Liverpool, to the happy reunion with Ella and the children awaiting him at home.

It was strange how someone he had known such a short time could have such an effect on his own life, but Sally Mather had appeared at the right time, and her kindness and common-sense approach had helped him sort a few things out in his mind. He had felt bad leaving her so soon after she had heard the devastating news about her poor, unsettled husband, but he knew she had her son and daughter to support her. He also had to see to his own family commitments back home.

As they came towards the house, he could see Larry and Hannah at the window waiting for him and his heart lifted. A few moments later they came out with Ella to greet him, and he was surprised when she laughingly told him she was going to blindfold him as they had a great surprise waiting for him.

Johnny did not know how to react when Ella took the scarf off which covered his eyes. He stood there in shock, looking from the bathroom which had been added to the house in his absence to Ella's delighted, grinning face.

'How . . . ?' he eventually said.

'How do you think?' Ella said, laughing. 'Aunt Nora, of course!' She looked over at Danny, who was standing in the scullery with Larry and Hannah, who were all smiles at the great excitement.

Johnny turned to look at Nora, his face white. 'I don't know what to say or think...'

'You don't need to say anything,' she told him. 'It's something that we all badly needed, and I was able to put my hands on the money. After I saw the lovely job the builders did for the people down the road, I did a little bit of investigation and it was all sorted out quicker than we could ever have hoped for. Seemingly, they're doing such great business with the bathrooms they know exactly what they're doing.'

He nodded, his jaw clenched in thought. 'This is – this is too much, Nora. It must have cost a fortune. We can't let you pay for all this.'

'Aren't I going to get good use out of it?' she said.

Johnny looked at her, and felt a wave of fear wash over him. Nora, he realised, had bought a long-term stake in the house with the bathroom. She had bought a long-term stake in all of their lives.

'Here, here!' Sean said, clapping his hands together. 'Can we use it straight away?'

'The toilet is OK, but not the bath and sink,' Nora told him. 'There are still some pipes to be connected, and the cement between the brickwork needs a few more days to dry out before they can put the plaster on.' She smiled.

'Daddy!' Ella said, putting her arm through his. 'I know it's a big surprise, but I don't know anybody who wouldn't be all excited about getting a new bathroom in.'

Sean put a hand on his father's shoulder. 'It's time to move into the new modern world. And we'll all be glad not getting frozen going to the jacks.'

Then, while everybody joined in with the laughter, Johnny suddenly felt he was like a cornered animal. If he acted any way other than happy, no one would understand. He hardly understood himself.

He turned around and forced a bright smile, then held his hands up in defeat. 'Well, I can't argue with you all. Of course it's brilliant. I was only worried about the money, and I'll sort that out with your Aunt Nora.'

'It's all paid for, done and dusted,' she said, with an airy manner.

He looked over at her now and nodded. 'We'll see,' he said.

Nora turned to the boiling kettle. 'You must be tired and hungry after travelling all night and going straight into work. We've pork chops and potatoes keeping warm, so if you all go and sit at the table inside, Ella and I will bring it in to you.'

'I'll head off now,' Danny said, going out into the hallway. 'I only called in to see your new bathroom, and me granny will have me dinner waiting on me.' He looked at Ella and winked at her. 'I'll see you tomorrow.'

Johnny and Sean went out into the hall too, and took their coats off and rolled up their sleeves, and then Johnny brought his travel bag into the living room to take out the toys and sweets they had brought back for Larry and Hannah.

After dinner, Nora left Ella to talk to her father in private in the living room. She took the younger two into the scullery to play with the colourful strips of plasticine that he had brought them, while she washed up.

'So it's all sorted, you're out working in Clerys every day now?' He shook his head as though finding it hard to take it all in.

'I know it's a shock for you that I decided to leave school,' Ella said, sounding breathless, 'but I had been thinking about it for a while.' She looked at his strained face and felt guilty. 'I would have waited until you came back, but the nuns were talking to me about ordering textbooks for next year, and I just had to make up my mind quick.' She shrugged. 'I had sent off a few job applications and I didn't expect to get anything so quickly. I thought you would be back and I would have talked it over with you before starting.'

Johnny looked at Ella. 'Clerys is a grand place to work, and if you're sure it's what you want...?'

'It is, Daddy. I love it. It's a brilliant shop with a great atmosphere in it. Most of the staff are really nice, and I look forward to getting up every day.'

'Well,' he said smiling at her, 'it sounds like you've done the right thing. There aren't many people who go to work and love what they're doing like that.'

She threw her arms around his neck. 'Oh, I'm glad you're OK about it – I was worried.'

Johnny hugged her tightly, knowing that Ella's freedom to fly on in her adult life with her new job in Clerys had clipped his own wings tighter than ever before.

He had a sudden urge to run down to the telephone box and pour all this out to Sally and ask if she had any other suggestions, but the poor woman had enough to worry about. The last day he and Sean had spent in Liverpool, he'd seen how anxious all the Mathers were, trying to find out more about how Bill had died.

Just before they left for the overnight boat, Sally told him how hard her husband's loss had hit her. 'Everyone says I lost the Bill we all knew and loved when he came back from the war,' she had said, tears streaming down her face, 'but I had always hoped he would come back. Not just for me, but for the kids as well. Every time I saw him wheeling the bike into the house I hoped and prayed that his brain would be back to the way it was. A right waste of time all those prayers were.'

Johnny looked out of the window now, remembering all the prayers he had said after Mary died. When he thought about it now, most of them had actually been answered. Hannah had recovered from the scalding. Her arm and leg would always bear the scars, but, with every passing year, they had faded.

His prayers for Sean and Ella had worked out. They were both now striking out on their own in the world as young adults, and as happy as you could expect given the difficult times they had been through.

And his prayer to find a substitute mother to his children had been answered by the presence of Nora Lamb. He wondered if he could now pray to his wife to forgive him for the terrible things he had done. Could he now pray for help to get rid of her?

Chapter Forty-Six

Sally Mather shielded her eyes against the early afternoon sun, to look out of the window of the hired car as they drove out from Balloch village, along the banks of Loch Lomond. She and David, and her daughter Karen, had one last stop to make before they headed back into Glasgow to catch the train home to Liverpool. A stop to find the exact place that Bill Mather was found.

They turned off the road onto a long narrow driveway.

'That's it straight ahead,' Karen said, pointing to the roof and turrets of the old Victorian building.

David turned to look at his mother. 'What do you think?' he said. 'Will we drive right up to the house or have a look around here?' He pointed back to the loch. 'They said it was across the road from the youth hostel, so I reckon it was down by the water there somewhere.'

'Well, we're not going to find the exact spot,' Sally said, 'but I really just wanted to see the hostel and the surrounding area he was in. He talked occasionally about the hostels, and I always remember him saying the one at Loch Lomond was his favourite. It was one he came back to year after year.'

There was a silence as they all thought of the man who had left them behind in Liverpool, while he spent most of his time on a bicycle going from one remote place to another, preferring to live amongst strangers.

'Well, let's drive up to the hostel,' Sally said. 'That will give us some idea of where we are.'

They went up the narrow, tree-lined drive until it suddenly widened, and they had a clear view of the side of the magnificent building.

'It's a fantastic place,' David said, slowing down again. 'It's absolutely huge – like a castle. I wonder if we can just go in?'

'The hostels are all closed at this time of the day,' Sally said, 'I think people have to be out between ten o'clock and four.'

'Well, there's a car parked over there,' Karen said, indicating to a gravelled area at the front of the building, in the middle of which stood an old, ornate fountain. 'We might as well go in and see if there's anybody there. If there's not, we can have a look around the grounds.'

They parked the car, then got out and stood for a few moments taking in the breathtaking views around them – the mansion house's formal gardens set on different levels, the patchwork of fields beyond, and looking further again to the glistening blue water of Loch Lomond. As she took in all the peaceful beauty, Sally knew exactly why Bill had come here.

She turned back to look at the magnificent old building, the tall, stained-glass windows, the castle-style turrets, the steps to the left side leading up to a conservatory, the steps to the right leading down into the landscaped gardens.

'The entrance is over there at the side,' David said. 'It's through that porch.'

As they walked towards it, the door opened and a man in his late fifties came out. He came to meet them, his hands on his hips and his brow furrowed. 'Can I help ye?'

'I'll do this,' Sally said. 'You two wait here.' She quickly went over to him and introduced herself, and he told her he was the assistant warden. They spoke for a few minutes, and as the conversation went on, his face and whole demeanour softened.

'Oh, God,' he said, his hand coming out to shake hers. 'I'm sorry to be meetin' you under these circumstances. I knew poor Bill and always looked out for him as soon as the fine weather came. A quiet and polite man, who always kept himself to himself.'

Sally felt a stab at her heart as she listened to the stranger describing the man she had loved and had borne two children by.

'I was here the day he was found,' he told her. 'As you probably know he was staying at the hostel and we knew something was wrong when he didn't turn up in the evening, and then again the next day. He had booked in for two weeks, and still had a week to go. He was one of the ones you could always depend on to be here when he said he was coming.' He shook his head. 'I still canny believe what happened, the shock when the police came to say they'd found him down by the water.'

'Could you show us where it was?' she asked quietly. 'We'd like to know where he spent his last few hours.'

'I can indeed,' he said, 'but would you maybe like to come in for a cup of tea or anything?'

Sally shook her head. 'Thanks, but I think it would be best to get this over and done with.'

The warden came with them in the car and they went back down the long hedge-lined driveway. He directed them until they were on a lane which led down to the edge of the water.

The car stopped and they got out, and then the warden led them up through a field towards a small copse surrounded by thick bushes. He pointed to the trees. 'I don't know if you want to go any closer, but it was in there he was found.'

Sally felt that same stabbing sensation again. She looked at David and then at Karen. Both had tears streaming down their faces as they stared at the lonely, painfully beautiful spot, where their father had taken his own life.

'The only good thing I can say is that Bill is now at peace,' Sally told Johnny when he rang her the following week. 'But it wasn't easy when we found out what had happened. We all thought it was an accident, that he'd been knocked off his bike. To find out he'd committed suicide was terrible.'

'I'm so sorry for your trouble,' Johnny repeated for the fourth time. 'I wish I was over in Liverpool now and could say it to your faces, instead of over the phone.'

'It's nice to hear your voice anyway,' she said, 'and I appreciate you ringing all the way from Dublin.'

'It's nothing,' he told her. 'I was looking forward to talking to you. Since I came home I've realised that I don't talk to anyone like that, I don't open up the same with other people...'

There was a silence and then Sally asked, 'How have things been with Nora? Have you had a chance to talk to her yet?'

He gave a sigh loud enough for her to hear over the phone and told her about the bathroom.

'Oh, Johnny,' Sally said, 'it sounds as though she's planning to be in your house for a long time.'

'She must have been thinking about doing the bathroom before I went away, because she had the money and the builders and everything organised to do it very quick.'

'You're going to have to speak to the poor woman before she makes any more plans that can't be changed.'

'I'm just waiting for the right time,' he said. 'I've already told her I'm going to sort the money for the bathroom, but I'm waiting for the right opportunity to say to her about getting someone else in to help while I'm at work.'

'What about Ella?'

Johnny then explained about Ella working in Clerys.

'I feel guilty,' he said. 'It's my fault. I wasn't thinking straight after Mary died, and I didn't think of the effect this might have on Nora. Taking her away from her home and life was selfish of me. I should have looked further down the line and after the first year was up I should have encouraged her to go back to Tullamore.'

'It's easy for any of us to see things in hindsight. We've all got things we would do different if we got the chance.'

Johnny walked back to the house feeling more positive than he had felt in a while. He would find the right time to talk to Nora and put things right.

Chapter Forty-Seven

Ella was up early on Wednesday morning – her day off – to go into Dublin with her Aunt Nora and the two little ones, to get them new clothes and shoes for going back to school in early September. She put on a navy and grey floral dress with a matching coat, which she had bought in the Clerys summer sale, along with navy court shoes. She tied her long blonde hair neatly back, and then pulled on a grey felt cloche hat. She liked to dress up more since she'd begun working in the department store, and had seen how well-dressed many of the customers were.

Her Aunt Nora complimented her taste, and showed her outfits she might like in her magazines, and Ella's friend, Nancy, had taken them to a discreet, second-hand clothes shop out in Ballsbridge, where they could buy upmarket clothes for far less than the shops, which helped stretch her wardrobe.

On the bus into town, Ella sat in one seat with Larry while Hannah sat with Aunt Nora in the seat behind.

'They have the cardigans and jumpers I've knitted, so we just need two warm skirts for Hannah and trousers for Larry,' Nora said, patting him on the head. 'The fellow will be as tall as me, soon, he's growing that fast.'

Hannah looked up at her aunt and smiled. 'Can we get sweeties and ice cream, Auntie Nora?'

'If you're good. And after we've got all your nice school things – sure it's a fine thing to be starting school, Hannah.'

'Dad gave me the money for all the things they need,' Ella said, 'and he's said you haven't to spend a penny on them.'

'We'll see,' Nora said, smiling. 'And don't forget you and I are down at the church tonight helping with cleaning the church and polishing the brass candlesticks.'

'Tonight?' Ella said. 'Oh, God! I thought it was tomorrow night. I've arranged to go to a show in town with Danny. He bought the tickets at the weekend.' She looked anxious now. 'I don't want to let Father Brosnan down.'

'Ah, don't worry,' Nora said, 'Mrs Murphy can come tonight instead.'

'Are you sure?'

'She's always happy to get out of the house in the evenings. She says she finds them so long on her own. I think the poor soul is lonely.'

'There's no fear of our evenings being long or lonely, is there?' Ella said. 'There's always something going on.'

Nora nodded. 'Oh, and don't let me forget to go to the haberdashery for buttons, and we said we might look at some blouse patterns for you.'

'That sewing machine you brought up from Tullamore has really come in handy, hasn't it?' Ella halted. 'Do you ever miss your old home?'

Nora shrugged. 'Not really. At times it's hard for me to even remember what my old life was like.'

Ella grinned. 'I'd say it was a lot quieter.'

'It was actually lonely too,' Nora said. 'I can understand how Mrs Murphy feels, and I'm a lot younger than her. Most nights when I came in I never saw a soul until the next morning at work. The highlight of my week was going for my shopping and going to Mass, and then of course, I loved coming up to visit you lot every fortnight or so, going for walks around the park with your mother.'

Hannah tugged on her sleeve. 'Auntie Nora,' she said, smiling up at her, 'Larry says you're our mammy now.'

Nora's face lit up. 'Did he now?'

Larry turned around. 'You *are* our mammy. The teacher in school said you do everything that a real mammy does. You help us with our reading and writing, and you make us sausages, and you say our prayers with us.'

Tears suddenly rushed in Nora's eyes. She looked at Ella and whispered. 'I've never thought of trying to replace your mother, I've never said anything to either of them to think like that.'

Ella's face crumpled. 'Oh, Aunt Nora, nobody would think that. The truth is, you *have* been their mammy. You've been with them since they were little, and it's only right they should think of you like that.'

'Well, I'm privileged,' Nora said, taking her hanky out now to dab at her eyes. 'I'm privileged to be a part of this family.'

Ella reached a hand back and squeezed hers. 'And you always will be a part of our family'

That evening, after they had all eaten, Ella discovered she had run out of hair lacquer. She put her coat on to go to the local shop for some and said she would take the two young ones along with her for a walk. Nora went into the scullery to wash up, while Johnny and Sean sat listening to the sports results on the radio.

A knock came on the door and Sean stood up quickly. He grinned at Johnny. 'That should be for me.' He went out to the door. 'Yes, lads,' he said, 'bring it right through.'

Johnny turned around to look, and saw two men coming in carrying a piece of furniture. 'What's all this?'

Sean came into the living room, pushing the table and then an armchair aside to make room for the men to put it down by the window. 'I got a bit of a surprise for us all,' he told his father. 'A radiogram. I thought it was about time we had one, so we can listen to records.'

'Begod,' Johnny said, an amazed look on his face, 'won't that be the best thing ever?'

Sean pressed a silver coin into the two lads' hands telling

them to buy themselves a drink, then he saw them out to the door and came back in.

Nora came along the hallway, to stand by the living room door.

'Well, what do you think?' he said, clapping his hands and rubbing them together. 'Martin was buying a new one for the shop, and he let me have this one for ten pounds. Wasn't it a bargain?'

'It's beautiful, surely,' Nora said, 'and won't it be great for you to play your own kind of music on, rather than depending on the radio all the time?' She paused. 'But that's an awful lot of money for you, Sean. Can I help you towards it?'

'Not at all,' he said. 'You're the last one I'd take money off, after all you give to us. And I was thinking that you would get great use of it during the day when you're here on your own.' He looked at his father. 'Isn't that right?'

Johnny nodded. 'It is indeed.' He went over to examine it now, lifting the lid to look at the record player and then opening the doors of the walnut-veneered cupboard below to check out the radio.

'I brought a few records home with me,' Sean said, going out to the hall. 'A Glenn Miller and a Nat King Cole, and a children's one for Larry and Hannah.' He came in carrying them and was just taking a record titled *Children's Favourites* from the sleeve when the front door opened and Ella and the younger two came in.

There was a great commotion when they saw the radiogram, and a few minutes later the children were clapping and dancing along to songs like 'The Ugly Duckling' and 'The Teddy Bears' Picnic'.

'Oh, this is brilliant,' Ella said, examining the record player. 'Nancy's older sisters have records, so I'll ask if we can borrow a few of them at the weekend.' She looked at the clock and tutted. 'I suppose I'd better get a move on; Danny will be here for me in twenty minutes. I'll have to drag him out when he sees all the records.' She lifted up the Nat King Cole record to look at the sleeve.

'Oh, look at the time,' Nora said. 'I need to hurry up too, I said I would call for Mrs Murphy.'

When she went out of the room, Ella turned towards her father. 'Daddy, can I have a word with you in the scullery?'

'Is there anything wrong?' Johnny asked.

'No, I just want to check something with you before I go out.' She looked at Sean. 'You come into the scullery too. We won't be a minute.' She looked at Larry and Hannah. 'Now, don't dare touch anything, just sit nice and listen to that lovely music.'

'Larry and Hannah said something when we were out,' she told them, when they were out of earshot. 'And I wanted to check it with you before saying anything.' She took a deep breath. 'They want to start calling Aunt Nora Mammy.'

Johnny's face paled.

'I think Larry just wants to be the same as the others in his class. The first time he said it I got a shock too, but when I thought about it ...' She shrugged. 'Where's the harm? It's different for me and Sean, because we were older and we knew our own mammy for much longer.'

'No,' Johnny said. 'No! She's not their mother. She's not even their bloody aunt!'

Sean and Ella looked at him in shock.

'What the feck are you going on about?' Sean asked. 'What's your problem?'

'Under no circumstances is she going to be called Mammy!' Johnny's eyes were almost bulging with rage and he was shaking his head vehemently. 'Under no circumstances at all.'

Ella put her hand on her father's arm. 'God, Daddy, what's wrong?'

He stretched his arm out and jabbed a finger up at the ceiling. 'She is not going to be here for a lot longer – she can't be. One of us can take them to school early, or we can ask Mrs Murphy, and we can get a woman in to mind them after school until we come in. They're old enough now and it's time she went back to her own place in Tullamore.'

Sean's hand came up to his mouth, and he shook his head as though he was too flabbergasted to speak.

Ella leaned in closer and whispered. 'Have you had a falling out with her or something?'

Johnny took a deep breath to still himself. 'No ... not as such.' How could he explain that it went far beyond falling out? How could he explain the horrendous situation he had found himself in? 'It's the bathroom and everything, the way she just went ahead and altered our house as though it was her own.' He closed his eyes and then moved his hands out in a slicing gesture. 'It's just hit me that she's planning on staying here for the rest of her life. It's not what I envisaged and it's not the right thing ... I feel she has me trapped. She'll have to go home.'

'I don't understand any of this,' Ella said. 'Aunt Nora's been so good to us all, we can't just throw her out. We were all talking about Christmas when we were at the shops today – can you imagine how Larry and Hannah will be if she's not here?'

Johnny ran his hands through his hair now, and then clasped them at the back of his head. 'I'm not saying straight away, but she'll have to go.'

Sean moved forward and grabbed his father by the front of his shirt. 'That's enough!' He put his face close to Johnny's. 'Have you forgot that woman saved our family? We were nearly being taken into the orphanage – we could all have been split up. I was so frightened of being put in reformatory I was planning on running away. If it hadn't been for her, God knows what would have happened to us all.'

'Get your hands off me!' Johnny said, stepping back in shock. He pushed his son away. They stood facing each other now, eyes locked in anger.

'Stop it!' Ella said, pushing between them. 'For God's sake!'

Then Johnny suddenly noticed that Sean was actually shaking. He gave a great sigh and looked away. 'Look, Sean,' he said, 'I don't want to fight with you over this.' He paused. 'I know what you're saying is right, and I appreciate all she's done up to now. It's the future I'm thinking of.'

Sean narrowed his eyes. 'No, you don't appreciate her,' he said, his breath coming in short pants now. 'There's more to this than you're telling us. Have you met another woman or something? Have you got your eye on one of the nurses in the hospital?'

'No,' Johnny said. 'There's no woman. It's not that. I'm just thinking about the long-term – Nora's future as well. It's not fair that she should be giving up the chance of meeting somebody herself.'

Footsteps sounded on the stairs and everyone stood in silence as Nora came down to lift her coat and hat. 'I'm going off to the church now,' she called in a cheery voice. 'I'll see you all later.'

When the front door banged shut, Ella turned to look at her father incredulously. 'You've got this all wrong. Aunt Nora has no interest in meeting anybody. She's just happy here being part of our family. She was nearly in tears this morning, when Larry said about her being like a mammy.'

A huge lump seemed to form in Johnny's throat, and he had to swallow several times before he could speak. 'Well,' he said, 'I understand what you're saying about the little ones and Christmas, but I'm just warning you...' He looked from Sean to Ella. 'If it goes on much longer, I don't think my nerves will be able for it.' He put his head down. 'There's a side to her you don't know.'

Sean pushed past him now, heading towards the hallway. 'No,' he said, 'it's more like there's a side to *you* that we didn't know.'

Johnny closed his eyes. He couldn't argue there. The only way they would understand was to tell them what had happened between himself and Nora. But how could he? They were too young to understand and they would blame him.

'Forget I said anything,' Johnny said now. 'We'll just carry on as we are.'

Chapter Forty-Eight

Nora walked into Clerys on a clear but cold Saturday morning in October and after a few stolen words with Ella, she went upstairs to the tearoom. She enjoyed coming into the department store more often now that her niece worked there. It gave her a sense of belonging, adding another place that was part of her new life in Dublin. Luckily, she hadn't run into anyone from Tullamore there again and she had pushed aside the memory of that occasion.

Veronica was already there, over by the window. Nora fluttered her hand in the air to indicate she had seen her, and was grateful to see her friend was on her own. On a couple of occasions Dominic had turned up with her again. That had always made her feel awkward, but in the last few months there had thankfully been no sign of him joining them. Nora knew her friend thought she and the shy, kind Dominic would have made a good match and couldn't understand Nora's indifference to him.

Veronica had even gone as far as to say, 'At our age, Nora, we have to look beyond love and romance, and think more about companionship, kindness and security.'

There was a time when Nora would have agreed with her, but that was before she had discovered an element which she now felt was imperative to a happy marriage – a passionate, sexual relationship. After her and Johnny's first clumsy encounter, something had awoken in her; a wanting, a sensuousness that she had never imagined women were capable of. And it was now clear to her that this intense desire for physical closeness was what had led certain women down a path of destruction. If you did not keep a firm control of it, Nora now knew it was a wanting that could almost consume you. It had consumed her thoughts at night and, at times, even during the day. At one point she had got very concerned about it, feeling the intensity of her feelings was not natural for a woman, and she had prayed hard for it to ease. And then things had changed.

For some reason, the opportunities for her and Johnny to be on their own at the weekends had dramatically lessened. And he had become more serious – more distant – which Nora had put down to him working regularly, and then going out again a few hours later to play with the band.

He was too tired to talk, he said, when he came home at the end of the night. And his attempts at not drinking so much were becoming more successful, but this meant he was also less relaxed and more inclined to feel guilty about betraying his wife. Nora had been entirely understanding, because she knew that the right time would eventually come for them. And the physical abstinence in the meantime had helped, because she found that the long gaps had helped to dampen down her desires.

As she approached the table in the tearoom now, Nora could tell that her friend was not in the best of form. She had taken care to do her hair and make-up as always, but there was a frown on Veronica's face and a dullness in her eyes that she had never seen before.

It wasn't long before Veronica told her the reason for her low spirits – that she and Frank Morrison had broken up. In fact, she had given him his marching orders. Nora was shocked: she had been expecting to hear news of an engagement any day now. But Frank, it seemed, placed more importance on saving money than anything else.

'In a nutshell, he was mean,' Veronica stated. 'It took me a while to cop onto it, but as the time went on I discovered he was nothing but a bloody old scrooge.'

Nora was taken aback and intrigued. 'In what ways was he mean?'

'Well, for a start, he was spending more and more time at my house because he got fed there and it saved him putting on a fire in his own place. And any time I suggested we went to the cinema, he said it was a waste of money when we could listen to the radio. He was the same with going out for a meal. He started saying that my cooking was far better than any restaurant, and weren't we better off eating at home?' Veronica, clearly agitated, prodded her finger on the table. 'And do you think he ever brought a bottle of wine to go with the meal, or a bunch of flowers?' Veronica shook her head emphatically. 'No, not after the first few times he came around. At first he forgot to bring the wine, then he forgot to stop at the shop, and then he stopped mentioning it at all.'

'I'm sorry to hear all that,' Nora said. 'You don't deserve it.'

'I'm glad I found out when I did. I got a narrow escape. I'm not surprised the girl he went out with for ten years ran off with somebody else. When I think about it, all that time and he never bought her an engagement ring? I should have heard the warning bells when we started going out, but I got carried away with the romance of it all.'

'What made you change your mind about him?'

'It was Dominic,' she said. 'I noticed when we were out together how well he treats me and women generally. And after a night when I'd cooked another meal for Frank and he had turned up with one arm as long as another, I realised that I was selling myself short. I suddenly thought that if I don't find someone who can treat me as well as Dominic, then I'd rather be on my own.'

Veronica went quiet as the waitress came towards them with their scones and tea, then she looked at Nora and attempted a smile. 'Well, it's all in the past now. I'm back to square one. Back to being "spinster of this parish" and all that.' She lifted her teacup and took a sip. 'Still, it's better than being taken for a total eedjit. I could have married him and he would have moved into my house and would be telling me to turn the heating off and go to bed early to save on the electricity.'

'Well, no one would ever take you for an eedjit, Veronica Fisher,' Nora said. 'You're a clever woman, and I'm sure the right man will come along. We're not over the hill yet.'

As they ate their scones and drank their tea, Nora brought her friend up to date about Sean and his singing over in Liverpool. She then told her about Ella and her job in Clerys, and said they might go past the handbag department on the way out, just to say 'hello'. 'Ella will be delighted to see you. She always says how well you look.'

'Ah, Nora, you're a tonic,' Veronica said, smiling fondly at her. 'You always think of something nice to say.' She paused. 'And I must return the compliment – genuinely now – and say you are looking the best I've ever seen you. Your clothes and make-up – everything looks lovely. You're like a different woman from the one I worked with in Tullamore.'

'I suppose in many ways I am,' Nora said, nodding. 'I have a whole new life now, a new family – everything. And of course, our lovely new bathroom. Thanks be to God I don't have to go outside to the lavatory any more.' She laughed and made the sign of the cross. 'It was the best investment I ever made. What was the point of hanging on to two fields down in Tullamore when we could use the money to improve the house in Islandbridge?'

Veronica's brow furrowed. 'Do you mean you paid for the bathroom?'

'Yes,' Nora said, 'I did. Didn't I tell you that before?'

Veronica shook her head. 'I thought you had just put something towards it.'

'You're getting mixed up with Ella's school fees. Johnny, Sean and I all helped out there.'

'God, you've certainly been very good to them. I didn't realise just how good.' She leaned across the table, her voice lower now. 'but you need to be careful with your money, you don't want to have it all spent on the Cassidys and have nothing left for your old age.'

Nora shook her head and smiled. 'What do you mean?'

'I mean when the time comes for you to go back to your own home in Tullamore. You'll need money to keep yourself then.'

'But I have no intentions of going back to Tullamore. Why would I? I have a family and a home here in Dublin now. This is my life.'

'But what about your house and farm?'

'I've actually been looking into selling them.' She gave a little shrug. 'There's no point in letting the place go damp and then trying to sell it in a few years when Sean and Ella are gone.'

'Are you serious?'

Nora smiled and nodded. 'I know it's a big step, and you're the first person I've told. It's all very confidential at this stage of course, but you're the one person I know I can trust.'

'Of course you can,' Veronica said. 'But I hope you are giving it a lot of thought, looking at your own future.'

'Well, I was thinking it might be best to actually sell it now, and if Johnny was to sell his house, and we put the money together, I think we could buy a very nice house in a nicer area.'

Veronica stared at her for a few moments. 'Let me get this straight,' she said. 'You are planning to spend the rest of your life in Dublin with Johnny Cassidy and his family?'

Nora suddenly looked coy. She lifted her white linen napkin and dabbed her lips, in case of any stray crumbs. 'Well, yes.'

There was a silence.

'But what if Johnny meets someone and decides to get married again? It's a few years now since he lost his wife, so he might be thinking along those lines soon enough.'

'He *is* thinking along those lines,' she said. 'We were making sure we gave it a decent length of time before making it public.'

'He's already met someone?'

'Yes, he has,' she said, her eyes sparkling. 'And it's me.'

Veronica sat up bolt straight. '*What?*' she gasped. 'You and Johnny Cassidy are getting *married?*'

Nora nodded. 'Eventually. It's a matter of time. Johnny and I both still feel we want to respect dear Mary's memory. We both feel it's just a little early yet to announce anything official.'

'I don't think you've ever told me such unexpected news – I don't actually know what to say.'

'Well, it's too early for congratulations, it could be a while yet. But, to be honest, I'm in no hurry. We're happy enough as we are for the time being. Johnny is busy working away in the hospital and I'm happy in the house.'

'And has it been going on long between you?' Veronica asked. 'I'm just thinking back to the time when Dominic asked you out. I wondered why you refused him.'

Nora bit her lip. 'Yes, it has been a while now. I hope Dominic wasn't upset?'

'No, he's grand. Oh, Johnny has been great to keep this all quiet at the hospital,' Veronica said now. 'There hasn't been a whisper of him seeing any women, and I know a few of the others had their eye on him.'

Nora did not say that hearing about other women fancying Johnny had already given her a few sleepless nights. 'Johnny is very private, on account of Mary's memory and the children, so I'll just remind you, please, not to mention this to anyone.'

'I won't say a word,' Veronica promised. She reached across the table and took Nora's hands in hers, then she gave them a little squeeze. 'And I do wish you both all the very best.'

Later, they stopped and had a few words with Ella at the bag counter.

Veronica could see how obviously fond of her aunt the young girl was. As they walked towards the front door she said, 'She's turned into a beautiful looking girl, hasn't she? And nicely spoken too.'

'Yes, she is beautiful,' Nora said, 'but Ella is not the type to let it go to her head. She's clever too, and she's done well getting such a good job. I'm very proud of her.'

As they parted at the door, Veronica suddenly put her hand on Nora's arm. 'Now, please don't take this the wrong way – I only have your best interests at heart. Don't go rushing into selling your house or anything like that until you are actually married. Don't throw your lot in with Johnny until you're one hundred per cent sure.'

Nora smiled at her. 'There's no need to worry about me at all. I know exactly what I'm doing.' She didn't mind the advice. In fact, she felt sorry for her friend, understanding that her current view of men was tainted by her experience with Frank Morrison. But there was no comparison between the two relationships. Being related to the Cassidys made all the difference. Nora was happy to share all she had with the family, and she had gone into the relationship with Johnny knowing what he was like, and knowing that he did not have two pennies to rub together.

But hadn't he already proved that he was willing to change? He had grabbed the chance of a decent job and had stuck at it, and, more importantly, he had sorted out his drink problem. The two main obstacles that she would have struggled with. Of course it meant he wasn't the same free and easy person he had been when he was drinking heavier, but that was no harm. Once they were married and sharing a bed, she knew they would soon resume the lovely intimacy they had so much enjoyed. She felt sorry for Veronica, and hoped she would be as lucky too.

A short while later, as she walked down O'Connell Street, Nora stopped to have a look in a shop window. She felt a warm glow inside as she studied the display of Silver Cross prams. This time next year, she and Johnny would be married. Any doubts she had harboured about it had been dispelled over the last few weeks. Her monthly period was now at least nine weeks late, and she had given it plenty of time to make sure. She was a woman who ran to a regular thirty day cycle, and could circle it every month on the calendar and be almost one hundred per cent sure. If she was this late, there was a very good reason.

Any doubts Johnny Cassidy had would also be dispelled as soon as she told him her news. She knew he was reluctant to commit to another marriage with anyone, reluctant to have another woman fill Mary's place as mother to his children. She had heard him and Sean and Ella, the night the new gramophone arrived, arguing about allowing the little ones to call her Mammy. And she had heard Sean and Ella standing up for her. She could hardly believe all the lovely things they had said about her. It was more than she had ever dreamed of – both that and the way the little ones had been so affectionate towards her earlier in the day.

She had heard bits of what Johnny had said, but she had deliberately not listened to it. She knew what men could be like – what married couples could be like. She had often heard her parents squabbling like children, saying awful things to each other that she knew they did not mean. From what she had heard, Johnny was in the wrong sort of mood and had come across a bit fractious and awkward as her mother had been on occasions. She knew that, after a while, things always settled down. Arguments were sorted out or gradually just drifted off.

He would, of course, do the right thing. He would not leave her to face the shame of being an unmarried mother. It would be unthinkable for him. They would do what hundreds of Irish couples did every year; they would have a shotgun wedding. And if people talked – let them. And by the time the baby came, she would be long married and no one in Tullamore would be any the wiser as to how long she had actually been married for. And for anyone who took the trouble to work out dates – she could not care less.

She and Johnny had been living under the same roof for several years now, and what had happened between them was the most natural thing in the world. They were only flesh and blood, after all. Nora smiled to herself. She wasn't looking for anything elaborate. Not at her age, and not under the circumstances. A quick, quiet morning wedding would do just fine. She had seen a lovely cream, lace-edged suit in Clerys that very day that would be perfect for it.

She glanced at the window again, and smiled at her reflection. This time next year she would be pushing one of these Silver Cross prams along the Dublin streets.

Chapter Forty-Nine

Nora waved goodbye to Hannah at the school gates and then stood and watched as the little girl made her way across the yard towards her class. She had already dropped Larry off at the boys' school, and was relieved that he had gone off without any problems, for there were odd mornings when he said he did not like school and didn't want to go. He would have preferred to be at home reading his books or using his vivid imagination to write and then illustrate his own little made-up stories.

Hannah was a different kettle of fish; she loved school and mixed much more easily. Everyone in the family was grateful for this, because an outgoing personality would help her deal with the scars still evident on her arm and legs. Nora smiled now, watching Hannah's blonde, curly head bobbing along towards two other little girls, who smiled delightedly when they saw her.

Nora turned and made her way back towards the shop to pick up the items on her list for dinner that evening. She acknowledged one or two mothers who she knew by sight, but did not stop to chat. She knew by looking at the younger women, some of them rather unkempt looking, that they were not her sort. Besides, it was one of her busy days at home when she had sheets and pillowcases to wash and dry, and hopefully get them ironed before she went back to collect Larry and Hannah at half past three.

The grocer filled one of her shopping bags with half a stone of potatoes, and in the other he packed carrots, flour, milk, a pound of cheese and a sliced fruit loaf. It was only when she got outside the shop that she realised the bags were fairly heavy, so she went as quickly as she could, stopping every so often to change hands as one bag was a bit lighter. The row of terraces had just come into sight when she felt the first cramp in her stomach. She immediately slowed down, and, as it eased, she reminded herself that she really needed to go and register at the local doctor's.

She had been putting it off because she dreaded all the inevitable questions about her not being married. But she knew she had to do it soon as time was moving on and she was almost twelve weeks pregnant. She had been afraid to go for a check-up any earlier in case she jinxed anything, but so far she had been perfectly well. She had also been waiting for the right moment to tell Johnny, and common sense told her she should first visit the doctor.

When she got into the house, she dropped the bags in the hallway, took off her coat and hat, then went in to the living room to flop in a chair. She sat for a few minutes, catching her breath, then she felt another cramp, more severe than the one before. A wave of alarm washed over her. She sat a while longer until it subsided, then she got up and went into the scullery to make herself a cup of tea. While she was waiting on the kettle to boil, she put bread under the grill to toast and then she went to a drawer and took out a packet of aspirin. She swallowed two down with a drop of milk.

After she had eaten she felt better, and her stomach had eased. As she went back into the scullery with her plate and cup she looked at the two heavy shopping bags leaning against the coat stand. She thought for a few moments and decided it was best to leave them until later, until she felt one hundred per cent back to herself. She put her apron on and went in to fill the sink for the washing, and then, as she was loading it into the sink, the door went. She sighed and went back out into the hall. It was Mrs Murphy with a parcel for her.

'It was delivered when you were at school with the childer,'

Rose said, handing it over. 'It looks like it's something from the catalogue.'

'It is,' Nora said. She had given up trying to retain privacy over certain things. She had realised that it was the price to be paid for help with the children and other smaller things. She had also got used to Mrs Murphy and didn't find her curiosity as irritating as she used to. 'It's just a few things that Ella and I ordered.'

'Been treating yourselves?'

'New, warm dressing gowns for the winter.'

'Lovely, I must do the same myself.' She paused. 'Are they candlewick?'

'Ella's is, mine is chenille.'

'And what colour did you go for?'

'I think mine is a wine-coloured one. Would you like to have a look at them?' Nora opened the door wider and stepped back inside. There was no point in wasting more time describing the damn things, she thought. It would be quicker and easier if she brought Mrs Murphy in and let her look at them while she checked the water in the sink.

They walked into the living room and Nora left the neighbour opening the parcel, while she went down to the scullery. She sprinkled the washing powder into the sink and threw in the sheets and pillowcases from her own bed, then went back to the living room.

'Oh, that's really lovely . . .' Rose said, lifting out the blue candlewick one. She checked the size. 'Although it wouldn't go anywhere near me. And how much was that?'

Nora tried not to grit her teeth. She would never ask anyone what they paid for things, her mother had always told her it was the height of ignorance. 'I think it was fifteen shillings.'

'Not bad,' Rose said. She put it down and then lifted out the medium-sized one, ordered for Nora. 'Now that's a bit better size,' she said. She ran her hand over the material. 'Oh, the chenille is lovely and soft. How much did you pay for that?'

'I think it was seventeen and six.' Nora was now irked at

Mrs Murphy for touching her dressing gown, but knew it was being fussy.

'I think it might be a bit long for me.' Mrs Murphy got to her feet to hold the garment up to herself. 'Ah, you can see it's trailing on the floor, I would need to take a few inches up on it—' She stopped and looked at Nora, who had suddenly bent over, one hand on her stomach and the other on her hip. 'Are you all right?'

Nora held her breath for a few seconds and then slowly exhaled. 'I've just got a bit of a cramp in my stomach,' she said. She straightened up and then stood for a few moments. 'I'll just go to the bathroom. I'll only be a minute.'

'Would you like me to make you a cup of tea? It might help.'

'Thanks, I'll put the kettle back on to boil as I'm going past.' She went out of the room slowly, leaving Mrs Murphy to examine the dressing gowns in more detail.

Rose had just put her arm into the chenille dressing-gown when she heard Nora cry out. She dropped it onto the chair and rushed out into the hallway. 'Are you OK?'

Nora came out of the bathroom, her face white. 'I'm bleeding – I'll have to go to the hospital.'

'Have you had an accident? Where have you cut yourself?'

Nora's eyes filled with tears. 'It's the baby! I think something might be wrong with the baby.'

Rose sat out in the corridor waiting to hear the news. She was still in a state of shock, trying to process what was happening. A driver had been kind enough to pull over when he saw her out in the middle of the road, trying to flag down any of the passing vehicles. She had helped Nora into the back and the man had driven them straight to the casualty department of St James's Hospital.

'Just try to keep yourself calm,' Mrs Murphy had said, patting her hand as they drove along. 'You'll be grand. Sometimes these things happen early on and then everything is fine.' When they arrived at the hospital a nurse took details from Nora and a short while later she was taken through to see the doctors.

Rose sat staring down the long, tiled corridor, wondering how she had missed the connection between Nora and Johnny Cassidy. She rarely missed anything like that. But in this case, if she was to stand in front of a judge and jury, she would have to say she had never seen or even suspected anything untoward going on between them.

She shook her head. Not in a million years would she have paired them up. She would have sworn that Nora wasn't the type to have thoughts in that direction at all. In fact, Rose presumed that the prim spinster was still as intact as the day she was born. Never did she in her wildest dreams foresee Nora Lamb being pregnant. Well, she thought, we certainly live and learn.

Nora lay flat on the examination table as the doctor gently pressed the lower part of her stomach. He eventually stood up, pushing his glasses up on his head.

'We've given you a thorough examination, Mrs Lamb,' he said, taking her hand and helping her to sit up straight, 'and checked for heartbeats and anything else which would indicate a viable pregnancy...'

'And how is the baby? Is everything OK?' She looked at him expectantly.

'I'm afraid to tell you that there is no sign of a baby and there never was. The bleed is menstrual.'

'It can't be. There has to be a baby!' Nora's voice rose. She closed her eyes and pressed the back of her hand to her mouth. 'I've missed two periods – it's never happened before.'

'That's not unusual, given your age. What that means is the body is preparing to go into menopause – the change of life – and it often does it gradually.'

'No!' Nora shook her head vehemently. She couldn't have lost her one and only chance. Even if physical relations were to start

287

again with Johnny, the doctor was telling her now she was too old to conceive. 'It can't be that, it can't be.'

'One of the first signs is bigger gaps between periods,' the doctor continued in a calm voice. 'It could take a year or even more, or this period could be your last. Many women start the change in their early forties, and you're forty-five.'

'Are there no more tests you can do?'

'We've taken a urine sample and blood tests, and we'll have those back in a few days.' He shook his head. 'But I'm almost one hundred per cent sure that you are just having a heavy period.'

Nora stared at him. All these weeks she had been certain there was a tiny baby growing inside her. It was something she had never dared to hope or dream might happen to her – even as a younger woman. All these weeks she had been planning the new life she and Johnny would have with this little person. Imagining herself taking the baby out in the pram, bathing it, looking on proudly as Ella held it in her arms. Taking photos of the baby with Larry and Hannah.

It was all fantasy. And she knew that the dream had ended today. She moved her gaze away from the doctor, then she bowed her head and started to cry.

Chapter Fifty

Mrs Murphy brought Nora into her comfortable, slightly shabby, living room. There were two velvet-covered armchairs on either side of the fire, and a small striped sofa which converted into a pull-down bed when it was too cold for Rose to sleep upstairs. There was a radio perched on a stool, and there were piles of newspapers on a half-moon table by the window, and a vase of dusty silk flowers.

While she waited on the kettle boiling, Mrs Murphy, conscious of her pernickety visitor, started straightening cushions and shifting the papers into a tidier pile. She even took a hanky from her pocket and ran it over the mantelpiece. She need not have troubled herself for Nora, sitting in one of the armchairs and still in a daze, took in nothing of her surroundings.

A short while later, Rose came back into the living room and handed her neighbour a large mug of hot whiskey with three large teaspoons of sugar in it. 'Get that down you and you'll feel a whole lot better.' She went back into the scullery and came out with one for herself. 'We'll both feel the better for it,' she said, sitting down in the chair opposite.

As she sat, her gaze directed down on the grey and red hearth rug, Nora felt another twinge in her stomach. This time she recognised it as the period cramps she had been having for over thirty years. Oh, how had she deluded herself! A wave of hopelessness washed over her. As tears once again prickled behind her eyes, she lifted the mug and took a good drink of the hot sweet liquid. She gave a few coughs as it hit her chest, and then she took another, bigger, mouthful and within a few moments she could feel the comforting warmth spreading through her.

A quarter of an hour later Mrs Murphy brought the second mug through for them. By that time, Nora had outlined the story of her and Johnny's relationship.

'You never told him about thinking you were expecting?'

'No, I was waiting until the doctor had confirmed it, and I was waiting to catch him at the right time.' She sighed. 'But in the last while we never seem to be on our own, and any time we are, he's very tired and not up to talking. I knew once I'd seen the doctor that he'd have no option but to listen. That he would have no option but to marry me.' She took another mouthful of the sweet, comforting whiskey. 'It makes me seem so stupid now, doesn't it?'

'No, it's anything but silly. You're not the first and you're not the last woman to think that having a baby would bring things to a head one way or another. And in a lot of cases, the men step up to the mark and get married.'

Tears suddenly filled Nora's eyes. 'Well, I won't be telling him anything now, will I? All that has happened is that I've been told I'm too old – I'm never going to have children of my own.'

'Can I ask you something?' Rose said. 'Did he ever approach you when he was sober?'

Nora shook her head. 'There was never the opportunity with the children around; it was always when he came in late from his music engagements.' A hint of a smile came on her lips. 'We would sit and have a little drink and listen to music on the radio.'

'And it only happened on three or four occasions, in all the time you've been staying here?'

She nodded sadly, then took another drink from her mug. 'That was all. It could go months before – before it happened again.'

'Did Johnny ever say anything to you about getting married? Or even mention about telling the family or other people about you and him? Making it official, like?'

Nora shrugged. 'He never talked about it afterwards at all; I think he felt guilty about poor Mary.' She looked at Mrs Murphy. 'He was always guilty and the next day he was always shy and awkward with me.'

'Did he bring the drink home with him?'

'The first time we sat up chatting, he brought wine home from one of the dances.' She stared out of the window now. 'After that, I usually kept a bottle in. I thought of it like a little treat since we never went anywhere together. I didn't mind, because I understood his situation, and I was giving him time to sort things out.' She sighed again. 'And then, when I thought we were having a baby, I thought it would be the one thing to make him, well, do the right thing.'

There was a silence now as Rose digested it all. There was no doubt about it, it painted a very sad picture for a grown woman. It was quite plain that Nora had ambushed a drunken Johnny. While he was certainly no saint in the matter, she knew, reading between the lines, that it had been offered to him on a plate. And, if he had really had any interest in Nora, he would have taken the opportunity to do what they did on a regular basis. Rose Murphy knew men, and she knew that few men living in such close proximity with a willing woman would go months unless they had no interest. And whilst she had no doubts that Nora had believed herself to be pregnant, she wondered if the dates were even right or if it had all been wishful thinking on the poor woman's part.

'Are you going to tell him what happened today?' Rose asked in a gentle tone.

'What do you think?'

'I think you need to have the whole thing out with him; you need to know where you stand.' She halted. 'And you're going to have to be prepared to take what he says. You can't force anyone into having feelings for you if they don't.'

Nora nodded. 'I'm afraid,' she said, her voice slurring a little with the whiskey. 'I'm afraid I've got this whole thing wrong. I'm afraid I've made the biggest mistake of my life – and made an awful fool of myself.' She stood up now, swaying as she did so. 'You won't say anything to anyone?'

Mrs Murphy shook her head. 'Not a word,' she said. 'I promise you.' As they walked to the door, she put her hand on Nora's arm. 'Don't be too hard on yourself, you've done a lot more good in that house than any harm you think. Those children wouldn't be where they are today without all you've done for them. Just give yourself a bit of time to work it all out.'

Nora walked down towards the Cassidys' house, and as she came near the door she felt in her coat pocket for the key. She had it ready to put in the lock when she hesitated. She thought for a few moments, then put it back in her pocket and set off walking at a quick pace. Every so often she swayed off her path, but she righted herself.

She walked for nearly fifteen minutes until she reached the church. She went up the wide steps at the front and then over to the side door. She paused for a few moments, gathering herself together, and then she pushed the heavy door open. The church was empty apart from an elderly woman up in the front pew of the main altar, and an elderly man in the pews over to the right in front of the side altar. Nora had a sinking feeling when she saw them. Two old and lonely people, seeking some comfort and solace from the empty, holy building – just as she was herself.

She quietly slipped into one of the back pews and knelt down and blessed herself, then joined her hands together and automatically went into a list of silent prayers – Our Father, Hail Mary, Memorare, Hail Holy Queen. The reciting of them helped to still her mind and her breathing. Then, feeling calmer, she opened her eyes and just knelt, staring around her at the altars and the walls, upon which hung painted sculptures of the Stations of The Cross. Then she knelt in an upright position, placing her elbows on the pew in front. She clasped her hands together, her fingers intertwining, and this time instead of rhyming off her prayers, she silently spoke to the Blessed Virgin as she would speak to a person.

Nora felt that Mary, as a woman and a mother, would

understand all the things she had gone through today. First of all she asked forgiveness for the sins of the flesh she had committed, and then she asked for understanding of her situation. She prayed then for the strength which she needed to accept that the longed-for baby was never going to happen. Then guidance as to what she should do now with regards to her relationship with Johnny Cassidy. Finally, with silent tears streaming down her face, she asked for help to get through the rest of this terrible day.

After a while she moved to sit up on the pew and stayed there for a while longer. She was in no rush; she would go straight from church to collect the children from school, which did not finish for another half an hour. She heard a door banging, and when she lifted her head she saw that both the other people were gone. She lifted her handbag and, taking a hanky out, rubbed it over her eyes and then dabbed her nose. Then, since there was no one else in the church to disapprove, she went back to her handbag and took out her compact.

She checked her face in the small mirror and thought it still looked red from crying, so she put some powder on and applied her lipstick. She held the compact out at arm's length and checked again, and thought she looked a bit better. By the time she walked down to school, she hoped that the worst of the redness and the puffiness around her eyes would have gone.

Then, just as she held the compact mirror up a bit higher for a last check, she heard a voice saying, 'Hello Nora, how are you?' She whirled around and saw two figures who had obviously entered the church as silently as she had. Father Brosnan was coming towards her, while Bridget – the one who had set her cap at Johnny – was going down the side aisle towards the vestry. As the priest came to sit in the pew beside her, Nora's face started to burn. How long had they been there? Had they seen her putting on her make-up in the church? If so, they would have thought her both irreverent and ridiculously vain.

'Are you keeping well?' Father Brosnan enquired.

Nora attempted a smile. 'Yes,' she said, 'I'm grand, thank you, Father.'

'And Johnny and the family?'

'Grand,' she repeated.

'I don't often see you in here during the day,' he said. 'Is everything all right? There's nothing worrying you is there?'

'No,' she said quickly.

'Don't mind me asking,' he said. 'It's just that people tend to come in when it's quiet if they want to make a special intention or say prayers for someone who is sick.'

'I was just passing by,' she told him, 'and I had time to spare before picking the children up from school.'

'Well, I'm glad to hear all is well...' He patted her hand. 'You've made a great job of those children,' he said, 'they're a credit to you.'

Nora looked at him. 'Do you think so? Do you think I've done something good?'

He leaned in towards her. 'Nothing short of a miracle,' he whispered. 'You've done a grand job with them all, and I'd say Johnny Cassidy will be grateful to you until his dying day.'

Nora felt a catch in her throat as she suddenly remembered the recent argument she had overheard between Johnny and Sean and Ella. Johnny had not sounded too grateful then. The thought brought tears back to her eyes, and for a fleeting moment, Nora felt like unburdening herself to this kindly priest. She felt like telling him everything that had happened between herself and Johnny, because something told her that he would understand, having been celibate himself all those years. She even wondered if she could ask him to hear her confessions, but something stopped her, a muddle of pride, embarrassment and shame.

She just could not bring herself to put the situation into words. When she had tried to explain it to Mrs Murphy it had come out wrong, and she guessed the elderly neighbour thought she had been foolish to get involved with Johnny at all. And Veronica had been the same when she told her about paying for the bathroom. She could not risk another person feeling that she was some sort of pitiable fool.

She blinked back her tears and straightened her back. 'Thank you for those kind words, Father,' she said. 'It means more than you know.' She looked at her watch. 'I must go and collect the children now.'

As she walked out through the church gates, Nora wondered if going into the church had been any help at all. She still felt a huge sense of loss about the baby that was never meant to be, and she was still just as confused about where she stood with Johnny. She needed something to stop her mind from racing, going over and over all the things she had said, all the things she had thought. Prayers and talking to the priest had not worked.

She stopped and thought for a few moments, and then she started walking again, more purposely this time. Five minutes later she stopped outside the off-licence. She put her hand on the door, hesitated, then went straight inside.

Chapter Fifty-One

Earlier that same Monday morning, the phone rang in the music shop and Martin went to get it. 'Ah, it's Sean Cassidy you're after,' he said. 'Hold on now and I'll get him.'

Hearing his name, Sean turned to look at his boss.

'It's for you,' Martin told him. 'You have a call from England.'

As soon as Sean put the receiver to his ear he recognised Ricky Hamilton's voice.

'Sean, a couple of good opportunities have come up,' he said, 'and I immediately thought of you. The Adelphi rang to offer you a regular spot, three nights a week, with great pay. Are you interested?'

'God, I don't know,' Sean said.

'Well, the next piece of news might help you make up your mind. If you can get over at the weekend, I have one of the guys from Stina Records coming up from London to hear a female vocalist I represent. When I told him about you, he said if you were around he would be interested in hearing you. What do you say?'

'I – I need a bit of time to think about it . . .'

'Well, I've got to get back to him tomorrow at the latest.' Ricky's tone was businesslike. 'So if you're not interested, let me know in the morning. And Sean, this is probably the biggest chance you're ever going to get from a well-known recording company. You do know that, don't you? If you're serious about your career you don't want to miss this opportunity. Stina have recently taken on some of the new American artists, and they're going down a storm. They're on every radio station in Britain at the moment. If they like what you do, then you could be the next big thing to hit the airwaves. If you have any ambition at all, you should grab this opportunity with both hands. I have a string of musicians and singers who would kill for this chance.'

'I know – I know. Look, I'll be back to you by tomorrow.'

'OK, ring as soon as you know. And you don't need to worry about anything, I'll look after you. I'll manage your career full-time. Liverpool will only be the start, I'll get you gigs all over the country. Ireland isn't big enough for your talent. If you turn this down, Sean, you're going to regret it.'

Martin, having heard the whole news from Sean, said, 'Why don't you go over to the hospital to see your father and talk to him about it now. He'll advise you, and the walk out might help you to think clearer. And don't be worrying about this place.' He smiled. 'You can always come home if it doesn't work out, but you might not get this chance again.'

Johnny, dressed in his porter's uniform, was just going into the staff canteen for his own break when he saw Sean coming down the corridor. His heart quickened, 'Is everything OK at home?'

'Everything is grand,' Sean said. 'I just wanted five minutes with you to talk something over.' They went into the canteen together and Sean explained about the phone call.

'Well, you don't need to ask me what I think,' his father said. 'Any performer would jump at the chance of meeting up with one of the recording companies. Go for it. Take it from some-body who knows how few get an opportunity like that. You'll always regret it if you don't.'

Sean suddenly smiled. 'I think I will go for it,' he said. 'As Martin at the shop said, I can always come back.'

'Ring Ricky this evening. Don't leave it until tomorrow.'

'What time do you finish?'

'Five,' Johnny said.

'I'll come and get you after work and we'll walk down to the Barley Mow for a quick pint and I'll phone from there.'

Johnny put his hand out and shook Sean's. 'I'm proud of you.'

After his first pint Sean rang Ricky and made arrangements to be over in Liverpool by Friday. After his second pint, and prompted by his father, he made a call to the Strand Café to check if Sally had a room spare for him.

'No problem booking me in,' he told his father, as they started on their third and last drink. 'She says it's a quiet time of the year.'

Johnny had been tempted to say he would have a few words with her himself, but he knew that Sean would be able to tell from the way they spoke that he had been keeping in touch regularly. After the last row about Nora, he felt it was safer to keep his business private. He would walk down later this evening or tomorrow and give her a ring when he was on his own.

It started to rain on the way back, so they quickened their step.

'I was just thinking,' Sean said, 'would there be any chance of you coming over to Liverpool with me for a week or two? Just until I settle in, like.'

'I don't know about that,' his father said. He was thinking of the money he was saving up to pay Nora back for the bathroom. 'Maybe in the New Year, when we've Christmas over. Sure, you'll be grand on your own. You know Liverpool well enough now, and the Mathers will be there to give a hand if you get stuck with anything.'

'I was thinking I might find something a bit fancier, maybe even get my own place.'

Johnny stifled a sigh. Typical of Sean to turn his nose up at a perfectly good place. He hoped he wouldn't start getting uppity with the Mathers the way he had with his own relations in Liverpool.

When they arrived at the house, just as Johnny went towards

the door, Ella swung it wide open. 'Where were you?' she demanded. 'You're half an hour late.'

'Woah, woah,' her father said, coming into the hallway. 'We had a bit of business to sort out. Is there something wrong?' Then he stopped. 'Are Larry and Hannah OK?'

'Yes, they are,' she said, 'but Aunt Nora's not.'

'What's wrong with her?' Sean asked.

Ella gestured towards the living room, and they followed her in. 'She's upstairs asleep now,' she said in a low voice, 'but when I came home she was sitting here with Mrs Murphy and she could hardly put two sensible words together. She was rambling and talking rubbish...' She took a deep, trembling sigh. 'Mrs Murphy has Larry and Hannah. She called up to the house for something, and when she saw the state Aunt Nora was in she took them down to her house until we sort things out.'

Johnny's face creased. 'I don't understand—'

'She was drunk!' Ella hissed. 'Blind drunk.'

'Oh, God.' Johnny's face drained white.

'I had to help her up the stairs, she was tripping and falling and everything, and saying stupid things. I couldn't believe she had got into such a state. She must have been drinking all afternoon.'

There was a noise and Sean pointed up at the ceiling. 'I think she's getting sick.'

'Quick, Ella,' Johnny said. 'Take a basin up to her. It's better if it's another woman.'

As Ella turned out towards the hall she said to her father, 'Mrs Murphy says you have to go down to her as soon as you come in.'

Johnny knocked on his neighbour's door and waited, his heart pounding, until she came to usher him inside. Larry and Hannah were kneeling at her coffee table with colouring books and pencils.

'We'll leave them there and go down into the scullery,' Rose told him. 'Did you see her?'

'Nora? No, I've just got in. Ella is upstairs with her.'

'She's in a bad way.' Mrs Murphy pursed her mouth tightly. 'I don't want to interfere in what's going on in your house, but I'm worried about the poor woman.'

'I don't know what's happened,' he said, looking bewildered. 'She was grand when I left this morning.'

'Well, she's been anything but grand all day. I don't want to go saying anything I shouldn't or go breaking any promises. All I'll say, Johnny, is you need to talk to her and straighten things out between the two of ye.'

Johnny's heart stopped. 'What did she tell you?'

'Enough. Enough to know that she's maybe read more into your living arrangements than you meant her to.' Rose held her hand up. 'Now, I'm not here to be judge and jury or anything like that, but you need to have a talk with her and clear the air.' She paused, thinking back to earlier in the day. 'In some ways, Johnny, you're a lucky man. You've had a narrow escape, it could be an awful lot worse.' She laid a hand on his. 'Speak to her when she's up to it. I'll keep the children for another while. I was just going to put some sausages on for them.'

He nodded. 'Thanks – you've been very good.' He moved towards the hallway, then he suddenly turned back. 'I don't know what to do – the whole thing has turned into a disaster.' His voice was strained now. 'I said to Sean and Ella a while ago that I thought she might be better off going back to Tullamore. I knew she was making plans for the long-term when she put the bathroom in, and I thought it wasn't fair to take it from her. I didn't want to give her the wrong idea and I've been saving since to pay her back. Never, in my wildest dreams did I think she would—' He shook his head and closed his eyes.

'Johnny, it takes two to tango. And from what I can gather, you did the dance.' She touched his shoulder. 'You're not the first man and you won't be the last – but you need to sort it all out now.'

Chapter Fifty-Two

Later that evening Johnny stood at the bottom of the stairs. This was the first time, in a long time, he and Nora had been in the house on their own. Sean had gone down to see Mrs Keating to tell her about going to Liverpool, and Ella had taken the younger two down to Danny's grandmother's house almost as soon as they'd got back from Mrs Murphy's.

Ella had been awkward when he asked her to take the children out of the house. 'But Danny was supposed to be coming up here tonight.'

'Well, I'm sure he won't mind you going there.' Ella still hadn't seemed happy, and he understood that she was upset and worried about her aunt being drunk and behaving in a way she wasn't used to, but he wished she had been more of a help than a hindrance.

He mounted the stairs now, his stomach churning. As he reached the top, he heard a noise. 'Nora?' he called, his voice croaky and uncertain. 'Are you OK?'

There was a silence then he heard her call back. 'Yes, I'm grand... thank you.'

He had to talk to her, but he didn't want to go into her bedroom. 'I'm making a cup of tea,' he said. 'Will you come down? They've all gone out, and I think we need to – to sort a few things out while we're on our own.'

'I'll be down in a few minutes,' she said, quickly cutting him off.

Nora sat up in bed and, as she did so, her head began to swim and a feeling of nausea rose up inside her. She sat for a minute or two until it subsided, and then, very carefully she moved to the edge of the bed. She waited another little while and then she stood up. She went to the wardrobe mirror and looked at herself. Her hair was dishevelled and flattened on the side she had slept on. Her lipstick was smeared and her face looked almost grey.

Old, old, old, she thought, as she stared at her reflection. Old and pathetic. A woman now starting the change of life. A woman too old to bear a child.

She closed her eyes to steady herself, then she moved over to Mary's dressing table to brush her hair and tidy herself up.

Johnny was waiting in the living room, standing with his back to the fire. A mug and Nora's china cup and saucer were on the side table along with a small plate of biscuits. 'How are you feeling?' he asked.

'Not great,' she said. 'But it's entirely my own fault. I'll soon get over it.' She sat down in one of the armchairs.

Johnny lifted the cup and saucer and brought it over to her, then he lifted the mug and sat down in the chair opposite. There was an awkward silence and he cleared his throat. 'I'm not sure what happened to you earlier,' he said. 'But I gather from Mrs Murphy that you were not well and maybe upset about something.'

She slowly nodded then lifted her cup to take a drink. As she put it back down in the saucer, her hand shook and the bone china made a rattling sound. 'I'm not sure where to start,' she said, 'but I suppose an apology for drinking too much would be the best place.' She looked over at him, but as usual, he was not able to meet her gaze.

'Well, I'm hardly the person to blame anyone for drinking too much, so don't worry about that.' He paused. 'I think it's more me that owes the apologies,' he said. 'And I should have said it a while ago and not let things carry on.'

'What do you mean?'

'About what happened between us on the couple of occasions

– after, after we'd been drinking. It should never have happened.' He faltered. 'It was wrong and I feel bad that we ever … When I think of how Mary would have felt if she knew.'

'No, no,' she said. She put her teacup down on the table. 'I do understand what you're saying, but we waited a decent length of time, and it's gone into years now. If people knew now, no one would think bad of us. We're only human, after all.'

'Nora, we can't let anyone know! It was a drunken mistake.' He looked her straight in the eye. 'And it can't ever happen again. If we're going to be in the same house for a while longer, we need to be one hundred per cent agreed on that.' He shook his head. 'It can't *ever* happen again. That's what I needed to say, and I'm glad now that it's out in the open and over and done with. We can put it all behind us.'

She could see how wretched and anxious he looked, and she wondered if he would ever get over feeling like this, if he would ever be able to live in the present and leave the past behind. She had to know why he was giving up on any future with her. She had to know *right now* where she stood.

'I was at the hospital today,' she suddenly heard herself say, 'and that's why I was upset. That's why I drank too much.'

His head jerked up. 'Was there anything wrong? Are you OK?'

'I thought I was losing our baby – but it was all a mistake.'

Johnny's face palled. 'What?' he said, his voice croaky and distorted. 'You're having a baby?' He dropped his head in his hands. 'Oh dear God!'

'No, I'm not pregnant – it was all an awful mistake.' She started to cry. 'But I really thought I was for two months and – and I was happy. Happier than I've ever been.'

'Nora!' Johnny suddenly shouted. 'This is fucking madness! Having a baby would have been the ruination of the family. How could we have told them? They would have been shocked and disgusted with the pair of us. Can you not see that?'

She looked up at him, tears streaming down her face. 'Did you ever care for me at all?' she asked. 'Was there ever anything there between us – any feelings – from your side?'

The sight of the sad woman in front of him and the fragility which he could hear in her voice softened his anger. He knew he had to handle things very carefully.

'Yes, I cared for you. I – I do care,' he told her quietly, 'but only in the way that a friend would care.' He shook his head. 'That was all it ever was. I never gave a thought to any carry-on between us, and I still can't work out how it happened.' He shrugged. 'But it did happen, and we have to put it in the past.'

She nodded her head, her gaze fixed downwards.

Johnny thought for a few moments, and then he moved to the edge of his chair to be nearer her. 'We would never have made a match for a hundred reasons. It was just because we were thrown together at a very difficult time. Our differences weren't so noticeable because we had the children to sort between us.' His voice was kind and gentle now. 'But you must know, we're very different types of people. You're clever and organised, and a professional woman, while I'm ...' He shrugged. 'I'm the opposite, and after a while I would have driven you mad. I don't know how Mary put up with me at times, but there was something there – something similar about the two of us – that made it work, through all the ups and downs. I doubt if I'm ever going to find that again.'

She nodded and tried to smile. 'Oh, dear Mary was a saint all right.' She knew he was handing her a little life raft, a face-saver, by pointing out his faults. And she knew she had to take hold of it, because if she didn't, only more catastrophes could follow.

'Well, I think the chat has straightened us out now,' Johnny said. 'I think we'll be grand from now on, and I hope you know how much I've appreciated your help here in the house and with the children.'

'Of course,' she said, 'and I'm sure you know I think the world of them.'

He nodded and smiled. 'And I will be paying you back the money for the bathroom. It would be wrong to take it from you.'

'I can afford it, Johnny, and it was only because I was used to one at home. I really would like to pay for it, if you'll let me. I'm sure you could put your money to good use for the family.'

'Well, we can talk about that another day,' he said.

Nora gave a little shudder when she thought of all the ridiculous plans she had had, like selling the house in Tullamore. What would Johnny think if he had known? No wonder Veronica had looked so shocked. Had Veronica guessed that she had got things so wrong? She then remembered the two women she met in Clerys whom she had bragged to about getting married. A wave of mortification engulfed her now. She had to close her mind against it all. It was just too much to bear.

'I know you meant well,' Johnny told her, 'and we've had more than enough apologies for the one day. Anything else we need to sort can wait until another time. We don't need any more changes just now.'

Again she nodded, but she was wondering what changes he was referring to.

'As long as you and me can be friends from now on, everything will be grand.' A relieved smile came on his face. 'Isn't that right?'

Nora managed the vestiges of a smile. 'Indeed.' She lifted her teacup up and drank a few mouthfuls. She would say no more. She would do everything she could from now on to retain any dignity she had left.

Chapter Fifty-Three

On Wednesday morning, Johnny moved out of bed around seven o'clock, having lain awake for most of the night. Everything that had happened over the last few days had circled round and round in his brain, until he could not bear thinking about it any more. What's done is done, he told himself, and everything that needed to be said has been said. He just wished his mind would believe him and switch off.

He went quietly out of the room and went downstairs. After doing his usual morning routine things, he wandered into the living room with a comforting mug of tea and looked out of the window. It was a dry, clear day, and the coming week was fore-cast for more pleasant late autumn weather. He looked across the road at the tall pine trees in the park, their branches slowly swaying in the breeze. He stood watching them, as though in a meditation, and as he did so, an idea formed in his mind. He would go to Liverpool with Sean.

He needed to get away from this situation to clear his head. It would take a while before he could approach the subject of Nora eventually moving out, and a break away from home would help put more distance between them. Work would not be a problem – he still had a few weeks' holidays to take – and although it would mean less time off over Christmas, he didn't mind that. As long as he had the actual day with the children he didn't mind going into work. The hospital was actually quite cheery during the festive time.

They would all be grand for a short while without him, and it was important to give Sean the bit of support he needed to get his career started off in Liverpool. He knew that, deep down, his oldest son wasn't as confident as he pretended to be. For all everyone told him how talented he was, he still spent his dinner times in the shop rehearsing on the piano and quite a few evenings down at Mrs Keating's going over and over his music again. He was too much of a perfectionist, Johnny thought, but it was his nature, and only time and experience would make him ease off.

As he stood drinking his tea, Johnny worked out his plans. He could use some of the money he had saved up for paying Nora back for the bathroom. She had made it plain last night that she would be desperately hurt if he did insist on paying her back, and he didn't want to make her feel any worse. He would go into work early this morning and have a word with his boss, see what they could sort out.

He had a quiet word upstairs with Sean before they both left for work, and told him his plans. 'I'd feel happier in my mind if I went over with you and was there to see you all settled in. I could probably manage around ten days.'

'That would be grand!' Sean said. 'And you have your brothers and all over there, so you won't be stuck if I'm in meetings or rehearsing.'

'Not at all,' Johnny said. 'I'll find plenty to keep me busy. And to be honest, I've not been feeling the best of late, and they say a change is as good as a rest.'

'You have been a bit run-down all right,' Sean said, then he gestured across to Nora's bedroom. 'How is she today?'

'Grand. She's downstairs getting the breakfast and doing all her usual things.'

'Do you know what made her take to the drink like that?'

'She kind of talked around in circles and it was hard to make sense of it,' Johnny hedged. 'Mrs Murphy said it was some kind of women's troubles, so I thought it was best not to enquire any further.'

Sean made an anguished face at the thought of female

307

problems. 'Well, it wasn't a bit like her, so I hope she's got over it and is OK now especially with us going away. Will we mention to her and Ella now that you're coming with me?'

'No,' Johnny said, 'Ella's not been in great form with all this, so I think it might be better if we wait until this evening. A day in Clerys and away from the house might put her in better humour.'

When he came back from work, after sorting his time off, Johnny and Sean told Nora and Ella about their plans. Johnny noticed that Nora looked a bit flustered and Ella's face had tightened the way it did when she was annoyed.

'When did you decide this?' Ella asked.

'Sean had asked me a few days ago when he found out he was going to Liverpool,' he explained, 'and at first I said no.' He looked over at Sean. 'But when I gave it a bit of thought, I decided it would be for the best if I did go. He might be like a film star to all the ones at the dances, but at the end of the day he's still only a snotty-nosed young lad, and needs his Daddy now and again.' He looked over at Ella. 'Are you OK about it?' he asked.

'Fine,' Ella said. 'I'm sure we'll all manage here on our own, won't we Aunt Nora?'

'Oh, I expect we'll just tick along as usual,' she said distractedly, then she moved to check on the potatoes on the hob.

Johnny thought he detected an edge to Ella's voice, and it suddenly crossed his mind that she might still be worried about what had happened with her aunt and feel anxious about being left on her own with her. He took the chance to talk to her about it later when Sean was down at Mrs Keating's, the children in bed and Nora had gone out to help with cleaning at the church.

'Are you OK about me going, Ella?' he checked. 'I wouldn't like you to feel we had gone off and left you or anything like that.'

'As long as it's only for a week or a bit more. I understand you wanting to go with Sean and see he's all settled, because I know what he can be like if anything goes wrong.'

Johnny moved forward now and took her in his arms, pleased when she leaned against him. 'There's nothing to worry about. Things will be just grand.'

It was later that evening, as they all listened to Larry read a story written for school, that Danny arrived at the house in his best coat, and, after hearing Larry's story about a lion in Dublin Zoo, he asked if he could have a private word with Johnny in the scullery.

'I'm a bit nervous saying this to you,' Danny said when they got there, 'but I know it's the right thing to do.'

Johnny looked at him. 'Go on,' he said, 'you'll feel better when you get it off your chest.'

'Well, it's actually about Ella.'

Johnny's heart speeded up.

'I was wondering – would you mind if we got engaged?'

Johnny looked at him in total shock. '*Engaged?*' he said. '*Engaged to be married?*'

The normally confident Danny took a step backwards. 'Yeah, if it's OK with you ...'

Johnny turned away and walked over to the window, looking out into the dark. He thought for a few moments ... then another few moments. Then he said a quick prayer to Mary that he was doing the right thing and turned around and said, 'Ella is so young. Are you sure? Are you sure you're doing the right thing?'

'Yeah,' Danny said. 'Absolutely.' His Adam's apple bobbed up and down with nerves. 'I've been in love with her since the first time I saw her.' He shrugged. 'Well, I met her when we were kids but I knew when I started talking to her that she was the only one for me. I wouldn't look at anyone else.'

'What about Ella? Does she feel the same about you?'

'Yeah,' he said, 'she does. It's what we both want. I know she's a couple of years younger than me, but she's mature for her age and knows what she wants. I got promotion at work on Monday and I told her at lunch time, and that was when I proposed, like. I was supposed to come down Monday night but it didn't suit, and anyway, I came tonight.'

Johnny felt a little wave of relief. That's what had upset her, having to wait a few more days to ask. 'If you want my opinion,' he said, 'I think you're well-suited, so I have no objections at all.' He came over to his future son-in-law now, and shook his hand.

'Aw brilliant!' Danny said, his face flushing red. 'I hoped you would say that.' He suddenly remembered. 'I hope you don't mind, but I brought a few beers down for us and a few Baby-chams to celebrate.'

'Mind?' Johnny said, grinning at him. 'I think it's proper order!' A little celebration he thought was just what they needed.

'I left them outside the front door,' Danny said, 'just in case.'

'Well, get out there quick in case somebody runs away with them,' Johnny told him.

As Danny went to the door, Johnny stuck his head into the living room and beckoned Ella to come out. He could see she was anxious. 'You can relax,' he told her, 'I'm happy enough.'

Her face lit up. 'Are you sure? I didn't know what you'd think.'

'He's a nice lad,' Johnny said, 'he thinks the world of you and he'll look after you. That's all that matters.' Then, as Danny opened the door and came in with his heavy bag, Johnny put his arms around her for the second time that day.

They went into the living room and told everyone the news, then Hannah was sent to Mrs Murphy's house to invite her to join them. Sean appeared and he helped sort the drinks, and got glasses of lemonade for Larry and Hannah.

'I'm so happy for you, Ella,' Nora said, taking both her hands in hers. 'When you find the right person early in life, you have many years of happiness ahead of you.'

As Ella hugged her aunt, she suddenly remembered the story about James Meehan, and how her aunt had lost her own first love. Then she remembered some of the strange things her aunt had said the other night when she was in her drunken ramblings. She had tried to block them out of her mind, but every now and again they came back, making her both wonder and worry. Sean interrupted them with tumblers of Babycham.

Ella caught her aunt's eye and Nora took a deep breath. 'Maybe I shouldn't...'

'Go on,' Sean said, 'A small Babycham isn't going to kill you, there's nothing in it.'

She glanced warily at Ella. 'Well,' she said, taking the glass from him, 'I suppose it *is* a celebration...'

Mrs Murphy came in carrying three-quarters of an apple tart she had baked that morning and a packet of Kimberley biscuits. After wishing the young couple all the best, she sat with a glass of beer, saying she would leave the two small spare bottles of the sparkling drink for Ella and Nora. She also whispered an apology to Johnny for not bringing something strong with her. 'I only had a bottle of sherry, and I thought maybe that wouldn't be the best thing after the other night.'

Johnny nodded and rolled his eyes. 'We're grand with just a drink or two each,' he whispered back.

Johnny gave a toast to the couple and after everyone cheered, Danny held his hand up. 'Thanks, everybody, and thanks Johnny for welcoming me into the family. I'm honoured, and look forward to being an official member when we've set a date for the wedding. We're going out this weekend to let Ella pick a nice ring.' He paused to smile over at Ella. 'And me Granny says she'll have you all down some evening next week and she's going to invite Nancy and Ella's other friends as well.'

'That will be lovely,' Ella said. She got on fine with Danny's grandmother now, and was used to her ways.

'We have another celebration here this evening,' Danny continued. 'I'd like to wish Sean every success with his new career over in my home city of Liverpool – where all the best people come from!' Everybody laughed. 'And we all look forward to hearing him on the radio soon.' He held his glass up and another cheer went up.

As Ella took a sip of her drink, she glanced over at her aunt in the corner, sitting with Hannah on her knee. She noticed her aunt was smiling and trying to look all jolly and happy, but something told her it was forced and unnatural. Then she saw a glint of a tear in the corner of Nora's eye and she was suddenly filled with a sense of foreboding.

Later, as she walked down to the end of the road with her new fiancé, he told her some news that only served to intensify the feeling of uncertainty.

'I got a letter from one of me aunties this morning,' Danny said, drawing her to a halt, 'there's been trouble at me mam's and she ended up in hospital with a broken arm.'

'Oh, God!' Ella said. 'What happened?'

'That bastard, Eric. They had a row and she ran upstairs and tried to shut the door on him, and he pushed it so hard she fell against the wardrobe and hurt herself. The only good news is that he's gone.' He shrugged. 'Although he could be back again next week. According to me Aunt Tilly, they've rows every other week.'

'Oh, Danny.' Ella reached up to put her arms around his neck. 'I feel terrible for you. You must be worried sick.'

'I do worry,' he said, 'but there's nowt I can do about it. Me being there only makes things worse.' He bent down now to kiss her on the forehead. 'Thank God I've got you, it's changed me whole life and given me something to plan for the future.'

'When I was young,' Ella said, 'I thought grown-ups could sort everything and make it all right. Now, I'm beginning to think they cause all the problems, and we're on the sidelines watching all the disasters and not able to do a thing about it.'

He pulled her closer to him now. 'You worry too much and think too much about everything. You need to concentrate more on yourself and all the good bits that happen. Everything will work out. It was me mam's own choice to take Eric and to stick with him.' He pressed his body closer to hers now. 'Just think, one of these days we'll be married and we won't need to stand at cold street corners to have a kiss and a cuddle any more. We'll have our own nice, warm bed to cuddle up to each other in.'

Ella felt a little wave of desire wash over her as she thought about it. 'You're right,' she said. 'We'll start planning for our own future together. I want us to be married in the next year or two and have our own place.'

'That would be the gear!' he said, beaming at her. 'And we start this week getting you an engagement ring. I'll get the money I've saved out of me post office account, you can pick anything you want.'

'That sounds brilliant,' she said, looking up at him. Her face went serious. 'But I'm not looking for a really expensive ring, I'd rather you left a bit of money in your account – just in case.'

'In case of what?'

'In case you want to go over to Liverpool. You might want to see your mam and the rest of your family.'

He held her out at arm's length now. 'Do you know something, Ella Cassidy? You're a real diamond of a girl, and I want the most expensive ring I can get you to show you how much I love you.'

PART THREE

Chapter Fifty-Four

They walked along the Liverpool docks in the semi-darkness of a chilly November morning, suitcases in hand. They had sat up most of the night as the boat had been packed and there wasn't room to lie down on a couch or bench. Sean had moaned, saying they should have paid for a berth where they could have had a bunk bed each and get a few hours' sleep, but Johnny had refused to waste the money, saying it would help pay towards their digs.

As the big city buildings loomed, a weary Johnny listened as Sean rambled on again about the new songs he had been practising and the things he was going to say to Ricky Hamilton. He advised his son to just listen and learn for the first few weeks and do anything he was asked. Sean agreed to an extent, but said he wanted to push his own ideas because otherwise he would get railroaded into singing stuff that he didn't want to.

As they walked up the familiar streets that led to the Strand Café, Johnny felt his heart start to lift at the thought of seeing Sally Mather again. Over the months since his last visit, he had spoken to her every week. He had listened as she poured out all her feelings about her husband's death and reassured her when she questioned herself. Recently, the conversation had lifted to lighter subjects and Sally had been delighted to hear they were both coming over again.

The café lights were on as they turned the corner and when they got to the door, Johnny could see Sally talking to a little dark-skinned lad aged around seven at one of the tables.

When she saw them come in, she came towards them with a warm smile. 'I'm sure I've seen you two soft lads somewhere before?'

She then took them to the table she knew Johnny liked down in the corner and took the breakfast order in to her daughter-in-law, then she brought them a large pot of strong tea.

'Who's the little lad?' Sean asked, nodding at the boy who was now busily writing something in a book.

'I'm looking after him for his mam,' Sally said. 'She wasn't feeling too well, so I said I would keep him last night. I'm only in for a few hours this morning, so I'll take him out later.' She poured Johnny's tea then Sean's.

'There's quite a few black kids around Liverpool, isn't there?' Sean mused. 'We never see many in Dublin. Are there a lot of black families in the area?'

'There's every kind here, love,' Sally said, 'but mainly Irish like yourselves.'

After he had finished eating, Sean said: 'I'm going to have a few hours' kip, then I'll give Ricky a call, and see what's happening.'

'I'll be up in a bit,' Johnny said. 'I'm going to take a walk out and buy a paper.'

As soon as he left Sally came over with a mug of tea. 'I've something I need to tell you,' she said. 'It never came up before, but the little lad over there is actually my nephew. Our Violet's son, Carl.'

'Carl? That's an unusual name, isn't it?'

Sally gave a long, low sigh. 'That's our Violet for you, never does things by half,' she said, an unusually bitter note in her voice. 'As if having a kid by an American GI wasn't enough, she had to give him a name that sticks out as well.'

'He looks a grand little boy,' Johnny said. 'He reminds me of our Larry the way he's sitting there writing away.'

'He's a lovely kid,' Sally said, 'I'm really fond of him. They've been living over in Manchester for the last couple of years, but she turned up again a fortnight ago, saying she had split up with her latest fella and was living at her friend's out on the Scottie Road. How long she'll be here for is anybody's guess. She's a bleedin' disaster area, always has been. She's man-mad, and was since she was fifteen. She's one of those women who's more bothered about doing her hair than doing her housework.' She shook her head. 'I was too embarrassed to tell you about her. But now I know you're not the kind of bloke to think bad of me because of what my sister did.'

'Of course I don't think bad of you.' Johnny wasn't sure what to say. 'What about the boy's father?'

'He's gone back to America years ago. And I don't blame him. He was mad about Violet, but she two-timed him and when she was expecting young Carl she didn't know whose kid he was until he arrived and she could see the colour. Anyway, he found out about the other fella before young Carl was born, and he broke it off with her, so he never even got to know he was his son.'

'She's not the first, and no doubt won't be the last to find herself in that situation.'

'There are times when I feel Carl's more sensible than she is. I don't know how he's turned out as well as he has.'

The café was quiet so they had more tea and then Johnny realised he hadn't told Sally about Ella. She was delighted to hear about the engagement and asked him if they had set a date.

'They're buying the ring at the weekend,' he told her, 'and I'm hoping they're not going to rush into anything too soon as she's only just sixteen.'

'Both of mine were married young, and touch wood,' she tapped her hand on the Formica table, 'they're doing fine so far. But you never know what life is going to throw at you.'

Johnny looked at her, and then gave a sigh. 'Isn't that the truth?' he said.

Chapter Fifty-Five

Nora walked up to Bewley's Café. She usually felt a little thrill coming into the city to meet her friend, but today she only felt anxiety. She needed to bring Veronica up to date on things, to let her know that the relationship with Johnny Cassidy was now over. She wanted to clear the decks of all the illusions and misunderstandings she had been living with for the last few years. It was time, she realised, to start living life in the here and now and forget all the fantasies.

When she had sketched the outline of the relationship break-up – citing differences in certain attitudes due to different upbringings – Veronica reached across the table and took her hand. 'I am so sorry to hear it's all over, and if it's any comfort, I know exactly how you feel. We can't settle for someone who we know isn't right for us. You have to be brave and let it go. As the saying goes – *To thine own self be true*.'

It was small comfort to Nora, because she knew that in her break-up with Frank Morrison, Veronica had been the strong one. She was the one who had refused to compromise and lower her standards just to have a man at her side. Nora knew that she had done the opposite. Over the years she had been harbouring delusions about Johnny, she had been prepared to cast aside her morals and values, and barter any pride she had left in order to have Johnny Cassidy at any price.

She did not tell Veronica any of this, instead weaving a story of her realising they did not have enough in common and that she was happier just being friends. Whether Veronica believed her or not, she was kind enough not to probe and make her feel any worse.

'Ah, well,' Veronica said, taking a bite out of her chocolate éclair, 'we're both back to square one, Nora. But at least we have loved and lost.' She smiled and said in a low, conspiratorial tone. 'We might be Misses, but we haven't missed a lot. And in all honesty, Johnny Cassidy is as handsome a man as you will find, and you will always have your memories. At least we won't go to the grave wondering.'

Nora had stared at her, wondering what she was inferring. She had never told her friend about the nature of her relationship with Johnny, and would never have divulged it to anyone had it not been for the unfortunate situation when Mrs Murphy was there. She decided not to ask Veronica what she had meant, as it might well backfire on her. Nora could tell that her friend wasn't going to pry further, and she was glad. She put her hand on Veronica's arm. 'I know you promised me before – but you won't ever mention about Johnny and me at work?'

Veronica shook her head. 'You have my word and I promise I never told anyone.' She sucked her breath in through her teeth. 'I only wish I had never told anyone about Frank.' She shrugged. 'It's nice to talk about it when it's all rosy in the garden, but it's not as easy when people want to know what happened when you break up.'

'Exactly,' Nora said. 'And we never really said anything to the children – you can understand how delicate the situation was. You were one of the few people I mentioned it to.'

'Of course,' Veronica said. She looked at her for a moment then said. 'Are you OK, Nora? I know it must have been hard on you, having all those plans then ...'

'I'll be grand,' Nora said quickly. 'It's done now, and we won't waste time going over it any more.'

On the bus back to the house, Nora did not feel the relief she had hoped for. There was still a sense of unease, a feeling of loss that she could not shake off.

Even though she accepted all Johnny had said, and had begun

to believe herself that they did not have enough in common to build a marriage on, she felt an emptiness that she had never felt before.

Over the next few days, as the feeling persisted, she felt she needed to talk it out again, and ended up sitting with Mrs Murphy for hours while Ella was working and the children were at school. She would have preferred someone nearer her own age, but there was only Veronica and she could not lose face with her by telling the whole story. It was important that the one true friend she had kept her good opinion of her.

'It's not really about what happened between me and Johnny,' she tried to explain to her neighbour, 'it's more about me. I just don't know what to do about the future. Since coming to live in Dublin, my life was full of plans. In the beginning it was looking after Hannah, making sure I did everything right to help her skin recover. And then all the little things I would plan for her and Larry, teaching them their alphabet and doing jigsaw puzzles and the like.' She smiled. 'And then, of course, there were the things I had to plan for the house – like making the rations stretch far enough for us all. And I had so many plans for what I was going to do with the house – and now they're all gone, for I feel I have no right to make plans any more.'

Rose Murphy had been kind. 'But you're still needed in that house, Nora, and, as far as I can see, you will be needed for a good few years to come.'

'But what if Johnny meets someone else? What if he wants to get married?'

Rose shook her head. 'He told me himself that he has not looked at another woman since Mary died.'

Nora had looked miserably down at the faded pattern in the hearth rug. 'It's all my own fault, and I know that. But I just can't stop thinking that I don't belong here any more, that I don't have the place in the family that I imagined. And there are times I'm beginning to wonder if I ever did.'

'Ah, now that's nonsense. Don't be talking like that,' Rose told her. 'You've been part and parcel of that family since you arrived. You're making too much of it all. Take your time to get over it while Johnny's away.'

As she stood ironing that afternoon, Nora mulled over the things they had discussed. She wondered now if a day down in Tullamore might be a good change of routine. It had been over a month since she had last been there and it would do no harm to check how things were with the house and the farm.

Then she suddenly thought of the two women from Tullamore she had met in Clerys and she cringed as she remembered how euphoric she had felt when she told them all about her romance and her new life in Dublin. If she met them, or anyone she worked with that they had told her news to, she would have to tell them that the wonderful new life she had described had all unravelled. She put the iron down on the board and sank her head into her hands, tears flowing down her face. Had there ever been such a deluded, foolish woman as herself?

Chapter Fifty-Six

Sean checked his tie in the mirror on the sitting-room wall and, after making a slight adjustment to the knot, put his hat on and stared at his reflection. 'Do I look all right?'

'Will you come away from that mirror?' his father said. 'It's going to break if you look into it much more.' He lifted another KitKat and began to unwrap it.

'Ignore him,' Sally said, laughing. 'You look a million dollars, Sean, like a film star.'

'Don't go making him more big-headed than he already is,' Johnny said, taking a bite from his biscuit.

'Right, I'll be off then,' Sean said, picking up his leather music folder.

'You know where you're going to, don't you?' Sally said.

'Yeah, it's the Phil, the Philharmonic Dining Rooms, and I was there before.'

Sally looked at the clock. It was nearly one now, and his meeting was at half past. 'It'll take you about quarter of an hour or twenty minutes to walk it, so you're in plenty of time.'

'I might pick up a taxi,' he said.

Johnny shook his head. Sean could spend money like it was going out of fashion. He got up from the table and went over to put an arm around him. 'Well, good luck to you anyway,' he said, squeezing his shoulder. 'And we'll look forward to hearing how you get on.'

After Sean left, Sally looked at Johnny. 'Do you fancy a walk out or maybe we could go for a drink or something? We can make sure we're back for around three. I wouldn't think he'll be back much before that.' She smiled. 'It'll be a change for me to have company, and if I stay here if they get busy down in the café, they'll be up looking for me.'

'Enough said,' Johnny told her. 'I'll be delighted to have a walk down the town with you.'

They had a walk around the city centre, stopping to look at both the magnificent buildings and the tumbled-down ruins, chatting as they went. The afternoon sky suddenly went grey and when it started to drizzle, they made for the comfort of the Queen's Head.

'Well, this is nice,' Sally said, holding her glass of gin and tonic up to touch Johnny's pint glass.

'You've no idea how nice,' he told her. 'I rarely have a drink in the afternoon these days, even on a Saturday.'

'I'm the same. I rarely go out at all, especially since Bill died.'

'Are you still finding it hard? I know we talked about it the other evening, but with Sean there, it wasn't as easy to talk as it is when we're on our own.'

She looked at him and then gave a little sigh. 'Oh, it's not easy, especially after the way Bill went.' Her eyes filled up. 'Every time I think of him lying out overnight in that lonely little spot...' She blinked several times. 'The only thing that makes me feel better is that it was a place he often talked about. One of the places he loved and went back to regularly. It was beautiful, right on the banks of Loch Lomond, overlooking the water.'

Johnny put his hand on hers. 'Try to remember the good times, it's what always helps me.' He noticed a tear sliding down her cheek and he instinctively moved closer and put his arm around her. As he drew her into him, she leaned her head on his shoulder and they sat there in silence for a few minutes.

'I'm really glad you came over again,' she whispered. 'Your phone calls were such a help to me after Bill died. They were the only little bright spark during the dark nights.'

'Well, I felt the same,' he said. 'Knowing I was going to be talking to you kept me going all week. And I always felt much happier when I came off the phone. And to be honest, Sean could probably manage on his own, but it was a great excuse to be able to come over to see you again.'

She looked up and caught his eye. 'What are we going to do, Johnny?'

'How do you mean?' He straightened up now.

'Well, I'm assuming from the way we've been talking – from the nice things you've said to me – that you have feelings for me. Am I right?'

Johnny swallowed hard on a lump that seemed to have just come into his throat. This conversation was one he had been avoiding. 'Of course I do,' he said, 'I think the world of you, and I enjoy every minute we spend together...' His shoulders suddenly slumped. 'Sally... I'm not sure what to say. I love being with you and I hope that, well, maybe in the future...'

Her face brightened. 'You don't have to say any more,' she said. 'We can't rush these things, we need to get to know each other properly before.' She held up her drink. 'Cheers, luv!'

As Johnny clinked glasses with her, he had a mixture of emotions. He was happy that this lovely woman had admitted to having feelings for him and wanted their relationship to continue. But a part of him was fearful of getting involved, of making a mistake. What had happened between him and Nora had terrified the life out of him, and although the situation with Sally bore no comparison, it was as if, by some sort of punishment, he had lost the right to connect with another woman again. The ghost of his mistake would always be there between them. As if by tainting Mary's memory they both had lost the right to any kind of happiness again.

'Are you OK?' Sally asked. 'Did I say the wrong thing?'

'No, not at all...' He looked at her now and felt like laying his head on her breast and letting her embrace and comfort him as she would a weary child, for the weariness he felt from carrying the guilty burden and having to live with it went deep into his bones. He closed his eyes. 'Sally, I'm not the man you think I am – I've made mistakes – well, one big mistake.'

There was a silence and then she whispered, 'Do you want to tell me?'

What if he did tell her? What if she was appalled and rejected him as even a friend? It would be no more than he deserved, but at least he would have told the truth for the first time in a long time. He would have taken a little bit of his dignity back. As he thought it through, he realised that he had not one thing to lose. He lifted his glass and drank half of it down in one go, and then he set it back down on the table and looked at her.

'The situation with Nora was worse than I told you. I was drinking much heavier than I should have been, and some-how...' He moved his gaze to the ceiling. 'Somehow, I ended up in a weird situation with her. The first time it happened I knew nothing about until the next morning. I was drunk and brought wine home from a function as a treat, just to thank her for being so good with the children and the house and everything. I was sleeping and I thought it was some sort of dark dream – but then a few weeks later she caught me when I came home drunk *again*.' He shrugged. 'This time she had bought drink in, and I should have known that it was odd because she wasn't a drinker – but I could hardly see straight, far less think straight.'

Sally looked startled by his revelation. 'I thought she was an older woman... old-fashioned. I didn't know you fancied her.'

'She is a bit older and old-fashioned, that's the terrible bit,' he said. 'I wasn't attracted to her at all. But, what I didn't realise is, she had never been with anybody before, and she read all sorts into it.'

Sally's face was white now. 'You mean she was a virgin?'

'I'm sorry,' he said, 'this is terrible for you to hear...'

'Go on,' she said, 'you might as well finish.'

Johnny went on then to describe how Nora had got it into her head that the late-night, drunken collisions actually meant something and she had somehow convinced herself that they were going to be married.

'Did you ever talk about it, like?' Sally asked.

'Never. The next morning it was never mentioned. In fact, for a while I kidded myself that it hadn't happened. I just put it to the back of my mind. In all honesty, it only happened a few times.' He looked beseechingly at her. 'I never planned it, and did everything I could to make sure I avoided her. She was up waiting for me every time I came in and usually with a bottle of sherry, but most times I went straight to bed. The last time was away back in the summer, and after that I cut down on the drink, and made sure there were no more opportunities.'

'And did she not get the message?' Sally looked bemused. 'Most women would kind of know if they were getting nowhere.'

'That's exactly what I'd hoped,' he said, 'but then she started all the business of putting the bathroom in and making plans for doing up the house. She thought she was sorting it out for her and myself – for a future together. And I was a pure eedjit – I had no idea.' He gave a sigh. 'She even told me she had hoped to have a baby – but thank God it wasn't true.'

'Oh, my God,' Sally said, 'It sounds like she was planning the whole thing.'

He held his hands up. 'It would be easy to blame her for everything, but I brought it all on myself by getting stupid drunk.' He looked at Sally. 'It gave me the biggest wake-up call I've ever had in my life. How poor Mary put up with me coming in from dances and weddings jarred every weekend, I don't know. All this now makes me feel I could have been better to her. Living with the guilt about that as well is terrible.'

There was another silence, then Sally said, 'Everybody makes mistakes...'

'Yes,' he said, 'and I'm trying to put it all behind me. I've been to Confessions... to different priests.'

'And did it make you feel better?'

'A bit, but it was hard trying to explain it all. One told me to remove Nora from the house and that would solve it all, but it's not that easy.'

'I went to Confession when Bill died,' Sally said. 'And although there were all the problems of how he died and where he was buried, one of the priests was really nice and understanding, and made me feel better about it.'

'Well, I'm glad you felt it helped you.' He sighed. 'It helped me for a while. I felt I had been forgiven, but it's not been easy. And in all fairness it can't be easy on her either, after what she sees as a big let-down. I tried to talk to Sean and Ella about her. I said we might get in a woman to look after the little ones for a few hours after school and let Nora go back to her own place and they went mad. Sean reared up on me, and they both said I was selfish and being hard on their poor Aunt Nora. And Larry and Hannah adore her too, so I'm on a hiding to nothing. I just can't seem to find a way out of it.'

'Oh, Johnny, it sounds terrible. Living in the same house every day with a secret between you must be a nightmare.'

'It is,' he said, 'especially when you have no one who knows and understands. I don't know how I would have coped without having you to talk to on the phone.'

She covered his hand with hers. 'Well, I'm right beside you now, and I'm listening. You can talk away as much as you want.'

He put his head down, hardly able to look at her. 'Are you sure you're still happy to sit with me, even after hearing all this? I don't know if I'm worth your time...'

'We're friends, Johnny – and friends help each other. You didn't judge my marriage when you heard how strange that was. And you were so kind when I told you about Bill taking his own life. Those phone calls helped me to get through that.'

He hesitated. 'I never imagined that I'd meet anyone who could take Mary's place.' He lowered his voice. 'Being with you makes me realise that, in time, I could start all over again.'

'That's good, Johnny. It means you're beginning to look forward again. And I feel in exactly the same boat.'

'But with you here in Liverpool and me in Dublin – and the whole mess I still have to sort out at home – what can we do?'

Sally looked down into her glass. 'There's no answer to that one. Not just yet.'

Chapter Fifty-Seven

Nora knelt by the side of the bed with her father's dark brown rosary beads wrapped around her fingers. Twenty minutes later, having said countless Hail Marys, she climbed into bed, exhausted. She did not feel any better. She did not feel as though anyone was listening to her prayers. It was not a new feeling, but the ritual made her feel she was doing something to overcome her present state of mind.

She had felt tired now for days, weeks, but her brain would not settle enough to let her sleep for more than an hour or two at a time. It kept going back to the baby... She now knew it had never been real, but it still felt like a huge loss to her. How, she wondered, did other women cope with having a baby stillborn or a miscarriage? She had never fully understood their grief.

The biggest loss was of her dreams of a very different life. A family life. One which would have included her nephews and nieces, with her and the baby at the centre of it. Instead, she was living in a house that no longer felt like her home. She knew the children cared for her, and she cherished the memory of the night that Sean and Ella had stuck up for her and demanded that she stayed. But now all hope was gone and she knew that she was not wanted by Johnny – and never would be – she had to start to dismantle that life and return to her old one. She would start the process tomorrow; she would go down on the morning train to Tullamore for the day and go to the twelve o'clock Mass. She could pick up milk and bread and maybe chops or something like that for dinner, and if she went down to the farm

Tim Dunne would give her a few potatoes and vegetables. She wouldn't need much, she was only cooking for one. Back to the old ways, she thought. Back to the lonely ways. She turned over in the bed now and let her tears fall into the pillow.

The morning was bright for November and thankfully dry and mild. Nora had dressed in a navy costume and her blue blouse with the pussycat bow, her grey tweed swing coat on top with a navy hat and gloves. She had put her usual make-up on, and her hair – which had been set in waves on Saturday – still looked fine. As she had given herself a last glance in the mirror before setting off for the train, she thought how much better she looked than when she had left Tullamore several years ago. How much better she looked than she felt inside.

It was when she was coming out of Mass that she saw Kate Thompson across the aisle in the church. The hospital receptionist was talking to an elderly couple, and when she spotted Nora she waved to her and gestured that she would see her in a few minutes outside the church. Nora gave a smile and a little wave back, and continued shuffling along with the crowd until she got outside. Without a backward glance, she quickly wove her way through the throngs of Mass-goers until she was outside the church gates, and then she rushed across the road.

As she walked up High Street towards her house, she knew she had behaved ridiculously, but it was better than standing outside the church telling a catalogue of lies. And she could have quite easily bumped into other people she knew, who would expect her to give them chapter and verse of her life up in Dublin. Thankfully, she met no one she knew in the shop at the corner, so she bought what she needed and then walked back to her house.

The afternoon wore away and she went upstairs to sort books she thought she might take back with her to read. She was planning on catching the last train back at seven o'clock. As she was checking through the bookshelves she came across some photo albums and she sat down to leaf through them. She passed another hour staring at old photographs and reliving old memories of her life in this house.

As she walked across the floor, Nora reckoned that the tapestry covered sofa and chairs were the harbourers of the damp fustiness she could smell. When she came back to live here she would throw them out and buy newer, brighter things. The thought of starting again hastened her step towards the mahogany cupboard by the side of the fireplace, where the drink was kept. The bottom cupboard, with a lock and key, held what she was looking for.

She fiddled with the small key, her hand shaking a little as she did so, until it opened. She stared at the array of bottles, gifts to her parents, some owned by her Uncle Bernard which she had salvaged from his home before it was sold.

Neither her parents or uncle had liked drinking at home, and she lifted the bottles one by one, examining the labels. She lifted a bottle of sherry, and when she pulled the corked top out, she was tempted by the sweet smell. But she had vowed to herself never to touch it again, after the spectacle she had made of herself. She put the bottle back and came out with a bottle of Tullamore Dew. She remembered how lovely it had been that evening at Mrs Murphy's. How comforted she had felt in the midst of all her misery. She had that same need again, plus she was cold in this house, and a nice hot toddy would help to keep her warm.

She took the bottle to the kitchen and then put the kettle on the cooker. She left it to boil and came back to the living room to look at the photographs. She smiled as she remembered family days out that were captured on film by her Uncle Bernard, down at Salthill with her mother and father, days out at Athlone and Fair Days in Tullamore. She had been in her twenties, then, and thought she had all her life in front of her, an exciting life with friends, a good job, and eventually a husband and children. She never thought that the days captured in the photographs would be the most exciting she would see.

She brought her mug of whiskey into the small room and

sat down in front of the electric fire. As she sipped it, she felt herself relax a little, and by the time she got to the bottom of the mug, she was warmed up and cosy. It was after five and she decided that she had time for another drink before heading for the train. She had drunk three-quarters of it when she felt her eyes start to flicker and just as she was telling herself she should move, her eyelids closed and she fell into the deepest sleep she had had for weeks.

It was half past nine when she eventually woke to the room in darkness, apart from the glow of the fire. It took her a few minutes to work out where she was and what time of the day or night it was. She moved to switch on the light, and could feel her head heavy from the whiskey. Then she checked the time and realised that she had slept for hours and that she had missed her train. She sat thinking about it for a while, and after considering her options about how to pass a message on to Ella – phoning the Guards, phoning the priest – she decided to do nothing. It was all too dramatic, and it would only draw attention to her private business. Ella would soon realise that she had merely missed the train. In fact, she thought, Ella might not be overly concerned. Danny usually came down on a Sunday night, and with Johnny and Sean gone, Nora thought she might feel in the way with the young couple on their own.

Why should she feel so guilty and concerned about staying away for a night? Sean had just walked in and announced he was going off to live in Liverpool, and just as quick Johnny had said he was going along with him for a little holiday. No mention of holidays for her. It was taken for granted that she would keep the home fires burning. Well, tonight, the only fire she was burning was the one in front of her.

She shrugged to herself as she pictured Ella now wondering what to do with the children for school in the morning. She would probably drop them off at school before work and organise Mrs Murphy or one of her friends to pick them up – if she had not returned by then.

Nora imagined that she would be filled with guilt for not

being there – but strangely, she didn't feel at all guilty. Never once had she let the Cassidy family down, not in all the years she had been living there. She had always been on hand for them all. But not tonight. Tonight she would put it all out of her mind, and go up to bed and catch up on her well-earned sleep.

She went into the kitchen again and made herself another strong, sweet whiskey. It had worked earlier on, taking her into the deep slumber she so desperately needed. As she walked upstairs with her mug, she decided she would make no plans for the morning. No alarm clocks, no rushing about the house to catch trains. She would just sleep and sleep and then take the day as it came.

Chapter Fifty-Eight

Sean looked at his father and Sally as they sat at the table close to the stage in the Adelphi ballroom on Sunday night. He had managed to get tickets for Sally and her family as well. 'Am I OK?' he asked. 'Tie straight and hair all right?'

'Perfect,' Sally reassured him. She turned to her daughter. 'Doesn't he look fantastic, Karen?'

'Absolutely,' she said.

'Go on, get on the stage,' Johnny told him. 'You look fine.' He sat back in his chair, feeling much more relaxed than he had on the previous occasion he had been in the hotel. With Sally sitting beside him, and her son and daughter and their spouses sitting around the same table, he felt as good as anyone else in the ballroom. In fact, he felt better than he had ever felt, because the hall was packed to capacity and the reason it was packed out was because of his son.

Word had got around that the Irish fella who had played back in the summer – the lad who did Frank Sinatra and that sort of crooning stuff – was back as a regular performer. And it wasn't just the crowds who had come to listen and dance to Sean's music, one of the main men from Stina Records was sitting at the next table with Ricky Hamilton. Tonight was Sean Cassidy's big night, and those who were in attendance would remember it for a long time afterwards.

There was a big round of applause as Sean took to the stage. He gave a brief wave and then he settled down at the piano, starting off with 'That Old Black Magic', then moving straight into 'The Continental', which soon got the crowd onto the dance floor.

Karen looked over at Johnny with her eyebrows raised. 'I heard he was good, but I didn't think he was as good as this. He's really the gear, isn't he!'

Johnny sat back, basking in Sean's praises. He had done the right thing encouraging him to come to Liverpool. He glanced over at the table where the fella from Stina Records was sitting, and he could see by the way he tapped his fingers on the table that Sean was going down well. As he moved on to familiar numbers by The Ink Spots and Cole Porter, David and Joanne got up on the floor and then Karen and her husband, Kevin joined them.

Johnny looked over at Sally. 'Shall we?' he said, smiling.

'Yeah,' she said standing up, 'let's show those young ones how to do it properly.' Then as they walked onto the floor she turned to him and said, 'I'm taking it for granted you can actually dance?'

Johnny laughed and swept her into his arms and they moved in perfect time to waltz around the floor. As they did so, he felt a surge of joy at the music and the dancing and he thought to himself, *This is how it should be. This is what I felt with Mary.*

After Sean had finished his first session, he came off the stage and went to sit with Ricky and the Stina fella. Johnny watched them out of the side of his eye, and could see them engaged in serious conversation. He hoped, for Sean's sake, that it was all going as planned. A quartet band came on for a while and people moved around the floor and over to the bar.

'The band is good,' Sally said to him at one point, 'but you can tell the crowd aren't as keen on them as they are on Sean. He has a unique voice, doesn't he?'

'I'm glad you think so,' Johnny said. He went to say something else, then he felt a hand on his shoulder. When he turned around, he saw the man from Stina Records.

'Simon Goodchild,' he said, holding his hand out. 'I've been here with Ricky, listening to your son. He has an amazing voice – and amazing talent. You must be very proud of him.'

Johnny sat bolt upright. 'Johnny Cassidy,' he said, 'yes, I am indeed proud of Sean – and delighted you've enjoyed his performance.'

'I certainly did. There aren't many singers who are as good on the piano as he is.' He crouched down by the side of Johnny's chair, so he could be heard without shouting over the music. 'I want him to come down to the studios in London for a recording test session, to see how he sounds. We'll sort out dates this week and Ricky will bring him down.'

'That sounds grand,' Johnny said.

'I think his voice will work well on the recordings,' Simon Goodchild said. 'In fact, I'm sure of it. He tells me he has some idea for new songs as well, and that he's written a few of his own.'

Johnny's eyebrows shot up. That was news to him, but he thought it best to keep that to himself. 'Well, Sean's music is everything to him,' he said, 'and has been since he was at school. Between you and me, he's a bit obsessed. A real perfectionist.'

'Obsession is good,' Simon said. 'The best artists usually are. I've given him a couple of new songs to look over for tomorrow afternoon – they're by an up-and-coming songwriter we have on our books. I think they might make a good match. Sean said he'll have time to run over them on the piano tomorrow before I catch my train back to London.'

Johnny laughed. 'Oh, he will. He'll be up half the night learning the lyrics to have them off pat. That's what I mean about him being obsessed.'

It was a full moon as they walked back to the café, the younger ones in front, chatting and laughing, and Johnny and Sally coming behind.

'It's great how Sean and David hit it off from day one, isn't it?' Sally said.

'I'm glad about that,' Johnny said. 'I feel happier leaving Sean

337

here, knowing he has people he gets on with. And even if he finds a place of his own, he can still go to the café and have a cup of tea with them anytime.'

Sally tipped his arm with her elbow. 'Look at them all gassing away to each other. They loved the music and the dancing tonight as well. I think they can't believe that they're walking home with the fella who was signing all the autographs earlier on.'

'I can't believe it either,' Johnny laughed. 'Did you see all the girls going up to him at the table, asking for song requests and then wanting to know if he had a girlfriend?' He shook his head. 'Some of them were very forward altogether.'

'That's modern day for you,' Sally said. 'Our Violet would be up there looking for an autograph too, and she's years older than him. Talking of her, she's heading back to Manchester – back to the boyfriend.'

'So it's back on again?'

'Yeah,' she said, nodding her head vigorously. 'That's what she's like. She drives me mad at times.'

They were just turning the corner onto Richmond Street when Sean came back towards them, holding his hands out. 'You're not going to believe it, but I forgot the music scores that Simon Goodchild gave me! I left them at the reception desk to make sure nothing happened to them.'

'You can collect them in the morning,' Johnny told him. 'They'll keep them safe for you.'

'No, I'm going to walk back and get them now. I wanted to look over the lyrics tonight. I won't be long. I'll see you in a bit.'

Johnny knew there was no point in arguing; besides, it meant he and Sally would get half an hour on their own.

They were back upstairs in the sitting room, sitting side by side drinking tea, when Johnny put his mug down on the table and turned to face her. 'I can't remember being this happy in a long time,' he told her. 'And I know I'm pleased with all that's happening with Sean, but a lot of it is down to being with you.'

Sally put her mug down too and turned towards him. 'You know I feel the same.'

Then, without another word being spoken, he moved closer and kissed her full on the lips. After a few seconds he moved back to look at her, to check it was OK, and when she smiled, he kissed her again – this time harder and deeper.

Sally felt his arms tighten around her and she wrapped her arms around his neck. It had been years since she had been kissed like this. So long, she could barely remember. It was almost as though she was thinking back to a different person. They kissed for what seemed a long time and then they both moved so they were lying on the sofa, their arms wrapped around each other.

'I've dreamed of this...' Johnny said. 'And it's even lovelier kissing you than I imagined.'

As he drew her into him, Sally tilted her head so he could kiss her again. His arms tightened around her and, as he kissed her more passionately, his hands slid gently up and down her back. As she moved closer to him she could feel the unmistakeable hardness of his ardour against her, and it sent a thrill through her that she hardly recognised. She felt his hands move to her waist and, after a while, the kissing slowed and he slowly moved one of his hands to cup her breast, asking if she was OK. She nodded and closed her eyes, enjoying all the wonderful fluttery feelings that were coursing through her.

Sally had just started to unbutton her blouse when she suddenly stopped. 'The phone,' she said, sitting up. 'It's ringing down in the café.'

'Who would be ringing at this hour of the night?' Johnny asked.

'I've no idea, but I better go down and see.' She got to the door and then it stopped. She shook her head and laughed. 'Typical, isn't it? I bet it was a wrong number. Some drunken soft lad looking for a taxi or checking if we're still open.' As she turned back, it started ringing again. This time she just moved quickly out into the hallway and back downstairs.

She came back five minutes later, her face white and serious. 'Something's happened to Sean,' she told him. 'His manager, Ricky wants to talk to you! Sean's all right, but he's been in a fight and the other lad has been rushed to hospital.'

'What?'

'Go downstairs and talk to him – he'll be able to tell you more about it.'

He rushed past her into the hallway and down the stairs to the café and over to the phone. 'Hello, Ricky, it's Johnny here,' he said.

'I've got bad news, Johnny, you need to come down to the hotel quick. The lad that Sean got into the fight with has just been taken to hospital – and it looks pretty serious. The police are here as well.'

'What in God's name has happened? He only walked down to pick up his music, and he was grand!'

'Johnny, you need to get down here before the police take him away.' Ricky's voice was low and insistent. 'Sean has just stabbed someone.'

Chapter Fifty-Nine

Ella came downstairs after checking on Larry and Hannah. She came into the living room and looked at Danny who was sitting on the couch.

'What am I going to do? It's eleven o'clock and there's no sign of her. She's never done anything like this before. She always sorts Larry and Hannah's school clothes on a Sunday night, leaves them out for them all clean and ironed.'

'Like you said, she must have missed her train or something.'

'But we can't be sure... what if she's had an accident and is maybe lying in her house in Tullamore and nobody knows she's there.'

'I don't know what to say Ella, but there's nowt we can really do. She hasn't got a phone or anything, so we'll just have to wait until she comes home tomorrow.'

She went over to sit beside him and he put his arm around her. 'I'll have to take them to school in the morning, but before I do I'll have to ask Mrs Murphy to collect them after school if Aunt Nora isn't back.' She put her hand up to her mouth. 'I'm worried sick in case she doesn't come back.'

'Was she just the same as usual when she went away this morning?'

'I wasn't up, but she was grand last night.' Ella leaned in closer to him. 'I'll just have to see what happens in the morning, but it's going to be really strange here in the house all night with just the three of us.' She squeezed his arm. 'I wish you could stay.'

'So do I, but me granny would kill me.' He started to laugh. 'If she even knew we were here tonight on our own, she'd be down here, armed with her sweeping brush, to chase me all the way back home.'

Ella sighed. 'It's not as if we're even doing anything wrong!'

Danny nodded out to the hall. 'Mind you,' he said, winking at her, 'if your Aunt Nora's not coming home, that means her room is empty – and it's a pity to let it go to waste...'

'Trust you!' Ella said, laughing and rolling her eyes. 'Well, you can forget that, there will be no proper hanky-panky until I have a wedding ring on my finger.'

'Well, if you're sure about that,' he said, grabbing her around the waist, 'the quicker we set the date for the wedding the better.'

Later, as she was seeing him off at the door, Ella said, 'You've hardly mentioned about your mam since you came in. I feel all this about my Aunt Nora has taken over. What are you going to do? The letter she sent you sounded like they're finished for good and she really wants you to go back home.'

'That's because she's feeling guilty now about picking Eric over me,' he said, 'but she did nothing to stop me going at the time and I was only fifteen.' He slid his arms around her waist. 'She could easily change her mind, you know. I know what me mam's like. What if I give up my job and then she takes him back? I'd never get one as good as that again.'

Ella gave a little cry. 'Oh, Danny, you wouldn't go to Liverpool and not come back, would you? I feel everybody's leaving me – our Sean is gone for good, I reckon, Daddy is over in Liverpool, and now my Aunt Nora has disappeared.'

'Don't be daft,' he said, shaking his head. 'Dublin is me home, especially now I have you. Besides, I've a good job in the printers and once we're married and all settled in our own place, I'm going to get a loan and start up me own business. I've loads of ideas for posters and pamphlets, and I know I could make a good go of it.'

'I know you will,' Ella said. She looked up at the dark sky, littered with stars now. 'You better go, your granny will kill you.'

'What about the ring?' he said. 'I know you didn't see anything you liked in O'Connell Street yesterday. Are we going to look in Grafton Street tomorrow during our dinner break?'

'Can I leave it until later in the week? I think I would be able to concentrate on it more when Daddy and Aunt Nora are back.'

'Okey-dokey,' he said, taking her face in his hands and kissing her. 'I still wish we'd made use of that empty bed...'

'Go away you!' she said, stepping backwards into the hallway. 'I'll see you tomorrow.'

As she closed the door, the smile slipped from her face. She was now in the house on her own with just Larry and Hannah, and it gave her a strange feeling. A feeling akin to what she had felt after her mother died. Whatever had happened to her aunt, she instinctively felt it wasn't good.

Chapter Sixty

It was a cold, grey Monday morning as Johnny and Sally walked down Richmond Street.

'I can't believe they took him away last night when he's clearly innocent.' His voice was choked. 'The thought of my boy, locked up here on his own all night.'

'It will work out,' Sally said. 'It's got to. And the solicitor that David rang this morning – Jeffrey Wilson – will be in to see him later.'

'I don't know what I'd have done without your help. You're probably wishing me and Sean had never come into your café that first morning. All this trouble that's happened—'

'Trouble finds us all at some time or another,' she said. 'It's certainly had no trouble finding me recently.'

Johnny squeezed her hand.

They slowed down now as they came to the police station.

'I'll go on inside now,' he said. 'It's nearly half past eight. It should be all right, they said before nine.'

His hand moved to straighten his tie and then brush both sides of the lapels on his good dark coat.

'Are you sure you don't want me to come in with you?'

'Not at all. This is no place for a woman.' He put his arms around her. 'Thanks for walking down with me, and I'll see you later.'

'Tell Sean we're all thinking of him.'

'I will,' Johnny said, moving away now.

As he walked up the steps into the building he felt his stomach clenching. He had always prided himself on having avoided trouble with the Guards as a young man growing up in Dublin. Having them come out to the house that time after Mary died, when Sean got into trouble stealing coal, had been a low point in his life. But, he could look back on it and see that Sean had been disturbed by losing his mother, and had lost the run of himself, as a lot of young lads do. But the situation now was a million times worse. This was serious business.

Last night a lad had been stabbed and Sean had been found with the knife. Johnny had only seen him for a few moments last night at the hotel before the police took him away, so Sean had barely had a chance to blurt out the full story.

He went in through the doors and over to the desk, explained his business to the sergeant, and was told to take a seat. Five minutes later he was escorted to the holding cells.

'I'm sorry, but you haven't long,' the sergeant told him as he unlocked the door. 'He's in court later this morning and there's probably a solicitor coming in to see him before that.'

Sean, his face pale and strained-looking, was sitting on the small single bed when the door opened, just staring straight ahead. Johnny went over and sat beside him, since there was no chair. There was the bed and nothing else.

'How're you holding up? Did you sleep at all?'

'An hour here and there.' He looked at his father, his eyes hollow and with dark rings around them. 'What am I going to do if they don't believe me?'

'They will,' Johnny said. 'Just go into court and tell them exactly what you told me last night.'

'But it's the woman I stopped to help that needs to tell them,' he said. 'She's the one that's caused all this by telling lies. He was beating the shite out of her – and now she's defending him. I can't believe she said it was me that must have had the knife. She said she's never known him to have a knife on him before.'

'She's saying that because she doesn't want him to be the one to get in trouble for carrying an offensive weapon.'

'Well, he had a knife in his back pocket, and when I heard her screaming and went over to help her, he turned on me straight away and pulled the knife out. He had no hesitation and he came at me with it.'

'The bastard,' Johnny said. 'And a coward, beating a woman.'

'That's what I thought,' Sean said, shaking his head. 'I wish I'd never stopped, but what could I do? She was shouting and screaming for help as I went past on the opposite side. At the beginning, I just thought it was a couple that were jarred and arguing, but then I saw him punching her in the stomach and grabbing her by the hair. I wish I'd just kept going now and ignoring it, as some other people further ahead did. But I was afraid of what he would do to her.' He threw his hands up in a gesture of hopelessness. 'What would you have done, Da?'

'The same as yourself, it being a woman.'

'I believe one hundred per cent if I hadn't got the knife off him he would have stuck it in me. No doubt about it. He then dived at me to get it back, and when we started wrestling on the ground, the knife must have got in the way.' He put his arm on his father's. 'God strike me down dead, Daddy, I never meant to stab him. That's exactly how it all happened.'

'Just tell the judge that this morning,' Johnny said. 'Tell it exactly the way you've told me and they'll have to believe you.'

Footsteps sounded on the corridor and the sergeant opened the door and stuck his head in. 'Five more minutes,' he said, then went back out.

'What am I going to do about the man from Stina Records?' Sean asked. 'I was to meet him this afternoon.' His shoulders slumped. 'When he hears about all this he won't be interested. He's not going to want to be involved with somebody that's just been put in jail. It'll be all over for me.'

'Stop talking like that, Sean,' his father told him. 'We'll get it sorted. I'll go down to the Adelphi and see Simon Goodchild myself and explain. He'll understand when he hears exactly what has happened. And when the truth comes out in court, you'll probably be let go this afternoon and it'll all be grand.'

As he heard his own words, Johnny wished he felt as certain inside, because things did not look good for his boy right now.

Sean looked him straight in the eye. 'I just hope you're right.'

'What's the latest?' Ricky Hamilton asked.

'He's in court later this morning,' Johnny said. 'And he's worried about missing the meeting with the lad from the recording company.'

'I'll sort it,' Ricky said. His face became serious. 'I know Sean is one hundred per cent innocent, but I can't promise anything now. Simon was really impressed with him last night, but today was his big chance to try out some new stuff – to show the range of his skills.' He looked at his watch. 'He'll be down for breakfast soon and I'll catch him there.' He looked at Johnny. 'Have you had anything yourself? Do you want me to organise something for you?'

Johnny waved his hand. 'No, I'm grand thanks.' The thought of breakfast did nothing for him, although it crossed his mind how easily people like Ricky Hamilton sorted things for other people. How well taken care of Sean would have been if this catastrophe hadn't happened to him. Money and business certainly talked.

'Sean has a solicitor sorted, doesn't he?'

'Yes,' Johnny said, nodding. 'My friends recommended one, and he's going in to see him this morning.'

'OK, then,' Ricky said, looking around him. 'You have my phone number – let me know as soon as there's any news – hopefully positive news.'

There was a slightly awkward silence and Johnny suddenly felt he had no place here without Sean.

He stood up and shook Ricky's hand. 'I'll be in touch as soon as I hear anything, and thanks for your help.'

At one o'clock Johnny and Sally walked back into the café, which was busy with customers. David came over to them.

'How did the court hearing go?'

347

'Remanded in custody for a week,' Johnny said, 'until they get all the witness statements.'

Sally slipped her arm through Johnny's. 'We just have to believe that the truth will come out.'

'Are you ready to eat?' David asked. 'I can send something upstairs for you.'

She looked at Johnny. 'You hardly ate anything this morning, it would do you good to have something now.'

When they were in the sitting room upstairs, Johnny sat down on the edge of the sofa. 'I can't think what to do first – I suppose I need to phone the hospital, and then hope Ella rings me tonight so I can tell her I'm not coming back until next week.'

'Will you tell her why?'

'I don't want to worry her. It might be best if I just say I've got to go to London with Sean or something like that.'

'See how it goes,' Sally said. 'And I know you don't want to think about her, but at least you know the kids are well looked after there with Nora.'

'That's true,' Johnny said. 'I can't take that away from her.'

Chapter Sixty-One

On Monday work dragged as Ella just wanted to get home and find out what had happened to her aunt. Just going on for half past five, Ella was tidying a glass display cabinet of leather purses when she saw a woman coming towards her. She smiled and pushed the door of the cabinet closed.

'Ella?' the woman said, 'I just wondered if I could have a quick minute or two with you?'

Ella realised it was her Aunt Nora's friend.

'I was just wondering how your Aunt Nora is?' Veronica said. 'I was supposed to meet her on Saturday but she cancelled it. I was just wondering was she all right?'

Ella's heart sank. 'I don't know, she didn't come back from Tullamore last night. I thought you were going to say she might have phoned you with a message.'

'Oh,' Veronica said. 'No, she hasn't been in touch with me.'

They looked at each other.

'I'm actually a bit worried,' Ella said. 'It's not like her. I'm hoping she'll be back at the house when I get home.' She bit her lip. 'I'm just worried she wasn't feeling well or something like that, and had no way of letting us know.'

Veronica nodded, a thoughtful look on her face. 'I hope she's OK – she's been a bit up and down recently.' She was wary of saying the wrong thing. Then she looked at Ella and thought that she was old enough to know what was going on in her own house. And if Nora wasn't well or upset, they had to do whatever could be done to help her. 'I was wondering if things were getting too much for her in the house, if she's finding it awkward now things have changed with your father?'

'How do you mean?' Ella asked.

'Well, I don't like to talk about their private business, but now things have changed between them – now they're not … I just wondered if she's decided to go back to Tullamore?'

Ella stared at her, her mind suddenly flashing back to the two women who had congratulated her aunt on getting married, to the night her Aunt Nora was drunk and rambling, and saying very strange things. 'Can I just ask you,' Ella whispered, her heart racing now. 'Has Aunt Nora told you there was something going on between her – between her and Daddy?'

Veronica felt her throat tighten. The girl obviously didn't know. She leaned in closer. 'Now, she told me in confidence, and I would never break that, but under the circumstances I'm worried about her.'

'I'm worried about her too,' Ella said, her eyes widening, 'because not one bit of that is true. I don't know where she's got the idea there was something between her and Daddy.' She gave a little shudder. 'Oh, my God – the thought of it!'

'Oh, Ella, your Aunt Nora told me they were more or less engaged and planning to get married in the not too distant future. She told me all this when she put the bathroom in. She was even talking about selling her house and farm in Tullamore and buying a nice big house in Dublin.'

'But it's not true!' Ella whispered heatedly, vague memories coming back of her Aunt Nora rambling on about people thinking she was too old to get married or too old to have a baby. She suddenly found it hard to breathe. She had to make herself stop and take as deep a breath as she could manage. She could not cope with this now. She was at work, and Miss Roarty could come over at any time. She blinked rapidly a few times to try to push the images out of her mind. 'There's never been a thing between them,' she said, moving her head from side to side. 'Never! Daddy's still not got over Mammy. Aunt Nora was just helping us all out…' She stopped now, as tears suddenly came into her eyes.

'Oh, God,' Veronica said, 'I didn't mean to upset you, but better you know the truth, because she can't be well if she's making all this up. Whatever was going on, or whatever she imagined, she did tell me recently that it's all over.'

Ella took a deep breath. 'Well, thank God for that, and I hope she is all right. Although if she really felt like that about Daddy, I don't know how things can ever be the same in our family again.'

Chapter Sixty-Two

Nora woke up to the sound of loud knocking on the front door. She looked over at the window, squinting at the bright sunshine that was slanting through the crack in the curtains. She lay for a few moments, wondering if she had imagined it, then when it started again, she sat up and made herself move.

Her head felt heavy and slightly dizzy as she got to her feet and went to the hook on the back of the door to retrieve her dressing gown. Then, barefoot she went down the stairs to open the door.

'Ah, it's yourself!' Tim Dunne said, smiling at her. 'I wasn't sure if you'd gone back to Dublin or not.'

Nora gathered the dressing gown around her neck. 'Not yet,' she said. 'Did you want me for something?'

'I was driving past and I just thought I'd see if you wanted a few eggs.' He held out a brown paper bag with string handles. 'There's a dozen there. I've wrapped them singly in newspaper, so they should be OK if you're carrying them back with you.'

She took the bag from him. 'That's very good of you, Tim,' she said, attempting a smile. 'I'll have one for breakfast. I haven't decided what I'm doing yet.'

His face became serious. 'Oh God, did I wake you? I never gave it a thought with it being twelve o'clock.'

Nora's heart lurched. 'Is it really that time?'

He checked his watch. 'Ten past twelve.'

'I've had a touch of a cold and I was awake during the night. I must have been catching up.'

He nodded, then he smiled at her. 'It will do you good.' He stepped backwards. 'Well, I won't keep you. I'd better be getting a move on.' Then, he turned back to her. 'I don't suppose – I don't suppose you'd like to catch a bite of dinner with me? I'm going down to Hayes Hotel and it would be grand to have a bit of company. To be honest, I've missed seeing you around the place. I looked forward to having the oul' chat when you were here.'

Something about the tone in his voice made Nora look up at him. Then she caught the shy but hopeful look on his face, and she realised the eggs were only an excuse to see her. Was it possible, she wondered, that he had feelings for her that she hadn't realised? She tried to process it quickly as she had no time to waste: what they had in common, which was only the farm. Whether she found him attractive: no, not at all. Whether they might be good companions for each other? She could not imagine sitting with him listening to Glenn Miller on the radio, going to the cinema with him, walking around St Stephen's Green with him. In short – kind though he was, she could not imagine a life with him at all.

She cleared her throat. 'Oh, that's very kind of you, Tim,' she said, 'but I'm going to go back up to Dublin in the afternoon. I have commitments there, the children to pick up from school, the evening meal to sort.'

Tim took another step backwards. 'No problem at all,' he said, tipping his cap as though he had just received good news. 'Maybe another time that suits better?'

'I've got to go and get my bath now,' she said, closing the door. 'And thanks again for the eggs, it was very kind of you.'

When she got inside, Nora took a deep breath. Who would have imagined it? She walked down to the kitchen, poured herself a glass of water, then glanced up at the clock. What would they be thinking back in Dublin? She had left them all high and dry for the usual Monday morning rush. Had someone taken Larry and Hannah to school? Who would pick them up? She would have to explain herself when she went back. The thought of it brought a wave of fatigue and she could not think about it any more. She should go back to bed – just for an hour – to shake off the muddled up feeling. She would decide what to do after that.

It was four o'clock when her eyes fluttered open again. This time, she actually felt rested. She went downstairs and made herself tea and a boiled egg and toast, and then she washed and dressed. When she came back downstairs she sat on the chair by the window and stared out, trying to work out what to do. She could just stay down in Tullamore, she thought, and see how long it would take until someone missed her, and came looking for her. Maybe they wouldn't even bother. They might all be glad to be rid of her. Johnny – well, Johnny had no use for her now. He had made that plain.

But then a picture of the two little ones came into her mind. Poor Larry, such a clever but sensitive little boy. She loved him as much as she could imagine loving her own child. And little blonde-haired Hannah, a lovely, sunny child. Just thinking about them brought a knot in her chest. As she looked out of the window, her vision slowly blurred as tears came into her eyes. She got up and went over to the sink where she had left the bottle of whiskey from the night before. There was still a reasonable amount in it. She lifted a mug and filled it halfway up, then she poured lukewarm water from the kettle into it and added two heaped spoonfuls of sugar.

She came back to the window and sat there, sipping and thinking. By the time she was on her second mug, she had come to her decision. She couldn't disappear forever from the children's life without sorting things out. It would be wrong and cruel. It would be like losing a second mother. But what kind of a reception would she get having disappeared and left them?

She drained the end of the toddy to bolster her courage and stood up, swaying as she did so. Who was going to question her? Who had the right to question her? She would answer to no one. She had lived her life for the Cassidys for long enough.

Once again, she looked at the clock. She might make the five o'clock train – and if they didn't treat her properly, she thought, she would come back to Tullamore and that would be the last they would ever see of her.

Chapter Sixty-Three

Ella walked quickly down to Mrs Murphy's house.

'No sign of her yet?' Rose asked. They stood in the hallway so that the children, who were in the living room, didn't hear them.

'Nothing. I think I might have to phone the Guards,' Ella said in a low, strained voice. 'I'm getting really worried now.'

'Don't be getting worried,' Rose said. 'She's only been gone one night, and if she's not home tomorrow we'll start to make enquiries. I was just thinking that we could ask Father Brosnan to ring down to the priests in Tullamore to check she's all right.'

'That's a good idea,' Ella said. 'At least we'd know one way or another. I'm still worried about the thought of her lying sick or something like that.'

'Come on down to the scullery, I have the kettle boiled and a nice warm apple tart just out of the oven. Larry and Hannah have had chips and fried egg, so they're grand.' She paused. 'Would you like me to make you some?'

'No thanks, I'm not a bit hungry.'

'Your father is due home tomorrow, isn't he?'

'He is, thank God,' Ella said, 'and he better not be planning any more trips away. My nerves couldn't handle it.' She looked at the kindly neighbour. 'I don't know what I would have done without you to help with Larry and Hannah today.'

'I'm more than happy to walk down to the school for them,' Mrs Murphy said. 'Sure, it gives me something to do, and gets me out of the house. The doctor is always telling me I need a walk every day for my blood pressure, so it's doing me more good than harm.'

Rose turned to pour the tea into the cups and when she came to the table with it, she saw the young girl wiping her eyes with her hanky. 'Are you OK, pet?'

'I don't know what to think,' Ella said, starting to cry now. 'My Aunt Nora's friend came into Clerys this afternoon, and she was asking about her, saying she thought she wasn't herself recently – and she said something about Daddy and Aunt Nora.'

'What? What did she say?' Rose's heart quickened.

'She said Aunt Nora gave the impression they were – they were going to get married.' She looked up at the neighbour. 'It's all nonsense, isn't it?'

'Of course it is,' Rose said. She thought the last thing Ella needed was something like that to worry about. 'I wouldn't pay any heed to that at all. She might have just been saying it, thinking about appearances for the church and that kind of thing. A man and a woman together in the same house? She might have thought it might be a way to give him peace from other women...'

None of it made any sense to Ella, but she couldn't very well say that. 'I'm going to talk to Daddy about it when he comes home, he needs to sort it all out.' She gave a little strangled sob. 'A while ago Daddy was talking about Aunt Nora, saying that it was maybe time for her to go back to Tullamore, and he said then that we didn't really know what she was like. I'm beginning to wonder if this is what he was talking about.'

'Ella, don't go meeting trouble halfway,' Mrs Murphy advised. 'She's a decent woman, and she's at a point in her life where sometimes things can get on top of you a bit. Think of all the good things she's done.'

'You're right enough. I'm maybe making too much of it.'

Nora felt a hand roughly shaking her shoulder and looked up to see a young man in a uniform staring into her face. 'What is it? What's going on?' she asked.

'C'mon, Missus,' he said, gesturing at her, 'you're in Dublin for the last ten minutes. People are waiting to get on the train and you need to get yourself off.'

Nora sat up and looked out of the train window. Then, slowly she got to her feet. She put her coat on and gathered the bags she had with her, then she moved out of the carriage. She stepped down off the train, stumbling as she did so. She went along the platform, trying to work out how she had got from Tullamore to Dublin. She had no memory of walking up to the train station or getting on the train. She was tired, she thought, so tired her mind wasn't clear enough to remember.

When she got through the station, it was raining and blustery. She stood for a moment, and then decided she would get one of the taxis parked outside the station. As the gentlemanly driver put her bags in the boot, she sat up straight, her mind going over the days, and wondering whether Johnny was back home yet or not. She then tried to remember what she had decided to say about her unplanned overnight stay. As they drove along she recalled that she would more or less tell the truth – which was always the best policy – and say she had been unwell and needed to sleep.

The driver brought her bags to the doorstep, and after he drove away, Nora took a deep breath and put her key in the lock. Once inside, she discovered the house was dark and empty. She called upstairs for Ella just in case, and then she went down to the scullery to unpack the items she had brought back from the house. At one point she went back out to the door to check there was no sign of anyone, and then she rushed back into the scullery to take the bottle of sherry from a bag and a glass from the cupboard. An emergency measure to relax her – and get her over the awkward return to the house. She filled another little one, and then went into the living room to turn on the lights and the radio. Someone, she noticed, had kept a fire going. As she unpacked the rest of her bags, she finished off her drink, washed the glass, and then – feeling much more relaxed and in control of her anxiety – put the half-empty sherry bottle in one of her bags and took them upstairs.

She came back downstairs just as Bing Crosby came on the radio singing. The cheery song lifted her spirits instantly. She straightened up cushions and the candlesticks on the mantelpiece, then came back into the middle of the room and, as the music energised her, kicked off her shoes. This was exactly what she had enjoyed with Johnny – the merriment, the throwing off of inhibitions – and although she knew that episode of her life was over, she would not settle for anything less with anyone else. She would rather spend her nights at home alone like this – singing along with the radio and dancing around – than settling with someone like Tim Dunne. The decision, fuelled by the whiskey and sherry, gave her a feeling of power and euphoria.

It was just at this very point that Ella and Mrs Murphy came past the window. The curtains were still undrawn and Ella came to a halt. 'Oh, no,' she gasped, pulling on the elderly neighbour's sleeve. 'Would you look at the state of her!'

Rose stared in the window, her mouth gaping as she watched Nora whirling around in her stocking feet, the hem of her skirt in her hand as though she were Isadora Duncan herself. Then, she saw her stumble and catch herself on the chair, and then, after a few seconds, start to shimmy in time to the music again. She blessed herself, 'Jesus, Mary and Joseph!' Then, she turned to Ella. 'Say nothing tonight. You won't get any sense out of her.'

When they got inside the house, the children went in to say hello to Nora and then, after being hugged and kissed with an unusual intensity, they were bundled upstairs to bed.

'I wasn't too well,' Nora explained to Ella and Mrs Murphy, a bright smile on her face which did not reach her eyes. 'I'd say it was a bad bout of the flu; it completely floored me last night and I slept for hours and missed the train.'

Rose looked at her, thinking that it was more likely the sherry that she stank of that had floored her.

'We were worried sick about you,' Ella said. 'We nearly

phoned the Guards or the priest in Tullamore to check you were all right.'

'Ah now, that would have been a bit extreme,' her aunt said laughing. 'I was hot and clammy all night, and then this morning I was aching all over and not fit to get out of bed. I dragged myself out this afternoon, and thankfully I feel a morsel better.'

Ella was saddened and confused, as she looked at the state of her aunt. Her voice was slurred from drink, her hair was dishevelled, there were black rings around her eyes from her mascara, and one of her toes was protruding through a hole in her stocking. Mrs Murphy had explained how the change of life could affect some women in strange ways – and she could now clearly see that something had tilted the balance of her aunt's mind.

'Why don't you take a Beecham's Powder and go up to bed early tonight again?' she said, her voice kind and concerned.

Nora joined her hands together as though in prayer, relieved that her explanation had been so well received. 'I think I will,' she said. 'I want to be up to take the little ones to school.'

'Now Nora,' Mrs Murphy interrupted, 'why don't you let me take them? I think you could do with a bit of a lie-in, and get yourself back to normal. Back to your old, organised self.'

Nora looked from one to the other. 'Maybe if we see how I am in the morning?'

'I'll call down before Ella goes to work, around half-eight, and we'll see how things are. Wouldn't that be the best?'

'Thanks,' Ella said, 'and would you mind staying for another ten minutes to let me run down to the phone box to ring Daddy? I just want to check what time he is due home tomorrow.'

'Sure, there's no need for Mrs Murphy to stay,' Nora said, waving a finger. 'I'll be here for the children.'

'Well, can't we keep one another company for a few minutes while Ella is out?' Rose said, smiling at her.

'Of course we can,' Nora said, and as Ella went to get her coat, she touched the side of her nose. 'And you and me might even have a little drink together. I brought a drop of sherry back with me, just in case.'

'A cup of tea would suit me better,' Rose said.

Chapter Sixty-Four

Johnny had decided not to worry Ella with the terrible news about Sean, but when he heard how upset she was about him not coming home, he was not so certain.

'You'll have to come home this week, Daddy,' Ella stated. 'Aunt Nora is not well. She disappeared for two days to Tullamore and never told us. I had to get Mrs Murphy to look after Larry and Hannah.'

'Holy Lord,' Johnny gasped. 'What's got into her an' all?'

'She's been acting strangely and...' She lowered her voice, even though she was in a public phone box and there was no one outside. 'She's been drinking again. She must have been drunk coming back up on the train to Dublin. You're going to have to talk to her when you get back home, and maybe get her to see a doctor or something.'

'God, Ella, I'm sorry to hear all that. How is she now?'

'She's still a bit drunk, but she's going to bed early, so hopefully she'll be back to her old self in the morning. If she's not, I don't know what I'm going to do.'

'Could you phone into work sick or something? Or get Danny to go in and tell them for you.'

There was a pause. 'When will you be back?'

Johnny took a deep breath. He knew only the truth would do. 'Look Ella, I didn't want to tell you, but we've got a problem here.' And he related the story about Sean and how he had ended up on remand.

'Oh, Daddy...' Ella started to cry. 'Poor Sean, and him only

362

trying to help that terrible woman, and now she won't help him! What if he gets found guilty and they put him in jail for years? He wouldn't be able for that. You know what he's like.'

'We'll just have to wait and see,' Johnny said, his heart leaden just thinking about it.

'What's happening to us?' she sobbed. 'I feel everything is going wrong for our family again. It's like when Mammy died, and I'm frightened.'

'You'll be grand,' Johnny said, trying to soothe her. 'You'll all be fine. I'll be home as soon as we get this sorted, but I can't leave Sean in a prison in England all on his own.'

'I feel terrible we're all separated.'

'You have Mrs Murphy there and Danny as well, don't you? He's your fiancé now, and will make sure everything is grand. Why don't you ask him to stay for a couple of nights? He can sleep in with Larry.'

Having Danny in the house would make a massive difference. He would be able to help manage Aunt Nora too. 'OK,' Ella said, 'I'll go down and see him now.' The pips suddenly sounded. 'Tell Sean I send my love and I'll see him soon...'

As she walked to Danny's she wondered why she had said that, because she didn't know when she would ever see her brother again. The next time he could be in an English prison cell, all on his own. By the time she reached the house, a plan had hatched in her mind. When Danny answered the door, she pulled on the front of his jersey to bring him outside, where no one could hear them.

'Have you still got the money for the engagement ring?' she asked him.

'Yes,' he said and grinned at her. 'Have you seen a ring you like?'

'No, I want us to use the money to go to Liverpool. Our Sean is in serious trouble and I want to see him, and you need to go and see your mother.'

He took a step back. 'What? Are you kidding me?'

'No, Danny, I'm not. We're both going to phone into work

tomorrow and say we've to go over to England for a funeral and we'll be back next week. I've got a bit of money saved too, it's not much but it will help.'

He stared at her now. 'You're dead serious, aren't you?'

Ella nodded. She quickly told him all about Sean and about her Aunt Nora going off the rails again.

'Ah, Jesus!' he said, 'poor Sean. Imagine him going through all that over in Liverpool on his own.'

'Thank God Daddy went with him,' she said, 'but something keeps telling me we all need to be together as a family to get through this. Will you come with me?'

'If that's what you want, then that's what we'll do.' He thought. 'There's a boat that goes in the morning to Holyhead in Wales, and we can get a train or bus from there to Liverpool. We won't need to book it at this time of the year. But what about a place to stay?' Danny suddenly thought. 'If Mam's all right and Eric's not back, I can probably stay there, but with us not married yet, we won't be allowed under the same roof. Will you call your relatives?'

'I've got the name of the bed and breakfast that Daddy and Sean are staying in. He left me the name with the phone number.'

'Do you want to ring him back and tell him we're coming?'

'No,' Ella said, 'he'll only try to talk me out of it. We'll phone when we arrive in Liverpool and then he can't do anything about it. I'm not going to say anything to Aunt Nora or Mrs Murphy until the morning. I'm going over to see our Sean, and nobody is going to talk me out of it.'

Chapter Sixty-Five

Johnny was sitting downstairs in the café when the door opened. It was a fairly quiet time in the afternoon, and he was drinking a cup of milky coffee and reading a newspaper, trying to take his mind off things, when he suddenly heard familiar voices calling, 'Daddy!' When he looked up, Larry and Hannah were coming flying towards him. They threw themselves in his arms, and while he was still staring at them in shock, he saw Ella and Danny following behind.

He cuddled the children first, and then when they were settled in chairs beside him, he looked up at Ella. 'What on earth are you doing here?'

'I've come to see Sean,' she said. 'I couldn't settle knowing he is where he is. And we all missed you too.'

Johnny stood up and wrapped his arms around her. 'You're a sight for sore eyes,' he said, his voice thick with emotion. They stood just holding onto to each other while Danny pulled a chair out at the opposite side of the table.

Sally saw the group and came over towards the table to serve them, not realising Johnny was in the middle of them. She stopped a few feet short of the table, wondering who they were. Then, not wishing to intrude, she turned away but Johnny beckoned her over. 'Sally, you're not going to believe this,' he said in a low voice, 'but this is my family, and they've come all the way over from Ireland to support Sean and check we're OK.'

Sally came towards the table, feeling a little apprehensive, as Johnny introduced them all. 'I'm delighted to meet you,' she said, smiling at Ella. 'Sean and your dad talked a lot about you and Larry and Hannah.' She looked at the two little ones. 'I'll bet you two are starving after that long journey, aren't you? Would you like some chips and a glass of orange? And what about some sausages? I've got those nice little ones that all the kids like?' She looked at Ella. 'What do you think, luv? You'll know best.'

'Oh, sausages and chips would be grand,' Ella said. She looked at Danny. 'And what about you? Are you going to eat now or wait until you get to your mother's?'

'I'll eat with you lot,' he said grinning. He picked up the menu and studied it for a few moments, 'D'you know what I really fancy? Scouse. It's ages since I've had it.'

'Ah, you're definitely a Liverpool lad,' Sally said, grinning at him. She looked at Ella. 'Your dad was telling me you got engaged, isn't that great news? Congratulations to you both. Now, before I put the order through to the kitchen, have you sorted anywhere to stay?' She looked from Johnny to Ella. 'I've got two empty rooms upstairs, so it's no problem. The girls can go in one and the lads in the other.'

'Are you sure you've room for me?' Danny asked. 'I could squeeze in at me mam's.'

'I've a twin-bedded room you and this lad can share,' she said ruffling Larry's hair, 'and a double for the girls.'

'Ah, that's the gear,' Danny said, winking at Sally. 'I'll go out to me mam's for the evening and then I'll come back here later on.'

'Thanks, Sally,' Ella said. She didn't mind Danny not staying at his mother's, as long as he actually went and saw her. And she was glad he would be there with her and the children to help her. 'We had a bit of a cheek turning up like this, without giving you any warning.' She looked at her father. 'I didn't know where we'd stay, but I thought if we got stuck we'd go out to our uncles in Bootle.'

'We'll all be grand here,' Johnny said, 'but we'll call out and see your uncles as soon as we get the chance, anyway.'

'Well, now that's all settled, I better get you fed and watered, then I'll show you where you're all sleeping.'

Ella looked at the warm, cheery woman who was organising everything for them, and suddenly felt a wave of relief wash over her. It was as if she had been holding her breath for days and suddenly found she could breathe.

After they had eaten, Johnny said he was going down to the solicitor's office to see if there was any news about the other people's statements. Danny set off to get the bus out to Anfield to see his mother and sisters and Ella reminded him to take two of the packets of tea they had brought over from Dublin, as it was still in short supply. She herself might take Larry and Hannah for a walk out to the shops before they closed, to buy them a book each.

Sally took off her apron and said she would go with her. 'Me daughter, Karen and her husband Kevin have just come in, so they'll take over serving.'

As they walked around Woolworths, Ella smiled to herself as she listened to Sally's friendly Liverpool accent which reminded her so much of Danny's. She was very good with the children and after Ella bought them books, she bought them a comic each as well.

Johnny came back, grim-faced, and quietly told Ella and Sally that the solicitor had explained that the lad who had been stabbed was still in hospital and not fit to give a statement yet. He'd been operated on and was recovering, but it might be a few more days before the police were allowed to question him. The woman who had been with him had given a statement to say she was unaware of her boyfriend owning a knife and that she still thought it was Sean's.

'We'll just have to wait and see,' Johnny sighed, 'and hope and pray something comes up.'

Danny came back around ten o'clock, and Ella could tell by his face that it had gone better than he had imagined. 'She looked well,' he told her when they were in the living room on their own, 'her arm is a lot better, and the good news is that Eric's got a job up in Glasgow and he's gone for good.'

A little note of fear suddenly came into Ella's mind. 'Did she ask you to come home?' She was relieved that Danny's mother was safe and well, and was glad to hear that the awful-sounding Eric was gone for good, but she was now worried that he would move back to Liverpool.

'She said she would love me to be nearer, but she understands I'm settled in Ireland now, and especially with us being engaged. She's happy that I'm with my granny and grandad and cousins, but she feels bad I was forced to go because of her and Eric.' He shrugged. 'I told her it's all water under the bridge now and no point in looking back. But she was really glad to see me and wants me to bring you out for tea one night so you can meet her and me little sisters.'

'That would be great,' Ella told him, hoping this was the start of a change in fortune for them all.

The following day, Danny took Larry and Hannah off for a tour around the city, while Ella went with her father to visit Sean in Walton Prison. Any optimism she had had drained away when she saw the old Victorian building that her brother was incarcerated in. Her heart raced as she and her father went through the gates and then waited outside the big wooden doors until they were escorted inside. They joined the scores of other visitors in a queue, many rough-looking and the sort that she expected to see in a jail, but there were other very decent-looking people like themselves, which made her feel a little better.

Eventually they were taken inside to an area with lots of tables and she spotted her brother sitting at one. Her instinct was to smile and wave, but when he saw them Sean put his head down and didn't look at them until they were sitting opposite.

'You shouldn't have come into a place like this,' was his greeting.

Ella looked at his strained, white face. 'I came because I miss you and I wanted to see you. And Danny wanted to come and see his mam anyway.'

Sean lifted his head, his chin jutting out. 'If I get found guilty, you'll be sick of seeing me in here. They could put me away for years.'

'You're not going to get found guilty,' Johnny told him. 'The police will be taking a statement from the other fella tomorrow or the day after.'

'He's not going to admit carrying the knife,' Sean said, 'and I'll end up going down for it. My so-called brilliant career will be down the tubes before it even got a chance to start.' His eyes filled up with tears. 'It's not fair,' he said. 'I only went to help the woman and look where it's got me.'

Chapter Sixty-Six

The following afternoon the five of them caught the bus out to Johnny's brother Joe's house in Bootle. Joe was the middle brother, and worked as a postman, so Johnny knew he would be home as he finished around three o'clock.

They had brought a box of biscuits and two packets of tea which Joe's wife Betty was delighted with. 'You're all welcome,' she said laughing, 'but the tea is the most welcome visitor in any house in Liverpool.'

After the tea and biscuits, Danny and Ella took the younger ones for a walk to give the adults a chance to talk in private.

Johnny repeated the story of what had happened to Sean, and Betty burst into tears. 'Oh, my God,' she said, 'if that was any of my lads I would be heartbroken, especially since he was only doing a good deed.'

'That's a nightmare altogether,' Joe said. 'And do you know anything about the lad that had the knife? His name or anything or where he comes from?'

'I think they said he was from Scotland Road,' Johnny said, 'but the name I just can't think of – it's not an Irish one anyway.' He stopped for a few moments. 'I think it was something like Bishop...' He clicked his fingers. 'That's it – Robert Bishop.'

'I'll ask around,' Joe said. 'What was the girl's name?'

'Ruby something. I never caught her second name.'

'Leave me the number of the café you're staying at,' Joe said, 'and I'll ask the lads when they come in from work, and we'll see if anybody knows them. In the morning I can ask the lads that deliver the mail around the Scottie Road area – you would be surprised what you get to hear on your rounds.'

The next day Ella and the children went with Danny to meet his mother and sisters, and after Johnny had been to visit a dispirited Sean again, he and Sally went into the Queen's Head to steal a quiet hour on their own.

'Your family are lovely, Johnny,' Sally said, taking a sip of her gin and tonic. 'And although it's not the circumstances we'd have liked to have met up, I'm delighted that they came over.'

'Well, it's made me see Ella in a new light,' he said. 'I hadn't realised just how grown up she was. She's taken charge of everything and was able to sort them all out to come over to Liverpool within a day. Fair play to her, when she makes her mind up to do something, she'll move heaven and earth until she gets it. And she couldn't have picked a better lad than Danny Byrne – he not only adores her, but he listens to her as well.' He stopped, then shook his head. 'If only poor oul' Sean was as well settled and had somebody by his side. That's what he needs. God, when I think of him stuck in that cell. His poor mother would turn in her grave.'

Sally squeezed his hand. 'It will all sort out, don't get yourself all worked up again.'

They were all together again in the café that evening, and as they were eating their chips and fish fingers, Larry and Hannah were full of chat about the rabbits they had seen in the cage, out at Uncle Joe's.

'And the people in Liverpool don't eat the rabbits, Daddy,' Larry said with big eyes. 'They have them as pets. Isn't that much better?'

'Could we get a pet one when we get home?' Hannah asked.

'We'll think about it,' Johnny said, 'but maybe a little dog would be handier.'

'You can practise with me granny's dog, Prince, when we get

back home,' Danny said, winking over at Larry. 'You can hold the lead next time we're going out for a walk.'

Larry lifted his eyes to look at Johnny. 'When are we going back home, Daddy?'

Then Hannah turned to him. 'And when are we going to see Auntie Nora again – I miss her.'

Johnny looked over at Ella, and as their eyes met, he knew they had to have the discussion about her before any more time passed.

They had just gone upstairs and settled the children down with their books when David came up to tell Johnny that he had four men asking for him at the café. 'Your brothers and two nephews – they said they would meet you over in the Queen's Head as soon as you're ready.'

'Do you want me to come with you?' Ella asked.

'It's up to you...'

'I'll keep an eye on the kids,' Danny said.

'And if you're not back,' Sally said, 'I'll get them sorted for bed.'

After Johnny bought everyone a drink and they were settled at a table at the back of the empty lounge, Joe started. 'We got some information about the lad Sean was in the fight with.' He gestured across the table to his sons. 'Gerry and Arthur here did a bit of investigating down in the White Horse and it seems that Bishop fella is well known for fighting.'

Gerry leaned his elbows on the table. 'And from what we've been told, he's no stranger to knives, either. He's been involved in a few incidents.'

Johnny put his hands on the table, palms up, 'So what does that mean?'

'It means you need to get down to your solicitor and let him know, and they need to put a bit more pressure on that girl,' Arthur said. 'And from what we've heard, it's not the first time he's given her a good belting. But the thing is, she'll be terrified

372

of him and won't want to tell about him carrying the knife and drawing it first, in case he takes it out on her later.'

'Well, she'll have to be made to tell the truth,' Ella said, her eyes glinting. 'And she needs to cop on about the type of lad she's running about with.'

'True for you,' Uncle Charlie said. 'I know what I'd do if it was a daughter of mine being treated like that.'

Johnny looked at his watch. 'I'm going to ring the solicitor, he said to call any time.'

'I'll come with you,' Ella said, finishing off her lemonade.

Joe nodded. 'We'll have another one while you're away, and you can let us know what he says.'

Johnny listened intently to Jeremy Wilson. 'Apart from what you've just told me,' the solicitor said, 'which will definitely help his case, I've also got some encouraging information for you. I've just come back from seeing Sean in the last half an hour. I went in to tell him that we have new evidence, and a new witness statement.'

'A witness to the fight?'

'Yes, it seems Mr Bishop and his girlfriend had an altercation in a pub in the city centre earlier on. There was a couple sitting next to them who heard him threatening her, and they left just after Bishop and the girl. They caught up with them on Church Street and they saw Bishop pushing and hitting the girl. They stayed on the other side of the street to avoid them, and in fact went down a side street so Bishop didn't see them. They saw Sean running over to try and help and they heard the girl shouting to Bishop to put the knife away.'

Johnny closed his eyes and leaned against the phone unit. 'Thank God,' he said, 'Thank God...'

'The police are out at the hospital now, talking to Bishop and hopefully getting a statement from him, and they're going out to see the girl he was with, to give her the chance to make a fresh statement.'

'What do you think? What if she sticks to what she already said?'

'I think the police will impress upon her the need to tell the truth – and the serious trouble she will be in if she's found guilty of perverting the course of justice.'

'What will happen now?'

'We just have to give it a bit of time; the police need to go over all the evidence again and, hopefully, we will have enough of a case to present to the judge.'

Johnny put the phone down now and blessed himself. Please God, he thought, that the tide was turning in Sean's favour.

Chapter Sixty-Seven

Veronica decided to call into Clerys again on the Wednesday after work to hear if there was any more word about Nora, only to be told that Ella had had to rush off to England for a funeral. She had also been told by the staff in the hospital that Johnny had rung in to say he had to stay over there longer than expected. There was no one that she knew who could tell her anything about Nora, so she decided to take the bus out to Islandbridge to see if she was back home.

She knocked at the door and waited, then she heard footsteps and a pale-faced Nora opened the door.

'Veronica!' she said, clearly flustered. 'What brings you out here?'

'You,' her friend said, smiling at her. 'If the mountain won't come to Muhammad then Muhammad must come to the mountain.' She raised her eyebrows and waited until Nora opened the door wider to let her in.

'Just be careful there with the case and bags,' Nora said, leading her into the living room.

When they sat down side by side on the couch, Veronica turned to her. 'Are you going somewhere? Or is someone else?'

'Well, I was actually going to let you know. I'm moving back to Tullamore.'

'But why? I thought you liked living in Dublin, you seem so settled here.'

'I do like Dublin very much,' Nora told her. 'But I have no place here any more. I'm not needed.' She gestured out into the hallway. 'I'm going to move my things back down over the next few days, taking a few bags on the train each time. I should have everything sorted by next weekend, before they all come back. If they come back.'

'Where is everyone else?'

'Gone,' she said. 'As you know, Johnny went over with Sean to Liverpool, and now Ella and the two children have followed them. Sean has run into a bit of trouble over there, and they all wanted to be with him.' She shrugged. 'It seems there was no point in me coming back from Tullamore; I'm not needed. The neighbour, Mrs Murphy, filled in for me when I was gone, taking the children to school and such like, and I think they would probably prefer her to do that from now on.' She turned to look out of the window. She could have given more explanation about Sean, but didn't want to go into all the dreadful details that Ella had told her and Rose the night before she left.

'Are you sure this isn't about you and Johnny and what happened between you?'

Nora was still for a few moments. 'I'm sure it has had some bearing in my decision, but it's only part of it.' She looked at her friend. 'I wasn't entirely honest with you about all that. In fact, I wasn't honest with myself, and I've only come to realise it this last few days.' She rolled her eyes and tried to smile. 'I think I got a bit carried away, read more into things than were actually there. I thought if we were a proper couple that it would be good for the family – I thought it would be better than Johnny bringing in a stranger one day.' She gave a sigh. 'But I was, shall we say, a bit naïve there. It would never have worked out between us. Not in a million years.'

'Well, I didn't like to say...' Veronica paused. There was no point in making her feel worse. She had learned the hard way, just as she herself had had to learn about Frank Morrison. And Nora had been kind to her at the time, so it behoved her now to extend the same kindness to her friend. 'And are you all right? I was very worried when I heard you hadn't come back from Tullamore and so was Ella.'

'It's all sorted now,' Nora said, turning towards the window. 'I wasn't very well, and things got on top of me a bit. I've been to the doctor yesterday and had a chat, and it seems the menopause can cause a bit of an upset.' It was actually a long chat with Mrs Murphy that had been of greater help, and she had taken her advice and gone to the doctor in Kilmainham.

'Oh, it can,' Veronica said. 'My mother was very badly affected with it. Lots of women are. But how are you now?'

'Calmer and easier.' She looked up at her friend. 'I can't say I'm looking forward to starting all over again in Tullamore, but I think it's my best option. I have the house and farm there...' Her voice trailed off as she imagined the long lonely days and nights in the house again. Her only chance of change there was to throw her lot in with Tim Dunne, which she knew would not be fair to him.

'Why don't you stay in Dublin? You could sell up and buy a nice place here. That's what you had planned before for the family here, so why don't you do it for yourself? What's to stop you? Dublin is a big place, you can move away from here, but still keep in touch if you want to.'

'But I wouldn't know where to start.'

'I would help you, and so would Dominic.' She stopped now, thinking, then a big smile suddenly broke out on her face. 'Instead of taking your things back to Tullamore, why don't you move in with me in Ballsbridge? It's just a nice little distance from here, and I have two spare rooms. Wouldn't that make more sense than you going back to the country?'

Nora said nothing for a few moments, then: 'Do you think it could work?'

'I do indeed. I was happy enough in Tullamore, but after being back here in Dublin, I wouldn't go back. There's far more for single women like us here, we have the theatre, a choice of cinemas, and all the lovely tearooms and shops like Clerys and Switzer's.'

As Nora listened to Veronica extolling all the great things about the city – all the things she herself appreciated about it, the realisation dawned on her that she would actually prefer to be in Dublin. And maybe if she was living nearby rather than in the house here with the Cassidys, she might not have to break off all ties, as she would if she went to Tullamore. If she were here, she could still see Larry and Hannah regularly.

'I really would ask you to consider staying,' Veronica said. 'Because I would miss you very much, Nora. I've come to think of you like a sister, and it was knowing you were here that helped me break away from Frank. I knew I would always have someone to share things with – someone who had the same outlook on things.'

'Oh, Veronica...' Tears came into Nora's eyes now, and her voice was cracked with emotion. She took her friend's two hands in hers and squeezed them tightly. 'You've made me see things more clearly and I think you are right. I think I would be much happier in Dublin. And I'd like to take you up on the offer of accommodation until I get the house and farm sold.' A wave of excitement and anticipation rushed over her. 'It's like all my prayers have been answered.'

'Well, rather than us have to lug all these things on the bus, why don't we walk down to the shops. I know you weren't planning on being here tonight, so if you go and get us fish and chips, I'll go to a phone box and ring Dominic and ask him to collect us in his car. If he comes around eight o'clock, then you'll be out in Ballsbridge and all settled in your new room tonight.'

Nora smiled and nodded. 'I don't know where to start thanking you,' she said. 'I'm so lucky to have such a good and understanding friend.'

'I'm sure you would do the very same for me if I needed your help,' Veronica said. 'We all get things wrong at times, and we all deserve a fresh start.'

Chapter Sixty-Eight

They came down the steps of the courthouse, Sean in the middle, Johnny and Ricky Hamilton on one side of him, Ella and Danny on the other.

'I can't believe how quick it's all just happened,' Sean said. 'In a cell at eight o'clock this morning, and it's only eleven o'clock now, and I've been in and out of court. It feels kind of unreal.'

Johnny felt almost dazed with relief. 'Thanks be to God that the witnesses came forward and the case was thrown out before it went to trial. The judge said it could have been a terrible miscarriage of justice if they hadn't given their statements when they did.'

'And now you're a free man again,' Ricky said, clapping Sean on the back. 'Just think, when you have your recording contract and you're famous, it will make a great story in the big newspapers. You'll get hundreds for telling it – and you'll come out of it all as a big hero for saving that girl.'

'I don't feel a bit like a hero,' Sean said. 'What kind of hero ends up in jail? I feel a right feckin' eedjit. But even though he caused it all, I'm relieved that the other fella is going to be all right. I don't know how I would have coped if he had died.'

'Ah well...' Ricky shrugged. 'Thank goodness it's all behind you now.'

'Are you OK?' Ella said, squeezing Sean's hand. When he nodded, she said, 'What do you want to do? Do you want to go back to the café for something to eat or go somewhere else?'

'We're in no rush back,' Johnny said. 'Sally took Larry and

379

Hannah over to her sister's in Manchester for the day, so they won't be back until tonight.'

As they walked into the street Sean suddenly clapped his hands and rubbed them together. 'I know what we'll do,' he said, smiling now, 'we'll go to the Adelphi!'

'The Adelphi?' Johnny said, looking at him as though he had gone mad.

'Yes,' Sean said. 'I need to go back there to pick up the music scores that Simon gave me to practise for the recording studio – and we'll celebrate the fact that the lying bastard didn't win and I've got my freedom back!'

'Sounds like a good idea to me,' Ricky said, 'and you can put the first round on my tab, because I'm delighted to have Sean back on track again. I didn't say at the time because things happened too quickly that night, but Simon Wilson said he heard enough to know that it's more or less a given they're going to sign him up.' He looked at Sean. 'That's if all this fucking fiasco hasn't put you off Liverpool? I'd hate to see you going back to Dublin because of what some low life did.'

'Not a chance,' Sean said. 'In fact, it's the very opposite. I gave it good thought when I was stuck in that cell, and I'm more determined than ever to make it big. What's happened has made me realise that no matter where you are – Dublin, Liverpool, London – there will always be good, decent people who will help you, and there will always be people who will try to pull you down.' He shook his head. 'I'm not giving up on my dreams and ambitions for anybody.'

'And talking about decent people – wasn't it good that it was your cousins who came up with stuff about that Bishop fella – as well as total strangers who heard about you being charged, and went out of their way to help you?'

Sean nodded and then made a little anguished face. 'I owe some apologies to Joe's lads,' he said. 'I didn't have much time for them when I was over before, but well, I'll make it up to them. I'll make sure they know I appreciate what they did.' His eyes filled up. 'I've an awful lot of people to thank for standing by me, and I'll never forget it.' He moved now to hug his father and then Ella.

'What else would we do?' Ella said, tears streaming down her face. 'Isn't that what families are for?'

Sean nodded. 'And I promise you both, I'll do everything I can to make you proud of me.' He looked over at his manager. 'Ricky once said to me, "they'll be listening to your music, all across the Mersey", well, I'm going to make sure of it.'

'By the time the recording comes around, and the records are released in the summer,' Ricky said, 'never mind the Mersey – they'll be listening to your music all across the Atlantic. You just wait and see.'

Chapter Sixty-Nine

Ella and Johnny were in the living room back at home in Island-bridge when the car pulled up outside and they went to the window to watch as Nora climbed out of the shiny black Ford.

'I'll get the door,' Johnny said.

Ella sat waiting, her hands clasped together. They had been home two days now, and she felt everything was strange without her aunt there. The house had felt so different on their return from Liverpool and they found the letter that Aunt Nora had left for them apologising for all her recent behaviour.

'Come in, Nora,' her father said, in a halting, but friendly tone. 'It's nice to see you.'

'And you too, Johnny,' she heard Nora say.

The door opened and her aunt came in. As soon as Ella saw the fragile look on her face and the slight tremble of her hands, she felt a sense of sadness.

Nora went straight over to her with outstretched arms. 'How are you, Ella? It's lovely to see you. It seems longer than a week.'

'I'm grand, Aunt Nora,' Ella said, hugging her back. 'And it's lovely to see you too.'

Johnny took Nora's coat and hat and then they all sat down. There was an awkward silence and then Nora held her hand up.

'The first thing I want to do is apologise in person to you both.' She turned to Ella. 'I am so sorry that you saw me in such a dreadful state on two occasions. It was unforgivable of me, and I let myself down badly. Worse, I let you all down, behaving like that and turning to drink.' She shook her head. 'God knows what got into me...'

'Nora,' Johnny said, 'you've already apologised in that very nice letter you wrote. We know you weren't yourself, and, I'm the last person that can criticise where drink is concerned.' He waved his hand. 'It's all forgotten.'

'It is,' Ella said. 'And after all you did for us – all the good things you did for this family – you don't need to say any more. I'm just sorry you weren't well and it was too late when we noticed, or I might have done more to help you.'

'And the same goes for me,' Johnny said. 'I should have talked more to you, and maybe we would have understood each other better. We should have both looked at the long-term. I have to hold my hand up to the fact that I was only thinking of what was good for the children after Mary died, and I should have looked at it from your angle as well. You put an awful lot into this family, Nora, and we will never be able to repay that kindness.'

Nora felt as though a huge weight was suddenly lifting off her. 'Well, I'm grateful to the both of you for your kindness and understanding – and there was an element of naïvety on my part too.' She halted. 'But enough of me, please tell me how Sean is?'

They quickly filled her in on the situation, explaining that he had put the court case behind him and was now more focussed on his music career than ever.

'I'll wet the tea now,' Ella said, getting up.

'Are you sure?' Nora checked.

Ella smiled. 'After all the tea you've made in this house, you deserve to have the odd one made for you.'

'Ah well, I won't argue with you.'

As she made for the scullery, she felt relieved that her aunt seemed more like her old self. Things seemed to be falling back into place again, although not in the exact way they had been before. As long as Aunt Nora still had a place in their family, whether she lived with them in the same house or not didn't matter. She had rescued them all in the dark days after their mother dying, and helped each one survive. For that alone, she deserved the gratitude and understanding they were now showing in return.

Ella was also grateful for the support Aunt Nora had given her and Danny. When others might have dismissed them for being too young to know what they were doing, Nora had appreciated how well-suited they were. She had pointed out how intelligent and kind Danny was, and how they laughed a lot together, which she said was very important. They had something special, Ella knew, and she was now going to concentrate on planning their future together. In the next few weeks they would definitely find the right engagement ring, and after that they would start thinking of a wedding date.

Whether their married life might involve spending more time in Liverpool, she wasn't sure, but she knew that whether they were beside the Mersey or the Liffey, they would make the very best of it.

When they were alone, Nora looked straight at Johnny and said in a whisper, 'You didn't tell her about – about what happened on those few occasions?'

Johnny lowered his eyes. 'No,' he said. 'What would be the point? She wouldn't really understand, and she would never see us in the same light again.'

'I agree.' There was another silence, and then she said, 'It would be best if it was forgotten by us both, and never mentioned again.'

'Indeed.' He smiled at her, and their eyes met in silent agreement. 'So, you've moved out to Ballsbridge? How are you finding it?'

'Ah, lovely.' She went on to tell him about Veronica's house and her brother's house in Donnybrook, then she mentioned about putting her own up for sale. 'I'm having an evaluation done on that and my uncle's farm next week, and if all goes well, then they will go on the open market. After that, I'll be house-hunting up in Dublin, somewhere near my friends.'

'I wish you all the best,' Johnny said, 'you deserve it. And I look forward to us all coming out to see it.'

'Of course,' she said, 'and I'm hoping that Larry and Hannah will come out to stay some weekends with me and during their school holidays.'

'You'll never get rid of them,' Johnny laughed.

Ella came in with a tray with fruit cake and biscuits and three mugs of tea. 'Who will you never get rid of?' she asked.

Nora went on to tell Ella her plans over the tea. When she had finished, she said, 'Now, what decision have you come to regarding looking after the children during the week?' She looked from one to the other.

'If you're sure you don't mind travelling out from Ballsbridge, then we were thinking if you did the three days a week you offered, maybe Monday, Wednesday and Friday – then Mrs Murphy can take them on a Tuesday and Thursday.'

Nora's face lit up. 'Well, that would be grand,' she said. 'The three days would still give a nice shape to my week. I'll cook the evening meal as I've always done, and have it ready for you both coming in from work, and we can all sit down together.'

'That would be great,' Ella said. 'We've had enough changes with Sean going, and it would be lovely to have you here as usual when we all come home.'

'What if you decide to go back to work?' Johnny asked. 'I wouldn't want you to feel obliged to help us with the young ones or anything like that.'

'I've no plans for working until I've all the business with selling the house settled and I'm in my own place in Dublin. Now, that could take months, or even the best part of a year.' She smiled at them. 'And who knows, I might decide not to go back to work at all. Whatever happens, I'll give you plenty of warning in advance, and we'll talk it all through, so each understands the other. Isn't that the best way?'

Johnny looked at her now and smiled. 'It is Nora, and we'll all make sure we stick to it.' She was like a different woman, calmer than he had ever known her, and yet more confident and open. He knew he was lucky the way things had turned out, because it could easily have gone the other way and ended in disaster.

He had taken Sally's advice about finding a new role in the family for Nora, rather than feeling awkward and cutting her out. For Nora's sake – and especially for Larry and Hannah's. Sally had helped him make his peace with the fact that both he and Nora had been to blame for what had happened, and now they'd faced it head on they could start afresh. 'She's done more good than she's ever done harm. And everything will be different now you're in separate houses.' And Sally had advised him never to mention their indiscretion to Sean and Ella. 'They will have enough to do, coping with the ups and downs of their own lives; they don't need to deal with something that can hardly be remembered.'

Sally Mather had been the best thing that had happened to him since losing Mary, and he would be eternally grateful that he and Sean had stumbled into the Strand Café that first morning. What the future held for them, neither of them knew, but she already had plans to come over to Dublin for New Year. He would save his money from his music for trips over to see her and Sean, and it would keep him away from the drink and give him something to look forward to.

There was no rush for anything, they would take things as they came.

He heard laughter, now, and he turned to the window and saw Mrs Murphy and the bobbing heads of Larry and Hannah as they passed by. He went to the door to open it for them, and his heart lifted as it always did when he saw the bright, happy faces as they came in. They immediately ran over to Nora, hugging and chatting to her, and vying with each other to tell her all about their time in Liverpool.

'Ah, you're all here,' Rose Murphy said, smiling broadly at everyone as she came in. 'And all busy drinking tea.'

'And no one asking if you have a mouth on you!' Johnny said.

'Ella just made a pot, so I'll go down to the scullery now and pour you a cup.'

'You know me,' Rose laughed, 'I've never refused one yet.'

She sat down at the table. 'Well,' she said, 'it's good to see you all back home together.' She smiled over at Nora, and gave her a little conspiratorial wink.

Nora smiled back and nodded. There was no need to say anything. Rose Murphy had been a lifesaver to her, and a great comfort. She had learned a lot from her neighbour and, even more importantly, she had learned a lot about herself. In future, she would no longer judge people by their looks, education or background. Good people, she now knew, came in all shapes and sizes. And anyone, from any background, could make mistakes. Nora had learned that the hard way, but Rose had been matter-of-fact about almost anything she had divulged to her.

She had unburdened herself to the older woman while the Cassidys were gone, in a way she had never done with another living soul. And, as she listened to the advice Rose had given her, things began to make more sense. Everyone, Rose said, was entitled to the odd burst of madness, and she was not alone. She had also made Nora laugh, when she gave accounts of her own indiscretions both with drink and men.

Before coming to live in Dublin, Nora would have been appalled, listening to such tales, but she had discovered that life had a way of levelling things off. Going off the rails for a while herself had taught her that drink affected people in different ways, and could lead to situations she had never envisaged. Especially someone like herself, who had led such a sheltered life. She could never have imagined that underneath all her correct and judgemental ways, lay buried the wants and desires that she had condemned other women for. And although there had been more to her dreams than sex, she now knew that given certain circumstances, even the most unlikely people could be drawn together for comfort or to fill some gap in their lives.

And it was also strange, she now knew, how friends could appear in the most unlikely places, and when you least expected it. Veronica had already proved that by suddenly appearing in Dublin, and not only being such a great companion, but a support through Nora's recent difficulties. And Dominic, her brother, couldn't have been kinder, picking her up and dropping her off in the car, and generally doing anything he could to help, while expecting nothing in return. He was a complete gentleman, and the more she got to know him, the more Nora discovered there was to him. She was lucky, she knew now, that he had continued to be friends with her after her earlier dismissal of him, while she was still infatuated with the idea of romance with Johnny. With distance and experience, she could now see that Dominic was, in fact, a more suitable match for her. It was too early to know if she could grow to have deeper feelings for him, ones that he might return, but the possibility was there. She looked upon it as a little adventure for the future in her new life.

Johnny appeared now with the tea for Mrs Murphy and they all made a joke of lifting their mugs in a toast. 'What are we toasting now?' he asked.

'To Sean,' Ella said. 'And to a number one hit on the radio when his record comes out'.

Johnny lifted his mug now. 'May his music be heard across the Mersey and all the rivers and seas in the world!'

They all cheered, then Nora held her mug out.

'To friendship and family,' she said, looking around them all, 'and may our happiest days, be yet to come.'

Acknowledgements

I would like to thank the staff at Orion, especially Laura Gerrard and Katie Seaman, for all their work on *Music Across the Mersey*. Also, Genevieve Pegg and Kati Nicholl for their editing skills which helped finely tune the manuscript.

I owe a debt of gratitude to Kate Mills for her support with *Music across the Mersey*, and for all her excellent work with my previous books for Orion Publishers.

Warm thanks to my dear friend, Bernie O'Sullivan, who helped me with research on Dublin in the early years. She drove me around the places she grew up in, guided me around the streets, and was constantly on hand to help with any queries I had. An inspiring woman and a true friend who always goes the extra mile.

Thanks also to the family of Freddy O'Connor – to whom this book is dedicated – especially his lovely daughter, Helen Murphy. When I met up with Freddy as I was researching the book, he was welcoming and more than generous with his knowledge and advice about Liverpool. He shared his books and photographs and his love of this great city, which helped me enormously. Freddy is a true Liverpool legend.

I would also like to acknowledge the constant support I have received from Offaly Libraries – especially County Librarian, Mary Stuart – and Offaly Arts Office.

Thanks to my family and friends in Ireland and UK for their continued support of my writing – especially my parents and my beloved son and daughter – Christopher and Clare.

As always, I have to mention my old college boyfriend, Michael Brosnahan for the support he gives me in countless ways. He is the backbone of our family and this year we celebrated 40 years of marriage – the best decision I ever made!

Finally, heartfelt thanks to all my readers from all over the world, who have kept me going year after year with their requests for yet another book!